THE WEDDING PARTY

What's not to love about a wedding?
Well, except for the I'll-never-wear-this-again
bridesmaid dress, going solo to the ceremony
when your date deserts you and those awkward
encounters with bridezilla…not to mention
the silly group dances. It's almost enough
to deliver a "no, thanks" on the RSVP!

But in this 2-in-1 collection, these women
know how to get the most out of every
wedding occasion. And once they meet that
really hot guy—just right for a sexy night of
fun—the party really begins.

So sit back and enjoy the celebrations as
these stories show that the wedding is the
perfect place to get something started!

HEIDI RICE

was born and bred and still lives in London, England. She has two sons who love to bicker, a wonderful husband who, luckily for everyone, has loads of patience, and a supportive and ever-growing British/French/Irish/American family. As much as Heidi adores London, she also loves America, and every two years or so she and her best friend leave hubby and kids behind and *Thelma and Louise* it across the States for a couple of weeks (although they always leave out the driving off a cliff bit). She's been a film buff since her early teens, and a romance junkie for almost as long. She indulged her first love by being a film reviewer for ten years. Then a few years ago she decided to spice up her life by writing romance. Discovering the fantastic sisterhood of romance writers (both published and unpublished) in Britain and America made it a wild and wonderful journey to her first Harlequin® novel. Heidi loves to hear from readers—you can email her at heidi@heidi-rice.com, or visit her website, www.heidi-rice.com.

USA TODAY Bestselling Author

HEIDI RICE

AND

CHARLOTTE PHILLIPS

Beach Bar Baby

and

The Plus-One Agreement

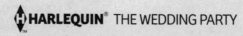

HARLEQUIN® THE WEDDING PARTY

Recycling programs
for this product may
not exist in your area.

ISBN-13: 978-0-373-60633-7

BEACH BAR BABY AND THE PLUS-ONE AGREEMENT

Copyright © 2014 by Harlequin Books S.A.

The publisher acknowledges the copyright holders
of the individual works as follows:

BEACH BAR BABY
Copyright © 2014 by Heidi Rice

THE PLUS-ONE AGREEMENT
Copyright © 2014 by Charlotte Phillips

Printed in U.S.A.

CONTENTS

BEACH BAR BABY

USA TODAY Bestselling Author

Heidi Rice

To all those people who asked me
when I was going to write Ella's story.
Now you know.
I hope it lives up to expectations!

ONE

—

Next time you book a holiday of a lifetime, don't choose the world's most popular couples' destination, you muppet.

Ella Radley adjusted her backpack and flinched as it nudged the raw skin that still stung despite spending yesterday hiding out in her deluxe ocean-view room at the Paradiso Cove Resort in Bermuda—AKA Canoodle Central.

Ella sighed—nothing like getting third-degree sunburn in the one place you couldn't reach to remind you of your single status. Not that she needed reminding. She stared in dismay at the line of six couples, all in various stages of loved-up togetherness, on the dock ahead of her as she waited to board the motor cruiser at the Royal Naval Dockyards on Ireland Island for what the dive company's website had promised would be 'a two-hour snorkel tour of a lifetime'. Unfortunately, she'd booked the tour when she'd first arrived nearly a week ago, before she'd been hit on by a succession of married men and pimply pubescent boys, napalmed all the skin between her shoulder blades and generally lost the will to have anything remotely resembling a lifetime experience.

Her best friend Ruby had once told her she was far too sweet and eager and romantic for her own good. Well, she was so over that. Frankly, paradise and all its charms could get lost. She'd much rather be icing cupcakes in Touch of Frosting's cosy café kitchen in north London—and laughing about what a nightmare her dream holiday had turned out to be with her business partner and BFF Ruby—than standing in line to take a snorkelling tour of a lifetime that would probably give her a terminal case of seasickness.

Stop being such a grump.

Ella gazed out across the harbour, trying to locate at least a small measure of her usual sunny outlook on life. Yachts and motor boats—dwarfed by the enormous cruise ship anchored across the harbour—bobbed on water so blue and sparkly it hurt her eyes. She recalled the pink sand beach they'd passed on the way in, framed by lush palms and luxury beach bungalows, which looked as if it had been ripped from the pages of a tourist brochure.

She only had one more day to fully appreciate the staggering beauty of this island paradise. Maybe booking this holiday hadn't been the smartest thing she'd ever done, but she'd needed a distraction... The trickle of panic crawled over her skin, making her aware of the familiar clutching sensation in her belly. She pressed her palm to the thin cotton of her sundress, until it went away again. She needed this day trip—to get her out of her room before the panic overwhelmed her or, worse, she became addicted to US daytime soaps.

The line moved forward as a tall man appeared at the gangplank wearing ragged cut-offs and a black T-shirt with the dive company's logo on it, his face shadowed by a peaked captain's cap. Ella stopped breathing, her eyes narrowing to minimise the glare off the water, astonished to discover that the steely-haired Captain Sonny Mangold, whose weathered face beamed out from the photo on the website, appeared to be in amazing physical shape for a guy pushing sixty. Talk about a silver fox. Not that she could see his hair from this distance.

Captain Sonny began to welcome each couple aboard, his gruff American accent floating towards her on the still, muggy air, and sending peculiar shivers up Ella's spine, even though she couldn't make out what he was saying. The couple ahead of her, looking affluent and young and very much in love, were the last to block her view. As the captain helped them both aboard Ella stepped forward, anticipation making her throat dry. She took in the staggeringly broad shoulders and long muscular legs encased in denim cut-offs as his head dipped to tick off the list on the clipboard in his hand. Wisps of dark blond hair clung to lean cheeks and a square, stubbled jaw, confusing her even more, then his head lifted.

All thoughts of nightmare holidays, canoodling couples and silver foxes blasted right out of her brain.

Goodness, he's stunning. And not much over thirty.

'You're not Captain Sonny,' she blurted, the wake-up call to her dormant libido blasting away her usual shyness too.

'Captain Cooper Delaney at your service.' The rich jade of his irises twinkled, and the tanned skin round the edges of his eyes creased. His arresting gaze dipped, to check the clipboard again. 'And you must be Miz Radley.' The laconic voice caressed her name, while his gaze paused momentarily on its journey back to her face, rendering the bikini she had on under her sundress half its normal size.

A large, bronzed hand, sprinkled with sun-bleached hair, reached out. 'Welcome aboard *The Jezebel*, Miz Radley. You travelling on your own today?'

'Yes.' She coughed, distressed as the answer came out on a high-pitched squeak. Heat flared across her scalp.

Good Lord, am I having a hot flush? Can he see it?

'Is that okay?' she asked. Then realised it sounded as if she was asking his permission.

'Sure.' His wide sensual lips lifted but stopped tantalisingly short of a grin—making her fairly positive he knew exactly how he was affecting her.

The blush promptly went radioactive.

'As long as you don't have any objections to me being your snorkel buddy?' He squeezed her fingers as she stepped aboard. 'We don't let clients dive alone. It's safer that way.'

The pads of her fingertips rubbed against the thick calluses on the ridge of his palm. And the tips of her already constricted breasts tightened.

'I don't have any objections,' she said, feeling stupidly bereft when he let go of her hand—and thinking that even on their ten-second acquaintance she'd hazard a guess that Captain Cooper Delaney was the opposite of safe. Why for the first time in a long time she should find that exhilarating instead of intimidating made her wonder exactly how stressed she'd been in the last week.

'How about you sit up front with me?'

It didn't sound like a question, but she nodded, her tongue now completely numb.

His palm settled on the small of her back, just beneath the line of her sunburn. He directed her past the other passengers as she struggled not to notice the hot tingles generated by his touch and the fresh scent of saltwater and soap that clung to him. Bypassing the single space left between the couples wedged onto the benches that rimmed the hull, he escorted her to one of the two seats in front of the console in the boat's cabin.

'There you go, Miz Radley.' He tipped his cap, the gesture more amused than polite thanks to that tempting twinkle, then turned to address the other passengers.

She listened to him introduce himself and the two

wiry teenage boys who were his crew for the day, then launch into a relaxed spiel about the twenty-five-minute voyage to the snorkel site called Western Blue Cut, the history of the sunken wreck they'd be exploring, the ecology of the reef and a string of safety tips. But all she really heard was the deliciously rusty texture of his voice while her mind wrestled with the question of exactly what being someone's snorkel buddy might entail.

It couldn't possibly be as intimate as it sounded. Could it?

But when he climbed into the seat beside her, his hand closed over the rounded head of the gear stick on the console and she swallowed past a constriction in her throat that felt a lot like excitement.

He adjusted the stick down, tapped a dial, pressed a button and the boat roared to life. She grabbed the rail at the edge of the console to stop from tumbling onto her butt. He slanted her an amused look as she scrambled back into her seat. Then hid his mischievous gaze behind a pair of sunglasses.

All the blood pumped back into her cheeks—not to mention the hot spot between her legs—as the motor launch kicked away from the dock, edged past the other boats in the marina, and left the walled harbour to skim over the swell towards the reef.

He flashed her an easy smile—that seemed to share a wicked secret. 'Hold on tight, miz. I'd hate to lose my snorkel buddy before we get there.'

The answering grin that flittered over Ella's lips

felt like her first genuine smile in months—filling up a small part of the gaping hole that had opened up in the pit of her stomach over a week ago.

Maybe going on a holiday of a lifetime solo didn't completely suck after all.

'Well, honey, you've certainly captured Coop's attention.'

Ella's cheeks burned at the comment from the plump middle-aged woman in bright pink Bermuda shorts and an 'I Found My Heart in Horseshoe Bay' T-shirt who joined her at the rail as the boat bobbed on the reef.

They'd reached their destination ten minutes ago and were waiting for Captain Delaney and his crew to finish allocating the snorkelling equipment before they dived in.

Ella had to be grateful for the respite, because sitting in such close proximity to the man for twenty minutes had caused her usually sedentary hormones to get sort of hyperactive.

'Do you know Captain Delaney?' she asked, hoping to deflect the conversation while studiously ignoring the blip in her heartbeat.

After careful consideration, she'd figured out that Captain Delaney's attention had nothing to do with her and everything to do with his job. She was the only single passenger on the boat, and he was just being conscientious, ensuring she got her money's worth and enjoyed the trip. They hadn't been able to talk much on the ride out because of the engine noise, thankfully. Those sexy—and she was sure entirely impersonal—smiles he kept flashing at her were more than enough to tie her tongue in knots. A reaction that had propelled her back in time to the excruciating crushes of her teens when she'd always been rendered speechless in the presence of good-looking boys.

This was precisely why she preferred guys who were homely and safe rather than dangerous and super-hot. Being struck dumb on a date could get old really fast.

'We've known Coop for nearly a decade,' the woman said in her friendly mid-western drawl. 'Bill and I been coming back to St George every year since our honeymoon in ninety-two. And we never miss *The Jezebel*'s snorkel tour. Coop used to work as a deck hand for Sonny as a kid, got his captain's stripes a while back. Now he just pitches in from time to time.' The woman offered a hand. 'Name's May Preston.'

'Ella Radley, nice to meet you.' Ella shook the woman's hand, comforted by her open face, and easy manner—and intrigued despite herself by the unsolicited insight into the hot captain's past.

She recognised May from the resort. May and her husband Bill, whom she liked too, because he was one of the few married men at Paradiso Cove who didn't have a roving eye.

'You're a cute little thing, aren't you? And with that lovely accent.' May tilted her head, assessing Ella in that direct and personal way that only American tourists seemed able to do without appearing rude. 'I must say, I've always wondered what Coop's type was. But you're quite a surprise.'

The blush headed towards Ella's hairline. 'I wouldn't say I'm his type.' Perish the thought; her heart would probably stop beating if she believed that. She might find him extremely attractive, but dangerous men had never been good for her mental health. 'It's just that I'm a woman on my own and he's being polite and doing a good job.'

May let out a hearty chuckle. 'Don't you believe it, honey. Coop's not the polite type. And he usually spends his time peeling the single female clients off him, not offering them a personal service.'

'I'm sure you're wrong about that.' Far from stopping, Ella's heartbeat hit warp speed—stunned disbelief edging out her embarrassment.

'Maybe, maybe not.' May's smile took on a saucy tilt, which was about as far from doubtful as it was possible to get. 'But this is the first I've ever heard of the snorkel-buddy safety rule. And that's after twenty years of coming on this tour.'

Ella bided her time while wrestling with May's shocking comment, until the captain and his two deck-hands had seen off all the other snorkellers. While fitting fins and masks, giving instructions about how far to stray from the boat, demonstrating some basic hand signals, advising people on how long they had before they should head back, and how to identify the paddle wheel from the wreck of the sunken blockade runner they'd come to see, Cooper Delaney appeared to be the consummate professional. In fact, he seemed so relaxed and pragmatic while handling the other passengers, Ella convinced herself May had to be mistaken about the snorkel-buddy rule—and wondered if she should even question him about it. Wouldn't she sound impossibly vain, bordering on delusional, suggesting he'd offered to partner her for reasons other than her own safety?

But then he turned from the rail, took off his sunglasses and his slow, seductive smile had all the blood pumping back into her nether regions.

She fanned herself with her sunhat. Goodness, either she was suffering from sunstroke or that smile had some kind of secret thermal mechanism.

He crossed the deck towards her, his emerald gaze even brighter than the dazzling expanse of crystal blue water.

'So, Miz Radley, you want to strip down to your swimsuit and I'll get you fitted up, then we can head out?'

He leaned against the console, his large capable hand very close to her hip.

She sucked in a sharp breath as her lungs constricted, only to discover the fresh sweat darkening the front of his T-shirt made his salt and sandalwood scent even more intoxicating.

Courage, Ella, just make a general enquiry so you know for sure where you stand.

'Is that absolutely necessary?' she asked.

'Fraid so. The salt water's bound to ruin that pretty dress if you don't take it off. You didn't forget your swimsuit, did you?' His smile tipped into a grin.

'No, I meant us snorkelling together.' Her nipples shot back to the full torpedo as his gaze drifted south. 'Is that necessary?'

One dark eyebrow lifted in puzzled enquiry, the smile still in place.

'It's just that May Preston said she'd never heard of that rule.' The words tripped over themselves to get out of her mouth before her tongue knotted again. 'You know, about it being necessary for people to snorkel in pairs for safety's sake...' She began to babble, her tongue overcompensating somewhat. 'I know it matters with scuba-diving. Even though I've never actually scuba-dived myself...' She cut off as his lips curved more.

Get to the point, Ella.

'I just...I wondered if you could confirm for me, why it's necessary for us to be snorkel buddies? If I'm only going to be a few yards from the boat?'

'Right.'

The word rumbled out and seemed to echo in her abdomen. He muttered something under his breath, then tugged off his captain's cap, revealing curls of thick sun-streaked hair damp with sweat flattened against his forehead.

'What I can confirm...' he slapped the cap against his thigh, the smile becoming more than a little sheepish '...is that May Preston's got one hell of a big mouth.

Which I'm going to be having words with her about as soon as she gets back aboard this boat.'

'It's true?' Ella's eyes widened, her jaw going slack. 'You really did make it up? But why would you do that?'

Cooper Delaney watched the pretty English girl's baby blues grow even larger in her delicate, heart-shaped face—and began to wonder if he was being taken for a ride.

Shy and hot and totally lost, with that tempting overbite, and her lush but petite figure, Ella Radley had looked cute and sort of sad when he'd spotted her at the back of the boarding line an hour ago. Then her skin had flushed a ruddy pink as soon as he'd so much as smiled at her and she'd totally captivated him.

That nuclear blush had been so damn cute, in fact, that he'd been momentarily mesmerised and the snorkel-buddy rule had popped into his head and then spilled out of his mouth without his brain ever even considering intervening.

But seriously? Could any woman really be this clueless? Even if she did have eyes big enough to rival one of the heroines in the manga comic books he'd been addicted to in middle school? And her nipples peaked under her sundress every time he so much as glanced at her rack? And her cheeks seemed to be able to light up on cue?

No way. No one was that cute. It had to be an act. But if it was an act, it was a damn good one. And he could respect that, because he'd dedicated his life to putting on one act or another.

Unfortunately, act or no, she'd caught him out but good.

Thanks a bunch, May.

He resigned himself to taking his punishment like a man, and hoped it didn't involve a slap in the face— or a sexual harassment suit.

'If I said because you looked like you could use the company,' he began, hoping that humour might soften the blow, 'would you buy it?'

The instant blush bloomed again—lighting up the sprinkle of freckles on her nose. 'Oh, yes, of course, I thought it might be something like that.' She shielded her eyes from the sun, tipping her chin up. 'That's very considerate of you, Captain Delaney. But I wouldn't want to put you out if you're busy. I'm sure I'll manage fine on my own.'

It was his turn for his eyes to widen at the earnest tone and the artless expression on her pixie face.

Damn, did she actually just buy that? Because if this was an act, it ought to be Oscar nominated.

No one had ever accused him of being considerate before. Not even his mom—and he'd worked harder at fooling her than anyone, because she'd been so fragile.

'The name's Coop,' he said, still not convinced that he'd got off the hook so easily, but willing to go with it. 'Believe me. I'd be happy to do it.' He tried to emulate her earnest expression. Although he figured it was a lost cause. He'd learnt at an early age to hide

all his emotions behind a who-the-hell-cares smile,
which meant he didn't have a heck of a lot of practice
with earnest.

Her lips curved and her overbite disappeared. 'Okay,
if you're absolutely sure it's not a bother.' The blue of
her eyes brightened to dazzling. 'I accept.'

The smile struck him dumb for a moment, turning
her expression from cute to super-hot but still man-
aging to look entirely natural. Then she bounced up
to pull her sundress over her head. And the punch of
lust nearly knocked him sideways.

Bountiful curves in all the right places jiggled entic-
ingly, covered by three pitifully tiny triangles of purple
spandex that left not a lot to the imagination—and
had that cheesy sixties tune his mom used to sing on
her good days about a teeny-weeny polka dot bikini
dancing through his head.

Damn but that rack was even hotter than her smile.
Her nipples did that bullet-tipped thing again and he
had to grit his teeth to stop one particular part of his
anatomy from becoming the total opposite of teeny-
weeny.

But then she turned, to drop her dress into the
purse she had stowed under the dash, and he spotted
the patch of sun-scorched flesh that spread out between slim shoulder blades and stretched all the way
down to the line of her panties.

'Ouch, that's got to hurt,' he murmured. 'You need
a higher factor sun lotion. The rays can be brutal in
Bermuda even in April.'

She whisked around, holding the dress up to cover her magnificent rack—and the nuclear blush returned with a vengeance. 'I have factor fifty, but unfortunately I couldn't reach that spot.'

He scrubbed his hand over the stubble on his chin, playing along by pretending to consider her predicament. 'Well, now, that sounds like a job for your snorkel buddy.'

A grateful smile lit up her face, and he almost felt bad for taking advantage of her...until he remembered this was all some saucy little act.

'That would be fabulous, if you don't mind?' She reached back into her tote and pulled out some lotion.

Presenting her back to him, she lifted the hair off her nape as he squeezed a generous amount of the stuff, which had the consistency of housepaint, between his palms, and contemplated how much he was going to enjoy spreading it all over her soft, supple, sun-warmed skin.

Well, hell... If he'd known the good-guy act came with these kind of benefits, he'd have given it a shot more often.

TWO

—

Do not purr, *under any circumstances.*

Ella bit back a moan as Cooper Delaney's work-roughened hands massaged her shoulder blades. Callused fingers nudged under the knot of her bikini to spread the thick sun lotion up towards her hairline. Tingles ricocheted down her spine as his thumbs dug into the tight muscles of her neck, then edged downwards. She trapped her bottom lip under her teeth, determined to keep the husky groan lodged in her throat where it belonged.

'Okay, I'm heading into the red zone.' The husky voice brushed her nape as his magic touch disappeared and she heard the squirt of more lotion being dispensed. 'I'll be gentle as I can, but let me know if it's too much.'

I could never have too much of this.

She nodded, knowing any further attempt at speech would probably give away how close she was to entering a fugue state.

'Right, here goes.'

Light pressure hit the middle of her back as his palms flattened against the burnt patch. She shuddered, the sting nothing compared to the riot of tingles now rippling across her skin and tightening her nipples.

'You okay?' The pressure ceased, his palms barely touching her.

'Yes. Absolutely. Don't stop.' She shifted, pressing back into his palms. 'It feels...'

Glorious? Blissful? Awe-inspiring?

'Fine...' she managed, but then a low hum escaped as he began to massage more firmly. His thumbs angled into the hollows of her spine, blazing a trail of goosebumps in their wake.

She'd been far too long without the touch of a man's hands. That fabulous sensation of flesh on flesh, skin to skin. She stretched under the caress, like a cat desperate to be stroked, the tingles rippling down to her bottom as his thumbs nudged the edge of her bikini panties. She closed her eyes, willing the firm touch to delve beneath the elastic, while the hot heavy weight in her abdomen plunged.

Arousal zapped across her skin, and she had to swallow the sob as the exquisite, excruciating sensations pounded into her sex after what felt like decades on sabbatical.

Then disappeared.

'All done.'

Her eyes snapped open too fast, making her sway.

His hand touched her hip, anchoring her in place—
and snapping her back to reality.

'Steady there.' The amused tone had the blush firing up her neck.

Oh, no, had he heard that strangled sob? Could he
tell she'd been hurtling towards a phantom orgasm?

Humiliation engulfed the need.

She was so going to unpack the vibrator Ruby had
bought her for the trip, and test-drive it in her room
tonight. Deciding she wasn't highly sexed enough to
need artificial stimulation had obviously been way off
the mark. And Ruby had once sworn by hers—before
she'd found her husband, Callum.

'That should keep you from getting barbecued
again, at any rate.' The rough comment intruded on
her frantic debate about the merits of vibrators. And
the blush went haywire.

She stretched her lips into what she hoped looked
like a grateful smile—instead of the first stages of
nymphomania. 'I really appreciate it.'

She watched as he snapped the cap onto the lotion
bottle. Only to become momentarily transfixed by the
sight of those long, blunt, capable fingers glistening
in the sunlight from the oily residue.

'There you go.' He held out the lotion bottle as another inappropriate jolt of arousal pulsed into her sex.

Locating her backpack, she spent several additional
seconds shoving the bottle back into it, pathetically
grateful when her hands finally stopped trembling.

Maybe if she drew this out long enough the blush might have retreated out of the forbidden zone too.

'Thank you, that was...' She groped for the right word—awesome being definitely the wrong word, even if it was the one sitting on the tip of her tongue.

'You're welcome.'

Her lungs seized at the glow of amusement in the deep green depths of his eyes. The blip of panic returned as she got lost in the rugged male beauty of his face—the chiselled cheekbones, the shadow of stubble on the strong line of his jaw, the tantalising dimple in his chin.

How could any man be this gorgeous? This potently male? It just wasn't fair on the female of the species.

The sensual lips twitched, as if he were valiantly suppressing a grin.

Get a flipping grip. The man offered to be your snorkel buddy, not your bonk buddy.

'So we're all set?' The rough question echoed in her sex.

'Unless you need me to return the favour?' She coughed, when the offer came out on an unladylike squeak. 'With the sun lotion, I mean. So you don't burn.'

The suggestion trailed off as his eyebrows lifted a fraction and the edge of his mouth kicked up in one of those sensual, secret smiles that had been making her breathing quicken all morning. It stopped altogether now.

Shut up. You did not just say that? You sad, sad, sex-deprived nymphomaniac.

'Forget it, that was a silly thing to say.' She raced to cover the gaff. 'I don't know why I suggested it.' Cooper Delaney's sun-kissed skin had the healthy glow of a year-round tan weathered by sea air. He'd probably never had to use lotion in his entire life. 'I'm sure you don't need to worry about sunburn. Perhaps we should just—'

'That sounds like a great idea.' The easy comment cut through her manic babble.

'It does?'

His lips kicked up another notch. 'Sure, you can never have enough protection, right?'

Was he mocking her? And could she summon the will to care while she was barely able to breathe?

'Um, right. I'll get the lotion, then.' She dived back into her bag, rummaging around for what felt like several decades as she tried to locate the lotion before he changed his mind. She found it just in time to see him lift the hem of his T-shirt over his head and throw it over the console.

All the blood rushed out of her brain as she stood, poised like the Statue of Liberty, clutching the lotion like Liberty's torch.

Oh. My. God. His chest is a work of art.

Sun-bleached hair curled around flat copper nipples as if to accentuate the mounds of his exceptionally well-defined pecs. She followed the trail down between the ridged muscles of his six-pack, then swallowed convulsively as the thin strip of hair tapered beneath the waistband of his cut-offs, drawing her attention to the roped sinews that stood out in bold relief against the line of his hip bones.

No wonder it's called a happy trail. I feel euphoric.

'Thanks, honey. I appreciate it.' His gruff words interrupted her reverie as he presented her with an equally breathtaking view of his back.

His spine bisected the slabs of packed muscle, sloping down to the tattoo of a Celtic Cross, inked across the base of his back, which peeked out above his shorts. Her gaze dipped lower, to absorb the sight of a perfectly toned male ass framed in battered denim.

She cleared her throat loudly, before she choked to death on her own drool. 'Is, um, is factor fifty okay?'

He lifted one muscular shoulder, let it drop. 'Whatever you've got is good.'

The low words seemed to rumble through her torso, making her pulse points vibrate.

She squeezed a lake of the viscous white liquid into unsteady palms. Taking a deep breath, she flattened her palms onto the hot, smooth skin of his back, while her lungs clogged with the tempting scent of cocoa butter and man.

The muscles tensed as she spread the thick lotion, and absorbed the heat of his skin, the steely strength beneath.

Moisture gathered in the secret spot between her thighs, which now felt as if it was swollen to twice its normal size.

As she spread the white liquid over the wide expanse of his back, and massaged it into his skin, she timed her breathing to the beat of the timpani drum in her ear, in a desperate attempt to stop herself from hyperventilating.

And passing out before the job was done.

Cooper touched Ella's arm, signalling with his index finger to draw her attention to the blue angel fish darting beneath the shelf of fiery orange coral. Her eyes popped wide behind the mask and her expressive mouth spread into a delighted grin around her mouthpiece.

As they hovered above the reef he watched her admire the brilliant aquamarine of the fish's scales, the white-tipped fins, and the pretty golden edging on the tail, while he admired the open excitement on her face and the buoyant breasts barely contained by purple spandex.

His groin twitched, the blood pumping south despite the chill of the seawater. The sudden flashback, of her stretching under his hands, her breathing coming out on a strangled groan as he caressed the firm skin, didn't do much to deter the growing erection.

He adjusted his junk, grateful for the wet denim of his shorts. Which had been holding him in check ever since he'd dived into the ocean, leaving Dwayne to fit Ella's flippers and snorkelling gear, before she spotted the telltale ridge in his pants.

They'd been out on the reef for over half an hour

now, and he'd mostly got himself under control. But the sight of that shy, excited smile, every time he showed her some new species of fish, or the barnacled wreck of the *Montana*, had been almost as mesmerising as the feel of her fingers fluttering over his bicep whenever she wanted to point something out to him, or the sight of all those lush curves bobbing in the waves.

The woman was killing him. So much so that his golden rule about hooking up with single lady tourists was in danger of being blown right out of the water.

As she pointed delightedly to a shoal of parrot fish flicking past he recalled why he'd made his golden rule in the first place.

Single ladies on holiday generally fell into one of two categories: those on the hunt for no-strings thrills, or those on the look-out for an exotic island romance. As both scenarios invariably involved lots of sex, he'd been more than happy to indulge in hook-ups with the clients when he'd first arrived on the island a decade ago. But back then he'd been eighteen going on thirty with a chip on his shoulder the size of a forest, not a lot of money and even fewer prospects.

In the intervening years, he'd worked his butt off to leave that messed-up kid in the dust. As the owner of a lucrative and growing dive-shop franchise, he sure as hell didn't need to look for acceptance in casual sex any more—or the hassle of pretending to be interested in more.

Which meant single lady tourists had been off limits for a while, unless he knew for certain they weren't after more than the one night of fun. Usually, it was easy enough to figure that out. In fact he'd become an expert at deciding whether a woman had lust or stardust in their eyes when they hit on him. But Ella Radley didn't fit the profile for either.

For starters, she hadn't exactly hit on him despite the obvious chemistry between them. And he still hadn't figured out whether that enchanting mix of artless enthusiasm, sweet-natured kookiness and transparent hunger was all part of an act to get into his pants—or was actually real.

Unfortunately, he was fast running out of time to make up his mind on that score. Sonny had two more fully booked tours scheduled right after this one. And with the old guy's arthritis acting up again, Cooper had agreed to step in and captain them. It was a responsibility he couldn't and wouldn't duck out of. Because Sonny and he had a history.

The old guy had offered him a shift crewing on *The Jez*, when he'd been eighteen and had just spent his last dime on boat fare to the island. He'd been sleeping rough on the quayside and would have sold his soul for a burger and a side order of fries.

He'd done a half-assed job that afternoon, because he'd been weak from hunger and didn't know the first thing about boats. But for the first time since his mother's death, he'd felt safe and worth something. Sonny had given him hope, so whatever debt the old guy called in, he'd pay it.

All of which meant he had to make a decision about Ella Radley before they got back to the dockyards. Should he risk asking her out tonight without being sure about her?

She swam back towards him, her eyes glowing behind the mask, then made the sign for okay.

He gave her a thumbs up and then jerked it towards the boat. They'd run out of time ten minutes ago. Everyone else would be back on the launch by now ready to head back to the mainland. Which meant it was past time for him to make his mind up.

But as she swum ahead of him, her generous butt drawing his gaze with each kick of the flippers, heat flooded his groin again, and he knew his mind had already been made up... Because his brain had stopped making the decisions a good forty minutes ago, when those soft, trembling hands had stroked down his spine and hovered next to the curve of his ass. And he'd heard her sigh, above the rush of blood pounding in his ears.

Ella gripped the rail as the launch bumped against the dock and her snorkel buddy sent her one of his trademark smiles.

He laid his palm on her knee and gave it a squeeze, sending sensation shooting up her thigh. 'Hold up here, while I get everyone off the boat.' The husky, confidential tone had her heart beating into her throat, the way it had been doing most of the day.

She forced herself to breathe evenly, and take stock,

while he and his crew docked the boat and he bid farewell to the rest of the passengers.

Do not get carried away. It's been an amazing morning, but now it's over.

The snorkel tour, the epic beauty of the reef and its sealife had totally lived up to the hype. But it had been Cooper Delaney's constant attention, his gorgeous body and flirtatious smile, that had turned the trip into a once-in-a-lifetime experience.

He'd made her feel special—and for that she couldn't thank him enough. Which meant not overreacting now and putting motivations into his actions that weren't there.

She gulped down the lump of gratitude as she watched him charm May Preston, and give her husband a hearty handshake. Once they'd gone, it would be her turn to say goodbye.

May waved, then winked—making the colour leech into Ella's cheeks—before handing a wad of bills to Cooper. He accepted the money with a quick lift of his cap.

A tip.

Shame tightened Ella's throat as Cooper folded the bills into the back pocket of the jeans he'd changed into. Of course, she should tip him. That would be the best way to thank Cooper for all his attention. And let him know what a great time she'd had.

She grabbed her backpack, found her purse, then had a minor panic attack over the appropriate amount. Was twenty dollars enough? Or thirty? No, forty. Forty, would work. After all, he'd surely need to share it out with the boys in his crew. She counted out the money, her palms sweating, hoping she'd got the amount right. She wanted to be generous, even though she knew that any amount couldn't really repay him for what he'd done.

For two amazing, exhilarating, enchanting hours she'd completely forgotten about all her troubles—and felt like a woman again, a whole, normal, fully functional woman—and for that no tip, however generous, could be big enough.

Slinging the pack over her shoulder, she approached him with the bills clutched in her fist. Now, how to hand it over without blushing like a beetroot?

He turned as she approached, that killer smile making her pulse hammer her neck. The appreciative light in his eyes as his gaze roamed over her had her bikini top shrinking again.

'Hey, there.' The killer smile became deadly. 'I thought I told you to stay put.'

She pursed her lips to still the silly tremble, unable to return the smile. 'I should get out of your way.'

'You're not in my way.' He tucked the curl of hair that had escaped her ponytail back behind her ear—in a casually possessive gesture that only made the tremble intensify. 'But I've got a couple more tours to run today. How about we meet up later? I'll be at a bar on the south side of Half-Moon Cove from around seven onwards...'

Blood thundered in her ears, so she could barely make out what he was saying.

'What d'you say?' he continued. 'You want to hang out some more?'

She nodded, but then his knuckle stroked down her cheek.

Panicked by the clutch of emotion, and the insistent throb of arousal, she shifted away from his touch. Time to make a quick getaway, before the lip quiver got any worse.

She thrust the bills towards him. 'I've had an incredible time. The tour was amazing. Thank you so much.'

His gaze dropped. 'What's this?'

'Umm, I hope it's enough.' Had she miscalculated? Was it too little? 'I wanted to thank you properly, for all the trouble you went to this morning.'

A muscle in his jaw hardened. And she had the strangest feeling she'd insulted him. But then he blinked and the flash of temper disappeared.

'Right.' He took the bills, counted them. 'Forty dollars. That's real generous.' She thought she detected the sour hint of sarcasm, but was sure she must be mistaken when he tipped his cap and shoved the bills into his back pocket. 'Thanks.' For the first time, the easy grin looked like an effort. 'I'll see you around, Miz Radley.'

The clutching feeling collapsed in her chest, at the formal address, the remote tone.

Had she just imagined the invitation for later in the

evening? Or, worse, blown it out of all proportion? Obviously it had been completely casual and she'd made too much of it.

She stood like a dummy, not knowing what to do about the sudden yearning to see the focused heat one more time.

The moment stretched out unbearably as he studied her, his expression remote and unreadable.

'I suppose I should make a move,' she managed to get out at last.

Get off the boat. He probably has a ton of things he needs to be doing.

'Well, thank you again.' *You've said that already.* 'It's been so nice meeting you.' *Stop gushing, you nitwit.* 'Goodbye.' She lifted her hand in a pointless wave that immediately felt like too much.

'Yeah, sure.' He didn't wave back, the words curt, his face blanker than ever.

She rushed down the gangplank, refusing to look back and make an even bigger ninny of herself.

THREE

—

Ella held the plastic column, flipped the switch. Then yelped and dropped it when it shivered to life with a sibilant hum. She signed and flicked the switch back down to dump the vibrator back in its box.

Damn, trying out the sex toy had seemed like such a good idea when she'd been with Cooper, while all her hormones were jumping and jigging under his smouldering stare.

But after their awkward parting, she wasn't feeling all that enthusiastic about discovering the joys of artificial stimulation any more.

Plastic just didn't have the allure of a flesh and blood man. Plus the way things had ended had flatlined all the jiggling. She just felt empty now, and a little foolish, for enjoying his company so much when it hadn't meant anything. She racked her brains to figure out what had happened. Because one minute he'd been laid-back and charming, oozing sex appeal, and asking her if she wanted to 'hang out' later and the next he'd been cold and tense and dismissive.

The phone rang, jolting her out of her dismay. She groped for the handset, grateful for the distraction, especially when her best friend's voice greeted her.

'Ella, hi, how's things in paradise?'

Ella smiled, happiness at the sound of Ruby's voice tempered with a surge of homesickness. 'Ruby, I'm so glad you called.' She gripped the phone, suddenly wishing she could levitate down the phoneline.

Other than this morning's snorkelling trip of a lifetime with the gorgeous—and confusing—Captain Cooper, her trip to Bermuda had been a disaster. She wanted to go home now.

'Is everything okay? You sound a little wobbly.'

'No, everything's good. I guess I'm just over paradise now.'

Ruby laughed, that rich, throaty, naughty laugh that Ella missed so much. 'Uh-oh, so I'm assuming you still haven't met any buff guys in Bermuda shorts, then?'

'Umm, well.' The image of Cooper's exceptionally fit body, his low-slung cut-offs clinging to muscular thighs, that mouth-watering chest gilded with seawater, and the devastating heat in his eyes, popped into Ella's head and rendered her speechless.

'You have met someone, haven't you?' Ruby said, her usual telepathy not dimmed by thousands of miles of ocean. 'Fantastic! Auntie Ruby needs to know all the details.'

'It's nothing, really. He's just a cute guy who was

captaining the snorkel tour I went on this morning. We flirted a bit.' At least, she thought they'd been flirting, but maybe she'd got that wrong too. 'But he's not my type at all. He's far too sexy.' She recalled his callused hands, massaging the thick suncream into her skin—and wondered if Ruby could sense her hot flush from the UK.

Ruby snorted. 'Are you on crack or something? There's no such thing as too sexy. Ever. And clarify "a bit"—does that mean there might be an option for more?'

'Well, he did sort of ask me out.'

'That's fantastic.'

'But I don't think I'll follow it up.'

Her mind snagged on their awkward parting. As flattering as Cooper's undivided attention had been, and as exciting as she'd found snorkelling with him— cocooned together in the exhilarating cool of the ocean as he used sign language to point out the different colourful fish, the sunken wreck of an old schooner and the majestic coral—it hadn't ended all that well.

She pictured again the tight line of his jaw when she'd handed him the hefty tip, and winced at the memory of his curt goodbye.

'Why not?' Ruby asked. 'I thought that was the whole point of this holiday. To have a wild, inappropriate fling and kick-start your sex life?'

'What?' Ella could feel the blush lighting her face like a Christmas tree. 'Who told you that?'

'You did. You said you needed to get away, and rethink your priorities. That you'd become too fixated on finding the right guy, when what you really needed was to find a guy,' Ruby replied, quoting words back to Ella she couldn't remember saying.

She'd been in a fog at the time, probably even in a state of mild shock after visiting her local doctor. She'd booked the holiday at the last minute, packed and headed for the airport the very next day, partly because she hadn't known how to tell Ruby her news. For the first time ever, she'd been unable to confide in her best friend, and that had been the scariest thing of all.

'I thought that's what you meant,' Ruby finished, sounding thoroughly confused now. 'That you were heading to Bermuda to get laid.'

'Not precisely.' Ella felt the weariness of keeping the secret start to overwhelm her.

'So what did you mean?' Ruby's sharp mind lasered straight to the truth. 'This has something to do with the doctor's appointment you had the day before you left, doesn't it? I knew something had freaked you out. What aren't you telling me?'

Ella could hear the urgency in Ruby's voice and knew her friend's natural tendency to create drama was about to conjure up a terminal illness.

'Whatever it is, you have to tell me, Ell. We can sort it out. Together. We always have.'

'Don't worry, Rube.' Ella began talking her friend down from the ledge. 'It's nothing terrible.' Or not that terrible.

'But it does have something to do with the appoint-ment?'

'Yes.'

'Which is?' Ruby's voice had taken on the stern fear-of-God tone she used with her three children, which instantly made them confess to any and all infractions.

Ella knew she wouldn't last two seconds under that kind of interrogation. Even from four thousand miles away. 'Dr Patel took some tests. I'll get the results on Monday.' She blew out a breath, the hollow pressure that had dragged down her stomach a week ago feeling as if it had become a black hole. 'But given my mum's history and the fact that I haven't had a period now in over three months, she thinks I might be going into premature menopause.'

'Okay,' Ruby said carefully. 'But it's just a possibil-ity? Nothing's certain yet?'

Ella shook her head, the black hole starting to choke her. 'I'm pretty certain.'

She'd done something cowardly in her teens, that she'd always believed she would be punished for one day. And sitting in Myra Patel's office, listening to her GP discuss the possible diagnoses, the prospect of a premature menopause had been both devastating, and yet somehow hideously fitting.

She placed her hand on her abdomen to try and con-tain the hollowness in her womb, and stop it seeping out and invading her whole body. 'I've left it too late, Ruby. I'm not going to be able to have children.'

'You don't know any such thing. Not until you get

the tests back. And even if it is premature menopause, a couple of missed periods isn't suddenly going to make you infertile.'

She did know, she'd known ever since she was eighteen and she'd come round from the anaesthesia in the clinic to find Randall gone. She didn't deserve to be a mother, because the one time she'd had the chance she'd given it up to please a guy who hadn't given a hoot about her.

'I suppose you're right,' she said, humouring Ruby.

'Of course I am. You're not allowed to go the full drama until you get the results. Is that understood?'

'Right.' Her lips wrinkled, as she found some small measure of humour in having Ruby be the one to talk her off the ledge for a change.

'Now.' Ruby gave an exasperated sigh. 'I want to know why you didn't tell me about this? Instead of giving me all that cryptic nonsense about finding a guy to shag.'

'I never said shag.' Or at least she was fairly sure she hadn't.

'Don't change the subject. Why didn't you tell me about this before? Instead of running off to Bermuda?'

It was a valid question, because they'd always shared everything—secret crushes, first kisses, how best to fake an orgasm, even the disastrous end to her college romance with Randall, and Ruby's rocky road to romance with the sexy barrister who'd rear-ended her car on a Camden street seven years ago and turned out to be her one true love. But Ella still didn't know how to answer it.

'I just couldn't.' Her voice broke, and a tear escaped. One of the ones she'd been holding captive for over a week.

'Why couldn't you?' Ruby probed, refusing to let it go.

'I guess I was feeling shocked and panicky and inadequate...' She sucked in a breath, forcing herself to face the truth. 'And horribly jealous. Of the fact that you have such a wonderful family and three beautiful children and I may never have any.' She let the breath out. There, she'd said it. 'I felt so ashamed to be envious of you. Because everything you have with Cal and the kids, you've worked for and you deserve.'

The self-pitying tears were flowing freely now. She brushed them away with the heel of her hand. Hoping Ruby couldn't hear the hiccoughs in her breathing. 'I couldn't bear for this to come between us in any way.'

'That's the most ridiculous thing I've ever heard.'

'Why?' The question came out on a tortured sob.

'Well, for starters, you don't want Cal. He's far too uptight and bossy for you. His insistence on being right about everything would make you lose the will to live within a week.'

'Cal's not uptight and bossy. He's lovely.' Ella jumped in to defend Ruby's husband, whom she adored, if only in a purely platonic sense—because he actually was a little bossy.

'Only because he's got me to unwind him on a regular basis, and boss him about back,' Ruby replied. 'But more to the point.' Her voice sobered, the jokey tone gone. 'You don't want my kids, you want your own. And if I deserve my little treasures—not that Ally and Max were particularly treasurable this morning when they decided to declare World War Three on each other using their Weetabix as nuclear warheads—then you certainly do.'

Do I?

The question echoed in her head, but she didn't voice it, Ruby's passionate defence counteracting at least some of the guilt that had been haunting her for over a week.

'You're going to make an incredible mum one day,' Ruby added with complete conviction. 'And, if you have to, there are lots of possible ways of achieving that.'

'How do you mean?'

'You know, like artificial insemination, IVF, donor eggs, surrogacy, adoption, that sort of thing.'

Ruby's matter-of-fact response shrank a little of the black hole in her belly. She hadn't considered any of those options yet, the prospect of infertility too shocking to get past. But why shouldn't she? If the worst came to the worst and Myra's diagnosis was correct?

'I guess you're right, I hadn't really—'

'But frankly,' Ruby interrupted, 'I think we're getting the cart before the stallion here.'

'Excuse me?'

'Ella, your biggest problem when it comes to having a child of your own is not the possibility of a premature menopause. It's the fact that every guy you've been out with since that tosser in college has been so mind-numbingly dull even I couldn't be bothered to flirt with them.'

Ella frowned, picturing the handful of guys she'd dated in the last decade. And realised that Ruby's outrageous statement might not actually be all that far off the mark—because she couldn't recall a single one of them with any degree of clarity.

When had dating become such an effort? And sex such a chore?

Was that why she'd had a rush of blood to the head at Cooper's casual suggestion of a drink later? Flirting with him had been exciting, exhilarating, and yet she'd totally freaked out when he'd offered her the chance to take it further.

What was that about? She was thirty-four, for goodness' sake, not ninety.

'The thing is, Ella,' Ruby continued, 'I know sexual chemistry isn't everything in a relationship—and Randall the dickhead is a case in point.'

Ella winced at hearing Randall's name spoken aloud—a name they'd both avoided speaking for sixteen years. But the gaping wound her college boyfriend had caused—which she'd believed then would fester for the rest of her life—had scabbed over in the years since. Because the mention of his name didn't hurt any more; it only made her feel ashamed, that she'd fallen for him so easily, mistaken a couple of really spectacular orgasms for love, and then let him bulldoze her into doing something she would later regret.

'But sometimes chemistry can come in very handy, if you need a serious pick–me-up in the dating department,' Ruby continued. 'Which brings us right back to Captain Studly from your snorkel tour.'

Didn't it just?

'So tell me again,' Ruby continued. 'Why exactly can't you take him up on his offer of a date?'

'Because I'm not entirely sure he meant it.'

'And why would you think that? Talk me through it.'

'Well, he asked me if I'd like to hook up for a drink at this local hang-out after he finished work at seven and I panicked.' She'd chickened out, because Cooper Delaney had been more man than she'd had the guts to handle in a very long time—it all seemed so obvious now. 'And then I had to get off the boat, because he was busy. But it was all very casual, and we never agreed on anything specific.'

Even if the memory of Cooper's offer of a date thrilled her now, instead of terrifying her, the memory of his face, closed off and impassive, when she'd said that final goodbye wasn't far behind.

'Did this local hang-out have a name?' Ruby probed.

'No, but I think...' She searched her memory; hadn't he told her where it was? 'Half-Moon Cove.' The location echoed in her head in his deep American accent. 'He mentioned it was on the south side of Half-Moon Cove.'

'Fantastic. That's all we need.'

'It is?'

'Yes, now shut up and listen to Auntie Ruby.' Ruby paused, and the tickle of excitement in Ella's belly began to buzz as if she were being stroked by the vibrator. 'Captain Studly most definitely did invite you on a date. Time and location are all the specifics you need. And you are flipping well going to go on it.'

'But what if—?'

'No buts.' Ruby cut her off. 'It's way past time Ella Radley started dating the sort of man candy that might actually have some hope of exciting her enough to get her past first base.'

'I've been past first base in the past decade,' she said, indignantly—even if she couldn't remember the events in any great detail. 'But I don't think—'

'Uh-uh-uh, didn't you hear the "no buts" stipulation?' Ruby paused, but not long enough for Ella to form a suitable response. 'That goes hand in hand with the "no panicking" initiative. If you feel yourself starting to hyperventilate because Captain Studly is too Studly, just think of him as a test run. You need to get your flirt on, Ella, and he sounds like the perfect guy to practise on.'

And just like that, the buzz in Ella's belly sank even lower and became a definite hum.

FOUR

—

'You sure you're okay here, ma'am? The Rum Runner isn't much for the tourists, just a local hang-out. I could take you to some nice places in Hamilton, where the cruise ships dock, no extra charge?'

'No, thank you, this is perfect, Earl.' Exhilaration fluttered in Ella's chest as she stepped out of the cab and surveyed the ramshackle bar at the end of the rutted beach road.

The twinkle of fairy lights on weathered wood added enchantment to the haphazard structure, which stood drunkenly, mounted on stilts over the water, as if it had downed one too many rum punches. The scent of the sea freshened the cloud of smoke and sweat as the customers spilled out of the saloon-style doors. The densely packed crowd smoked and chatted on the porch, while she could see couples dancing inside past the tables, swinging and swaying to the infectious soca beat, making the boardwalk pound beneath her sandals.

'You're sure this is the only place on the south side of Half-Moon Cove?' She handed Earl, her taxi driver, his fare and a generous tip through the cab window.

'Uh-huh.' Unlike Cooper, he sent her a wide smile as he tucked the money into the top pocket of his Hawaiian shirt. 'Cove's yonder.' He nodded towards a wide beach that began past the rocks at the end of the country road.

Edged by palm trees and vines and curving round the headland into the darkness, the cove lived up to its name, looking impossibly romantic as moonlight shimmered off the gently lapping surf.

'Ain't no other bars down here that I know of.' Pulling a card out of his pocket, he handed it to her. 'You give Earl a call when you need to get back. Not much traffic this way.'

After waving him off and watching the cab lights bounce out of sight down the unpaved road, she slipped the card into her bag, and slung the strap over her shoulder. Then she sucked in a fortifying breath and let it out in a rush.

Whether or not Cooper was here, she intended to enjoy herself. Ruby had given her the pep talk to end all pep talks, back at the hotel.

It was way past time she started living again, took the power back and charted her own course when it came to choosing the men she dated. And stopped boring herself to death with safe and secure and invited a little danger in. Bermuda with its colourful, chaotic nightlife and studly boat captains had to be the per-

fect place to start. Not least because if tonight went
tits up, this particular dating disaster wouldn't be able
to follow her home.

Ruby's words of dating wisdom had bolstered her
courage as she'd showered, and waxed, and moistur-
ised, and primped and perfumed. After far too much
debate, she'd picked out an understated ensemble of
skinny pedal-pusher jeans, heeled sandals and a lace-
edged camisole. She'd pinned up her unruly hair, and
plastered on a lot more make-up than she usually
wore—as per Ruby's specific instructions—then dug
out her favourite waterfall earrings and the cascade of
cheap but cheerful bracelets she'd bought at Camden
Market two weeks ago to complete the outfit.

The simple ritual of getting ready had helped temper her terror with a heady cocktail of excitement and
anticipation.

Edging past the people milling around on the porch,
she made her way to the bar. She'd have a couple of
drinks and then, if Cooper didn't show, she could always ring Earl back and call it a night. At least she
would have got to see something of the island before
leaving.

The Rum Runner had a funky, relaxed vibe that reminded her of Sol's Salsa Joint on Camden Lock where
Ruby and she and their wide circle of friends had once
congregated on a Friday night to kick back after the
working week. Ruby didn't go out much any more because of the kids, and most of their other friends had
settled down and/or moved away in the last few years,

so she'd slowly stopped going to Sol's too, but she'd always loved to dance and it occurred to her she'd missed the weekly ritual.

Her hips swung in time to the blast of horns and the fast infectious drum beat as the band on the stage in the far corner went into another number. She grinned as she wound her way through the packed tables—the soca rhythm an irresistible blend of joy and seduction—and felt the optimism that had always been so much a part of her personality seep back into her soul.

Slipping past a group of loudly dressed guys at the bar, she smiled back when one of them touched his beer bottle to his forehead in a silent salute.

'What'll it be, miz?' a barman addressed her once she had managed to inch past the crush of people and found a spot to rest her elbows on the bar. The thin layer of sweat on his dark skin made the red ink of the snake tattoo on his bicep glisten.

She tapped her toe to the bass guitar riff while checking out the names of the drinks scrawled on the chalkboard behind him—only a few of which she recognised. 'What would you recommend?'

'For you?' The lilting Caribbean accent matched the friendly twinkle in the barman's *café-au-lait*-coloured eyes. 'Only a Rum Swizzle will do.'

'That sounds wonderful.' She had absolutely no clue what that was. But tonight Ella Radley was on a mission, to get her flirt on and set it free. And for that, a Rum Swizzle sounded like just the ticket.

He returned a few minutes later and presented her

with a tall icy glass of tangerine-coloured liquid, garnished with a chunk of pineapple, a swirl of orange peel and a maraschino cherry. She took a sip and the potent flavour of rum, fruit juice and liquor zinged off her tastebuds. So that was why they called it a Swizzle.

'Delicious,' she shouted over the music. 'How much do I owe you?'

'Not a thing.' A gold tooth winked in the pearly white of his smile. 'Your first Rum Swizzle in my place is always on the house.'

'You own this bar?'

He nodded. 'Sure do.'

A shot of adrenaline rushed through her to add to the hit from the rum. And Ruby's voice seemed to whisper in her ear.

Above all be bold—and seize the initiative—flirting is much more fun if you own it.

'Do you know a guy called Cooper Delaney?'

'Coop? Sure I know Coop. What do you want him for?' He sounded a bit put out. 'That boy's nothing but trouble.'

That was what she was counting on, she thought, the adrenaline more intoxicating than the Swizzle. She took another fortifying sip of the delicious concoction. 'Is he likely to be in tonight, do you think?'

She heard the eagerness in her tone but didn't care if it made her sound tarty. Discovering her inner flirt would be so much easier with a guy she already knew could make her hormones wake up and jiggle. And considering they'd been in hibernation, like, for ever, she needed all the help she could get.

The bartender's gaze was drawn to something past her shoulder. 'Yeah, he'll be in tonight.'

'Really, you're sure?' she said, then bit her lip.

Dial down on the tarty—that sounded a bit too eager.

'Uh-huh.' His dark gaze returned to her face.

'Back off, Henry. You're poaching.'

Ella spun round at the deep, wonderfully familiar accent—and the shot of adrenaline went into overdrive. Cooper Delaney had looked super-fit that morning in ragged denim, but he took fit to a whole new level in a dark blue polo shirt and black jeans. But then her head carried on spinning and she started to tilt.

A tanned hand shot out to grasp her upper arm and hold her upright. 'Damn it, Henry, how many of those things have you given her?'

'Only the one.' The barman, who Ella's slightly fuzzy brain had registered must be called Henry, sounded affronted.

'Oh, yeah?'

Ella blinked, hearing the edge in Cooper's usually relaxed tone. Was he mad about something? And what did it have to do with Henry, the benevolent barman?

Cooper slapped a couple of bills onto the bar with enough force to make her jump. 'That's for the rum punch, man. The lady's with me.'

Really? Fabulous.

So she hadn't imagined his offer of a date. The spurt of joy at the thought was quickly quashed, though, when his fingers tightened on her arm and he slanted her a look that didn't seem particularly pleased to see her. 'We're out of here.'

'But I haven't finished my drink.' She pivoted on her heel, making a grab for her glass. But missed as he hauled her away from the bar.

'You've had enough.'

Henry shrugged and shouted after them, 'Sorry, miz. I told you he was no good.'

'You didn't have to pay for that,' she said, racing to keep up with his long strides as he marched past the tables and headed out into the night, dragging her along in his wake. 'Henry said it was on the house.'

'Yeah, I'll just bet he did.' Was that a snarl?

A succession of people called out a greeting to him or shouted across the crowd, but other than throwing back a quick wave of acknowledgement he barely broke stride. By the time they stepped off the deck and he swung her round to face him, she was breathless, the happy glow from her Swizzle fading fast.

'Okay, let's have it.' His shadowed face looked harsh in the half-light from the bar as he grasped both her arms, and made full use of his superior height. 'What are you doing here?'

'I...' And just like that her tongue swelled up, rendering her speechless. And all Ruby's advice about how to put her flirt on got washed away on a tidal wave of mortification.

He didn't look remote, the way he had when they'd parted that morning. He looked upset.

She'd made a terrible mistake—coming here when he hadn't really meant to...

'Because if you've come all the way out here to give me another smackdown, don't bother. I got the message the first time, sweetheart. Loud and clear.'

Smackdown? What smackdown?

'I should leave,' she blurted out, suddenly wishing that the worn floorboards of the bar's deck would crack open and swallow her whole. Or better yet whisk her back to her nice, quiet, ocean-view room at the resort.

Sticking to safe might be dull, but at least it didn't get you into these sorts of pickles. She'd never managed to piss off any of the guys she'd actually dated to this extent.

She sent a wistful glance back at The Rum Runner—the joyous dance music pumping out into the night. The lively bar had contained so many exciting possibilities less than five minutes ago. But as she stepped past him he didn't let go.

'Hey, hang on a minute.' The edge had left his voice. 'You didn't answer my question.'

'Was there a question in there?' she asked.

He didn't look mad any more, which she supposed was good.

But as his emerald gaze raked over her the focused attention made her breasts tighten. Humiliating her even more. Obviously her nipples were completely immune to his disapproval.

But then his wide lips quirked. 'It was never meant as a smackdown, was it?'

She tugged herself loose, and stepped back—starting to get annoyed. Okay, so she'd misinterpreted his offer of a date. Although how she had, she still wasn't sure. And her big coming-out party was officially a washout—but did he really have to gloat? And what was all this nonsense about a smackdown? 'I really have to go.'

She went to walk round him again. But his large hand wrapped around her wrist and drew her up short. 'Hey, don't... Don't go.'

He stood so close, the delicious scent of seawater and soap surrounded her. Making it a little hard for her to process the words. Was he apologising now? After all but biting her head off? 'Captain Delaney, I don't think—' she began.

'Call me Coop,' he murmured, the husky tone sending those tempting shivers of reaction back up her spine.

She drew in a breath, not able to recall a single one of Ruby's careful instructions as he stared down at her with the glint of appreciation in his eyes—and fairly sure she didn't want to any more. This evening had turned into a disaster.

She might as well face it, she would never be as good a flirt as Ruby, even if she took a degree course. She huffed out a breath. 'Listen, I genuinely thought you asked me here, and I had such a nice time this morning, I don't want to sour it now.' She hooked a thumb over her shoulder, feeling stupidly bereft at the thought of her party night ending so soon, and so ignominiously. 'But I really think I should go now.'

Because I'm a little concerned you might have a border-line personality disorder.

She came here to see you. You dumbass.

Warmth spread across Cooper's chest like a shot of hard liquor but was tempered by a harsh jolt of regret as he registered the wary caution in Ella's eyes—which looked even bigger accented with the glittery powder. Her lips pursed, glossy with lipstick in the half-light, as if she were determined to stop them trembling, cru-cifying him.

What the hell were you thinking? Behaving like such a jerk?

Even he wasn't sure what had gripped him when he'd walked into the bar and spotted her chatting with Henry, with that flushed excitement on her face. But the word that had echoed through his head had been unmistakable.

Mine.

And then everything had gone straight to hell.

Of course, his crazy reaction might have had some-thing to do with the severe case of sexual frustration he'd been riding ever since she'd stepped aboard the boat that morning, but that hardly excused it. And the truth was he'd been handling it just fine, until the mo-ment she'd handed him that wad of bills on the dock.

That was the precise moment he'd lost his grip on reality.

He'd been snarky and rude, acting as if she'd offered to kick him in the nuts, instead of giving him a forty-dollar tip.

He accepted tips all the time, to hand over to the kids who crewed the boat. Just the way Sonny had done for him when he was a kid.

He'd founded his business on the generosity of tourists like May Preston and her husband, who came back every year and always showed their appreciation way above the going rate. But when Ella had done the same, somehow he'd lost it. Instead of seeing her generosity and thoughtfulness for what it was, he'd been thrown back in time to the humiliation of his high-school days and the never-ending stream of dead-end jobs he'd taken on to keep him and his mom afloat. Back then, his teenage pride had taken a hit every time he had to accept a gratuity from people he knew talked trash about his mom behind his back. But he'd brushed that huge chip off his shoulder years ago, or at least he'd thought he had.

Why the weight of the damn thing had reappeared at that precise moment and soured his final few moments with Ella, he didn't have a clue, and he didn't plan to examine it too closely. All that mattered now was that he didn't blow his second chance with her.

That she'd come down to The Rum Runner at his suggestion was one hell of a balm to his over-touchy ego. The least he could do now was show her a good time. And given how cute and sexy she looked in those hip-hugger jeans and that skimpy tank it wasn't exactly going to be a hardship.

He raked his hand through his hair, trying to grab hold of some of his usual charm with women, and think of how best to engineer his way back into her good graces after acting like such a douche.

Then he recalled how she'd been moving that lush butt while chatting to Henry, rocking her hips in time to the music. His pal Oggie's band played the opening sax solo, backed by the manic drum beat, of their best dance track. And he hoped he had his answer.

'You can't go back to the hotel. Not before you've danced to some real Bermuda soca with me.'

'I don't know...'

She glanced back at the bar, but he could hear her hesitation.

'Sure you do. It'll be fun.' He took her hand, lifted it to his lips and buzzed a quick kiss across her knuckles. 'You've come all this way. And I've acted like a jerk. So I owe you.'

'That's really not necessary.' She chewed on her bottom lip, the indecision in her voice crucifying him a little more.

'Sure it is. One dance. By way of an apology? That's all I'm asking.'

The shy smile was enough to tell him she'd forgiven him. But the sparkle of anticipation was tempered by caution. 'Okay, I don't see how one dance could hurt.'

'Awesome.' He placed his hand on her waist to direct her back into the bar, the spike of lust making his throat go dry when her hip bumped his thigh.

'It may be thirsty work, though,' she shouted above the bump and grind of drums and bass. 'Perhaps I should go back and get my Rum Swizzle?'

'Let's work up a sweat first,' he said, placing firm hands on her hips as he slotted them both into the packed dancefloor, the sweat already slick on his forehead. 'I'll buy you one later.'

Dancing with her was bound to be really thirsty work, but he didn't plan to let her have any more Rum Swizzles. Those damn things were lethal, especially on an empty stomach—and with her tiny frame and that little stumble at the bar after only half a glass, he would hazard a guess Ella Radley was a really cheap drunk. He wanted her fully conscious for the rest of the night, so he could enjoy her company—and anything else she wanted to offer him.

Her perfume—a refreshing mix of citrus and spices—drifted over him as she placed her hands lightly on his shoulders and rolled her hips to the riotous bass beat in a natural, unaffected rhythm that was more seductive than original sin.

She grinned up at him, the cute smile a tempting mix of innocence and provocation, then jerked up on her toes to shout in his ear. 'Aye-aye, Captain. But be warned. I'm on a mission tonight to get whatever I want.'

His hands tightened on her hips as her belly

bumped against him and his groin throbbed in time to the music. 'Not a problem, sweetheart.'

Because so am I.

'That's enough of that.' Coop lifted the sunshine drink out of her hand and held it easily out of reach. 'I want you able to walk out of here.'

Ella sent him a mock pout, but couldn't disguise her happiness as his gaze settled on her face. The way it had been doing all evening, with a gratifying combination of possessiveness and desire.

They'd danced until they were breathless to the band's medley of soca anthems, then eased into the seductive moves of the soul tunes when they slowed the pace later in the evening.

It was well after midnight now, and the bar had begun to empty out. His large group of friends, most of whom had come over to their table to banter with Coop or introduce themselves to her, had mostly drifted away, leaving only a small group of die-hard couples on the dance floor still bumping and grinding with gusto and a scatter of people by the bar.

She'd danced with a few of the other guys, enjoying that relaxed, casual camaraderie that reminded her of her own friendship group back in Camden. But most of all she'd enjoyed the feel of Cooper's gaze on her throughout the evening—that said to everyone they were a couple. That—how had he put it?—she was with him, for the night. It had made her feel as if she belonged here, even though she was thousands of miles from home.

But more than that, his constant attention and that quick easy smile had both relaxed her and yet held a delicious tension, a promise of what was to come. Because she had no doubts whatsoever about where this was all headed. The smouldering looks, the proprietary touches, the irresistible scent of him, tangy and salty and spicy, wrapping around her in a potent blend of pheromones and sweat. And the delicious press of his erection outlined by the slow, seductive, sinuous moves of his muscular body as they danced.

The coil of desire had been pulsing in the pit of her stomach for hours now. Ready for him to make the next move—and if he didn't, she was ready to take the unprecedented step of making the move for him.

It was official. Ella Radley's flirt was now fully operational, the intoxicating buzz of the Rum Swizzles nothing compared to the glorious buzz of anticipation.

'And where exactly would I be walking to?' She arched an eyebrow, her tone rich with a confidence she'd thought had died inside her a lifetime ago.

His thumb brushed her cheek, his irises a mesmerising moss green in the bar's half-light. Resting his forehead on hers, he closed his fingers over her nape, that wandering thumb caressing the frantic pulse in her neck. 'My hut's down at the other end of the cove. You ready to take a stroll with me in the moonlight?'

It was the invitation she'd been waiting for, but the surge of excitement still made her giddy. She could already feel those rough, capable fingers on the slick flesh between her thighs. She wanted to taste him, touch him, inhale that delicious scent, and take the impressive ridge in his pants inside her. Her sex clasped and released, hollow and aching with the need to be filled.

Touching her lips to his, she licked across the seam of the wide, sensual mouth that had been driving her wild all day. The shot of adrenaline was as stimulating as the pulse of reaction when she heard him drag in a ragged breath. His fingers plunged into her hair, then clasped her head so his tongue could plunder.

She let him in, her tongue duelling with his as they sank into the ravenous kiss.

He broke away first, the pants of his breathing as thready as her own. 'I'm going to take that as a yes.'

She nodded, not sure she could speak around the joy closing off her throat.

Standing, he gripped her hand and hauled her out of her chair. He tossed a few dollars on the table, and sent Henry a parting salute. She waved her own goodbye at the barman, who was stacking glasses, a rueful smile on his face.

'See you around, pretty lady.' Henry waved back, shouting over the murmur of goodbyes being thrown their way by the bar's other remaining patrons. 'And don't you be doing anything I wouldn't, Coop.'

Coop dragged her outside, sending her a wicked grin over his shoulder as the night closed over them. 'Given what you would do, man,' he whispered for her ears alone, 'that gives me a hell of a lot of options.'

For some strange reason she found the comment riotously funny, her chuckle blending with the fading beat of music and the sound of the rolling and retreating tide as they stepped off the deck onto the beach. He laid his arm across her shoulders, tugged her into his side to lead her along the sand and into the darkness.

Crickets and night crawlers added an acoustic accompaniment to the flickering light of the fireflies in the undergrowth and the hushed lap of the water. She kicked off her sandals, picked them up, and let her toes seep into the damp sand.

The walk in the moonlight he'd promised went past in a blur, neither of them speaking, the only sound the sea, the insects and the rhythmic bump of her own heartbeat. A one-storey shack raised over the beach on a wraparound deck appeared as if by magic out of the undergrowth on the edge of the sand. A lamp suspended from the porch rail shone like a homing beacon, illuminating the rudimentary clapboard structure.

He dropped his arm from around her shoulders, to lace his fingers through hers and lead her up the steps onto the porch.

'You live here?' she asked, enchanted by the spartan dwelling.

'Yeah, mostly.' He held open the screen door to reveal a large, sparsely furnished, but tidy room. A sofa with well-worn cushions made up the living area, while a large mattress, the sheets neatly folded across the bottom, stood in front of the open deck. A tiny kitchenette cordoned off by a waist-high counter took up the hut's back wall, next to a door that she deduced must lead to a bathroom.

But it was the open deck, blending the hut's interior with the beach outside, that took her breath away. The silvery glow of the moon dipped over the horizon, shimmering over the water and making the dark sand look as if it disappeared into oblivion. The fresh scent of sea and salt and exotic blooms only added to the feeling of wild, untamed freedom that was so like Cooper himself.

'It suits you,' she said.

He huffed, the half-laugh both wry and amused. 'Why? Because it's cheap?' he said and she heard the cynical edge.

'No, because it's charming and unpretentious and unconventional.'

He turned up the lamp, giving the modest hut a golden glow.

Walking to the open deck, he closed two large shutters and then slid the screen door across, cocooning them in together against the Caribbean night. Only the sparkle of moonlight and the sound of surf and chirping insects seeped through the slats.

'Don't want to risk getting our butts bitten off by mosquitos,' he said, crossing the short distance back to her.

She laughed, the rough stubble on his jaw ticklish

against her neck as he gripped her hips and nuzzled the sensitive skin beneath her ear.

'Especially such a cute butt,' he added, giving the butt in question an appreciative squeeze.

She wrapped her arms around his lean waist and slipped her fingers beneath the waistband of his jeans, to caress the tight muscles of the backside she had admired that morning in wet denim. 'I can totally get behind that sentiment.'

He chuckled, warm, callused palms sneaking under her camisole to glide up to her ribcage and send a series of tremors through her body.

'Flattery will get you everywhere,' he said. Before placing his mouth on hers at last.

Releasing his bum, she lifted arms lethargic with lust and draped them over his broad shoulders; driving her fingers into the soft curls at his nape, she let him devour her. He angled his hips and the thick ridge in his pants rubbed against her belly.

Oh, yes, I want this so much.

To be taken, to take. She wanted to let her body do the asking and have his answer, in the primordial mating ritual of two animals in need of an endorphin fix. The fact that she liked him, that he seemed a genuinely nice guy, didn't hurt. But right here, right now, as the building firestorm made the pulsing ache in her sex unbearable, and her nipples tighten into hard, swollen nubs, all she really cared about was satisfying the driving hunger.

His large hands rose from her waist to frame her

face and she revelled in the primitive need making his eyes darken and the muscle in his jaw flex and release.

'Before we take this any further...' he trapped her against the hut's wall, the heavy ridge thickening even more '...I need to know if you're on the pill.'

Crushing disappointment cut through the fog of rum and arousal. 'You don't have any condoms? I don't either, I didn't think—'

'Hey, don't panic,' he interrupted. 'I've got condoms.'

'Oh, thank God.' Relief gushed like molten lava between her thighs.

'But I'm a belt and braces kind of guy. Condoms break.' He scooped her hair off her neck, pressed those clever lips to her collarbone, shattering her concentration. 'That's how I happened. I'm not looking to father another me.'

She heard the note of regret, and had the sudden urge to soothe. 'But you're so beautiful.' She cradled his lean cheeks between her palms, drew her thumb over one tawny brow and grinned into those piercing emerald eyes—which had crinkled at the corners with amusement. 'Your mother must have been so pleased to have you,' she said, loving the rasp of the manly stubble on his cheeks as all her inhibitions happily dissolved in the sweet buzz of Rum Swizzles and pheromones. 'Even if you were an accident.'

She heard his chuckle. Had she said something funny? She hadn't meant to.

'Not really.' He sent her the secret hey-there-gorgeous grin that he'd sent her when they were underwater and exploring the reef. Then it had flattered her, as if they were the only two people in the whole ocean allowed to explore its treasures; now it made her heart muscle squeeze and release, exciting her.

'Has anyone ever told you you're great for a guy's ego when you're hammered?'

'I'm not hammered,' she said, sure she wasn't. He'd only let her have two more Rum Swizzles, which he'd insisted on mixing himself behind the bar. And they hadn't tasted nearly as alcoholic as that first one. Plus she'd pigged out on the popcorn shrimp, some delicious jalapeño cheese things and the chips and dips and other nibbles that had appeared at their table as if by magic between dance sets. Right now she was pleasantly buzzed, but her senses felt heightened, more acute, not dull or fuzzy.

He touched his nose to hers. 'If you say so, miz,' he said in a perfect echo of Henry the friendly barman's Bermudan accent.

The spontaneous laugh turned to a staggered moan as his hands snuck under her camisole and cupped her breasts.

'Oh, yes.' She arched into the bold caress as his thumbs brushed her nipples, making the rigid peaks ache. 'That feels fabulous.'

He laughed. 'Stop distracting me and answer the damn question.'

She opened her mouth to ask what question, but then he plucked at one pulsating nipple, rolling it between his thumb and forefinger, and all that came out was a groaned, 'Yes.'

'Hallelujah.'

His teasing fingers left her breast to drag her top over her head. And unclip the hook of her bra. He tugged his shirt over his head and tossed it over his shoulder, revealing the naked chest that she'd imagined touching all day.

Hallelujah indeed.

He boosted her into his arms, her back bumping the wall, as he wedged the hard ridge between her thighs, pressing it against the damp gusset of her jeans. She gripped his shoulders, her head spinning from the sensory overload. Then he ducked his head to capture one thrusting nipple between his lips and suckled hard.

Fire roared down to her core and she writhed, swivelling her hips to increase the pressure of his magnificent erection on that hot, sweet, swollen spot.

He blew across her wet breast, the cool air making it tingle and tighten more. 'Damn, but you're gorgeous.'

'So are you,' she said, admiring the bulge of his biceps as he held her up, the bunched pecs and sculpted abs, and the happy trail that bloomed into a forest of dark blond curls where his low-slung jeans had slipped down under the pressure of her clutching thighs.

'Can I see you naked? Please?' she asked.

His answering laugh sounded strained. 'I guess so, seeing as you asked so nice.' He dropped her suddenly, clutched her arm as she stumbled. 'Race you.'

She giggled as he hopped around on one foot, wrestling to get his boot off.

'Don't just stand there.' He tossed the boot across the room. 'Lose the damn pants or you'll have to pay a forfeit.'

Unbuttoning her jeans, she slipped them over her hips, going for the full stripper effect as she wiggled out of them, and loving the way his nostrils flared as he lost the other boot.

His wicked grin spread, and her heart rate accelerated, as he unhooked his trousers, shoved them down and kicked them off, not once taking his eyes off her.

Her gaze caught on the magnificent erection, standing proud in the nest of tawny curls. 'Wow...that's... really rather exceptional.'

He laughed. 'Have I told you, I love your accent?' He inclined his head towards the last piece of clothing she had on. 'Now lose the panties, before I rip them off.'

She whipped them off, twirled them on her finger and flung them away with a flourish.

'Good job.' He grabbed her wrist and dragged her to the bed, lying down beside her on the surprisingly comfy mattress.

She shivered, the light breeze coming through the shutters scented with the ocean.

His thumb trailed down her sternum. Then circled one heavy breast. She lifted up on her elbows to kiss him. The taste of the cola he'd been drinking all evening was as sweet as the weight of that exceptional erection cradled against her belly. Anticipation roared through her system. It had been so long since she'd felt this sexy, this aroused, this playful.

Ruby was right: why had she always been so serious about sex after college? She planned to correct that right now—she licked into his mouth, loving his staggered groan—with this gorgeous, hot, wonderfully reckless guy who was a gift she couldn't wait to unwrap.

His hands framed her face, his fingers plunging into her hair. She wrapped greedy fingers around the thick erection, slid her hand from root to tip, assessing its girth, its length, imagining it embedded into that aching, empty place between her legs.

But he swore softly as her thumb glided over the plump head, gathering the slick drop of moisture—and grabbed hold of her wrist, to tug her hand away.

'I'm way too close for that, sweetheart, but how about…?' His voice trailed off as he traced his thumb between her breasts, circled her belly button, then delved into the hot, aching flesh of her sex.

Moisture flooded between her thighs.

She drew her knees up, let her head drop back, her sobs of pleasure loud over the sound of surf and the rustle of the breeze against their sweat-slicked bodies.

He circled and toyed with the slick nub, teasing the perfect spot. 'That's it, baby, I want to see you come for me.'

One large, blunt finger entered her, then another pushed in beside it, stretching her, stroking the walls of her sex as his thumb continued to play, to provoke.

Sensation fired across her skin, trapped her breath under her breastbone. The coil of need tightened like a vice, the pleasure turning to devastating, delicious pain as it built to impossible proportions but wouldn't let her go.

Clinging to his shoulders, urging him on, she pumped her hips into his hand, riding that wonderfully devious touch as she gave herself up to the riot of sensations.

Then he moved down on the bed, and disappeared between her knees. She shouted out in shock and delight as his tongue lapped at her swollen clitoris. Then he captured the slick nub between his lips and sucked. The coil yanked tight and then exploded in a dazzling shower of sensation. She sobbed—the long, thin cry of completion trapped in her throat as his mouth drove her through the last magnificent swell of orgasm.

She pressed her legs together as he lifted his head, collapsing back to earth. Shuddering and shaking, she opened her eyes as he grinned down at her, his lips slick with her juices.

The rumbled hum of his approval folded around her heart like a caress.

'Sweeter than a Rum Swizzle,' he whispered, the sensual, playful grin even more beautiful than the rest of him.

The sight was so unbearably erotic, gratitude swelled in her chest, turning her voice into a throaty purr. 'Thank you.'

His lips tipped up at the edges. 'No need to thank

me, baby, the pleasure was all mine.' He placed a kiss on the tip of her nose. 'But we're not finished yet,' he added, reaching across her to grab a foil packet from a glass jar on the upturned crate that doubled as a bedside table. He held it up. 'You want to do the honours, or should I?'

She lifted it out of his hand, her mouth watering at the thought of exploring that magnificent erection. And silently thanking him again for keeping things light and fun. 'Let me.'

She pushed his shoulder, until he lay on his back, that proud erection jutting up towards his belly button. Holding the packet in her hand, she licked the new bead of moisture off the tip. Savouring the taste of him. And eager to torment him the way he'd tormented her.

But the guttural groan was followed by a harsh expletive and before she could take him into her mouth he clasped her cheeks to hold her back.

'I'm sorry, sweetheart, but we're going to have to save that for later. I'm not Superman—and I don't want to disappoint you.'

He couldn't possibly disappoint her, she thought. But only laughed at his look of panic. 'Are you sure you're not Superman?'

'I used to be...' The confident smile returned as he rolled on top of her and snagged the condom packet out of her hand. 'But you're zapping all my superpowers.'

Ripping the foil with his teeth, he sheathed himself quickly, before nudging her thighs apart and settling between them. She felt the bulbous head nudge at her entrance as he held her hips, angling her pelvis.

She groaned as the thick shaft speared through the tight sheath, overwhelming her senses as her slick, swollen flesh stretched to receive him.

At last he was buried deep, pushing at her cervix. She gasped, astonished at the fullness, and how right, how exquisite it felt. She stroked his nape with unsteady fingers, enjoying the weight of him, the feeling of intimacy, and unity.

'I think you've boldly gone where no man has gone before.' She laughed, surprising herself with the ridiculous comment. But her heart felt so full, her body so magnificent, impaled on his. Could she come again? So soon after an orgasm? She certainly never had before, but with Cooper anything felt possible.

He swore, panting, the sinews of his neck straining beneath her fingers as he began to move. 'Damn it, woman, don't quote *Star Trek* at me now,' he grunted, between thrusts. 'Can't you see I'm trying to Klingon here.'

She snorted a laugh that choked into a sob as he stroked a place deep inside that triggered another unstoppable rush towards orgasm.

Goodness. I have a G-spot. Who knew?

'Touch yourself,' he demanded. 'I want you to come with me.'

She spread her own folds, blindly rubbing the stiff nub as he directed, feeling wild and untamed, greedily pursuing her own pleasure as the wave became sharper, sweeter, more glorious.

She rode the crest, his ragged grunts matching her loud moans, and soared towards oblivion with tears of joy and laughter—and staggered astonishment—hovering on her lids.

She drifted back to consciousness, the euphoria of afterglow slowly replaced by discomfort from the thick penis still lodged inside her.

He lifted off her, making her groan as her tight flesh struggled to release him.

'That was seriously awesome.' Flopping over onto his back, he lay with his arm over his face. 'You're incredibly tight.'

She felt herself blush, an odd combination of pleasure and acute embarrassment at the intimate comment. 'Only because you're so big,' she said, trying to find the playful tone again.

'While my ego and I thank you for that...' he dropped his arm to find her hand and thread his fingers through hers '...I'm not that much bigger than the average guy.'

The blush glowed. Maybe it wasn't just his size that had made him feel so large. Maybe it was because she hadn't done it with anyone in at least a year. And certainly never with that much energy or enthusiasm.

He turned onto his side, and cupped her cheek, his palm cool against her heated flesh. 'Has it been a while?'

She blinked, disconcerted by the perceptive comment. 'Are you a mind-reader?'

He touched her cheek, the tender, curious smile more seductive than the tangy scent of sex that surrounded them. 'How long?'

She huffed out a laugh, the embarrassment burned away by a new surge of arousal. 'Far too long, it seems.'

He hooked his thigh over her legs, shocking her when something stiff prodded her hip.

'Is that...?' She looked down, stunned to see him hard and ready again still sheathed by the condom.

He lifted her chin, grinning. 'Yeah, it is.' The cheeky grin—not to mention his astonishing powers of recuperation—made him seem very boyish. Too boyish.

'How old are you?' she asked, before she could think better of it.

His lips tilted. 'Nearly thirty.'

She propped herself up on her elbows. Good grief, he was still in his twenties. 'How nearly?'

'I'll be twenty-nine next month. Why? You planning to give me a present?' He cupped her breast, licked at the nipple. 'I can think of something I'd love to see gift-wrapped.'

'You're twenty-eight.' She scooted back. 'But that's... practically a toy boy.'

He chuckled, then grabbed her shoulders and shoved her onto her back, anchoring her in place with one hard thigh. 'Oh, yeah? So how old are you, then?'

'I'm thirty-four,' she said, indignantly.

His gaze drifted over her face. 'You don't look it.'

There didn't seem to be any judgment in the tone, but still she felt...embarrassed. 'Well, I am.' Maybe it was only six years but it felt like the wrong six years. 'Let me up.'

'Not going to happen, old lady,' he teased.

She struggled, trying to buck him off, but he didn't budge. 'Please, this feels awkward now.'

'Why? You're at your sexual peak. And so am I.'

Given the now-prominent feel of his erection, she had to agree. 'I know, but it feels weird.'

'It's not weird, it's cool.' He rubbed his shaft against her hip—making it fairly obvious he wasn't put off in the slightest by her vintage. She looked down at the thrusting erection. 'Although FYI, I'm not a toy boy,' he added. 'You're a damn cougar.'

A laugh popped out before she could stop it, but cut off when he cupped her sex. His fingers delved, stroking her oversensitive clitoris, the touch light and fleeting but enough to send shock waves of need echoing through her.

She thrust her fingers into his hair as he opened her thighs to position the impressive erection against her entrance. 'Well, I suppose, if you put it like—'

Grasping her hips, he thrust deep in one long, smooth, all-consuming stroke, stealing her breath and cutting off any more pointless protests.

Oh, sod it.

Six years was nothing, she decided, especially once he'd established a slow, lazy, teasing rhythm that quickly became more intoxicating than the rum.

* * *

Hours later, Ella struggled to focus on the radiant glow of dawn peeping through the shutters. Contemplating the tenderness between her thighs and the soreness in other, previously unknown and now thoroughly exercised muscle groups, she conceded that, while the years might not be a problem, the mileage definitely was.

'I should go,' she mumbled, her fuzzy brain latching onto the fact that lingering past daybreak had the potential to be a lot more awkward than their age difference.

But when she lifted one tired limb, a muscular forearm banded round her midriff from behind and hauled her back into his embrace.

'Nothing doing,' Cooper's sleep-roughened voice murmured against her hair. His big body cocooned her, his chest solid against her back, the soft hairs on his thighs brushing the backs of her legs and the softening erection still prominent against her bottom.

She debated arguing with him, but couldn't fight the thundering beat of her pulse, the fatigue dragging her into oblivion or the novelty of being held so securely. Maybe she could stay and snuggle, for a little bit? Grab one more hot memory to sustain her through the difficult truth she would have to face when she got home?

This was her holiday of a lifetime, after all, and Cooper Delaney—toy boy extraordinaire—her passport to no-holds-barred pleasure.

She relaxed, warmed by the comfort of his embrace. 'All right, but I'll go soon.'

Her lips tilted into a smile as he grunted. 'Shut up and go to sleep.' His forearm tightened under her breasts. 'You're going to need to get your strength up, my little cougar. This toy boy isn't finished with you yet.'

She choked out a laugh—that became a wistful hum as his arm became slack and her own body drifted towards sleep.

Colourful images collected behind her eyes—the glitter of pink sand beaches, the darting sparkle of blue-finned fish, the tangerine glow of fruit juice and rum, and the piercing jade of Cooper Delaney's eyes.

She swallowed to relieve the clutching sensation in her chest, and tumbled headlong into the rainbow dream.

FIVE

——

'Hey, Coop, get your butt out of bed, it's past eleven. And I've got exciting news.'

The muffled musical voice intruded on Ella's dream. She squeezed open an eyelid, grateful when the brittle sunlight hitting her retinas didn't appear to be accompanied by any pain, despite the definite thumping in her head.

Flopping over onto her back, she squinted at the empty bed beside her, the rumpled sheets striped by the sunlight slanting through the shutters. And heard the thumping again. This time, though, it was definitely not in her head, but coming from the hut's door, which shook on its hinges as the same musical voice from her dream, lilting with the lazy rhythms of a Bermuda native, shouted: 'No use hiding, man. Henry told me you'd be here.'

Ella shot upright, clasping the bed's thin sheet to her naked breasts, and swayed as several questions bombarded her at once.

How long had she been asleep? Where were her clothes? Where was Coop? And who the heck was that woman banging on the door?

The answer to number one was hours, if the brightness of the sunlight was anything to go by. Scrambling out of bed as furtively as possible, she located her clothes in a neatly stacked pile on the arm of the sagging sofa, answering question number two. Questions three and four remained a mystery though, as she dressed as soundlessly as she could manage while continuing to scan the hut for any sign of her host.

She jumped as the banging began again.

'Hey, I can hear you in there. Avoidance won't do you a damn bit of good.'

Rats, do you have bionic hearing?

She waited a few more strained seconds, while debating opening the shutters and escaping onto the deck, but eventually discarded the idea—given the girl's hearing capabilities.

The banging continued, and her not entirely settled stomach churned. What if this girl were Cooper's girlfriend? Or his wife? Was that why he'd disappeared? Because what did she really know about Captain Studly, except that he was gorgeous, knew how to dance the soca and had magic fingers, a very inventive tongue, and a huge and permanently stiff...

Don't go there.

Squaring her shoulders, she swung the door open ready to face the consequences, to be greeted by a stunningly beautiful barefoot young woman of about twenty, wearing a pair of Daisy Dukes, a T-shirt with the message 'Don't Mess with a Libran', tightly braided hair decorated with multicoloured beads, and a stunned expression.

'Hi.' She craned her neck to search the hut's interior, having gained her composure a lot faster than Ella. 'Is Coop around?'

'Um, no, apparently not,' Ella replied, opting for the only answer she could give with any confidence.

'Uh-huh?' The girl gave her a thorough once-over that had the heat steaming into Ella's cheeks. 'I guess he's up at the big house.'

The big house? What big house?

'Sorry to wake you,' the girl said. 'Henry didn't tell me Coop left the Runner with company last night. Just that he headed for his beach hut. Suppose Henry was messing with me. And Coop.'

And me, thought Ella, annoyed by Henry the barman's joke, and acutely embarrassed that this girl now knew she was the sort of woman who got picked up in bars.

What had seemed wildly romantic last night, now felt pretty tacky.

Ruby had encouraged her to let her inner flirt loose, but there had definitely been no mention of getting tipsy on rum cocktails, then getting nekkid with Captain Studly and jumping him four…no, five…oh, heck, make that at least a half-dozen times during the night.

'You Coop's new lady?' The girl interrupted Ella's panicked reappraisal of her behaviour.

'Um, no, we're just...' *What? Snorkel mates? Dance partners? Bonk buddies?*

The burning in her cheeks promptly hit maximum voltage as she searched for the appropriate term while recalling in X-rated detail exactly how intimately she and the invisible Coop had got acquainted last night, after very little provocation. 'Friends,' she finished lamely.

With benefits. Gold-standard benefits.

The phrase hung in the brisk morning air unspoken, but not unfigured out if the girl's frank appraisal was anything to go by. 'Do you know when he's going to be back?'

Hardly, seeing as I have no clue where he is.

'I'm afraid not.'

'Could you tell him I stopped by? I'm Sonny's daughter, Josie, and I—'

'Why don't you come in and wait for him?' Ella shoved the door wide, determined to make a fast getaway, before this situation got any more awkward. 'I was just leaving.'

Josie sent her a doubtful look as she stepped into the room. 'You sure, I—'

'Absolutely positive,' Ella replied, grabbing her bag from the hook by the door and slipping past the girl, before she could ask any more unanswerable questions.

'You want me to give Coop a message?'

Ella paused on the porch, the clutching sensation she'd had as she fell asleep the night before returning. 'Would you tell him thanks?' She cleared her throat, the stupid clutching sensation starting to squeeze her ribcage.

For being a friend when I needed one, she added silently as she jumped off the hut's porch and her feet sank into the wet sand.

Josie called out a goodbye and she waved back as she set off down the beach. But she didn't glance back again. Knowing it would only tighten the band squeezing her chest.

She'd had an amazing night. Maybe she'd gone a little off piste from Ruby's plan—and discovered the liberating powers of flirtation, soca dancing, Rum Swizzles and sweaty, no-strings sex in the process. Okay, make that a lot off piste.

But it was all good.

Give or take the odd heart murmur.

'Up you get, Sleeping Beauty, breakfast is served.' Coop bumped the hut's door open with his butt, keeping a firm hold on the tray his housekeeper had piled high with freshly sliced fruit, French toast, syrup and coffee. It had taken Inez a good half hour to assemble everything to her exacting standards—and quiz him mercilessly about his 'overnight guest'—during which time he'd got stupidly eager to see Ella again. Enough to question why he hadn't just woken her up and invited her to his place for breakfast.

The fifteen-acre estate that overlooked the cove, and the two-storey colonial he'd built on the bluff, were a symbol of who he was now. And he was super proud of it—and all he'd achieved, after ten long, back-breaking years of dawn wake-up calls refurbing second-hand equipment, long days spent out on the ocean running back-to-back dives, late nights getting his brain in a knot at the local community college studying for his MBA, all while keeping a ready smile on his face to schmooze a succession of tourists and corporate clients and bank managers and investors.

His business—Dive Guys—had made its first million-dollar turnover five years ago, and he'd celebrated by buying himself a brand-new motor launch, and the beach hut he'd been renting since his early days with Sonny. Three years later, he'd expanded the franchise across the Caribbean and had finally had enough to invest in the construction of his dream home on the land he'd bought behind the hut. He'd moved into Half-Moon House two years ago—but still couldn't quite believe that all those years of work had paid off in a wraparound deck that looked out over the ocean, five luxury en-suite bedrooms, a forty-foot infinity pool, a mile of private beach and an extremely nosey housekeeper.

Normally, he loved showing the place off to women he dated.

But when he'd woken up with Ella cuddled in his arms, he'd decided to keep the place a secret until after he'd finessed Inez into cooking a lavish breakfast for his overnight guest.

There had been something so cute and refreshing about Ella's breathless enthusiasm when she'd got a load of his first place the night before. She wasn't the only woman he'd brought to the hut, but she was the only one who had appreciated its charm and overlooked the used furniture and lack of amenities.

For some weird reason it had felt good to know all she'd seen was him—not Dive Guys, or the things it had afforded him.

'That looks real tasty, Coop. You shouldn't have bothered, though—I already grabbed a crab patty up at the Runner.'

Coop swung round, nearly dropping the tray, to find Sonny's daughter, Josie, perched on one of his bar stools. With her long legs crossed at the knee and a mocking smile on her lips, she should have looked all grown up, but somehow all he ever saw was the fresh kid he'd met a decade ago and who had made it her mission in life to be a thorn in his side ever since.

'Josie, what are you doing here?' He dumped the tray on the counter, sloshing the coffee all over the French toast, as he took in the empty bed in the far corner, and the empty couch where he'd folded Ella's clothes into a pile not more than thirty minutes ago. 'And where the hell is Ella?'

Josie's grin became smug as she snagged a chunk of fresh pineapple off the breakfast tray. 'So that's Sleeping Beauty's name. I always wondered if she had one.'

'Ha, ha,' he said without heat, used to Josie's teasing.

'She's very pretty. But kind of shy. Not your usual type.'

'Where is she?' he asked again, not happy at the news that Josie had met her. Somehow he didn't think someone with Ella's insta-blush tendencies would appreciate being caught in his bed by a smartass like Josie. 'Please tell me you didn't say anything to make her bolt.'

Josie sucked on the pineapple, shaking her head. 'Uh-uh. She bolted all on her own. Seemed kind of spooked that you'd disappeared.'

He ran his fingers through his hair. Damn it, he'd only been gone a half-hour and Ella had looked totally done in. After the workout they'd both had last night he would have bet she'd be comatose for hours yet. The thought had him eyeing his uninvited guest. 'You woke her up, didn't you, you little...?'

He made a swipe for Josie, but she leapt off the stool and danced out of his reach, laughing. 'What's the big deal? You don't date the tourists, remember? In case they get ideas.'

Not Ella.

The thought popped into his head, and had him stopping dead in front of Josie—the quest for retribution dying a quick death.

What was with that? Sure Ella had been sweet, and eager and inventive in bed, but how had she got under his guard so easily? Knowing what he did about tourists who liked to slum it in neighbourhood bars, how come he had never thought of Ella as one of them? And why had he crept out of bed and harassed Inez into making her breakfast? He didn't have a romantic bone in his body. Not since... He stared at the ruined toast, the creeping sense of humiliation coming back in an unpleasant rush of memory.

Not since the evening of the junior prom in Garysville, Indiana, when he'd stood like a dummy on Amy Metcalfe's porch, his neck burning under the collar of the borrowed suit, and a corsage clutched in his sweating palm that had cost him ten of his hard-earned dollars, while Amy's old man yelled at him to get lost, and his prom date sent him a pitying smile from the passenger seat of his half-brother Jack Jnr's Beemer convertible.

'Don't you want to know why I'm here?' Josie stared at him, her usual mischief replaced with excitement. 'I've got news.'

Shaking off the unpleasant memory, he clamped down hard on the dumb urge to head out after Ella. 'Sure? What news?' He tossed a piece of papaya into his mouth, impressed with his own nonchalance.

The smile on Josie's face reached ear-to-ear proportions. 'Taylor popped the question last night and I said yes.'

'What question?' he said, trying to process the information while his mind was still snagged on Ella and why the hell she'd run out on him. Wasn't Taylor that pimply kid Josie'd been dating for a while?

Josie's eyes rounded. 'Damn, Coop, even you can't be that dumb. The "Will you marry me?" question. Duh.'

Coop choked on the mango chunk he'd just slung

in his mouth. 'You've got to be kidding me?' His eyes watered as his aggravation over Ella's sudden departure was surpassed by horror. 'You're way too young to be getting married.' Plus marriage was for chumps—and Josie was a smart kid—what was she thinking?

Josie whacked him hard on the back, dislodging the chunk and nearly dislocating his shoulder. 'I'm twenty,' she said, indignantly. 'Taylor and I have been dating for four years.' She propped her hands on her hips, striking the Wonder Woman pose he knew meant she was about to start lecturing him. 'And we love each other. Marriage is the obvious next step. So we can think about babies.'

'Babies!' he yelped, as a blood vessel popped out on his forehead and began to throb. 'You cannot be serious?'

'Just because you're dead set on being the Oldest Player in Town,' she countered, 'doesn't mean everyone's that cynical and immature.'

'I'm immature?' he snapped. Seeing her flinch, he struggled to lower his voice, and regain some of his usual cool.

But damn it, first Ella's disappearing act, and now this? Had all the females in Bermuda been hitting the crazy sauce while he slept?

'Honey, I'm not the one planning to get hitched when I'm still in college.' Not to mention have a parcel of rugrats. Was she nuts?

The look she sent him went from pissed to pitying.

'Why does the thought of that terrify you so much, Coop? Maybe you should try it some time yourself?'

'What? Marriage? And kids?' he scoffed, barely suppressing the shudder. 'No way.'

'Not that, not yet, but...' Josie searched his face, the pitying look starting to annoy him now. 'Couldn't you at least try dating the same woman for longer than a week?' Her eyes shadowed with concern. 'Haven't you ever thought there might be more to women than just hot and sweaty sex?'

'Damn it, give me a break.' He slapped his hands over his ears. 'Don't talk to me about that stuff—my ears are bleeding.' He'd never kept his dating habits a secret, but Josie butting into his sex life was just wrong. On so many levels.

She glared at him. 'So who's being immature now?'

He dropped his hands, having to concede that point. 'Fine, you win that one, but conversations about sex are off limits, okay?' The last thing he needed was some snot-nosed kid giving him dating advice.

'Okay, truce.' She surprised him by backing down. 'I'll butt out of your business. You're a hopeless cause anyway.' She sighed, to emphasise the point. 'I didn't come here to argue with you, I came to tell you Taylor and I want to set the date for August tenth. If you're good with us using your land to do the ceremony on the cove near the Runner?'

'Sure, of course, no problem,' he said, feeling about two feet tall all of a sudden. He hadn't meant to piss on her parade; the wedding announcement had just come as a shock, that was all. How the heck had Josie grown up without him noticing?

'I also wanted to ask you to be my witness,' she added. 'If you think you can contain your horror long enough to sign the book?' The shadow of uncertainty in her gaze shaved another foot off his stature. Hell, he hadn't meant to be that much of a grouch.

'You sure you want the Oldest Player in Town there?' he murmured, relieved when she sent him a cheeky grin.

'Only if he promises not to hit on the bridesmaids.'

The thought of hitting on anyone brought back thoughts of Ella. And the pang of regret sliced under his ribs. She had to be long gone by now.

He raised his hand as if taking a mock oath. 'I do solemnly swear not to hit on the bridesmaids.'

'Cool, we're all set, then.' Josie grinned, then planted a kiss on the tip of his nose. 'I'll keep you posted on the wedding plans. I better hit the road, though.' She rolled her eyes. 'You have no idea how much work goes into organising a wedding in under four months.'

And he didn't want to know, he thought silently, but decided to keep that information to himself.

'Oh, by the way,' she said as she reached the door. 'Sleeping Beauty left you a message before she ran off.'

'Yeah?' The bubble of hope expanded under his breastbone. 'What message? Did she tell you where she's staying?' Maybe if she had, he could give her a call? Get Inez to make a fresh batch of French toast, or better yet some lunch?

Josie shook her head. 'She just said to tell you thanks.'

'That's it?' The bubble of hope deflated, making his voice sound flat and dull.

Josie nodded, her expression thoughtful as she studied him. 'If you wanted to contact her, Henry might know where she's staying if she was at the Runner last night. You know how talkative he is.'

'No, that's okay, it's no big deal,' he replied, and willed himself to believe it.

'Are you sure?'

He forced out a laugh. 'Sure, I'm sure. Not my style.' He didn't get hung up on women, even ones as cute and sexy as Ella. 'Oldest Player in Town, remember?'

Josie rolled her eyes again. 'Oh, yeah. How could I forget?'

But after Josie had left, and he had dumped the ruined breakfast spread in the trash and collapsed onto the bed, the joke nickname didn't seem all that funny any more. Especially when he got a lungful of the light, refreshing, lemony scent and the earthy smell of sex that still lingered on the sheets.

SIX

—

Ella plucked the tray of Triple Indulgence Brownies out of the industrial oven and dropped it gingerly on the counter—her tummy hitching up towards her throat as the aroma of melting chocolate surrounded her. The rich decadent scent tasted like charcoal on her tongue. Clasping her hand over her mouth, she sliced the brownies into twelve chunks, perched the tray on the window sill to cool, and rushed into the café, her stomach wobbling alarmingly.

Taking deep, measured breaths, she berated herself and her stupid nervous tummy as she stacked the batch of mini-chocolate tarts she'd made earlier—which thankfully didn't smell too strongly. Ruby would be here any minute and the last thing she needed was more searching looks and probing questions from her business partner—because she'd barfed all over the shop again.

She'd been tense and out of sorts for weeks. Ever since she'd got back from Bermuda and got the diagnosis she'd been dreading from her doctor, Myra Patel. That she was no longer ovulating at regular intervals—which explained the now five months without a period—because the onset of premature menopause was now a reality.

But she thought she'd come to terms with it. Or at least found a strategy to deal with her loss. Even though her biological clock was now ticking at triple time—and Myra had told her that her chances of conceiving naturally were probably remote, and getting remoter by the second—she had referred her to a specialist. Plus she and Ruby had discussed the feasibility of other options, when and if she found a life partner.

The good news was, after her wild night with Coop, there was every reason to be a lot more cheerful about her prospects when it came to relationships. Or at least sexual relationships.

Coop.

Her stomach clutched and released, the queasiness returning.

Maybe it was about time she admitted that her fertility problems weren't the only thing that had had her down in the dumps? That her nervous stomach wasn't just a symptom of her stress over the test results she'd got from Myra two months ago, but also her ridiculous overreaction to her one night with Cooper Delaney.

Somehow, she'd got fixated on him, picking over every minute detail of their day and night together—instead of assigning the experience to its rightful place in her past, and moving on with her real life.

So what if he'd disappeared the following morning, without leaving a note to say where he'd gone? They'd had a one-night fling. He'd owed her nothing. They lived thousands of miles apart, and he was only twenty-eight, for goodness' sake. Not that their age difference had bothered him... Then again, maybe it had, more than he'd let on. Could that be why he'd disappeared so abruptly? Before she'd even woken up? Without bothering to say goodbye?

She folded the oven mitt she'd used into the drawer and slammed it shut.

Stop right there, you're doing it again.

The hollow feeling of inadequacy opened up in her stomach, and the weary ache in her chest pinched her heart.

Maybe if she had left him a note...

She sighed and glanced up to see Ruby and Cal standing together on the pavement outside the shop— bidding each other goodbye as they did every morning before Cal headed for the tube station and his work as a top defence barrister in the City. The hollow weight became a gaping hole as she watched them.

Ruby threw her head back and laughed at something her husband had said. Callum said something else, that seemed to make her laugh more, but then he gripped the lapels of her coat and jerked her up onto her tiptoes, before silencing the laughter with a hungry kiss.

Ella felt the nasty dart of envy as Ruby's arms wrapped around Cal's neck to pull him closer. The kiss heated to scorching, Cal's hands finding Ruby's bottom beneath the hem of her coat. Anyone passing by would have mistaken them for newlyweds, instead of a couple who had recently celebrated their seventh wedding anniversary and had three very energetic children ranging in age from two to six.

Ella dropped her chin, and concentrated on rearranging the cookies on the display, feeling like a Peeping Tom as the nausea pitched and rolled in her belly. The doorbell tinkled, then the creak of the café door opened and slammed shut followed by the click of Ruby's stilettos on the tiled floor.

'Sorry I'm late. I'll close up today to make up for it.' Ruby's voice sounded upbeat and pleasantly mellow, as it often did first thing in the morning. Ella frowned, dusting icing sugar over the tarts. Hard to remember now that her business partner had once been the biggest grump on the planet until she'd downed at least two cups of coffee in the morning, but that was before her fender bender with Callum Westmore nearly eight years ago.

'That man sweet-talked me back into bed,' Ruby added with a huff. 'After Helga picked up the kids.'

'Poor you,' Ella muttered under her breath, then bit her lip to contain the sour note of sarcasm, and the bile rising up her throat.

What was the matter with her? She'd always been so happy for Ruby and Cal. It wasn't as if their path to true love had exactly been smooth. And as for Max and Ally and Art, Ruby and Cal's three irrepressible children, she adored them. And adored having a special place in their lives as their favourite 'auntie'. That relationship would only become more treasured if the possibility of a childless future became a reality.

'Ella, is everything okay?'

She put down the icing sugar to find Ruby watching her. Far too closely. Oh, no. Had she just heard that cutting remark? How was she supposed to explain it? 'Yes, of course...'

'Are you sure? You're a rather strange colour.'

'Really, I'm perfectly—' The gag reflex struck without warning, punching Ella's larynx and slamming her stomach into her throat. She slapped her hand over her mouth, and raced around the counter and into the restroom—getting there just in time to lose in the toilet the tea and dry toast she'd managed to force down that morning for breakfast.

'Okay, deep breaths.' Ruby rubbed Ella's spine as the nausea retreated. The cool cloth felt glorious on the back of her neck as she dragged in several deep breaths.

'How's your stomach? All finished puking?'

'Yes, I think so.' Ella pressed her hand to her belly to double-check. But her stomach seemed to have settled after the retching, the strong scent of the disinfectant in the toilet nowhere near as abrasive as the brownie scent had been earlier.

Ruby flushed the toilet and anchored her arm around Ella's waist. 'Good, then let's get you more comfortable.'

By the time they'd both settled in the two armchairs at the back of the café, Ruby's careful scrutiny had Ella's cheeks burning.

'Any idea what caused it?' Ruby asked.

Ella took a moment to examine the hands she had clasped in her lap.

'From that delightful shade of rosé on your cheeks I'm guessing you do know.' Ruby's hand covered hers and squeezed. 'But you don't want to say.'

'It's silly.' Ella shrugged, forced to face her friend. 'I'm totally overreacting to a stupid holiday fling— which didn't mean anything.'

'Of course it meant something. You wouldn't have slept with him if it didn't. You're not the casual-sex type.'

Ella breathed a heavy sigh. 'Kind of annoying that I didn't figure that out before I decided to jump into bed with him for a night of casual sex, isn't it?' The clutching sensation in her chest was back with a vengeance. 'I miss him. I wish I'd hung around to tell him goodbye properly. Got closure. Then maybe I could stop giving myself an ulcer thinking about him constantly.'

Ruby nodded, her expression far too intuitive. 'All excellent points. But can I suggest another possible explanation for the puking?'

Ella frowned. Why was Ruby looking at her like that? As if she was struggling to suppress a smile. 'There is no other—'

'Because you're no more the highly strung, give-yourself-an-ulcer type than you are the casual-sex type.'

'Your point?' Ella replied a little sharply.

'Look, you've been stressing about your holiday fling for weeks, I know that. But isn't it at all possible—given the extremely hot description you gave me of your bedroom aerobics with Captain Studly—that what we just witnessed might be something more substantial than a nervous tummy?'

'Such as?'

'Morning sickness.'

Ella stiffened. 'You know that's not possible.'

'According to Dr Patel it isn't impossible.'

Ella's frown became a scowl. 'It's only a very slight possibility. And we used condoms the whole time.'

'As did Cal and I before we got pregnant with Arturo,' Ruby shot straight back.

'It's not the same thing.' The sour note was back. 'You don't have any fertility issues.'

'I still think you should do a pregnancy test, just to be sure.'

Ella straightened in the chair. 'I am sure.' Sure what the result would be. And even surer that bringing back memories of another pregnancy test that she'd taken with Ruby years before would only make her current misery seem even more insurmountable.

'Well, I'm not.'

Ella threw up her hands. 'Yes, well, I don't have a pregnancy test and I don't have time to go and get one because we open in half an hour.' Maybe if Ruby wouldn't listen to her, at least she'd listen to reason.

'That's okay, because I do.' Reaching into her handbag, Ruby produced a blue and white chemist bag from which she pulled out a telltale pink box.

'Where did you get that?' Ella stared, her hurt and astonishment turning to dismay.

'Ella, you've been sick three times this week now.' Grabbing Ella's hand, Ruby slapped the box into her palm.

Ella wanted to refuse, but as she stared at the box she felt her will power crumbling in the face of Ruby's determination.

'Just go pee on the stick.' Ruby closed Ella's fingers around the box. 'Don't overthink this. Whatever the result is, we'll handle it. But denial is not the answer. I'll wait here.'

Ella stood up, her stomach folding in on itself, as the last of her will power ebbed away on a wave of exhaustion. 'Okay, fine, but you may be waiting a long time.' She frowned at her best friend. 'I am so not in the mood to pee on demand right now.'

It took fifteen torturous minutes before she could get out of the toilet.

'I left it on the vanity in there.' She washed her hands in the shop's sink and dosed them with antibacterial gel. 'Don't forget to dispose of it before we open,' she added, brushing the stupid sting of tears off her cheek.

'Ella, don't cry. You need to know for sure.'

She didn't dignify that with an answer, but simply set about filling the icing bag with cream-cheese frosting. She needed to be ready for the nine a.m. rush when they opened in fifteen minutes. She so did not have time for this rubbish.

She was still busy adding cream-cheese frosting in decorative swirls to the carrot cake when Ruby dashed back into the café a few minutes later. 'I think you better look at this.'

'Don't bring it in here,' she said crossly. 'It's covered in pee.'

'I know that,' Ruby replied. 'But it's not just any pee, it's pregnant-lady pee.'

'What?' Frosting squirted across the counter as her fingers fisted on the bag involuntarily. And her heart jumped into her mouth.

'You heard me.' Ruby held the pee stick in front of Ella's face like a talisman. 'See that strong blue line? That means Ella's going to be a mummy in exactly seven months' time. You're going to be ringing in the new year with your very own bundle of fun.'

She couldn't focus, thanks to the sheen of shocked tears misting her vision. 'But that's not possible,' she murmured, her voice hoarse.

Ruby laughed. 'Um, well, clearly it is. Pregnancy tests don't lie.'

Ella's unfocused gaze raised to Ruby's smiling face. 'I should take another one. It might be wrong.'

'Take as many as you like, but there's no such thing

as a false positive with these things. I took six tests with Art. And they all came out exactly the same. Assuming it was definitely you who peed on that stick, it's definitely you who's pregnant.'

Ella collapsed into the chair beside the cash register. Her knees trembling now almost as violently as her hands—which clutched the bag of frosting in a death grip as it dripped onto the floor.

'I'm going to have a baby.' The words sounded fragile and far away, as if they had been said by someone else, as if they could be extinguished if she said them too loudly.

Ruby stroked her back as she crouched beside her and wrapped her hand round Ella's wrist. 'Yes, you are.'

The tears welled and flowed, her whole body shaking now, at the memory of a similar test so long ago. The joy then had felt scary, terrifying, but so small and sweet. This time it didn't feel small, it felt huge, like a living, breathing thing that couldn't be contained within her skin, but so much more scary and terrifying too.

Dumping the pregnancy test in the bin, Ruby washed and dried her hands, then tugged a couple of wet wipes from the dispenser on the counter. 'I take it those are happy tears?' Ruby took the icing bag out of Ella's numb fingers and began cleaning the mess of cream-cheese frosting with the wipes.

Ella nodded, the lump in her throat too solid and overwhelming to talk around.

'Am I allowed to say I told you so, then?'

Ella's eyes focused at last, and she swept her arms round her friend's shoulders and clung on tight, too overwhelmed to care about the smug smile on Ruby's face.

'I don't deserve this chance.' She sobbed as Ruby hugged her.

Ruby moved back, and held her arms. 'Don't say that.' She gave her a slight shake. 'What you did then, you did for the right reasons.'

Ella folded her arms over her stomach, as if to protect the precious life within and stop the guilt from consuming the joy. 'I'm not so sure about that.'

Ruby tugged a tissue out of her pocket, to dab at Ella's eyes. 'You were eighteen years old Ella, you had your whole life ahead of you, and it was a mistake. You made the only choice you could in the circumstances.' She placed the damp tissue in the palm of Ella's hand, rolled her fist over it, and held on. 'Don't you think it's about time to forgive yourself?'

She would never be able to forgive herself, not completely, but that didn't mean she couldn't protect this child with every fibre of her being. This time she wouldn't mess it up. 'I want to.'

Ruby's lips quirked. 'Okay, next question. Because I'm going to assume the "Do you want to have this baby?" question is a no-brainer.'

Ella bobbed her head as the small smile spread. 'Yes, it is.'

'Brilliant. So next question, how do we contact Captain Studly? Do you have like a card for his tour company or something?'

'What? No.' The joy cracked, like the crumbling top of a newly baked muffin, exposing the soft centre beneath. 'We can't tell him. He doesn't need to know.'

'Calm down.' Ruby gripped her fingers tight. 'There's no need to panic. You don't have to do anything yet.'

The memory of his voice, smooth, seductive, husky, and so sexy asking, 'Are you on the pill?' seemed to float in the air around the café, mocking her.

What happened if she told him and he reacted the same way Randall had? He was still in his twenties; he lived in a beach hut; he picked up women in bars. He was exciting, reckless, charming, sexier than any one she'd ever met, and probably the least likely guy on the planet to welcome news like this.

'And he's not necessarily going to freak out the way Randall did,' Ruby said, doing her mind-reading thing.

Oh, yes, he will.

'I don't want to risk it.' She tugged her hands out of Ruby's. 'Why do I have to tell him?'

'Because it's his baby, and he has a right to know,' Ruby said, in that patient I-know-what's-best voice that she'd acquired ever since having kids. Ella had always thought it was so sweet. Now she was finding it more than a little patronising.

'But suppose he'd rather not know?'

'How can you possibly know that?' Ruby replied.

She opened her mouth to tell Ruby how he'd asked

her if she was on the pill and how the correct answer had somehow got lost in the heat of the moment. But then shut it again. She didn't want Ruby to think she'd deliberately tricked him, because she hadn't. But even thinking about that conversation now made her feel as if she had, which would only tarnish the perfection of this moment.

'He lives in Bermuda. I don't need his support.' Especially as he didn't have any money. 'I'm more than solvent on my own and—'

'That's not the point. He's the baby's father. By not telling him you're not giving him the choice, or the baby the choice to know him when it gets older. Think of how much it screwed up Nick when he found out our dad wasn't his biological father,' she said, reminding Ella of her brother Nick, who had run away from home in his teens when he'd discovered the truth about his parentage and had only recently come back into Ruby's life.

'It's not the same thing at all,' Ella protested. It wasn't as if she planned never to tell her child who its father was; she just didn't see why she had to tell the father right this second.

'I know it's not, but what I'm trying to say is you can't keep those kinds of secrets. It's not fair on either one of them.'

Ella wanted to say life wasn't fair. But the truth was she'd never believed that. Life could be fair, if you made the effort to make it so.

She wanted to deny he had any right to know. This

was her child. Her responsibility. And she didn't want to consider his rights, his reaction. But even as the panic sat under her breastbone, ready to leap up her throat and cut off her air supply, she pictured Coop's face, the genuine smile, those emerald eyes twinkling with humour, and knew that not telling him would be taking the coward's way out.

While she never would have planned to have a child alone, that was what she'd be doing—because fate had handed her this incredible gift. And while it was very likely that Coop wouldn't want to know about this baby, she had to at least give him the option of saying no. Because she had to give her child the chance to know its father. However slim that chance might be.

Ruby patted her hand. 'How about we leave this discussion for another day? You really don't have to do this yet.'

A loud tapping had them both turning to see the whole of the Hampstead Heath Mother and Baby Stroller Work-Out Class crowded around the door, looking sweaty and dishevelled and in desperate need of light refreshments.

Jumping up, Ella headed round the counter, to flip the sign on the door to open and welcome them in. As they smiled and wheeled their babies proudly into the café, chatting about the Hitler who ran the class, Ella smiled back, amazed to realise the lethagy that had dragged her down for days had vanished.

'Wait, Ella, are you sure you don't want to go home

and rest? I can handle the Yummies,' Ruby offered as she joined her behind the counter.

Ella grinned back at her, the ball of panic lifting too.

She had time to think about how to tell Cooper; how to break the news to him without making him feel responsible. And really, while the thought of what she had to tell him wasn't easy, the fact that she had a reason to speak to him again felt surprisingly good. 'No need. I feel great.'

Ruby laughed back, her own face beaming with pleasure. 'Just wait till tomorrow morning when you're crouched over the toilet bowl again. Actually, we better get some buckets for the duration.'

Ella spent the morning chatting to the mums, serving tea and freshly baked cakes and cookies, whipping up a succession of speciality coffees, while she admired their children, and struggled to contain the silly grin at how totally amazing her life suddenly was.

She'd speak to Cooper soon. Ruby was right: it would be wrong not to. But it had been an accident. And really, she didn't need to think about all the particulars just yet. Right now, all she really had to do was bask in the miracle occurring inside her. And focus on making sure she gave her baby the best possible chance to thrive. And if that meant eventually finding the courage to tell its father about their happy accident, she'd do it, somehow.

SEVEN

'Ouch. Damn it!' Coop yanked his hand out of the casing, and threw the wrench down on the deck. Blood seeped from the shallow gash at the base of his thumb, through the thick black smear of engine grease. He sucked on it, getting a mouthful of grit to go with the metallic taste of his own blood.

'What's all the cussing for?' Sonny's head peered out from the captain's cabin.

'That damn propeller just took a chunk out of my hand,' he snarled. 'Cussing's required.' He boosted himself onto the deck. Tying the rag he'd been using to clean off the drive shaft around the injury, he sent his friend an angry glare. 'That lug nut won't budge—probably because it's been rusted on for thirty years.' With his hand now pounding in unison with his head, after one too many drinks last night at The Rum Runner, he was not in the mood to be dicking around with Sonny's ancient outboard motor.

Sonny tilted his head to one side, sending him a

calm, searching look. 'Someone sure got out of bed the wrong way again this morning.'

Coop ignored the jibe. So what if he hadn't been on top form lately? Ever since a certain English girl had left him high and dry, her lush body and eager smile had got lodged in his frontal lobe and it had been interfering with his sleep patterns.

Going back to The Rum Runner last night for the first time since Ella had run out on him had been a mistake. Henry had started jerking his chain about 'his pretty lady', and he'd somehow ended up challenging the guy to a drinking contest. Staggering home at three a.m., and being violently ill in his bathroom had only added injury to the insult of too many tequila slammers and too many nights without enough sleep.

No wonder he wasn't at his sunniest.

'Isn't it about time you got rid of this bucket?' he said, letting out a little of his frustration on Sonny's boat.

Sonny stroked the console with the affection most men reserved for a lover. 'My *Jezebel*'s got plenty good years in her yet. And with Josie's wedding to pay for, she's going to have to make them count.'

Coop knotted the rag with his teeth, his temper kicking in. They both knew *The Jezebel* hadn't seen a good year since Bill Clinton had been in the White House. And that he'd offered to bankroll Josie's wedding a million times and Sonny had stubbornly refused to accept the money. But after a morning spent with a raging hangover trying to fix the unfixable when he should have been going over his business manager's projections for the new franchise in Acapulco, he wasn't in the mood to keep his reservations about Josie's nuptials to himself any longer either.

'What is Josie getting hitched for anyway? She's only twenty and they're both still in college. What are they going to live on?'

'Love will find a way,' Sonny replied with that proud paternal grin that had been rubbing Coop the wrong way for weeks. Hadn't the old guy figured out yet he was shelling out a king's ransom to kick-start a marriage that probably wouldn't last out the year?

'Will it?' he asked, the edge in his voice going razor sharp.

Sonny nodded, the probing look sending prickles of unease up Coop's spine and making his thumb throb. 'You know, you've been mighty bitchy for months now. Wanna tell me what's going on?'

Months? No way had it been months since his night with Ella. Had it? 'This isn't about me, Sonny,' he said, struggling to deflect the conversation back where it needed to be. 'This is about Josie doing something dumb and you not lifting a finger to stop her.'

'Josie's known her own mind since she was three years old,' Sonny said without any heat. 'Nothing I could say would stop her even if I wanted to.'

Coop opened his mouth to protest, but Sonny simply lifted up a silencing finger.

'But I don't want to stop them. Taylor's a good kid and she loves him. And it's not them I'm worried about.' Sonny rested his heavy frame on the bench next to Coop, his steady gaze making the prickles on Coop's spine feel as if he'd been rolling in poison ivy. 'You're the one hasn't been right ever since the night you picked up that tourist girl in the Runner.'

'What the...?' Coop's jaw went slack. How did Sonny know about Ella? The old guy was always butting into his personal life, because he was a romantic and he thought he had a right to. But he'd never spoken about Ella to anyone. Did Sonny have X-ray vision or something?

'Josie says you seemed real taken with her the next morning. But she'd run off? Is that the thing? You miss her?'

Damn Josie—so she was his source.

'It's not what you think.' Coop scowled, trying to cut the old guy off at the pass before this conversation got totally out of hand.

He didn't miss Ella, and he wasn't 'taken with her'. Whatever the heck that meant. It was nothing like that. She'd just got under his skin, somehow. Like an itch he couldn't scratch. He could wait it out. Give it a couple more weeks and surely the almost nightly dreams he had, about those bright blue eyes wide with enthusiasm, that sunny smile, that lush butt in the itsy-bitsy purple bikini...

He thrust his fingers through his hair, annoyed by the low-level heat humming in his crotch as the erotic memories spun gleefully back—and the weird knot under his breastbone twisted.

'It was a one-night hook-up,' he continued, trying to convince himself now as much as Sonny. 'We hit it off. But only...you know.'

Just shoot me now.

He shrugged. He wasn't about to get into a discussion about his sex life with Sonny. The old guy had given him chapter and verse as a teenager about respecting women, and he didn't need that lecture again. One thing was certain, though: Josie was dead meat next time he saw her for putting him in this position. Whether she had a ten-grand wedding to attend in five weeks or not.

'I don't think Ella and I are going to be declaring any vows,' he said, going on the defensive when Sonny gave him that look that always made him feel as if he had a case to answer.

He did respect women. He respected them a lot. Sonny just had a quaint, old-fashioned idea that sex always had to mean something. When sometimes all it meant was you needed to get laid.

'She lives thousands of miles away, we only spent one night together and she wasn't looking for anything more than I was. Plus she was the one who ran out on me.'

Sonny's eyebrow winged up, and Coop knew he'd said too much.

'I see. So you're the boy that can have any woman he wants. And she's the girl that didn't want you? Is that what's got you so upset?'

'I'm not upset.' Coop flexed his fist, his hand hurting like a son of a bitch. 'And thanks a bunch for making me sound like an arrogant jackass.'

Sonny smiled, but didn't deny it, and Coop felt the flicker of hurt. 'You're a good-looking boy with more money than you need and a charming way about you that draws women like bees to a honeypot. You've got a right to be arrogant, I guess.'

'Thanks,' Coop said wryly. He didn't kid himself, Sonny hadn't meant it as a compliment.

Money wasn't something that floated Sonny's boat; it was the one thing they still argued about. Because as far as Coop was concerned, money mattered, more than pretty much everything else. It made everything easier, oiled every cog, gave you options, and that all-important safety net that he'd lacked as a kid. He'd craved it for the first twenty years of his life. But now he had it, it meant more to him than just the luxuries, or the good times he could buy with it. It meant respect. Status. It showed people that he wasn't the worthless little trailer-trash nobody he'd once been. But best of all it meant he didn't have to rely on anyone but himself.

He liked Sonny, respected the guy more than any other guy he had ever known, but, the way he saw it, Sonny had way too many responsibilities in his life—to his five kids, his three grandkids, all his friends and acquaintances, not to mention Rhona, the wife he'd had by his side for over thirty years. Maybe that worked for Sonny, he certainly didn't seem to mind it, but, as far as Coop was concerned, that wasn't something he was looking for. A man could be an island—if he worked hard enough and had enough money to make it happen—and life was a lot easier that way.

'Aren't you headed to Europe next week?' Sonny pushed on, not taking the hint. 'Why not look this girl up and see how she's doing?'

Coop stared blankly at his friend. He'd thought about it; of course he had. He had a meeting with some financiers in St Tropez who wanted to talk about franchising options for Dive Guys in the Med. It was only a short hop from there to London, where Ella lived. But...

'I don't know. if I went all the way out to London just to hook up, she might get the wrong idea.' He sure as hell didn't want Ella thinking this was more than it was.

'Why would that be bad?' Sonny's rueful smile made Coop feel about as smart as the lug nut he'd been trying to shift all morning. 'If she's the woman of your dreams.'

'Damn, Sonny, Ella is not the woman of my dreams,' he shot back, getting exasperated.

What was with Sonny? Was all this wedding garbage messing with his head and making him even more of a romantic than usual?

He hardly knew Ella. And he didn't have dreams about women. Well, not apart from R-rated ones. For the simple reason that he was more than happy being an island.

'If you say so.' Sonny shrugged, undaunted. 'But

my point is you need to go get your sunshine back.'
Sonny jerked his thumb over his shoulder, indicat-
ing the glimmering turquoise water that stretched towards the horizon. 'And if it's across that ocean that's
where you oughta be.' His smile thinned. 'Because until
you do, you're not a heck of a lot fun for anyone to be
around.'

Coop frowned as he finally got the message. So that
was it. Sonny wanted him out of the way while him
and his family geared up for Josie's big day.

He felt the sharp stab of hurt. But guessed the old
guy had a point. He had been pretty grouchy the last
couple of months. Sleepless nights and sexual frustration could do that to a guy. And whatever was going
on between him and Ella, it didn't seem to be getting
any better. 'Have I really been that bad?' he asked.

Resting a solid hand on his shoulder, Sonny gave
it a fatherly pat. 'Boy, you've been bitchier than when
you were working all hours to set up your business.'

'Sorry.'

Sonny squeezed his shoulder. 'Don't be sorry, man,
go do something about it.'

Coop nodded. What the hell? Trying to talk some
sense into Josie and her folks about the wedding was
a lost cause. And he could do with more than the two-
day break he'd planned for his trip to the Med. Why
not book a flight that routed through London? Stop
over for a few extra days, book a suite in a classy hotel,
see the city, and if he happened to be in Ella's neighbourhood at some point, why not look her up? If she

wanted to throw some more sunshine his way—and maybe give him an explanation as to why she hadn't stuck around to say goodbye—why should he object?

As Sonny had said, he'd never had a woman walk out on him before now. That was most probably all this was really about. And if that made him an arrogant jackass, so be it. He needed to do something to get himself the hell over this hump he seemed to have got hung up on. So he could come back to Bermuda ready to smile through his teeth during his best friend's daughter's wedding.

What was the worst that could happen?

'Stop eating the merchandise! I don't care if you've got a cookie craving.'

Ella hastily wiped the white chocolate and macadamia nut evidence off her mouth. 'Sorry, I can't help it.'

Ruby sent her a superior look from the cappuccino machine, where she was busy whipping up a storm of decaf lattes and skinny mochas for the tennis foursome who had just arrived after a grudge match at the heath.

'You should be sorry. I'd love to know how you've barely gained an ounce.' Her gaze dipped to Ella's cleavage, displayed in the new D half-cup bra she'd splashed out on the previous week. 'Except on the bust.' Her eyes narrowed. 'Despite having consumed your own weight in confectionery in the last week.'

Ella grinned as she arranged the freshly baked passionfruit florentines on the 'treat of the day' display.

'I'm simply making up for lost time. I could barely keep anything down for three solid weeks.'

Ella stroked the compact bulge that made the waistband of her hip-hugger jeans dig into her tummy. Even though she could not have been more ecstatic about the pregnancy, revelling in every change it brought to her body, puking her guts up every morning had got old fairly fast. And running a cake shop, where the cloying aroma of sweetness and the bitter chicory scent of coffee had been hell on her hypersensitive sense of smell, had been a particular brand of torture she had been more than happy to see the back of. Now she could simply enjoy all the other changes—well, all except one.

Her sex drive seemed to have mushroomed at the same pace as her bosom—if the lurid dreams she had most nights, in which a certain Cooper Delaney was a key player, were anything to go by.

Only last night, she'd woken up in a pool of sweat, her skin tight and oversensitive, her already enlarged nipples swollen and her engorged clitoris pulsing with the need to be touched. She'd never been all that self-sufficient, sexually speaking, before she'd met Cooper, but she'd had to take matters into her own hands more than once in the last few weeks, while visualising Cooper's honed, ripped body driving into her and hearing his deep laconic voice growling 'touch yourself' in her ear.

Heat boiled in her cheeks, at the memory of last night's frenzied and sadly dissatisfying orgasm. And the guilt that had followed. Was it possible that her body was playing tricks on her, constantly bringing up these carnal memories of her child's father to push her into contacting him the way she'd planned to do weeks ago?

But that was before she'd done an Internet search on him. And a simple investigation to discover his contact details had brought the panic seeping back.

Because putting Cooper Delaney's name and the words 'Bermuda' and 'snorkelling' into the search engine had brought up ten whole pages of references, not just to him but to Dive Guys, the phenomenally successful franchise he owned and operated in most of the Caribbean. A company that had been listed on the New York stock exchange for over three years and was—according to an article in *Time Life* magazine— one of the fastest-growing start-ups in the region.

She'd been in shock. Then she'd been upset that he hadn't trusted her enough to tell her the truth about himself... Then she'd thought of the secret child in her womb and she'd begun shaking so hard she'd had to lie down.

Coop Delaney wasn't a part-time boat captain and all around beach bum living a free-spirited, laid-back, itinerant existence on a Bermuda beach—he was an exceptionally rich and well-connected businessman with the money and influence to buy and sell her and Ruby's little cupcake bakery several hundred times over.

How could she tell a man like that she was carrying his child? And not expect him to make demands? Demands she might not want to agree to? If he'd been the Coop she'd thought he was, she would have phoned him weeks ago. But now...

'Check out the suit in the window.' Ruby's appreciative whistle woke Ella from her stupor. 'That guy's got shoulders even a happily married woman can appreciate.'

Ella's gaze skimmed the top of the cookie display to see a tall man, with closely cropped hair step into the café. Recognition tickled her spine, then thumped into her chest as he lifted his head and shockingly familiar emerald eyes locked on hers.

She blinked rapidly, sure this had to be an apparition conjured up by her guilty conscience—but then his sensual lips quirked and the warm spot between her legs ignited.

'Hi, welcome to Touch of Frosting, Camden's premiere cupcake bakery. What's your guilty pleasure this morning?'

Ella vaguely processed Ruby's familiar greeting through the chainsaw in her head. 'Coop?' The word came out on a rasp of breath.

'Hey there, Ella.' The apparition winked, which had heat flushing to her hairline, before it addressed Ruby. 'You must be Ruby. The name's Coop. I'm a friend of Ella's.'

He held out a deeply tanned hand in greeting as Ella heard Ruby's sharp intake of breath.

'Hi.' Ruby skirted the counter and grasped his hand

in both of hers. 'Cooper Delaney, right? It's so fabulous to actually meet you.'

Ella heard the perk of excitement in Ruby's voice and the laconic ease in Coop's—and everything inside her knotted with panic.

'Ella told you about me, huh?' His voice rumbled with pleasure as the green gaze settled on her.

Say something.

Her mind screamed as she absorbed the chiselled perfection of his cheekbones, the tawny brows, the twinkle of amusement in those arresting eyes, and the full sensual lips that tilted up in a confidential smile. Arousal gripped her abdomen as blood pumped into her sex.

But then she noted all the things about this man that didn't fit: the slate-grey single-breasted suit, the clean-shaven jaw, the short, perfectly styled hair that was several shades darker with fewer strands of sun-streaked blond.

She shook her head, a bolt of raw panic slamming into her chest as he passed his palm in front of her face. He was speaking to her.

'Hey there, Ella, snap out of it. How you doing?'

I'm pregnant. And I should have got in touch with you weeks ago to tell you.

She opened parched lips, but couldn't force the words out.

'Ella's great, she had her first—' Ruby began.

'Shut up, Ruby!' The high-pitched squeal shot past the boulder lodged in her throat. Ruby's eyebrows rose to her hairline but thankfully she obeyed the command, while Coop's grin took on a curious tilt.

Ella skidded round the counter, galvanised out of her trance.

Get him out of here, then you can tell him. Sensibly, succinctly, and privately, without an audience of tennis players, yummy mummies, two giggling schoolgirls and your super-nosey best friend.

She owed him that much.

'I'm taking a half-day, Rubes.'

Ruby's brow furrowed.

Oh, dear, she'd have some explaining to do to Ruby, too. But that could wait, she thought, as she came to a halt in front of Cooper.

She tilted her head back, the effect of that lazy smile shimmering down to her toes. How could she have forgotten how tall he was? Taking a deep breath in, she got a lungful of his delicious scent.

He smells the same. Hold that thought.

But then the aroma of spicy cologne and soap and man triggered a renewed pulse of heat and the shudder of reaction hit her knees.

She grasped his arm, as much to stay upright as to propel him back out of the door before Ruby spilled any more confidential information. The bulge of muscle flexed beneath the soft fabric of his designer suit— which didn't do much for her leg tremors.

He glanced at her fingers and grinned, pleased with her haste. 'It's great to see you too, Ella.' That he didn't seem particularly fazed by her fruitcake behaviour helped to calm some of the tension screaming across her shoulder blades. 'I was just in the neighbourhood,' he added. 'And I figured we could catch up over....'

'That's wonderful, Coop,' she interrupted. 'But let's go somewhere private so we can talk properly.'

'Sounds good.' His hooded gaze suggested he had made a few assumptions about her eagerness to get him alone. And talking was not at the top of his current to-do list.

The stupid tingles raced across her skin.

Do not hold that thought. You need to keep a clear head.

She crossed to the door, still clinging onto his arm, but stopped in her tracks when he didn't move with her.

She swung back, ready to beg. 'Please, my flat's just round the corner. I have coffee. And cupcakes.'

Her gaze flicked over his shoulder to Ruby, who had crossed her arms over her chest and was staring at her, the concern on her face making Ella feel small and foolish.

'Cupcakes, huh?' He laughed, but then his hands cupped her elbows, forcing her to relinquish her death grip on his arm. 'I'm a sucker for cupcakes,' he purred, then yanked her onto tiptoes. 'But first things first.' He dipped his head, bringing his lips tantalisingly close. 'Don't I rate a "welcome to London" kiss?'

Before she had a chance to confirm or deny, his mouth settled over hers, and every thought bar one melted out of her head.

Yes, please.

His tongue coaxed her lips open in hungry strokes, then tangled with hers. The shaking in her legs shot off the Richter Scale but his arms wrapped around her waist, holding her steady against the lean, hard line of his body. His scent enveloped her, clogging her lungs as she clung to him for balance, and drank in the glorious urgency of his kiss.

As they broke apart she heard the smattering of applause from the group of mums in the corner. The heat rose up to scald her scalp—but he was smiling at her with that appreciative, sexy twist of his lips she remembered so well from Bermuda and she swallowed down the renewed bolt of panic.

She had so much to tell him, and she still had no real clue how he would respond. But kissing him again, having his arms around her, had felt so good, she refused to allow her doubts to resurface. She was having this beautiful man's baby—and it felt like fate somehow that he had come to London to see her.

He dropped his arms and slid one warm palm into hers. 'Let's get out of here.' He brushed his lips across her ear lobe. 'I'm dying to taste your cupcakes.'

She grinned, sure her cupcakes weren't the only thing he planned to taste. 'You're going to love them.'

She waved goodbye to Ruby, who sent her a wary smile back, then mouthed, 'Tell him.'

She nodded, sobering a little.

'Great to meet you, Ruby. I'll bring her back in one piece. I swear.' He sent Ruby a farewell salute as he opened the café door for her and she stepped outside.

The sky was dark and overcast, a summer storm brewing, but excitement rippled.

Against all the odds, Cooper Delaney was here. And she would get the chance to tell him her news face to face. Now the initial shock had faded, she knew it was the best possible scenario. She could prepare him properly, before she told him. Explain exactly how it had happened and how much it meant to her, and make sure he understood he didn't have to be a part of the life growing inside her if he didn't want to be. That he had no obligations.

But surely him turning up here had to be a sign. Of something good. He'd come all this way to see her, and he'd kissed her with such fervour. The chemistry between them was still so strong, so hot. And there had been definite affection in his gaze too, the way his hands had steadied her, held her close.

He hadn't forgotten her, any more than she had forgotten him.

He slung an arm across her shoulders. 'Lead the way, my little cougar. But put a fire under it,' he said, casting a wary glance at the ominous thunderclouds overhead. 'It looks like we're about to get soaked.'

She chuckled, giddy with anticipation and tenderness, as a fat drop of rain landed on her cheek. 'My road is the second on the left.' The crash of thunder startled her for a moment, then the deluge of fat drops multiplied into a flood, drenching her T-shirt and jeans in seconds.

Laughing, she darted out from under his arm, the

chilly summer rain plastering her hair against her cheeks and running in rivulets between her breasts. 'Come on, toy boy. I'll race you there,' she said, before sprinting off in a burst of energy.

They would work this out. Nothing bad could happen today. She was sure of it.

'Come back here...'

Cooper raced up the shadowy stairwell guided by that pert ass outlined in wet denim, his own shirt sticking to his chest.

He tripped, cursed, then finally caught up with her, his crotch throbbing now. Running with a hard-on was never a good idea, but he'd been waiting months to get his hands on her again.

Her light, infectious laugh bubbled through his blood, doing weird things to his equilibrium as he followed her into the shoebox apartment at the top of the stairs. He slammed the door behind him, taking in the compact living room, the kitchen counter, the couch covered in colourful cushions. Then grabbed a hold of one hundred pounds of wiggling, giggling female, and refused to let go.

'Got you.' He held her close, taking the time to study the open, heart-shaped face, the huge blue eyes that had haunted his dreams for weeks.

Maybe he had missed her, more than he thought.

'And you're not getting away from me any time soon,' he declared. Although she wasn't exactly trying too hard.

His lips captured hers in a hungry kiss, while he peeled off the drenched cotton T-shirt to discover the damp lemon-scented female flesh beneath.

He cupped her generous breasts, the pebbled nipples digging into his palms through her bra, then pinched the swollen tips, while his mouth drank in her soft grunts of excitement.

Her fingers threaded into his hair, tugging him back. 'I have to tell you...' Her voice came out on a whisper. 'We have to talk.'

'Later.' He nipped her bottom lip. 'Sex first. Then cupcakes. Talk after that.'

He delved to find the hook on her bra and sent up a silent prayer of thanks as it popped open. Dragging the wet hem of her T over her head, he ripped off the sodden bra.

When she was bare to the waist, her breasts heaved with her staggered breathing, the large reddened nipples like ripe berries, sweet and succulent.

'Those are even hotter than I remember.' He lifted his gaze, saw the flush of colour on high cheekbones, the blue of her eyes dilated to dark, driving need.

Cupping one heavy orb in his palm, he licked round the peak, heard her moan, then bit tenderly into the swollen tip, his erection now huge in his pants.

Her back arched as she thrust into his mouth, moaning softly as he suckled harder.

Finding the zipper of her jeans, he yanked down the tab, and delved beneath the clinging, constricting fabric to cup her. She sobbed as his fingers widened the slick folds, and touched the heart of her. She bucked, then grasped his wrist.

'Stop!' she cried. 'I'm going to come.'

'That's the general idea.' Panic clawed at his chest. If she said no now he was liable to die.

She stared at him, her need plain in the wide pupils, the staggered pants of breath. 'I want you inside me. It's been too long.'

'Not a problem.' He chuckled, relief flooding through him as the tension in his groin begged for release. 'Then let's get naked. Fast.'

The sound of frantic cursing, of tearing fabric, of buttons hitting the linoleum flooring filled the small room as they wrestled to get their wet clothes off as fast as humanly possible.

After what felt like several millennia she stood naked before him, her gaze darkening further as those bright eyes dropped to his groin. His erection twitched, the pulse throbbing at its tip, steady and relentless.

He lifted her against the wall of the apartment, wedging himself into the space between her thighs. Clasping her generous hips, he assessed those spectacular breasts. She'd gained some weight since their night in Bermuda and it suited her—the belly that had been so flat across her hip bones now pillowing his erection.

The dumb wave of regret that her body had undergone that small change and he hadn't been there to see it, to witness it, passed over like a shadow then disappeared as her breasts pressed into his chest—demand-ing more friction. He ducked his head, to suck at the pulse point in her neck, which beat in frantic flutters. Her addictive scent surrounded him, lemon and spice and all things nice.

His lips curved, holding her as she hooked toned legs around his waist. Her fingers threaded into the short, damp hair at his ears.

'I haven't got any condoms,' he admitted, his mind trying to engage with the need to slow the hell down. To think through the driving urge to sink into her tight heat. He hadn't had time to stop and pick any protec-tion up because he'd come straight from the airport. And he hadn't figured things would get this hot, this quickly. But could he risk it? Just this once? She was on the pill? 'You okay with me using withdrawal? I'm clean, I swear.'

He felt her nod, and lifted his head to see her eyes, glazed with an emotion that made his heart thud against his chest wall like a sledgehammer.

'So am I,' she replied

It was all the permission he needed. His shaft jerked against her belly from the kick of desperation. Palming her buttocks, and angling her pelvis as best he could, he thrust home in one long, solid glide. Her slick, wet sex stretched to receive him, then massaged him like a velvet vice. Her head dropped back, thudding the wall, as he began to move, the thrusts jerky, desperate, the need quickly becoming too fast and furious, the need so raw and draining he couldn't slow down, couldn't stop now if his life depended on it.

She sobbed, her fingernails scraping his back as she clung on. Her muscles began to milk him, and he knew she was coming.

Don't pull out. Not yet. Hold on. Damn it.

His seed boiled, driving up from his balls, hurling him closer and closer to the cliff edge, her sobs of completion beckoning him to come faster, harder. And a tiny part of his mind screamed to the animal inside him.

Now. Pull out, now.

He wrenched himself free. Dropping his head against her shoulder, kissing the salt, sweet taste of her neck, the pain of separation as devastating as the brutal, unstoppable roll of orgasm as his seed pumped into the welcoming softness of her belly.

'Damn, that was even more awesome than I remember.'

Ella's gaze shimmered back into focus as a rough palm touched her cheek and blunt fingers sank into her hair. Those deep emerald eyes searched her face, making her chest tighten.

She nodded, gently, feeling stunned, her sex still clenching and releasing from the intensity of her orgasm. Seemed absence didn't just make the heart grow fonder.

'Yes,' she whispered, her throat raw from the wellspring of emotion.

His lips curved, and he placed a tender kiss on her forehead. 'Come on.' He hefted her into his arms, bracing his forearm under her buttocks as she held onto his shoulders. 'Let's grab a shower. Then I want a cupcake.'

'But we still need to talk,' she murmured against his neck.

'Sure. But first I want to see that magnificent rack covered in soap suds.'

She chuckled, resting her head on his shoulder, and draping her arms around his neck, her emotions too close to the surface to protest. Surely a few more minutes of intimacy, of getting reacquainted, wouldn't do any harm—she'd waited this long already?

Locating the tiny bathroom at the back of the flat, he put her down to twist on the shower. But kept one hand on her hip, as if he were afraid she'd run off. She remembered leaving him, that morning with only a thank you. And felt the renewed trickle of guilt.

The water gurgled and spurted out of the shower head, the stream thin and underwhelming.

'Is that as good as it gets?' he remarked.

She smiled. 'This is British plumbing we're talking about. That's the equivalent of Niagara Falls.'

His quick grin lifted her spirits and made the trickle of guilt dry up.

'At least it's hot,' he said, testing the temperature before he hauled her into the cubicle.

'Not for long.'

He grabbed her lemon verbena soap off the ledge, and worked up a lather, his hair plastered to his head, his eyes wicked with intent. 'Then we better get this party started.'

Gentle hands cupped her breasts, lifting and testing the weight as his thumbs glided over pebbled nipples. The heat pulsed and tugged between her thighs.

She took the soap to wash him in return, putting all the emotion she felt into the task as her hands stroked the lean, muscular slopes of his abdomen, explored the roped sinews that defined his hip bones. She took his penis into her palm, felt it lengthen and harden as she caressed it.

Blood surged into her tender clitoris, and she knew she wanted him again, already, surging deep, the delicious decadent stretching feeling of his flesh entering hers. Touching her womb where their child grew.

Soon he would know, and, whatever his reaction, surely it would be okay, when this closeness, this physical joining felt so good, so right.

But then he lifted her breasts, the cooling water sluicing away the soap, and said, 'I like the extra weight—it looks great on you.'

The approval in his gaze had the wave of guilt flopping over in her stomach. She couldn't wait any longer. It wasn't fair to him, or to their child. She drew away from him, her back wedged against the wall of the cubicle.

'We need to get dressed. I have something I have to tell you.'

'Okay.'

He flipped off the shower control, but took hold

of her wrist as she opened the cubicle door. The sudden silence felt deafening, despite the blood roaring in her ears. He tugged her towards him as he stepped out behind her, tucked a finger under her chin, lifting her gaze to his. 'What's up? Is something wrong?'

'No, I just...' She gulped past the tightness.

Not yet. Get yourself together first. You need to tell him gently. Carefully.

Her gaze dropped to his erection. She certainly couldn't function, let alone think clearly, while he was standing naked in front of her, visibly aroused.

'I just need a minute.'

His grip had loosened, his gaze puzzled, but not yet wary. She pulled her hand free, headed for the door. 'Shall we get dressed? I can meet you in the living room in ten minutes? Make you that coffee I promised?'

He shrugged, grabbed a towel from the rail to wrap around his waist. 'Sure.'

She darted out of the door before he could change his mind.

'All right, let's have it, what was so important we couldn't finish what I was busy starting in the shower?'

Ella smiled at the rueful tone, and glanced up from the cupcakes she was busy arranging on a plate.

He stood with his legs crossed at the ankles, leaning against the kitchen counter. He'd changed into a pair of faded jeans and a black T-shirt, which must have been in the bag he'd had with him. Had he come straight from the airport, then, to see her? She felt a renewed spike of optimism, of hope.

She'd figured so many outcomes for what she was about to tell him, but none of them had included the possibility that he might be pleased with her news. Yes, it would be a shock, but why had she assumed it would necessarily be a disaster?

She never would have guessed he would come to London, or the chemistry between them would have remained as hot for him as it still was for her.

'Why don't you sit down?' She gestured towards the living area. 'The coffee will be ready any minute.'

His brows lifted, the rueful grin taking on a mischievous tilt. 'It's not coffee I want.' Stepping close to hold her chin, he gave her lips a quick peck. The kiss felt casual and affectionate. The hope swelled in her chest. 'But we'll play it your way, for now.'

He settled on the sofa, while she fussed over the coffee for another precious few minutes, getting her thoughts lined up.

Finally she couldn't put it off any longer. Sitting on the opposite sofa, she placed the plate of cherry-chocolate cupcakes on the coffee table and poured him a cup of coffee. She had a momentary wobble when he told her he took it black, and it occurred to her how much she didn't know about him.

Don't chicken out now. Telling him is the first step to finding out all those things you don't know.

She took a long fortifying sip of the fennel tea she'd made for herself. 'I'm not sure where to start,' she began, galvanised by the thought that she was excited about taking this new step.

He lifted a cupcake off the plate. 'Then why don't you start by telling me why you ran out on me?'

'I didn't,' she said, frowning at the slight edge in his voice. 'I woke up and you were gone. I figured you'd run out on me.'

'Damn, seriously?' He looked genuinely stunned, which was a balm to her ego.

'Well, yes. And I felt uncomfortable with your friend Josie there.' She remembered the spike of dismay and asked, 'Who is she, by the way? She seemed to know you exceptionally well.'

His eyebrows rose and his lips crinkled. 'Are you jealous?'

Colour stained her cheeks.

He chuckled. 'Josie's like a kid sister. An annoying kid sister. Believe me, you've got nothing to be jealous of.'

'I didn't say I was jealous.'

'Uh-huh.' He sent her a confident smile. And she huffed out a laugh. The tension in her chest easing.

He took a large bite of the cupcake, held it up. 'Damn, that's good.' Finishing it off in a few quick bites, he placed the paper casing on the plate. 'So why don't you spill it, whatever it is you have to talk about. Before we get back into the shower.'

The colour in her cheeks flared again, under his watchful gaze. 'Okay, it's, well, it's sort of hard to say right out.'

She gulped down the new lump in her throat.

'Yeah? That doesn't sound good.' He sent her a crooked smile. 'I really hope you're not going to tell me you're married.'

She laughed, the tension dissolving a little. 'God, no, it's nothing like that. It's...' She examined her fingers, suddenly shy rather than scared. Wouldn't it be amazing if he was actually as excited about this as she was? 'Actually, I'm pregnant. That's why, well, I've gained some weight.'

The crooked smile remained, but the curiosity in his eyes turned to astonishment as his gaze dipped to her breasts and then her belly. He straightened on the sofa, his mouth opening. Then closing. Then opening again. 'You...? You're expecting a kid? You don't look pregnant.'

She waited for the obvious next question, but he just continued to stare at her belly.

'Well, I'm only twelve weeks, so it doesn't show much yet.' She placed her hands on the slight swelling, suddenly keen to emphasise it for his benefit.

His head lifted. She'd expected surprise, even shock when he made the connection; she'd even prepared herself for annoyance, and anger. What she hadn't prepared herself for, though, was the way the relaxed, sexy charm had been ripped away to be replaced by complete horror. 'Tell me you're not saying what I think you're saying?'

Her pulse throbbed painfully in her neck, and she

cradled her abdomen, the urge to shield her child, instinctive. She couldn't speak, so she simply nodded.

He leapt up from the sofa like a puppet who had been rudely jerked on stage. The vicious swear word echoed around the tiny room. 'You have got to be kidding me? It can't be mine—you said you were on the pill.'

She'd expected this accusation, on the numerous occasions when she'd had this conversation in her head. But all the careful explanations, the reasoned arguments, the excuses absolving her all seemed to pale into insignificance in the face of his frantic denial. And all she could manage was, 'I know, I realised when I found out you may have got that impression, but I—'

'You lied to me?' He stepped forward, the stance threatening.

Somehow she knew he wouldn't hurt her, not physically, but she could see the turmoil of emotion and it made her insides tangle into tight, torturous knots, the guilt that she'd kept so carefully at bay for weeks creating a yawning chasm in the pit of her stomach.

'Why the hell did you lie?' He dug his fingers into his hair, sending the damp strands into deep furrows. 'Unless... Hell... You wanted to get knocked up? Is this a set-up? You figure I'll pay you off?'

The accusation came so far out of left-field, she hadn't seen it coming before it had smacked into her chest and hurled her heart into her throat. 'What? No. I never...' Her denial choked off at the contempt in his eyes. 'You used a condom—how could I have planned it?'

'I knew the cute and clueless act was too good to be true. But I fell for it anyway.'

'What act? What are you talking about?'

'Drop it, okay. You've got what you wanted.' His eyes slid back to her belly, the light in them harsh and resentful. 'My bun in your oven.'

'No, you don't understand. It was never planned.' The justification, the explanation at last came tumbling out. 'The pregnancy was...is an accident. It was all so rushed and...I didn't think it would matter that I wasn't on the pill.'

'You didn't think it would matter?' His voice rose to a shout. 'Are you nuts? I told you I didn't want to risk it. What the hell about that did you not understand?'

'No, that's not what I meant. I didn't think I could....' She faltered, unable to reveal the truth about her medical history, her fertility issues, the test results she'd gone to Bermuda to escape. She couldn't tell this stranger about any of that; it would make her too vulnerable, too raw, especially now, with her throat already aching with unshed tears.

'You don't have to be involved.' She scrambled to justify, to explain, to avert the terrible feeling of loss. 'I've made the decision to have this child. I want it. Very much.' Her hands shook, the trembling having moved up from her toes, to her knees and across her torso.

Don't you dare cry.

Why hadn't she said all of this to start with, before she'd told him about the pregnancy? He obviously thought she was some kind of gold-digger. If she could just make him understand he didn't have to feel responsible for this child, everything would be okay. But even as she told herself it, a part of her was dying inside at the knowledge that Cooper Delaney hated her now.

'I just thought you should know.'

'Right, so now I know,' he snarled. 'Thanks for that. And what the hell am I supposed to do with the information? You've told me a part of me is going to be walking around on this planet and I don't get to have any say in that?'

She shook her head, the tears drying up inside her. *Stay firm. Stay strong. Don't break, not this time.* 'No. No, you don't.' She firmed her lips to stop them trembling. 'I won't have an abortion. And nothing you can do or say will make me.'

He flinched. 'Who said anything about an abortion?'

'I won't do it. I want this baby very much. If you don't, that's okay. You never have to have anything to do with it.'

'Yeah, right.' Marching past her, he grabbed his bag off the floor. 'Like that's going to work.' He slung the leather holdall over his shoulder and opened the door. Rain slashed down in angry currents against the hall window. But the summer storm that had seemed so cleansing, so perfect, so passionate only hours before, now appeared grey and dark and oppressive.

He sent her one last scathing look over his shoulder, the look of betrayal in his eyes palpable. And then slammed the door behind him.

She sank down against the wall, her legs too shaky to hold her, and pressed her forehead into her knees. And listened to his footfalls, heavy on the stairs, fade away into nothingness.

Coop stumbled out onto the street, his heart hitting his ribcage hard enough to shatter bone. Rain slashed at his face as he dumped his bag on the sidewalk and smashed his fist into the brick wall that marked the perimeter of her apartment building.

Pain hurtled up his arm, lanced across his knuckles, but went some way to dulling the terrifying emotions consuming him.

You dumbass. What the hell were you thinking? Coming here? Trusting her?

He sucked the battered knuckles, and picked up his bag in the other hand.

He hailed a cab, jumped in out of the rain and shouted through the grill, 'Take me to a hotel.'

'How about the Renaissance, sir? It's pricey but very plush.'

'Sure, great, whatever,' he croaked, his voice hoarse, his whole body starting to shake. He didn't give a damn where he went—he just had to get away from the memory of those big eyes glossy with unshed tears.

But then he caught the glittering pink logo on the window of Ella's cupcake store as the cab sped past it.

The panic boiled in his gut as the taste of her lingered on his tongue and the residual heat throbbed in his crotch. Mocking him.

He sank his head into his hands and wanted to howl with pain and frustration.

God help him, it didn't matter what he did now, or how much money he made or how fast he ran—he could never ever be an island again. And it was all his own damn fault.

EIGHT

—

Coop stared at the glittery pink lettering on the front of the diner, and then past it through the glass. He spotted Ella in front of the counter, busy chatting to a customer, her hand resting casually on her belly—and swallowed to ease the thickening in his throat.

Play it cool. No more freak-outs allowed.

He'd spent a night in the gothic splendor of the five-star hotel overlooking St Pancras Station, not sleeping a wink, as he went over every single thing she'd said, and every single thing he'd said. And he'd come to a few important—if shattering—conclusions.

He didn't have the first clue what he was supposed to do about the bomb she'd exploded in his nice, easy, island life. Correction: his formerly nice, easy, island life. Fatherhood was something he hadn't planned for and didn't know a damn thing about.

And he hated not knowing, because it reminded

him too much of his childhood. The dead weight of responsibility, the relentless pressure of being constantly trapped without a way out and that terrifying feeling of insecurity, of never knowing if he would be strong enough, smart enough, man enough to make things right for his mom.

He didn't want to live through all that again. And he hated that he would have to now.

And because of that he'd panicked yesterday, when Ella had told him her news—and had dropped a pretty big bomb on her in return.

Because however much he might want to blame all this on Ella, he knew now—once he'd taken the time to examine all the facts—that he couldn't. He also knew he couldn't just walk away from his own kid and forget about it—the way she'd suggested—because that would make him no better than his old man. And he was pretty sure he couldn't do that and live with himself afterwards.

All of which left him with only one option. Suck it up, stop whining about what he couldn't change and try to deal with it.

And the only way he could do that was to deal with Ella first.

Forcing the trademark 'never-let-them-see-you're-scared' smile he'd perfected as a kid onto his lips, he pushed open the door. But as Ella's gaze locked on his and her eyes went wide with distress his step faltered, his heartbeat stumbled and the thickening in his throat got a hell of a lot worse.

* * *

'Coop?' Ella bit into her lip, the tremor of shock and anxiety almost as overwhelming as the wave of relief.

She'd never expected to see him again, had convinced herself that his angry departure was for the best. She'd told herself over and over again during a long night spent on the phone to Ruby, and then lying in bed staring at the crack in her ceiling, that she couldn't make Coop want to be a father—any more than she could make him forgive her for something she hadn't done. So it would be pointless and futile to contact him again.

'We need to talk,' he said, his deep voice slightly strained but with none of the explosive anger from their last encounter. 'Can you take a break?'

She nodded, too stunned to speak, then glanced round the shop to locate her business partner. Ruby stood chatting to a young couple to whom she'd just delivered a couple of chai lattes. But then her head came up and she spotted Coop. All traces of the genial hostess disappeared as she marched back across the café.

'What do you want?' Ruby stepped behind the counter to stand shoulder to shoulder with Ella. 'Haven't you done enough?'

'I'm here to talk to Ella, honey, not you,' Coop said, the casual tone in direct contrast to the challenge in his eyes.

'Well, "honey"...' Ruby sneered the endearment, squaring up for a fight '...you're going to have to go through me to get to her after the immature way you behaved yesterday.'

'It's okay, Ruby.' Ella touched her friend's arm, emboldened by her support—even if it was counterproductive right now.

The last thing she wanted was for Coop to find out how much his accusations had hurt her, or how she'd dissolved into a quivering wreck after his departure. Showing that kind of weakness would only put her on the defensive. 'Coop's right—we need to talk. Is it okay if I take a few minutes?'

'Are you sure?' Ruby asked.

'We'll need more than a few minutes to sort this mess out,' Coop interrupted before she could reassure her friend. 'I've got a car waiting outside to take us back to my hotel, so we can have some privacy.'

This mess.

Ella's heart shrank. Her baby wasn't a mess. But if that was the way Coop saw it, then sorting out his involvement—or rather the lack of it—would be fairly clear cut. And she supposed she should be glad that he seemed prepared to do that much.

'Why do you need privacy?' Ruby interrupted again. 'So you can shag her and then have another temper tantrum like a two-year—'

'Ruby, please, don't.' Ella raised her voice, grateful for the spark of indignation. 'I'll be fine. All we're going to do is talk.' She wasn't about to make the mistake again of believing the strong physical attraction between them meant an emotional connection too.

She really didn't know this man. His volatile reaction last night had proved that. This 'talk' would be a chance to find out more about him—while also reassuring him that her expectations of him were zero as far as the baby was concerned.

Ruby continued to eyeball Coop for several pregnant seconds, but, instead of rising to the provocation, he grinned.

'You heard the lady.' He slung his hands in his pockets, the picture of nonchalance as he raised an eyebrow, the challenge unmistakable. 'All we're going to do is talk.' His gaze landed on Ella and the unwanted hum of awareness seared through her body. 'This time.'

'How are you? Is everything okay with the kid?'

Ella turned, to find Coop watching her from the opposite side of the cab as it crawled down Camden High Road. After persuading Ruby that she was woman enough to handle a private chat with her baby's father, she'd been careful to seat herself as far away as possible from him. But the tentative enquiry and the flicker of concern knocked her off balance again.

'Yes, everything's good.'

'I just wondered because...' he paused to clear his throat, looking more uncomfortable than she'd ever seen him '...I was kind of rough with you. In your apartment. You know, before you told me.'

She blinked, puzzled. He hadn't been rough, not until after he'd heard the news and then only verbally. But then it dawned on her what he was referring to.

Their frantic lovemaking against the wall. The blush climbed into her cheeks and heat pulsed in her sex at the visceral memory. While a matching, much more dangerous warmth tugged under her breastbone.

'Oh, no, everything's fine, really. Sex isn't a problem in pregnancy—as long as we don't start breaking furniture it should be okay.' The blush launched up to her hairline as it occurred to her what she had implied. 'Not that we're likely to be...well, you know.'

The sensual smile was even more unsettling. 'Yeah, I get it.' He tapped his fingers against his knee. 'Listen, I owe you another apology.'

She struggled not to be seduced by the smouldering look he appeared to be sending her, which she decided had to be an optical illusion. After their argument yesterday, he wasn't likely to jump her again. And she definitely did not plan to jump him.

'What for?' she said, unable to deny the tiny trickle of hope at his conciliatory tone. The less acrimony between them, the more chance they had of making this talk as painless as possible.

'For losing my temper. For freaking out when you told me...' his gaze dipped pointedly to her belly '...about your condition. For making out like this was all your fault.'

Relief was sharp and sweet at the heartfelt words. 'So you don't believe I got pregnant to set you up any more?'

He had the grace to look embarrassed. 'Not once I'd examined the facts. I figure opening that first condom packet with my teeth probably wasn't the smartest thing I've ever done.' His gaze fixed on her. 'And after what happened yesterday, I'm guessing even if you had told me the truth about being on the pill, I would have risked it. Things had got pretty hot by then already.'

The muscles of her thighs melted as the pesky hum of reaction shimmered down to her core.

'I appreciate your honesty.' She nodded, accepting his apology with deliberate formality, while crossing her legs in an attempt to ease the ache in her sex.

Not going there. Remember?

'I owe you an apology, too.' She heaved a sigh, knowing she was hardly blameless in the misunderstandings that had arisen between them.

'Yeah?' He arched a questioning brow.

'I should have corrected you...' The blush fired up her neck as his lips quirked, the sensual knowledge in his smile not doing a thing to cool the hot spot between her thighs. 'But I wasn't really paying a lot of attention to the conversation at that point.'

'You and me both.' The low comment was husky with intimacy.

She cleared her throat. *Hormones behave. Now.* 'But to be honest, I really didn't think it would make any difference because...' She hesitated. 'I've had some fertility issues. Believe me, the chances of me getting pregnant were extremely slim.'

He frowned. 'How slim?'

'Well, if my doctor's reaction is anything to go by

when she confirmed the pregnancy, I think we might be talking lottery-winning odds.'

'Damn. Seriously?'

She nodded, smiling at his reaction. He sounded more stunned than pleased, but it still felt good to share such an important moment in their child's life with him.

'When did you find out?' he asked, and her smile faded.

Blast.

'Um...' She glanced out of the window as the pristine new Eurostar terminal at St Pancras Station inched by.

'You know, that you were knocked up?' he prompted, obviously thinking she hadn't understood the question.

She studied the station's redbrick Victorian grandeur as they turned onto Euston road, desperate to avoid his unsettling gaze and the equally unsettling question. He'd been honest with her, and she knew she owed him the same courtesy, but would telling him the truth break this momentary truce? Obviously, she should have contacted him weeks ago, and she hadn't. If only she hadn't been such a coward.

'What's the deal, Ella?' he probed, already sounding suspicious. 'How long have you known about this?'

She sighed. 'Four weeks.'

She tensed at the muffled curse as the cab stopped outside the station hotel.

'Great.' He didn't say another word, just paid the

cabbie and ushered her into the Renaissance's grand lobby area.

Every time she'd passed the historic hotel since its renovation a few years ago, she'd wondered what it looked like inside. But she barely registered the lavish vaulted ceiling or the plush interior design as his palm settled on the small of her back, and he directed her to the elevators.

His suite on the third floor had a spiral wrought-iron staircase that curved onto a second level, and original Gothic arched windows that looked down onto the station concourse. But as he poured out the bottle of sparkling mineral water she'd requested into a glass filled with ice it wasn't the hotel's palatial elegance she found intimidating.

'Okay, so now I want to know—why the delay?' He helped himself to a cola from the room's bar. 'Because I've got to tell you, I'm not feeling real happy about the fact that you've known about this kid for a month and you didn't get in touch.'

She'd been expecting the question ever since they'd arrived. And had prepared an answer. But she paused to take a hasty gulp of the icy, effervescent water.

She didn't want to tell him how she'd initially panicked about his reaction. Because then she'd have to tell him about Randall, and the child she'd lost. And she didn't see how that would serve any purpose now. Except to make her look bad. And she looked bad enough already.

'Stop stalling, Ella,' he murmured, watching her

over the rim of his glass. And she had the disconcerting thought again that he seemed to be able to read her a lot easier than she was able to read him.

'All right,' she huffed, perching on a bar stool. 'If you must know, I did an internet search to get your details, so I could contact you.' This wasn't lying, she justified, it was simply failing to tell the whole truth. 'And, well...' Okay, maybe this part of the truth made her seem a little pathetic. But pathetic she could live with.

'And...?' he prompted, as if he didn't already know what she was going to say.

'I thought you were a freelance boat captain who lived in a one-room beach shack. I wasn't expecting to discover your name mentioned as one of the top young entrepreneurs in the Caribbean. It was disconcerting.'

He sent her an unapologetic smile.

What was so funny?

'And totally unexpected,' she added. 'I needed time to adjust to that before contacting you. So I waited, probably a bit longer than I should have.'

'A bit?' The grin spread as he propped himself on the bar stool next to her and nudged her knee with his. Crowding her personal space. 'Four weeks is an awful lot of adjustment time, don't you think? And you never did contact me, honey. I came to you.'

'There was an awful lot to adjust to.' She raised her chin. He'd tricked her, and pretended to be someone he wasn't. Surely she was entitled to be a little miffed about that? 'It made me realise that I didn't really know anything about you, and that scared me.'

'You knew the important stuff.' He ran his thumb across her bottom lip.

'Don't.' She jerked back, the sudden touch almost as shocking as the tenderness in his eyes.

'You scare pretty easy, don't you, Ella?' The probing gaze made her feel as if he could see through her T-shirt and jeans to the naked, needy girl she'd once been. 'Why is that?'

She tried to regulate her staggered breathing, unable to take her eyes off his.

Sexual desire was something she could handle. Would handle. But she didn't want to need him. To need any man. Not again.

'Do you think we could talk about the baby now?' she said. 'I have to get back to work.'

'Sure.' Coop shrugged, the tension in his shoulder blades nothing compared to the kick of need in his crotch.

Damn, he wanted her again: that lush mouth on his, those hard nipples grinding against his chest, the hot, wet heat gripping him like a velvet glove.

And he was pretty damn sure she wanted him too.

He could smell her arousal, the spicy scent of her need, ever since she'd climbed into the cab and sat stiffly in the far corner, as if she was worried she'd spontaneously combust if she got too close.

She still fascinated him, and excited him. And even though he kept telling himself hooking up with her again had the potential to turn this mess into a total disaster—another part of him was thinking this mess couldn't get much bigger if it tried. So why should they deny themselves? Only problem was, he wasn't sure if that part of him was the part that was supposed to be doing the thinking, or a part that was positioned a lot further south.

He had to admit he was also very curious, as well as kind of touched, by her reaction when she'd discovered the truth about Dive Guys and his wealth. Wouldn't most women feel entitled to hit him for some kind of compensation? Especially once they found out how much he was worth? Instead of that she'd 'needed time to adjust'? What was with that? One thing, it sure didn't make him feel any better about having accused her of setting him up.

He poured the last of his cola into his glass, took a long swig to buy himself some time and figure out what to do now.

She hadn't said anything, the expectation in her face tempered by wariness. As if she was worried about what he was going to say, but determined to put the best possible spin on it.

'The way I see it, Ella,' he began, acknowledging that it was definitely a strike in his favour that she was so easy to read, 'however this happened, we're both going to be parents of the same kid. And you're right, we don't know nearly enough about each other.' He let his eyes wander over her torso, vindicated by the bullet points thrusting against the tight cotton of her T. 'Except in the most basic sense.' He slugged down the last of the cola, and let the cool caffeinated liquid soothe his parched throat. 'How about you come back to Bermuda for a couple of weeks?' The offer came out of his mouth before he'd really had a chance to consider it, but it instantly felt right when her eyes lit up with delighted astonishment. 'And while you're there we can iron out how we're going to handle stuff once the kid's born.'

'You want to be involved? In the baby's life?' She sounded so overjoyed, he had to bite the inside of his mouth to keep from grinning back at her. Was it really going to be that easy?

'Of course I do. It's my kid too, isn't it?'

'Well, yes. Yes, it is.' She flattened her hands across her abdomen, in that protective gesture that he was beginning to realise was entirely instinctive. And totally genuine.

His heartbeat slowed at the evidence of how much the baby meant to her already, even though it was probably no bigger than a shrimp. Then fluttered uncomfortably, at the knowledge that his child was unlikely to ever mean that much to him.

He could do responsibility, and loyalty, and commitment, up to a point. But the kind of blind faith and trust you needed to care about someone more than you cared about yourself? Forget it. He knew he'd never be able to do that again.

'What on earth do you mean you're going to Bermuda?' Ruby stared. 'For how long?'

'I'm not sure, probably only a fortnight. He suggested I get an open ticket, but I doubt it'll take longer than that.' Although she had to admit she'd been impossibly touched when he'd sounded concerned that two weeks might not be enough time to sort out 'all the baby stuff'.

'Are you completely bonkers?' Ruby propped her hands on her hips, the belligerent stance one Ella recognised.

'He's invited me and I think it's a good idea.' She sprinkled edible pink glitter onto the swirl of buttercream icing. And placed the finished cupcake onto the tower she was assembling for a nine-year-old's birthday party, refusing to make eye contact with her friend. She'd expected this reaction. It didn't mean she was going to enjoy dealing with it. She hated arguing with Ruby. 'We're having a child together. I'd like him to be involved if he wants to be, but I need to know a lot more about him to make that a realistic possibility. Especially as we live so far apart.' She'd thought it all out, and it all made perfect sense.

Ruby tapped her foot. 'So why can't he stay in London so you can sort all that out here?'

Ella sighed, and wiped sugary hands on her apron. 'He has a business to run.'

'So do you.' Ruby went straight for the jugular.

'I know it's not a good time.' Ella faced her friend, and shook off the sting of guilt. They were already having to take out a loan to cover the extra staffing costs while she went on maternity leave, but... 'It will be good for Sally and Gemma to have a trial run with you supervising before I have the baby and I've got enough saved to cover the cost of their wages while I'm away.'

'You know very well this has nothing to do with the money,' Ruby pointed out. 'What about your antenatal appointments? What if something happens with the baby?'

'Coop's arranged for the top obstetrician on the island to handle my care while I'm there.' Even if he had gone a little pale when she'd mentioned the problem. 'But it's unlikely to be more than a couple of weeks. I'll still only be four months when I get back.'

'Fine, well, now for the biggie.' Ruby threw up her hands in exasperation. 'What about the fact that Cooper Delaney is a complete jerk who accused you of being a gold-digger, and a liar and had you in floods of tears less than twenty-four hours ago? How do you know you can trust him not to be a jerk again once you're stuck in Bermuda with him?'

I don't.

Ella pushed away the doubt. He'd lost the plot when she'd told him about the baby, but he'd apologised for that and she knew he meant it. And anyway, this really wasn't about her. 'He's the father of my child and he's giving me a chance to get to know him better. Surely you can see I have to take it?'

'Umm-hmm. And you don't find it the tiniest bit suspicious that twenty-four hours after totally flipping out about this pregnancy he suddenly wants to be so intimately involved in it...' Ruby paused for effect '...and you.'

'Maybe.' Of course she'd thought about it. After the initial euphoria at his offer, she'd calmed down enough to realise his sudden interest in the baby might not be the only reason he'd asked her to come to Bermuda.

But that didn't alter the fact that he was the father of her child. And she did want him to be involved. And that going to Bermuda was the only way to find out if they could make that happen.

'You're absolutely determined to do this, aren't you?' Ruby sounded pained.

'Yes.'

Ruby cursed sharply, defeated. 'I guess it's my own fault. If I hadn't interfered and encouraged you to nail Captain Studly in the first place, you wouldn't be in this situation.'

Ella grasped Ruby's cheeks, forcing her gaze back to hers. 'What situation? Getting the chance to have a child of my own? Getting to experience the miracle of becoming a mum? Something I was sure would never be possible? That situation?'

Ruby sent her a lopsided smile. 'Okay, point taken. But do me a favour, okay?'

'What favour?'

'Don't let all your happy over the pregnancy blind you to the truth about what's really going on with him. You have a tendency to always want to see the best in people, Ella. And that's one of the things I love about you. But try to be a little bit cautious this time.'

'If this is about what happened with Randall, you don't have to worry.' Ella threaded her fingers through Ruby's and held on. 'I'm not going into this blind. I learnt that lesson when I was eighteen I'll never fall in love that easily again.' She'd made that mistake with Randall, and her baby had paid the price. 'But I refuse to go into this scared either.'

She needed to take some risks, to solve the fascinating enigma that was Cooper Delaney. A man who had the laid-back, laconic charm of a beach bum, but had the drive and ambition to build a multimillion-dollar empire from nothing. A man who could worry about the child growing in her womb when they made love, and yet look at her with a hunger that burned right down to her soul.

She wanted to understand him—to know how he really felt about this pregnancy and this baby and her—but only so he could play an active role in her child's life.

She wasn't looking for anything else. She was sure of it.

NINE

—

'How was the trip?' Coop reached in to grab her suitcase as Ella stepped out of the air-conditioned taxi into the sheltered carport rimmed by palm trees and flowering vines at the back of his property.

She fanned her face with the wide-brimmed straw hat she'd bought at the airport as the afternoon heat enveloped her. Bermuda in April had been in the mid-seventies and pleasantly hot; in late July it was hitting the high eighties and seemed to be sucking the life-force right out of her tired limbs.

'Good. Thank you.' She huffed to stop her sweaty hair sticking to her forehead as Coop paid the driver and waved him off.

The truth was it had been better than good, when she'd arrived at Gatwick Airport to discover the economy class ticket she'd insisted on purchasing herself, despite several terse emails from Coop before she left London, had been upgraded to first class. The added benefits of a three-course cordon bleu meal and a fold-down bed had made the eight-hour flight pass in a haze of anticipation. But now she was here, the impact of seeing him again was making the crows of doubt swoop like vultures in her stomach.

'I appreciated the upgrade, but you really didn't need to do that.' She wanted to make it absolutely clear she did not expect him to bankroll her.

Picking up her suitcase, he slung her carry-on bag under his arm. 'Sure I did.' His gaze skimmed down to her midriff before he sent her an assured grin. 'No baby of mine travels coach.'

The vultures in her stomach soared upward to flap around her heart and she stood like a dummy, stupidly touched by the reference to their child.

'Come here.' Resting his hand on her waist, he directed her towards the wooden steps that led out of the carport and into the back of the house. 'Let's get you out of this heat.'

The stairs led to the wide veranda of a white, wood-framed house that rose from the grove of palms to stand on a rocky outcropping. She'd admired the modern, two-storey colonial structure as they wound down the drive from the main gate. Up close, the building was dominated by the large windows covered by louvred shutters. The house appeared cool and airy even before they stepped off the veranda into a palatial, high-ceilinged living area that opened onto a wrap-around porch, which looked down onto the cove below. Dumping her bag and suitcase at the base of a curving staircase that led to the second level, Coop leaned against the balustrade and smiled. In a faded red and black Bermuda College T-shirt and ragged jeans, his bare feet bronze against the oak flooring, he looked more like the beach bum she remembered than the suited executive she'd found so intimidating in London.

'So what do you think? Better than the hut, right?'

She swung round to take in the view and give herself a moment to regain the power of speech. Expensive, luxury furnishings—including a couple of deep-seated leather sofas, a huge flatscreen TV, a bar framed in glass bricks and a walled fireplace—adorned the tidy, minimalist living area. She stepped through the open doors onto the deck, hoping that the sea breeze would cool the heat rising up her neck. And spotted the edge of an infinity pool, sparkling on the terrace below the house. Steps carved into the stone led down through the grove of palms and banana trees, probably to the beach at Half-Moon Cove.

The cosy, ramshackle beach hut where they'd conceived their child had to be down there somewhere—but felt light years away from the elegance of his real home.

'It's incredibly beautiful. You must have worked very hard to earn all this in under a decade.'

He joined her on the deck, resting his elbows on the rail beside her hip and making her heartbeat spike.

'So you've been checking up on me?'

She studied the sun-bleached hair on his muscular forearms—lost for words again.

She'd expected to be a little intimidated by his wealth—especially after the first class travel over. She hadn't expected to feel completely overwhelmed. Not just by the staggering beauty of his home, but by him too. And the staggering effect he still had on her.

'The Internet is a glorious thing,' she murmured.

Unfortunately all the articles and news clippings about the meteoric rise of his business had contained virtually no information about his personal life. Or his past—bar a few photos of him escorting model-perfect women to island events. And once she'd discovered those, her enthusiasm for playing Nancy Drew had waned considerably.

'The journalist from *Investment* magazine said you were the Rags-to-Riches King of the Islands,' she said. 'She seemed very impressed with your business model.' And not just his business model, Ella had decided, from all the detailed prose about his muscular physique and sparklingly intelligent gaze.

The grin as he glanced her way was quick and boyish. 'Yeah, I remember her. As I recall she hit on me.'

'I'm not sure I needed to know that,' she blurted, before getting control of the sting of jealousy.

He straightened away from the rail. 'Just so you know, I didn't hit on her back.' He skimmed a knuckle down her cheek. 'I like to be the one doing the chasing.' He tucked his finger under her chin. 'Except when it comes to pretty little English cougars who go trawl-ing in beach bars.'

Her pulse sped up to thud against her neck, and the spot between her thighs melted. 'I didn't come back to Bermuda to hit on you again,' she said, trying hard to sound as if she meant it. Sleeping with him would only distract her from the real reason she was here.

He clasped the rail on either side of her hips, box-ing her in.

'Then how about I hit on you?'

She gasped as he pressed warm, firm lips to her neck. Lust shot through her like a jolt of electricity—connecting the soft tissue under her chin to the bun-dle of nerves that lay dormant in her sex.

Except, it wasn't dormant any more.

The sensations spread like molten lava, incinerat-ing everything they touched as he explored her mouth in bold, determined strokes.

She sucked on his tongue, savouring the tangy fla-vour of him, the groan of desperation. Her fingers flexed against the lean muscles of his abdomen as roughened palms stroked under her blouse. His fin-gers wrapped around her waist to yank her closer. She shuddered, her sensitive, pregnancy-engorged breasts pressed against the hard wall of his chest.

Sure fingers cupped her breast, then tugged at one hard peak and hot need arrowed down to her sex, the desire erupting like a volcano.

'Wait, Coop.' She wrenched herself free. 'Please, stop

a moment. I need...' She sucked in a breath, her lungs on fire, alongside the rest of her. 'I didn't come for this.'

Did she?

But as his heavy-lidded gaze met hers the heady rush that had been lapping at her senses ever since the car had pulled up to the house surged.

'So what?' He clasped her hand, and headed for the staircase.

He took the stairs two at a time. She could have resisted, could have told him no, but instead she found her feet racing to keep up with him.

He led her into a wide room on the first floor, with a huge four-poster bed draped with gauzy white curtains, and double doors that opened out onto a veranda.

He tugged her into his arms. 'I want you,' he murmured, his voice so low she almost couldn't hear it above the distant sound of the ocean, and the pounding in her eardrums. 'You want me.' His gaze dropped to her midriff. 'We've made a kid together. Why shouldn't we do this?'

She couldn't find a coherent response as the desperate desire to be touched, to be taken in that wild way only he seemed capable of, consumed her.

He jerked off his T-shirt, kicked off his jeans, and then wrestled off her clothes before lifting her, naked and yearning, onto the bed.

Her hands splayed across his wide chest, sank into the blond curls of hair across his nipples. She had to slow him down. Get her mind to engage.

Ruby had warned her not to get distracted, not to fall straight into bed with him. And here she was, less than an hour off the plane and already naked and willing.

'Shouldn't we think about this?' She struggled to hold him back, but the question broke on a soft sob as he cupped her mound. Blunt fingers probed the slick flesh, gliding over the perfect spot.

She bucked, cried out, pleasure radiating across her skin.

The light in his eyes became feral in its intensity. 'You're soaking wet, Ella. What's there to think about?'

Her breath rasped out as he stroked her into a frenzy, caressing the burning nub. Then rolled her over onto her stomach. Raising her hips, he positioned her on all fours, the thick erection nudging her entrance.

'I'll be gentle.' He lifted her hair off her neck, cradled her body with his to nip her shoulder. 'I promise.' Her heavy breasts swayed and he captured them, holding her steady. 'Now tell me you don't want this as much as I do?'

'You know I do.' She moaned, stretched unbearably, as he plunged. Her pulse thundered like an express train in her ears.

Need and desperation pummelled her. She couldn't breathe, couldn't think, the coil yanking tight inside her as he began to move. Pulling out, thrusting back, going impossibly deep, the rhythm torturously slow but steady, relentless, stealing her breath. Her hands fisted in the bedclothes, her body battered by the building waves of pleasure. Sure fingers squeezed her nipples, then he reached down, to open her folds and touch the too-sensitive nub of her clitoris.

Pain and pleasure combined as he shot her to peak. The titanic wave crashed over her as his rhythm built and accelerated. She heard him shout, getting even bigger inside her, before the hot seed pumped into her. He let her go at last and she collapsed onto the bed, her body shaky, her mind dazed, her heart pounding against her ribs with the force and fury of a wrecking ball.

She rolled away from him, feeling stupidly fragile. 'You didn't use any protection,' she murmured.

'Not much point now. That horse has already bolted.' He whispered the words against her ear as his forearm wrapped around her waist and his body cradled her. 'You okay? I didn't hurt you, did I? I was trying to be gentle but I got kind of carried away towards the end.'

She shook her head, struggling to talk round what felt like a wad of cotton wool in her throat. 'No. It felt good.' And scarily intense.

One large hand cupped her breast, his thumb grazing the sensitive nipple. She flinched, the stiff peak too tender for attention.

'I'm sorry.' His thumbs drew back, to trace slow circles around the areola, avoiding the tip. 'The plan wasn't to jump you straight off. But I've missed you.'

'The plan...' She lurched onto her back, dislodging his hand. 'You planned this?'

'Yeah. I guess so.' He propped himself up on an elbow to look down at her, his gaze roaming over her face. 'Why? Is that a problem?'

'I don't know.' She tried to gather her thoughts and make sense of them, while the rush of afterglow still pumped through her system. 'I just thought...'

'What? That this wouldn't happen?' He brushed his fingers across her forehead, tucked the tendrils of hair that had escaped her updo behind her ear. 'Honey, I figure whenever we're on the same continent it's sort of inevitable. So why fight it?'

It wasn't the answer she had been looking for, the one she thought she should have wanted. But as soon as he said it she knew it was the truth.

'Yes, but...' She stared at him. 'That really isn't the reason I came here.'

'So why did you come?'

With her sex still aching from the intensity of their lovemaking, her breasts tender from the pinch of his fingers, and emotion coursing through her system, the answer didn't come as easily as it had when she had been lying in that fold-down bed across the Atlantic.

'To get to know you,' she murmured. 'To find out if you want to be a dad. How involved you want to be. I don't want sex to complicate that.'

'To complicate it?' He chuckled. 'The way I see it, sex is pretty much the only simple thing there is about all this. And we're good at it.' He shrugged, his gaze flicking to her midriff. 'We're going to have to work on the other stuff, because I don't have any easy answers for you there.'

For a moment he looked lost, and the lump of emotion became impossible to swallow down. Was she pushing him too hard, expecting too much, by being here?

'You don't know how you feel about the baby?' she asked, feeling foolish and a little ashamed of her naivety. Why had she been so quick to assume his decision to invite her here meant he must already have feelings for the baby? He'd been thrown into this situation against his will. Of course he'd be confused, maybe even a little resentful.

'Not really.' He flopped back on the bed, stared at the canopy above their heads. 'All I know is I don't want to mess up, like my old man did.'

She turned to him, ready to probe a little. 'How did your father mess up?'

His gaze locked with hers and for a moment she thought she saw something, but then it flicked away again. 'By not being there, I guess. I never met him. It was just my mom and me.'

'I'm sorry.' Her heart sank at the defensive 'don't go there' tone. And the news that he had been abandoned as a child by his own father. No wonder he'd reacted so violently to the news of her pregnancy. Had the horror she'd thought she'd seen been nothing more than blind panic?

She touched his forearm. 'You're not like that. If that's what you're worried about? Because you're already trying to do the right thing.'

He looked at where her fingers touched his arm, then up at her face, his expression blank now and unreadable. 'You always this much of an optimist?'

His tone was flat, but she refused to let it bother her.

'I try to be,' she said, smiling. 'I don't consider that a bad thing.'

She wanted this child; he was still coming to terms with the fact of it. She had to remember that. Give him time. And space. And not give up hope. His cynicism made complete sense, now she'd had that brief glimpse into his childhood.

'So, what was your mother like?' she asked.

He shook his head, smiling back at her. 'Forget it, Little Miss Sunshine. How about you tell me something about your folks, first? I don't see why I have to do all the talking.'

He'd hardly told her anything, she thought, but she didn't call him on it. Surely telling him more about herself could only increase the intimacy between them, and make it easier for him to open up too?

'Okay, well...' She paused, his question triggering memories of a time in her life that she barely remembered now, but had been so painful once. 'Funnily enough, I think it was watching my parents and seeing what they went through that made me an optimist.'

'How come?'

'Because they had an incredibly acrimonious divorce when I was eight.'

His eyebrows shot up. 'And that made you an optimist?'

'Well, yes. Because it taught me how important second chances are,' she continued, choosing to ignore the sceptical expression. 'They'd tried to stay together for me and my brother and it had been a disaster. Children always see more than you think.' She sighed, remembering the whisper arguments, the bitter silences, the terror and confusion when she and her brother had been told Daddy would be moving out. 'I missed my dad terribly and it was awful to see my mum so sad and angry all the time. But then, eventually, they both found the people they were meant to be with. And I ended up with a stepmum who makes to-die-for chocolate cake and a stepdad who drove me and Ruby to cookery fairs without complaint. It totally transformed them both, made them much better people and much better parents. Because they were finally happy.'

He rolled onto his side, and suddenly she became aware of his nakedness, and hers, and the low-level hum of arousal that always seemed to be there. He placed a warm palm on her hip, slid it up to cup her breast. 'That's sweet,' he said, the comment only mildly condescending. Then he ducked his head, to lick a pouting nipple. 'But not as sweet as you are. You know, your breasts look incredible. Have they got bigger?'

Right, it seemed their deep and meaningful conversation appeared to be over. She knew a distraction technique when she heard one—and felt it hardening against her hip.

'Yes, they have...'

He leant down and sucked at the tip of her breast, gently, provocatively.

'The obstetrician says it's to do with the pregnancy hormones,' she continued, trying to focus despite the glorious feel of her nipple swelling against his tongue. 'They're much more sensitive too.'

He grinned up at her. 'Awesome.'

Wrapping his lips around the stiffened peak, he drew it against the roof of his mouth. Her fingers plunged into his hair as she held his head and gasped, the pleasure almost too intense to bear now. 'Oh, God...'

His growing erection nudged her belly, and she reached to stroke the shaft instinctively. But as she brushed her thumb across the bead of liquid at the head, rejoicing at his growl of need, her stomach rumbled loudly.

'Enough.' He gave a strained laugh, carefully dislodging her hand. Then kissed her fingers, his smile mocking. 'I guess I'm going to have to offer you food. I don't want you passing out your first day.'

At the mention of food, her stomach growled again. Colour tainted her cheeks as he laughed. 'How about you go grab a shower, and I'll put out the food my housekeeper prepared for us? We can eat out on the deck.'

'I'd like that,' she said, suddenly grateful for the respite, and the chance to examine all the emotions careering through her system.

Although she'd discovered in the last twenty minutes that he had a few 'issues' about his role as a father to overcome, it felt good to have got her first proper glimpse of the man behind the confident façade he wore so well. And exciting to know that they'd already started to establish a new intimacy between them.

Despite all Ruby's dire warnings not to confuse her joy about the pregnancy with anything else, she wasn't the least bit worried about jumping back into bed with Coop.

The one good thing about her terrible experience with Randall was, she'd never be delusional enough to mistake hot sex for love again.

Just because Coop looked great, smelled amazing, knew how to hit all her happy buttons—endorphin-wise—had sperm supersonic enough to impregnate her virtually barren body, and made everything inside her gather and tighten when he looked at her a certain way, she knew she could remain totally objective about their relationship. Such as it was.

Her main priority was the baby. And that would never change.

She lay back in the bed, and took a moment to appreciate the delicious view of Coop's naked backside as he tugged his jeans back on. And stifled the sigh as the pale strip of defined muscle disappeared behind battered denim.

Her stomach fluttered as if it were filled with hyperactive butterflies when he leaned down to press a kiss to her lips. 'Supper will be served in twenty minutes, Little Miss Sunshine. Don't be late.'

'Aye aye, Captain.'

He strolled out, and her gaze dipped back down to that beautifully tight butt—while the swooping sensation in her stomach bottomed out.

Okay, maybe sleeping with Coop would be a tiny bit distracting, but surely they were going to need some light relief from all the heavy stuff they had to deal with? And the truth was, the intimacy of sex seemed to be a great way to get him to lower his guard.

She squinted as the setting sun dipped lower and the light peaked past the four-poster's gauzy curtains onto the bed. In fact, now she thought about it, maybe she should consider it her duty to seduce him as often as possible.

Damn, you nearly blew it.

Coop put the last of the platters Inez had prepared on the outdoor table. The generous plate of lobster salad, Inez's salted crab cakes and colourful sides of fruit salsa, fried plantain and cornbread had saliva gathering under his tongue.

Good, hopefully Inez's mouth-watering spread would keep his mouth and hands busy when Ella came down for her supper. He uncorked a chilled bottle of

Pouilly Fuissé and splashed a couple of slugs into a glass before planting the bottle in the ice bucket next to the table.

Time to cool the hell down.

What the hell had got into him? He'd seen her less than a week ago. Had made love to her less than ten days ago. And yet, he'd jumped her as soon as she'd arrived.

One gasp of breath, one look from those trusting eyes and he'd been all over her like a rash. His first night with her had already caused more problems than he knew how to solve. And now he was losing all his cool points too? What the hell?

He gulped the pricey wine without tasting a single drop—the thought of the baby going some way to dousing the heat in his pants.

She loved this kid already; he could see it in the dreamy look every time she mentioned it. And then there were all those questions about how he felt about the baby. Making him pretty sure she wasn't going to be impressed with his initial thought that maybe his role in the child's life could be limited to setting up a hefty college fund and giving her a monthly allowance to cover her expenses.

On the balcony above, the white cotton curtains billowed out of the open balcony doors caught by the early evening breeze off the ocean. The sound of running water drifted down from the guest room's shower.

The image of Ella, naked and flushed, her rosy nipples begging to be sucked, swirled into his brain.

He drained the glass. Snagged one of the patties off the plate, wrapped it in some arugula and stuffed it in his mouth.

Enjoy it, Delaney, because crab cakes are the only cakes you're going to be sucking on for the rest of the night.

He needed to keep his wits about him. And not fall into the trap of getting hot and heavy about anything other than the sex. Until he had some answers to Ella's questions.

With that in mind...

Picking his smartphone off the table, he keyed in his housekeeper's home number. When Inez picked up he told her to take a holiday for a couple of weeks, all expenses paid. He could hear the suspicion in the older woman's voice—Inez had six grown kids and eight grandbabies and was nobody's fool—but after checking he'd remember to water the plants and suggesting a local girl to come in and do the laundry and cleaning while she was away, she finally took the bait.

Then he rang Sonny, listened to a lengthy update on the wedding arrangements, and then told his friend that he wouldn't be around for a while and if he needed anyone to help out with tours to contact his business manager. Then he carefully layered in a request to tell Josie he'd be mostly off island till the wedding.

He knew Josie was likely to be his biggest problem. Like any annoying little sister, that girl was more curious than the proverbial cat, had got into the bad habit of thinking she could drop in on him any time unannounced—and had an even bigger mouth than Inez.

He tucked the phone into the back pocket of his jeans. And dispelled the small tug of guilt. Ella would get to meet all his friends at Josie's wedding in three weeks' time if she was still here, but until then it would be better if they both kept a low profile.

Their little heart-to-heart and that poignant insight into her childhood had been unsettling and he didn't want any more weird moments like that again if he could avoid them.

When she'd told him about her parents' break-up, the urge to take away the unhappiness in her eyes had been dumb enough. But much worse had been the freaky feeling of connection. Because he remembered exactly what it was like to be scared, to be confused, to feel as if your world were being ripped apart and there wasn't a damn thing you could do about it. When he was a child, his mother's black moods, those dark days when she couldn't function, or when she cried—usually after his father had been by to screw her for old times' sake—had scared the hell out of him.

He'd almost told Ella about it. Thank God, he'd managed to stop himself just in time. Because the last thing he needed was them sharing confidences about stuff that meant nothing now.

He'd ridden out the storm long ago and he'd survived. And Ella had too.

But, unlike Ella, his takeaway from his childhood had been nowhere near as sunny and sweet as hers. And that made her vulnerable in a way he hadn't really considered until now.

Ella was an optimist, unrealistic expectations came with the territory, and he didn't want her getting any unrealistic ideas about him and what he was able to offer her and the kid.

But that didn't mean he didn't enjoy seeing that bright light in her eyes, or knowing she thought more of him than he knew was there. He certainly didn't plan to extinguish that light unnecessarily. Plus, after way too many bruising fights and angry words in his youth, and all those endless pointless arguments with his mom to get her to see the truth about his old man, he'd also become a big fan of avoidance when it came to talking about your feelings.

Especially if you had nothing to say on the matter.

Getting Ella together with Sonny and Josie and telling them about the baby would just create loads of unnecessary drama. He shivered as goosebumps pebbled down his spine at the thought. Because neither one of them could keep their noses out of his business and they had an opinion about every damn thing. And Inez was one of the biggest gossips on the island, so it made sense to keep her out of the loop too. He didn't want anyone knowing his business before he knew it himself.

He put the glass down at the soft pad of footsteps on the stairs and glanced up, his pulse slowing to a harsh, jerky beat as Ella walked towards him.

The filmy dress she wore blew around her legs. The bodice only showed a small amount of cleavage, but he could still make out that magnificent rack and the bullet-tipped nipples outlined by the snug fabric.

Well, he guessed that was some compensation—however many problems this pregnancy was going to cause in the long term, he could totally get behind the changes his child was making to her body now.

He put a dampener on the thought when she opened her mouth in a jaw-breaking yawn. He needed to keep his dick under control tonight, at least until she'd slept off the effects of her flight. And suffering through another sleepless night might make him think twice before losing his cool with her again.

'Hi, this looks amazing,' she said, surveying the table. 'I'm so hungry I could eat a horse.'

'You're not the only one.'

She laughed, that musical lilt that had beguiled him from the get-go. 'Why do I have the strange feeling it's not a horse you want to eat?'

Smart girl.

He took her hand, kissed the knuckles. 'As much as I'd like to eat you, tonight, it's probably best if you stay in the guest room.' He pulled out her chair so she could take a seat. 'Alone.' He bit down on the groan as she tucked the pretty dress round that tempting butt.

'You don't have to do that.' The furrow of surprise and disappointment on her brow was almost comical. 'Unless you want to,' she added, as if his wanting her was actually in doubt.

'Honey, you've just got off an eight-hour flight.' He forced himself to be noble and ignore the growing ache in his crotch. 'It's the early hours by my count in the UK and...' He was about to point out that she was pregnant, but stopped himself. No need to bring up that topic unnecessarily. 'And I don't want to wear you out,' he finished.

The heart-pumping smile brightened her whole face. 'That's very considerate of you.' Wasn't it just? 'But I should warn you, I'm not good with jet lag. I'll probably wake up at the crack of dawn.'

He allowed himself a firm kiss, of exactly two seconds' duration. Because any longer would only increase the torment. 'Once you're awake, you'll find me in the bedroom at the end of the veranda.' Most likely wide awake and ready for action. 'I'm sure I can figure out a way to cure your jet lag.' She blushed prettily and his voice lowered. 'Sleep therapy happens to be a speciality of mine.'

'I'll bet.' The eagerness on her face crucified him. 'I'm sure that will come in handy, come cougar time.'

He chuckled, the sound rough, as he pulled up a chair and began piling the food onto their plates. He listed the different dishes Inez had prepared, reeled off some suggested activities she might like to try in the next couple of days, and neatly sidestepped a couple of questions about the snorkel tour. And Sonny.

To stay focused on eating the food and not her, he kept in mind that, while tonight would be torture, downtime now would be rewarded by lots of uptime from tomorrow morning onwards.

He quizzed her about her business and as many

other generic topics as he could think of before her eyelids began to droop. He showed her back up to the guest bed after supper, and kissed her on the cheek— and had to be grateful that she was too exhausted to do more than smile sleepily back. Especially when her scent invaded his nostrils, and it took every last ounce of his will power to step back and close the door after her. Just before the door clicked shut, he heard the soft sound of her flopping onto the bed they'd shared less than an hour ago—and his knuckles whitened on the door handle.

It took a couple of seconds but he finally let go.

Tucking his clenched fists into his pockets, he headed down the hall to the library at the other end of the house, feeling more noble than Sir Galahad.

Booting up the computer on his desktop, he ran a search on the effects of pregnancy on a woman's body in the first and second trimester. Might be good to do some research—Ella said sex in pregnancy was safe, but, considering how much sex they were likely to want, he didn't want to be making any demands on her she couldn't handle.

But he couldn't concentrate on the information, his impatience for the night to be over growing as the endless minutes ticked by. The thought that every one of those minutes shortened the time they had left together only irritated him more.

What was up with that?

They had as much time as they needed. She'd agreed to buy an open ticket. And very few women had kept his interest for more than a couple of dates. So it stood to reason that, no matter how cute and fascinating and hot he found her, or how much baggage they had to sort out with the baby, having her in his home would get old soon enough.

So why the heck was he was already worrying about her departure?

TEN

—

'Wow, that was *a-mazing*!' Ella shoved up her mask and hit the release button on her tanks. She laughed, her mind still reeling from all the images she'd seen and absorbed in the last thirty minutes. She'd thought snorkelling on the reef had been a life-time experience, but her first scuba-dive had topped it.

Darting fish, waving coral, the dappled sunlight shining through the waves and the pure white sand sparkling under her flippers.

'Here. Let me.' Coop grabbed the air tanks and set them on the boat's deck before shrugging off his own equipment.

'I almost had a cow when I saw that shark.' She shuddered, the laugh breathless at the memory of the majestic creature gliding by beneath them. 'What kind was it? It looked enormous.'

She unzipped the snug wetsuit, struggled out of the top half.

'Tiger shark, about seven feet.' Cooper sent her a

mocking smile as he climbed out of his own suit. Water glistened on his tanned chest, diverting her gaze. 'Not much more than a baby. Nothing to freak out about.'

'You're joking—that was no baby,' she replied, indignant. 'And I didn't freak out.' *Much.*

He chuckled and grabbed her wrist, to pull her into his embrace. 'I guess you handled yourself pretty well.'

His palm touched her cheek and she felt the giddy rush of pleasure from the intense study. 'For a rookie,' he whispered, before his lips covered hers and she forgot to be mad.

They were both breathless when they came up for air. Her heart beat in an even more irregular rhythm than when she'd spotted the tiger shark.

'So, you want to do that again some time?' His hands settled on her waist, his thumbs brushing her hips above the half-off wetsuit. 'Sharks notwithstanding.'

'Yes, please. And I loved the shark.' He chuckled at her enthusiasm. 'It was so beautiful and exciting.'

But not as beautiful and exciting as you, she almost added, but stopped herself just in time. She'd been on the island ten days now, and it was getting harder and harder not to let her feelings run away with themselves. With his damp hair falling across his brow, those handsome features gilded by sunlight, and the lean muscles of his six-pack rigid against her palms it was even harder to remember why she shouldn't let them.

She'd had an incredible time so far. When she'd

been here in April, she'd stayed almost exclusively at the resort. And had no idea that she'd missed so much of what the island had to offer. The colonial elegance of the pastel-shaded houses and cobblestoned streets in St George, the exhilaration of a motorbike ride to a secluded cove, the luxury of an impromptu picnic lunch at a beach café.

But best of all had been Coop's attention and his willingness to spend so much time with her. Every day he'd laid on a new adventure to experience. And apart from a few hours spent in his study each day to deal with his business, he'd hardly left her side.

She hadn't expected him to be this enthusiastic about showing her around—or how much she would enjoy his company. She felt young and carefree and bold, excited at the prospect of trying out new things that she might have been too cautious to try out before.

Yesterday morning he'd announced she was learning to scuba-dive. Then he'd devoted most of the day to teaching her. Fitting her out while demonstrating all the equipment, giving her endless lessons in how to breathe through the regulator in the pool, running through all the safety routines, and the intricacies of buddy breathing.

They'd managed a short training dive yesterday from the beach, but today he'd taken her out on the motor cruiser.

And the thirty-minute dive had been spectacular. Every second of it.

But even her first scuba-dive in Bermuda couldn't top the wonder of spending her nights and the long lazy mornings in bed with Coop. The man had skills in the bedroom that were quite simply phenomenal— making love to her with care and dedication one minute and hungry intensity the next.

Of course, during all the fun and frolics, she'd been careful to keep reminding herself that this trip wasn't about her and Coop but about the baby—which hadn't been all that hard to do, for the simple reason that she hadn't made a lot of progress in that area at all.

He talked about their baby and the pregnancy, but only in very generic, impersonal ways. In fact, he was so guarded on the subject whenever it came up now, that she had begun to wonder if all the new activities, all the wonderful experiences hadn't been arranged to distract her from any mention of why she was really here.

She hated herself for being suspicious of his motives, for doubting his sincerity in any way, but most of all she didn't understand why he would even want to do that. What possible reason could he have to avoid the subject? When he'd invited her to his home specifically to talk about it? It didn't make any sense.

'You want to go back out tomorrow?' he asked, brushing her hair back from her face.

The flutter of contentment pushed aside the foolish moment of doubt.

She was being ridiculous. How could he be avoiding talking to her, when they were together so much of the time? 'Could we go out again today?'

He tapped her nose. 'No way. Half an hour's enough. You're a beginner and...' his gaze flicked to her abdomen and he took his hand from her waist '...you know.'

It was an oblique reference to the baby, but a reference nonetheless, so she decided to go with it. If she had concerns, maybe it was about time she voiced them. She knew she had a tendency to avoid confrontations. Probably a lay-over from her early childhood, when her parents had spent so much of the time arguing—and the hideous breakdown of her relationship with Randall.

But if the thought of the baby made Coop uncomfortable, the only way to get over that was to stop letting him avoid the subject. And when she'd Skyped Ruby the day before, her friend had told her in no uncertain terms to stop worrying and confront Coop about the issue.

'I called the obstetrician this morning,' she said as casually as she could manage. 'The one you lined up for me. She said scuba-diving would be absolutely fine.'

'Yeah, you told me. But it's still not a good idea to push it.'

'I didn't know you'd heard me,' she said, trying not to mind the abrupt dismissal as he set about hanging the air tanks on their frame. 'I arranged to go in for a check-up on Monday, by the way,' she added, but he didn't look up, engrossed in checking the gauges. 'If you want to come with me?'

That had got his attention, she thought, as his head shot up. 'Why?' There was no mistaking the flicker of panic. 'Do I need to? Is there something wrong?'

'No, of course not, but...' While his concern warmed her, the panic was another matter. 'I thought you might like to come—she might do a scan and you could see the baby.'

'Right.' He turned away, went back to concentrating on the equipment. 'Why don't you shimmy out of that wetsuit?' He threw the request over his shoulder. 'Then we can head back before you start to burn. It's hot as hell out here.'

She inched the wetsuit down her legs, sat down on the boat's bench seat to struggle out of the clinging black neoprene. 'So you'll come to the scan? On Monday?'

She handed him the suit and he draped it over the bench seat next to his.

'Yeah, maybe, I don't know. I'll have to see how I'm fixed.' He met her eyes at last, the 'don't get too excited' tone in his voice loud and clear. 'When's your appointment?'

The lack of enthusiasm was almost palpable and she had the sudden premonition that he was only asking for the information so he had time to come up with a viable excuse.

'Two-thirty.'

'Damn, that's a shame. I promised Sonny I'd come over that afternoon. I'll have to miss it.'

Her heart stuttered. So now she knew for sure. She

had not imagined his reluctance. She drew in a deep breath, determined not to back down again in the face of his stubbornness.

'I see.' She tugged her beach tunic on over her bikini, the ocean breeze making her shiver despite the heat. 'I could rearrange the appointment for later. Why don't I come with you to see Sonny? I'd love to meet him.'

The sides of his mouth pinched—making the strain to maintain the easy smile on his lips more visible. 'No need for that. I'm helping him strip an old motor. It's not going to be any fun.'

She felt the dismissal like a slap that time. She'd asked before about his friends on the island. And he'd closed her down on that subject too. She'd been here for over a week and she hadn't met anyone he knew. When she'd suggested going back to The Rum Runner the previous evening, he'd explained that he didn't want Henry hitting on her again, then picked her up and dumped her in the pool. Once he'd dived in after her and then 'helped' her out of her wet clothes, the request had quickly been forgotten.

She watched as he began to pack the equipment into the box at the end of the boat. The panicked beat of her heart richocheted against her chest wall.

Stop freaking out and ask him. Avoidance isn't the answer. You can't handle this if you don't know what's going on.

'Don't you want me to meet your friends?'

He swung round on his haunches, his eyebrow arching up his forehead. 'Huh?'

'It just seems a bit strange—' she forced the comment out, past lips that had dried to parchment '—that wherever we go we never seem to bump into anyone you know.'

She saw the flash of guilt in his eyes before he was able to mask it.

'They don't even know I'm here, do they?' she asked, but from the flags of colour on his tanned cheeks she already knew the answer. The fact that he hadn't told anyone about the baby either went without saying. She clamped down on the feeling of unease though. She mustn't overreact. Just because he hadn't told them yet, didn't mean he would never tell them.

He swore softly and stood up. 'Not yet.'

'I see.' She swallowed. 'Do you plan to tell people? Eventually?'

'Yeah, sure. I just wanted to keep you to myself for a while.' He held her arm, his voice lowering to a seductive purr as he caressed the sensitive skin on the inside of her elbow with his thumb. 'You remember Josie, Sonny's daughter, the kid that woke you up when you were in the hut?'

She nodded.

'She's having a big wedding on the beach next Saturday. We'll have to go to that, I'm one of the witnesses. Everyone will be there.'

He went back to sorting out the equipment.

'Oh, okay. That's good,' she said, although the way he'd said they would 'have to go' made it sound as if he wasn't too happy at the prospect. 'But it might be

nice to see them before that?' she pushed. Obviously
she had overreacted, but something about the whole
thing still bothered her. Was he planning to keep their
relationship a secret until then? 'Because, you know,
it might be a bit weird me turning up at this wedding
pregnant with your child, if no one knows me.'

'Do you think they'll be able to tell?' He dropped the
wetsuit he'd been packing as his eyes shot down to her
tummy. 'You're not showing too much yet.'

What?

The feeling of unease was replaced by the shock of
vulnerability.

'Well, no, maybe not, but...' The words got caught
behind the silly lump of emotion. Which had to be
the pregnancy hormones, making her feel ridiculously
oversensitive. But she couldn't stop the thoughts coming, now that the dam had broken. 'Why don't you
want them to know?'

'Hey, what's the matter?' He stood up, the concern
in his eyes almost making her back down again. 'It's
not that big a deal. Believe me, it's just easier not to
tell them yet.'

She stared at him. Was he actually serious?

Yes, it might make it easier for him, but how would
it be easier for her? Wouldn't it make things awkward
at this wedding if someone did notice? And asked questions about her condition? She knew they weren't a
proper couple, that she shouldn't get too invested in
their relationship. That they were just having fun with
each other while sorting out what to do about their

shared child. But the fact was, she'd been here for ten days, and they hadn't actually sorted out anything yet. Not even how he was going to introduce her to his friends.

Was she his girlfriend? His wedding date? A holiday fling? Or just another of his temporary bonk buddies? Maybe being the mother of his child didn't give her any relationship rights, but surely it ought to afford her a tiny iota of respect?

'The thing is, Coop,' she began, trying not to let the hurt show, 'I can't see how not talking about the baby is making it easier for me. I can't stay here indefinitely, you know, and—'

'Damn it, Ella, you've only been here a week. We can't rush this stuff.'

'*Rush it*? Coop, I've been here ten days!' she said, exasperated now. 'And we haven't talked about the baby at all.'

'Because we've been busy, doing...' he paused '...other stuff,' he said, so emphatically that she suddenly realised she'd been right to be suspicious of the endless round of activities. 'Stuff that you said you enjoyed,' he added, grudgingly, sounding a little hurt.

'I did enjoy them. I loved every single minute of them,' she rushed to reassure him, but then noticed he didn't actually look *that* hurt. 'But that's not the point. We could have talked about it in the mornings before we went out. Or in the evenings when we got back.'

'Uh-huh, well, we've been pretty busy then too.' His gaze raked down her figure, making her whole body warm. And it occurred to her that the relentless schedule of daytime activities might not have been his only distraction technique. 'And I don't recall you complaining about that either,' he added. 'Especially when I had my mouth on that succulent little clit this morning.'

Hell. That did it.

She glared at him—the succulent nub in question throbbing alarmingly now in unison with her distended nipples. 'You sod.' He'd been playing her all along. And she'd been too dazed by her own lust to see it. 'You've been seducing me deliberately, haven't you, to stop me from discussing it? I knew it.'

'Hey, calm down. I have not.' His lips quirked. 'I love sucking on your clitoris, remember?' He reached for her arm, but she jerked it out of his grasp. Not finding the joke—or the fact that her clitoris wouldn't stop throbbing—remotely amusing any more.

'I suppose the next question is why? Why would you do that? Unless...' Her temper faded, and then collapsed, at the stubborn, defensive look on his face.

Oh, no. Not that.

She heaved a heavy sigh when he didn't say anything, scared to say it, terrified that she might be right, but knowing she had to ask. 'If you're having second thoughts about being involved with this baby, Coop, you need to tell me.' She met his gaze, the flags of colour on his cheeks shining beneath his tan. 'I want you to be part of its life, very much.'

Maybe she still didn't know much about how he really felt about parenthood, but the things she had learned about him in the last week had convinced her of that much. His generosity, his intelligence, the quick wit that always made her laugh, the care he took with her, his need to look out for her and protect her and the capable, patient way he'd taught her how to scuba-dive, not to mention that reckless, dangerously exciting streak that made her feel bold too, made her sure he would make a wonderful father. 'I'm not here to force a connection on you that you don't feel.'

She couldn't make him want to be a father, however much she might want to. That wouldn't be fair on him, and it certainly wouldn't be fair on her child.

'If you're not ready to discuss this yet, it's probably best if I just leave.'

The calm, rhythmic sound of the ocean lapping against the side of the boat stretched across the silence. She flinched as he raked his fingers through his hair and broke the silence with a bitter curse.

What the hell did he say to that?

She was looking at him with those big round trusting eyes. And he knew he hadn't been honest with her, or with himself.

But he didn't want her to leave. Not yet. He wasn't ready. And he did want to figure out what to do about the kid. But the more she'd talked about the baby, the more inadequate it had made him feel, until the problem had become so huge he'd clammed up completely. Plus, it had been so damn easy just to get lost in her and forget about all that. She was so cute and funny and engaging. Everything he showed her she loved; everything they did together she threw herself into with a complete lack of fear. She was smart and funny and resourceful and so eager and responsive. Especially in bed.

But she was right: he'd played her, even if he hadn't really intended to. And now he owed her an explanation.

'Come here, Ella.' He tried to take her into his arms, the guilt tightening his throat when she grasped his forearms to hold him off.

'Please, just give me a straight answer, Coop. Don't try to sugar-coat it, okay. I can take it.'

He wasn't so sure of that. 'I swear, no more messing you about.'

He sat on the boat's bench seat, and gently pulled her into his lap, pathetically grateful when she didn't resist him again.

'There's no need to make up excuses.' She cupped his cheek and the guilt peaked. 'I understand if you feel overwhelmed.'

He covered her hand and dragged it away from her face. 'Stop being so damn reasonable, Ella.'

She stiffened in his arms. 'This isn't about being reasonable. It's about being fair. I don't want to force you to shoulder a responsibility you don't want.'

'Damn it, Ella, who the hell ever told you life was fair?'

It scared him how easily she could be crushed, especially by a guy like him—who always looked out for himself first.

She tried to rise, but he held her tight, pressed his forehead into her shoulder. 'I'm sorry, don't go...' He sucked in a deep breath, prepared to admit at least some of the truth, even though the feel of her butt nestled against his groin was having a predictable effect.

What he wouldn't give right now to strip off the light cotton dress and feast on her lush body—and get the hell out of this conversation. But he couldn't carry on lying to her.

He rested his head back against the seat. Stared at the blue sky, the swooping seagulls, the clean bright sunlight. And felt the darkness he'd spent so long running away from descend over him like a fog.

He forced his head off the seat to look her in the face. 'Hasn't it ever occurred to you that I might not be cut out to be a dad? That you and the kid might be much better off without me?'

'No, it hasn't,' she said and the total confidence in her voice sneaked past all the defences he'd put in place over the years. 'I realise you're not as ecstatic about this pregnancy as I am. But that doesn't mean you won't be a good father when the time comes. If you're willing to try?'

'I want to try, but I just don't know if...'

'There aren't any guarantees, Coop, not when it comes to being a parent. You just have to do what comes naturally and hope for the best.'

'I guess, but you'll be a lot better at that than I am,' he said, able to appreciate the irony.

'Maybe you should ask yourself why you're so insecure about this. Would that help?'

'I doubt it.' He definitely didn't want to go there.

'Is it because of your own father? And the fact that you never knew him?' she said, going there without any help from him. 'Is that it?'

He shook his head. Damn, he'd have to tell her the truth about that too, now. 'I did know him. I guess I lied about that.'

'Oh.' She looked surprised, but not wary. Or not wary yet. 'Why did you lie?' she asked, as if it were the most natural thing in the world.

'Because I didn't exactly *know* him,' he clarified, trying to explain to her something he'd never understood. 'I knew of him. And he knew about me.'

'I don't...' she said, obviously struggling to figure it out.

'I grew up in a small place in Indiana called Garysville,' he said, reciting a story he'd denied for so long, he felt as if he were talking about some other kid's life. 'Towns like that, everyone knows everyone else's business. My old man was the police chief. A big deal with a reputation to protect, who liked to play away from home. Everyone knew I was his kid, because I looked a lot like him. And my mom didn't exactly keep it a secret.'

'But surely you must have talked to him? If it was such a small town.'

And you were his son.

He could hear her thinking it. And remembered all the times he'd tortured himself with the same question as a boy.

'Why would I?' The old bitterness surprised him a little. 'He was just some guy who came over to screw my mother from time to time. She told him I was his. He didn't want to know.'

'He never spoke to you?' She looked horrified. 'But that's hideous—how could he not want to know you?'

Like father, like son, he thought grimly. Wasn't that what he had thought about doing to his own kid? When he'd figured money would be enough to free him of any responsibility for his child.

'Actually, that's not true, I did speak to him once. Six words...' He forced the humiliating memory to the surface, to punish himself. 'You want to know what they were?'

Ella's heart clutched as Coop's face took on a cold, distant expression, the tight smile nothing like the warm, witty man she knew. She nodded, although she wasn't sure she did want to know. He seemed so unhappy.

'Do you want fries with that?' The brittle half-laugh held no amusement. 'Pretty tragic, isn't it?'

Her heart ached at the flatness of his tone. 'Oh, Coop,' she said, the sharp pain in her chest like a punch. No wonder he was so reluctant to talk about the baby. It wasn't fear of the responsibility; it was simply a lack of confidence.

'I worked nights at a drive-thru in town when I was in high school,' he continued, still talking in that flat, even tone that she was sure now was used to mask his emotions. 'My mom was finding it hard to stay in a job, she had...' he paused. '...these moods.' He shrugged. 'Anyhow we needed the money. He drove in one night with his family, about a month after I'd got the job. He ordered two chilli dogs, two chocolate malts and a side order of onion rings for his kids. Delia and Jack Jr.'

She wondered if he realised how significant it was that he'd remembered the order exactly. 'You knew them?'

'Sure, we went to the same high school. Not that we moved in the same circles. Delia was the valedictorian, Jack Junior the star quarterback. And I hated their guts, because I was so damn jealous of the money they had, the choices.' He huffed out a bitter laugh. 'And the Beemer convertible Jack Jnr got for his sixteenth birthday.'

And the fact that they had a father, your father, and you didn't, she thought, her heart aching for him.

'He looked me right in the eye and said no, they didn't need fries, then he paid and drove on. He never came to my window again.'

She heard the yearning in his voice and the punch of pain twisted.

No wonder he'd worked so hard to get away from there, to make something out of his life. Rejection always hurt. It had nearly destroyed her when Randall had rejected her, but at least she'd been an adult. Or adult enough. She couldn't imagine suffering that kind of knock-back as a child. Every single day. To have it thrown in your face that you weren't good enough, and never knowing why.

The casual cruelty of the man who had fathered him, but had never had the guts to acknowledge him, disgusted her. But his bravery in rising above it, in overcoming it—surely that was what mattered. Why couldn't he see that?

'But you've got to understand, Ella. I'm not sure I'm a good bet as a father. Because I'm a selfish bastard, just like he was.'

She wanted to tell him that he was wrong. That he wasn't selfish, he was only self-sufficient, because he'd had to be. And that she admired him so much for having the courage to rise above the rejection. But she knew it wasn't only admiration that was making her heart pound frantically in her chest.

She touched his cheek, felt the rasp of the five o'clock shadow already beginning to grow at two in the afternoon. 'Do you really think you're the only one of us who's scared, Coop? The only one who thinks they won't measure up?'

He stared at her. 'Get real, Ella. You've loved this kid from the get-go. You've made it your number one priority from the start.' His gaze roamed over her face. 'How would you feel if I told you I'm pretty sure I only invited you here because I wanted you. Not the kid?'

The desire in his heavy-lidded eyes made the heat pulse low in her abdomen. 'If that doesn't tell you what kind of father I'd be, I don't know what the hell does.'

She smiled, utterly touched by the admission. 'Actually I'm flattered. And rather turned on.'

'Seriously, Ella. For once, I'm not kidding around about—'

'I know you're not.' She cut him off, then gripped his cheeks, pressed her forehead against his, and prepared to tell him something she had never wanted him to know. 'How about if I told you that when I was eighteen I got pregnant and I had a termination? Would you still think I don't have some pretty persuasive reasons to doubt my own ability as a parent?'

She forced her gaze to his, willing him not to judge her as harshly as she had always judged herself.

His eyes widened, but he looked more stunned than disgusted. 'That's your big revelation? Big deal. You were eighteen. Why would you want a kid at that age?'

She shook her head. 'But you don't understand. I did want it.' She rested her palm on her belly, emboldened by the new life growing there to talk for the first time about the one she'd lost. 'I wanted it very much. Which is why this child means so much to me now.'

'Okay, I get that.' He threaded his fingers through hers, the acceptance in his eyes unconditional. 'But you can't punish yourself now for a choice you made at eighteen. Having a baby at that age would have screwed up your life.'

She wanted to take his comfort, his faith in her,

but she couldn't, not till he knew the whole truth. 'But that's not why I did it. I had the abortion because Randall ordered me to. He insisted. He said either I lose the baby, or I would lose him. And I chose him. Over my own child.'

A tear slipped over her lid, and he brushed his thumb across her cheek.

'Ella, don't cry.' She heard the tenderness and knew she didn't deserve it. 'This Randall was the father?'

She nodded, tucked her head onto his shoulder. 'Pretty pathetic, isn't it?'

'Not pathetic,' he said, nudging her chin up with his forefinger. 'You were young and scared. And given an impossible choice by that bastard. That's his bad, not yours.'

Ruby had always said the same thing to her, when she'd tortured herself with what ifs after the procedure. But now, for the first time, she felt herself begin to accept it.

Coop rubbed the tight muscles at the base of her neck. 'I'm guessing Randall didn't stick around once he'd got you to do what he wanted.'

'How did you know that?'

'Because the guy sounds like a selfish, manipulative jerk.' He sighed, then brushed her hair off her forehead, and his lips tilted in a wry smile. 'It takes one to know one.'

'You're nothing like him.'

'I don't know—I freaked pretty bad when you told me about Junior. And I've been doing my best to avoid the subject ever since.' He rested his hand on her belly, rubbed it gently back and forth. It was the first time he'd ever touched her there, and the flood of warmth caught her unawares.

'Yes, but you apologised for flipping out the very next day,' she pointed out. 'Even though you were still reeling from the news. And you've never tried to pressure me the way he did. That makes you a much better man than Randall ever was.'

The half-smile became rueful. 'I don't know about that.' She opened her mouth to protest, but he lifted a finger to her lips, silencing her. 'But I'm glad you think so. How about I come to the scan on Monday?'

The smile in her heart at the suggestion was even bigger than the one she could see reflected in his eyes. 'Okay, if you're sure?'

She knew what a big leap this was for him, so she was doubly pleased when he took a deep breath, then nodded. 'I guess so. I can't guarantee I'll know what I'm doing, but I'd like to be there anyway.'

'That's wonderful, Coop.'

His fingers threaded into her hair as he captured her lips in a tender kiss. But what started as gentle, coaxing, quickly heated to carnal as she opened her mouth and flicked her tongue against his.

She felt the satisfying swell of his erection, coming back to life against her bottom as she feasted on him—and let him feast on her.

He drew back first, to flick his thumb across the stiff peak of her nipple. But when she tried to reach for the front of his shorts and the stiff length inside, he grabbed her wrist to hold her off.

'Not a good idea.'

'Why not?' she said, the rush of emotion only intensifying her eagerness.

He kissed her nose. And she felt the tiny sting. 'Because you're getting a little pink around the edges, and I don't want you getting a sunburn. It's liable to cramp our style.'

He lifted her off his lap, to walk to the boat's console.

'Why don't we just go below decks?'

'For what I've got in mind, we're going to need a bigger bed.' He grinned over his shoulder and fired up the boat's engine. 'Now sit down and grab a hold of something. I'm going to see how fast I can get this thing back to base.'

She did as she was told, impossibly pleased that his eagerness matched her own, before he whisked the steering wheel round and hit the accelerator. The rush of wind lifted her hair and made the sunburn on her nose tingle as the launch bounced over the swell, hurtling them back towards the dock below his house at breakneck speed.

Her heart pumped to a deafening crescendo as she held on for dear life and watched him steer with practised ease. And the tightness that she hadn't realised had been making her chest ache for days released. Everything was going to be all right.

She faced into the wind, felt the spray of water hit

her cheeks, and gave herself up to the excitement, the exhilaration pumping through her system.

She glanced back as the boat slowed to approach the small dock that stood below the back steps up to his property.

'Tie her up,' he shouted and she grabbed the thin nylon rope, climbed onto the dock and began looping the rope round the post while he switched off the engine.

His gaze locked on hers, telegraphing his hunger as she finished knotting the rope. Desire settled like a heavy weight as he stepped off the boat. The playful urge to tease hit her and she sped off towards the house.

'Hey, where the hell are you going?' he yelled, his feet hitting the deck behind her as he gained ground. 'Come back here.'

Catching her, he swung her round in a circle. And cut off her laugh with a kiss that promised all sorts of delicious retribution.

Her tongue tangled with his as she opened her mouth to take the kiss deeper and dug greedy fingers into his damp hair. *No more doubts, no more panicking, no more holding back,* she thought as he broke the kiss to lift her into his arms.

'Got you,' he murmured.

Euphoria slammed into her at the possessive tone. She clung onto his neck and whispered, 'Hurry up.'

'I am hurrying, damn it,' he huffed, climbing the

steps two at a time with her cradled in his arms. 'You're heavier than you used to be, pregnant lady.'

She beamed at him, impossibly pleased by the silly joke.

Everything would be okay with the baby now, because she understood where his insecurities were coming from and knew he was at least willing to try to work all those problems out.

And while they were doing that, why shouldn't they see if there could be more? He'd given her a painful glimpse into his past—had let his guard down and let her in. And she'd done the same. Her heart stuttered painfully at the thought of all the possibilities that she hadn't considered, hadn't let herself consider. She'd been so cautious up to now, mindful of Ruby's warning not to let her heart run away with itself. But was it really necessary to carry on being so careful? When they'd taken such a huge step forward today?

She clung to his shoulders and kissed the soft skin beneath his chin.

'Behave,' he growled as he staggered into the living room and headed for the stairs. 'We're not there yet.'

She laughed as he boosted her in his arms to take the stairs, the euphoria intoxicating as she imagined just how far they could go, now she was ready to take the leap.

ELEVEN

'You smell so good.'

Strong arms wrapped around Ella's waist from behind. She shivered as Coop nipped playfully at her ear lobe, then glared into the bathroom mirror.

'For goodness' sake, I'm trying to put my face on here.' Slicking another coat of gloss on bone-dry lips, she gave him a not exactly subtle jab with her elbow, which only made him chuckle.

'Stop freaking out, you look great.' Warm palms skimmed over the light silk of the dress she'd found in a boutique shop in Hamilton after a fraught shopping expedition yesterday, then settled on the curve of her stomach. 'How's Junior?'

A little of her aggravation dissolved, pushed out by the feel of his hands, stroking where their child grew, and the tender enquiry in his gaze as it met hers in the mirror.

'Junior's fine.' She smiled back at him. She knew he was still feeling his way, still nervous about stepping into a role he hadn't prepared for, but he'd been eager and attentive during the scan five days ago, firing questions at the obstetrician.

When the doctor had asked them if they wanted to know the sex, he'd deferred to her, but she could see how keen he was to know the answer and had decided to go with it—maybe knowing the sex would make the baby more real to him. When the doctor had pointed out their child's penis, she'd been glad she had, because she hadn't been able to stop laughing when he'd whispered with stunned delight, 'For real? The kid's hung like a horse.'

She turned in his arms, pressed her hands to his cheeks. 'But Junior's not the one who's about to meet all your friends for the first time.' She dropped a hand to her stomach, the jumpy sensation nothing to do with the child growing inside her.

Because while Coop's attitude to their child had become everything she could have hoped for, the euphoria of that day a week ago, when she'd been sure they were beginning to form a more tangible bond between the two of them, had faded considerably.

'I want them to like me,' she murmured, not quite able to keep the resentment out of her voice. She'd tried in the last week to make him understand this was important to her. And he'd resolutely refused to even meet her halfway, ignoring or deflecting her repeated requests to introduce her to anyone he knew. Just as he'd continually ignored her suggestions that she should book her flight home soon.

So here they were, on the evening of his friend's wedding, and she had no idea where she stood, not just with his friends but with him too. 'I would have preferred to at least have met some of them.'

'You already met a few of them at the Runner on our first night,' he said, in a familiar argument.

'That was four months ago!' she replied, her patience straining. 'And I hardly talked to any of them.'

'Quit panicking—they're going to love you,' he murmured, dismissing her concerns again. Lifting her hand, he pressed a kiss into the palm. 'You know what you need?'

'A Valium, maybe?' she said, only half joking.

'Nuh-uh.' One warm palm settled on her leg and then skimmed up under her dress, to cup her buttock. 'I've got a better way to help you unwind.'

His thumb sneaked under the leg of her panties, making the pulse of heat flare, as it always did. She grasped his wrist and halted the exploration—determined not to be sidetracked again. 'Stop it, Coop. We haven't got time.'

His lips curved. 'Sure we have.' Dropping his head, he kissed the pulse point in her neck, the one place he knew from experience would drive her wild. 'You're just kind of uptight. This'll help.'

'No, it won't,' she said, but the protest trailed off as he cupped her, the heel of his palm rubbing the bundle of nerves and giving them the friction they craved.

'We can't...' She gasped, blindsided by the inevitable swelling in her sex, the rush of moisture, as one thick finger snuck past the gusset of her panties and slid over her yearning clitoris. 'I don't have time to shower again.'

'Then don't.' His clever fingers played with the swollen nub. 'I love you with that just-screwed look.'

The words registered through the haze of heat, and her temper flared. Flattening her palms against his chest, she shoved him back, shaking with frustration—and no small amount of fury. 'Get off me. How old are you, for goodness' sake?'

'What the hell are you so mad about?' He looked genuinely nonplussed. 'You want to—you know you do.'

Given that his fingers were slick, he probably thought he had a point, which only made her more mad.

Feeling the threat of tears stealing over her lids, she pushed him aside to storm out of the bathroom.

'Damn it, Ella! What the hell did I do?'

She swung round, slapping her hands on her hips, desperate to keep the anger front and centre to disguise her hurt.

'I'll tell you what you did. You never once took my feelings into account about this. If I'm nervous and uptight it's because I didn't want to go to this event not knowing anyone. I realise we're not a couple, not really, but I thought...' She blinked furiously.

She had thought what exactly? That they were a couple, that there had been something developing between them in the last few weeks that had nothing to do with their child. But how could she know that, when he was so determined to avoid anything even resembling a serious conversation?

'Of course, we're a couple,' he said grumpily, making the stab of uncertainty under her breastbone sharpen. 'We're going to this damn fiasco together, aren't we? But I still don't see why we can't make love now if we both want to.'

Because we wouldn't be making love. Or at least, you wouldn't be.

The anger and frustration collapsed inside her, consumed by anxiety. She'd leapt over the cliff days ago convinced that he would catch her. But had she jumped too soon, reading far more into his actions than was actually there?

'The reason we can't make love...' she spoke the words slowly, succinctly, willing herself not to let an ounce of her distress show '...is because we don't have the time. And I'd really rather not turn up at this wedding smelling like some woman you've just screwed.'

He swore, his expression hardening, and she thanked God for it. She'd rather deal with his temper now than risk letting him see the emotion beneath.

'That's not what I meant and you damn well know it.'

She sighed, starting to feel shaky and knowing she couldn't maintain this façade for long. 'I think we should just go, I'm sure it'll be better once I get there.'

He raked his hand through his hair, the temper disappearing as quickly as it had come—as it always did with Coop.

'Okay, I guess you're right.' He pulled his smartphone from the pocket of the dark linen trousers he'd donned for the occasion and checked the time. 'The ceremony's in thirty minutes. Josie will murder me if I'm late.'

He escorted her down the steps to the beach, as if he were handling an unexploded bomb. But as they passed his beach hut, then walked together the mile along the sand towards The Rum Runner, retracing the steps they'd taken on their first night together, he threaded his fingers through hers.

Fairy lights strung through the palm trees twinkled in the distance as the strains of music and merriment drifted towards them on the breeze. Her heart lifted at the romantic sight.

No wonder she'd fallen for Coop so fast. He was such a good man, in so many ways. Easygoing, affable, charming, energetic and always striving to do his best. Unlike Randall. But she knew he also had a host of insecurities, which he worked hard to keep hidden. Maybe his attempts to keep things casual didn't come from a lack of feeling? Perhaps he just needed a little more time? She could stay a few more days before booking her flight home.

After all, she hadn't even told him yet that her feelings had deepened, intensified. Maybe if she did...?

'I've been dreading this damn wedding ever since Josie told me about it four months ago,' he murmured, interrupting her thoughts.

'Why?' she asked, sensing his nervousness, and able

at last to let go of her own. Surely meeting his friends didn't have to be bad.

'At first, I thought it was because she's still just a kid,' he said, his gaze fixed on the wedding party in the distance. 'But now I think it's the thought of promising to be with someone for the rest of your life. It spooked me. Why would anyone want to do that?'

She followed the direction of his gaze to see the beautiful young woman she'd met at his hut four months ago in the middle of the crowd of people on the beach. Her long-limbed frame was displayed to perfection in a short ivory satin gown, and her face glowed with love and excitement.

'Because they love each other? And they want to be together?' she heard herself say, willing him to believe it. 'It's not hard to make a promise to love someone if they love you in return.'

'Do you really believe that?' He glanced down at her, the look on his face remote in the fading light. 'After the number that Randall guy did on you?'

She flinched at the statement. She could have said that she had never truly loved Randall, that what she'd felt for him had been infatuation, a pale imitation of what she already felt for Coop. But the cynicism in his voice was like a body blow and she hesitated.

'Come on.' He squeezed her hand, and began to walk. 'Let's get this over with, then we can go home and do something much more interesting.'

But as he drew her towards the party the red glow

of dusk and the twinkle of fairy lights didn't seem quite so romantic any more.

'So she came back?'

Coop looked up from the plate he'd been piling high with Henry's famous goat curry, to find Josie, her face radiant with love, grinning at him.

'Hey, kid. Congratulations.' He scooped her up with his free arm as she giggled and kissed his cheek. 'You look amazing,' he said as he put her down again, and she did him a twirl.

'Old enough to be getting hitched?'

'All right, you've got me there,' he admitted.

The ceremony had been several hours ago, and somehow watching her and Taylor standing together before the minister, with Ella gripping his hand to stop his fingers shaking, hadn't been as bad as he'd thought. In fact, it had been kind of touching.

Or it would have been, if listening to the wedding vows hadn't made him feel like such a jerk, for taking out his frustration on Ella when they'd been walking along the beach. He didn't know what the hell had got into him, mentioning that guy she'd dated, especially after that dumb argument they'd had back at the house.

He shouldn't have tried to jump her like that, but the truth was he'd been feeling edgy and tense for days now, ever since she'd started talking about booking a flight home, and the only time that feeling went away now was when they were making love.

'So where's Mr Josie?' he asked Josie, stifling his impatience to get back to Ella.

He needed to chill out about her. He'd left her with Sonny and Rhona less then twenty minutes ago; she'd be good with them for a while. Sure, she'd been more subdued than usual tonight, but she was probably just tired—the kid had been restless last night and she hadn't been able to get comfortable. Once he'd got her something to eat he'd take her home and make slow, lazy love to her. And everything would be okay again.

'Taylor's over with his buddies,' Josie said wryly. 'Boasting about the swordfish he landed last week.'

'Damn, you already sound like an old married couple.' Coop chuckled.

'That's the general idea.' She smiled. 'Talking of couples, why didn't you tell anyone Ella was visiting?' Josie observed, wiping the easy smile off his face.

He turned back to the buffet, the direct question unsettling him. 'Maybe I didn't want anyone bothering us,' he said, trying to inject some humour into his tone, but not quite pulling it off.

Josie's fingers touched his arm. And he glanced over his shoulder to see the serious expression on her face. Uh-oh, this couldn't be good. 'Is the baby yours, Coop?'

He dumped the plate on the table, and grasped her forearm, pulling her away from the crowd of people behind them. 'How do you know about that?' he whispered furiously.

'Because it's obvious. Especially if you know how petite she was four months ago.'

He thrust his hand through his hair. 'Damn, please tell me you haven't said anything to Ella.'

He knew she'd wanted him to tell people before she met them. If she found out they'd guessed about her condition, she'd be hurt—and that had never been his intention.

'Of course I haven't. It's not something you can bring up in a conversation with someone you've only met twice.' Josie tugged her arm out of his grasp. 'But damn, Coop, why the hell didn't you say something? If the baby's yours? Why keep it a secret? And why keep Ella's being here a secret too?'

'Because...' His mind snagged—because he'd wanted to keep things as light and non-committal as possible. Because dealing with the baby had felt like enough already. But even as the excuses sprang into his head they sounded like just that. Excuses. 'Because it's complicated,' he managed at last.

'Why is it complicated?'

'Because she lives in London,' he said, reciting the reasons he'd been giving himself for weeks, but didn't seem to fit any more. 'She's only here for a couple of weeks and it was an accident. And we hardly know each other.' Although that too didn't seem true any more.

He did know Ella: he knew how much he liked to wake up and spoon with her in the morning. How much he'd come to depend on her smile, that sunny, optimistic outlook that was so unlike his own. How addicted he'd become to her company, her enthusiasm, her bright, lively chatter about anything and everything. 'She's going to have the baby...' he paused, then soldiered on '...because we both want it.'

The admission might have surprised him, but for the rush of emotion as he recalled feeling those flutters against his palm the night before, when Ella had been snuggled against him. And seeing that tiny body on the sonogram five days ago, as the doctor had counted all his son's fingers and toes.

How had that happened? Somehow, in the last few weeks, the thing that had terrified him the most didn't terrify him any more; it excited him. He actually wanted to be a dad. But more than that, he wanted to be with Ella in a few months' time, when her body became round and heavy as it cradled their baby.

Damn, was that the reason he didn't want her to leave? It seemed so obvious now he thought about it. No wonder he got edgy every time she mentioned going back to the UK. He wanted her to have the baby, his baby, here in Bermuda. He knew he could do this thing now, and he didn't want to miss a moment of it.

'We're trying to work stuff out,' he said, seeing Josie's eyes go round with astonishment at his declaration. 'And we don't need anyone butting into our business while we're doing it.'

'Okay, I get that.' Josie nodded, surprising him. 'But I still don't see why it's that complicated, if you both want to have this baby.'

'Coop!' They both turned to see Rhona, Josie's mom, descending on them.

'Hi, Mom,' Josie answered.

Rhona fanned herself with the hat she'd been wearing during the ceremony. 'Coop, honey, I thought I should tell you, Ella went off home.'

'What? Why?' The low-level feeling of panic that had been bugging him for days resurfaced in a rush. 'Is she okay?'

'I think she's just tired.' Rhona sent him a sharp look. 'Now, don't take this the wrong way, honey, but is that girl expecting?'

Oh, hell.

'I've got to go, Rhona,' he said, ignoring Josie's muffled snort of laughter and Rhona's question before he got bombarded with a million more. He'd have a lot of explaining to do next time he saw them, but that could wait.

Bidding both women a hasty goodbye, he rushed out of the bar, and broke into a run as soon as he hit the beach.

He needed to get home, and tell Ella she didn't have to go home, that he wanted her to stay—for the baby's sake. She'd be sure to welcome the news, because she always put the baby first, and having two parents had to be better than having just one.

As he jogged up the beach steps to the house he saw the light in the bedroom window and grinned.

I love it when a plan comes together.

She was still awake. He'd tell her about his plans for their future and then they could finish what he'd been trying to start before the wedding.

'Hey, Ella,' he shouted up the stairs as he heard the

whizz-bang of the fireworks Sonny had organised to finish the celebrations on the beach. Glancing over his shoulder, he caught the dazzle of light and colour as a shower of golden rain cascaded into the night sky. 'You missed the fireworks—how about we watch the display from the terrace?' He bounded up the stairs, then strode down the corridor. 'I've got something I have to tell you.'

But then he pushed the door open and spotted Ella, her arms full of silk panties, and her neatly packed suitcase laid open on the bed.

His grin flatlined as all the adrenaline that had been pumping round his system during his jog home slammed full force into his chest.

'What the hell do you think you're doing?'

TWELVE

—

Ella whipped round at the surly shout, her heart jumping into her throat at the sight of Cooper, looking gorgeous and annoyed, standing in the doorway, his face cast in bold relief by the coloured lights bursting in the sky outside.

She folded her underwear into the suitcase, flipped the lid closed and took several deep breaths to slow her galloping heartbeat. 'I'm packing,' she said. 'I've booked myself on the night flight to London. It leaves at eleven.'

'What the...?' The expletive echoed round the room as he slammed the door shut. 'When exactly were you planning to tell me this? Or weren't you planning to tell me? Is that why you ran off early from the wedding?'

She stiffened, stunned by the anger, and the accusation. 'No, of course not. I planned to tell you when you got back. It's just...' She chewed on her lip, determined not to fold again under the pressure of her own inse-

curities. She'd let him dictate the terms of this relationship—or non-relationship—right from the start.
But it was only as she'd had to stand by his side and
listen to his friend recite her vows, while enduring the
speculative looks of all his friends, that she'd begun
to realise how little she'd been prepared to settle for.
Because she had lacked the courage to demand more.

'I think we need some space,' she continued. 'There's
something I have to tell you and—'

'Yeah, well, I've got something to tell you.' He cut in
before she could get the words out she'd been psych-
ing herself up to say all evening. 'I want you to stay,
to move in with me.'

'What?' She sat down on the bed, her legs going
boneless as her insides tumbled with an odd combination of hope and astonishment at the unexpected
offer. 'You want me to stay? Seriously?'

She hadn't been wrong: there had been something
developing between them, and he'd seen it too. Of
course, she couldn't just abandon her life in London,
but that he would even suggest such a thing had to be
a very good sign that his feelings had deepened too.

He took her arm, drew her up. Touching his forehead to hers, he settled his hand on her neck, to stroke
the flutter of her pulse. 'Of course. You're having my
kid. I want to be there for you both, not thousands of
miles away.'

It took a moment for her to hear the words past
the delighted buzz of anticipation. 'But that's...' She

struggled to clarify, to make sure she'd understood. 'You only want me to stay because of the baby?'

His lips quirked, his brow wrinkling in a puzzled frown. 'Yeah, of course, what else is there?'

There's me. I need you to want me too.

She stepped out of his arms, the blow both shattering and painfully ironic. When she'd first arrived in Bermuda, hearing him say those words would have felt like a miracle. But now they felt desperately bittersweet. How could she accept his offer, when she wanted so much more?

She looked into those jade-green eyes that she had come to adore, but held so many secrets, and said the only words she could. 'I can't stay, Coop. It's not—'

'Why not? Is it because of your business? I get that...' He touched her waist, trying to reassure her, but only making her heart shatter a little more. 'We can work out the logistics. I'll need to be in Bermuda for the summer season, but otherwise I can come to London. I've got money, whatever we need to do to make this work—'

'That isn't it...' She placed her hand on his cheek, loving him even more if that were possible. He was a generous man, who wanted to do the right thing for his child.

'Then what is it?' he asked.

'This isn't about the baby. It's about me, and you.'

'What?'

She swallowed, knowing she needed to tell him, and

hoping against hope that he wouldn't freak out when she did. 'I think I'm falling in love with you.'

He dropped his head back to hers, let out a rush of breath and then, to her total astonishment, he chuckled, the sound deep, and amused and self-satisfied. 'Damn, is that all?'

She stepped back. 'It's not funny. I'm serious.'

He shrugged, his lips tipping in that seductive smile that she had once found so endearing. 'I know you are—so what? That's good, isn't it? If you love me you've got to stay, right?'

'Not if I don't know how you feel about me?' she heard herself say, the question in her voice making her feel needy and pathetic.

'Don't be dumb. It's obvious how I feel about you. I like having you around.' He held her waist, tugged her back into his arms. 'I've invited you to move in, haven't I? At least until the kid's born.'

She braced her hands on his chest, hearing the qualification. 'But that's not enough.'

His brow furrowed. 'Why not?'

'Because I need more than that. You're asking me to make a major change in my life, to move thousands of miles away from everything I know on what sounds like a whim.' The emotion clogged in her throat at the look of total confusion on his face.

'What do you want me to say? That I love you? Is that it?' The bitter edge in his tone made the traitorous tears she'd refused to shed sting her eyes. 'If you need me to say the words I will.'

'This isn't about words.' She drew back. 'It's about emotions. It's about you being honest with me about your feelings.'

Coop stared at Ella's earnest expression, saw the glitter of tears in those trusting blue eyes and felt the panic that he had kept at bay ever since his mother's death start to choke him.

He didn't do emotion, he didn't even talk about it, because it reminded him too much of the deep, dark, inescapable hole where he'd spent most of his childhood.

'You don't know what you're asking,' he said, desperately bartering for time, scrambling around for a way to avoid the conversation. 'I'm not good at that stuff.'

'I know that, Coop.' She sighed, the sound weary and so full of despair it cut right through his heart. 'And I understand. I took a huge knock to my confidence too when Randall rejected me. If I hadn't, it wouldn't have taken me so long to tell you all this. But you have to understand. I can't come and live with you, bring up a child with you and all the time live in some kind of weird limbo where you get to call all the shots because—' she lifted her fingers to do air quotes '—you're "not good at this stuff".' She stood up, brushed her hands down her dress in a nervous gesture he recognised. 'I need to call a cab.'

She turned to pick up her case from the bed. He dived ahead of her, gripped the handle. 'You don't need a cab. You're not going tonight.'

She blinked, the sheen of tears crucifying him. 'Yes, I am. I have to go. I'm tired and we both need space, maybe once—'

'Don't go.' His voice cracked on the word. 'It's not that I don't want to talk about it, it's that I can't.'

'Why can't you?' she asked, the tone gentle but probing, scraping at the raw wound he'd thought had healed years before.

'Because I'll mess it up. Because I'll say the wrong thing, or I'll say it in the wrong way. They're just words—they don't mean anything. What matters is what we do, not what we say to each other.'

She nodded, but he could see the concern in her gaze, and felt as if she was looking through the veneer of charm and confidence and seeing the frightened little boy cowering beneath. 'Coop, whatever made you think that there's a wrong and a right answer?'

She laid a palm on his cheek, but he jerked back. Terrified of being drawn into that dark place again.

'You say that, but there is a right answer. If there wasn't I wouldn't have given her the wrong one. I told her I loved her, that I could look after her, but it didn't change a thing.'

She watched him, her unwavering gaze so full of the love he knew he wasn't capable of giving back, all the panic imploded inside him until all that was left was the pain.

'Who are you talking about, Coop?'

His heart hammered his ribs as he dropped his chin, fisted his fingers to stop them shaking and murmured, 'My mom.'

* * *

Ella stared, unable to speak around the lump wedged in her throat. She could see the painful shadow of memory in his expression, and wished she could take it away. Reaching for his hand, she folded her fingers around his and held on. 'Can you tell me about her?'

He cleared his throat, but he didn't pull his hand out of hers. 'There's not a lot to tell. She had an affair with my old man, he gave her the standard line about leaving his wife. And she got pregnant with me, before she figured out he was lying.'

'He sounds like a very selfish person,' Ella said, then remembered how he'd once compared himself to his father. 'And nothing like you.'

'Thanks.' He sent her a half-smile, but it did nothing to dispel the shadow in his eyes. 'Anyway, he wasn't interested in me, but he carried on screwing my mom from time to time, so she convinced herself he loved her.' He shrugged, but the movement was stiff and tense, and she knew he was nowhere near as relaxed as the gesture suggested.

She pressed her hand to his chest, desperate to soothe the frantic beats of his heart. 'You don't have to tell me any more, if it upsets you. I understand.' His mother had obviously fallen in love with a man who had used her and carried on using her. Was it any wonder that after witnessing that throughout the years of his childhood, he'd be cynical about love himself? And wary about making any kind of commitment. 'I shouldn't have pushed you. It wasn't fair.'

'Yeah, you should have.' He covered her hand. 'And I don't think you do get it, Ella.' He sighed. 'The thing is, she was so fragile. She wanted something she couldn't have and she had these dark moods because she couldn't cope with that. At first, when I was really little, she'd have the odd day when she couldn't get out of bed, and she'd just cry and want to hug me. But as I got older, it got worse and worse, until she couldn't hold down a job. I tried to make things better for her. As soon as I was old enough, I got a job. I figured if I could make enough money...' He stared into the darkness, the hopelessness on his face devastating. 'But I couldn't. Whatever I did, whatever I said, it was never the right thing.'

'Coop,' she murmured, desperate to try and take the hopelessness away. 'It sounds as if she suffered from depression. Money can't cure that.' Or a child's devotion.

'I know, but...'

She leant into him, the love welling up her chest as he looped his arm round her shoulders. 'What happened to her?'

She heard him swallow, the sound loud in the stillness of the night. 'I came home from the graveyard shift at the drive-thru one night and found her in the bathroom. She'd taken too many of the pills she used to sleep. I called the paramedics, but it was too late.'

Ella pulled back, the tears soaking her lashes. 'I'm so sorry that you found her like that.' And that he'd had such a bleak childhood. No wonder he'd been so determined to protect himself—he'd suffered so much, at such a young age. 'But surely you must see that you weren't to blame. Whatever you said or didn't say, it wouldn't have made a difference.'

'Hey, don't cry.' He scooped the tear off her lashes. 'And I guess you're right. But that's not the reason I didn't want to tell you about her.'

She swallowed down the tears. 'So what is?'

'I didn't want you to know what a coward I am.'

'A coward?' She didn't understand: he'd done his best; he'd stuck by his mother and tried so hard to make her life easier, better. 'How can you say that when you did everything you could for her?'

'Maybe I did. But I'm not talking about her. I'm talking about us.' His lips tipped up in a wry smile. 'The thing is, even though I loved my mom, and I was sad when she died...' he gave his head a small shake '...you know what I felt most when I stood by her graveside?'

She shook her head, confused now. What was he trying to tell her?

'Relief.' The word came out on a huff of breath. 'I was so damn glad I didn't have to be responsible for her any more.' He cupped her cheek, brushing the tears off her lashes. 'For years after her death, I used to have this recurring nightmare that I was standing by her grave and her hand would come out and drag me in with her. Because that's what it felt like when I was growing up, being trapped in this big dark hole that I could never get out of. So I ran and I kept on running. Once I landed here, I devoted myself to making money, until I had enough to make the nightmares go away. But I never realised until this moment that in a lot of ways I never stopped running.' His hand stroked down to rest on her stomach.

'I'm sorry that I didn't tell everyone about you, and the baby. And that I'm not good with stuff like this. But if you'll just give me another chance, I'll try not to be such a damn coward again. Because I don't want to keep running any more.'

She stared at him, her heart bursting with happiness and giddy relief. Maybe it wasn't a declaration of undying and everlasting love. But she'd had one of those before and it had been a lie. Coop's declaration meant so much more.

'I think maybe we both need to stop being cowards,' she said. 'I should have had the guts to tell you straight away that my feelings were changing, that I wanted more, instead of panicking about how you would react.'

His hands framed her face, to pull her gaze back to his, and the approval she saw there was as intoxicating as the heat. 'You were just scared. Believe me, I get that. Just so long as you're not scared any more?'

She bobbed her head in answer to his question, far too emotional to speak.

'Cool.' He wrapped his arms round her waist, the solid feel of him making heat eddy up from her core to add to the joy.

She threaded her hands through the short hair above his ears, tugged his head down to hers and poured out everything she felt for him in a kiss full of happiness and desire and the rush of emotion that no longer had to be denied.

When they finally came up for air, he cradled her cheeks. 'So will you cancel your flight? I know you've got to go home soon, but when you do I'd like to come too, until we figure out how we're going to work this out. I'm not good at making promises. But I know I want to be with you, not just because of the baby, but because...' He ducked his head, swore softly under his breath, the flags of embarrassed colour on his cheeks sweet and endearing and impossibly sexy. 'Hell, I'm pretty damn sure I'm falling for you, too.'

She laughed, the sound rich and throaty and full of hope as she clung onto his neck. 'All right, but only on one condition.'

The quick grin on his lips sparkled with a heady combination of tenderness and wickedness. 'Seriously, you've got another condition? That's pushing it.'

'I'll stay on the condition that I get to give you that just-screwed look I adore.'

He laughed. 'Yup, definitely pushing it.'

He was still chuckling when he dumped her on the bed a few minutes later and got to work giving her what she wanted.

EPILOGUE

—

'That water is so warm, it's incredible,' Ruby said as she reached for one of the beach towels and patted herself dry.

Ella shielded her eyes against the sun to smile at her friend from her spot on the lounger. 'I know, but we should probably call the guys in soon, or we're going to have some very cranky kids on our hands later.'

Ruby turned towards the sea, her smile crafty. 'Yes, but they are going to sleep like the dead, once their fathers have put them to bed.'

Ella laughed, her gaze following Ruby's out to the shallow surf, where Cooper and Ruby's husband Callum were busy playing some kind of splashing war with their children. Cal ran forward, with his four-year-old Arturo clamped to his back like a limpet, while his daughter Ally shouted instructions and charged by his side. Her older brother Max seemed to be in cahoots with Cooper, who had their two-year-old son Jem slung on his hip, as he and Max launched a new offensive against the Westmore invaders. Jem's delighted chuckles were matched by the manic pumping of his little legs as his Daddy scooped up a tidal wave of water with his free arm and drenched Ally, Cal and Arturo in one fell swoop.

Ella grinned at the comical scene as Max began to do a victory dance.

She loved having Ruby and Cal and their family visiting them in Bermuda for the summer—especially now that she and Cooper had made the decision to move here permanently and sell the flat Coop had bought in Camden just before Jem's birth. It had been a major wrench finally agreeing to let that part of her life go, not least because she knew she would miss her best friend terribly, but as Jem got older they'd decided that jetting backwards and forwards between their two home bases was too confusing for him—and getting him over the jet lag every few months nothing short of a nightmare.

'Do the daddies know they're on bedtime duty?' Ella asked as the splashing war went into a new phase, Ally, Cal and Arturo apparently refusing to concede defeat. She suspected both men were going to be even more exhausted than the kids come bedtime if the war carried on much longer.

Ruby settled on the sun lounger next to her and sent her a wicked grin. 'They won't have a choice when I tell them you and I still have lots of important business to conduct concerning the new Touch of Frosting opening in Hamilton.'

'But I thought we got everything sorted yesterday?' Ella said, remembering the fabulous brainstorming session they'd had discussing recipes and displays for the opening of her new bakery in two weeks' time, which Ruby and her family were staying to attend.

'Yes, but they don't know that, do they?'

Ella laughed. 'Ruby, you're nasty.'

'I try,' Ruby replied, smiling back. Then she reached over to take Ella's hand, her smile becoming hopeful. 'So, Ella, you've been so upbeat, I'm assuming you got good news from the specialist last week?'

Ella gripped her friend's fingers, and let the moment of melancholy pass before replying. Ruby knew she and Coop had been trying for another child for over a year, so of course she would ask. 'Actually, it wasn't the news we wanted.'

Ruby sat upright, her smile disappearing. 'Ella, I'm so sorry. I shouldn't have brought it up, I just assumed...'

'No, that's okay.' She tugged Ruby's hand to reassure her. 'Really, it is. We knew it was a long shot.' She allowed her gaze to drift over to her two precious guys, still playing like loons together in the surf with the Westmores, and the smile that was never far away returned. 'It would be incredibly selfish of me to expect another miracle in my life.' She paused, the smile getting bigger. 'After the two I already have.'

Because she considered Coop to be as much of a miracle as their baby. He'd rescued her, she thought, in so many ways, and she'd rescued him. They had both found something wonderful together, not just in Jem but with each other, something made even more wonderful by the fact that they hadn't even realised it had been missing from their lives until they'd found it.

'Even so,' Ruby said, 'it seems such a shame it should be so hard for you to have more children when you make such incredible parents.'

'I know,' she said, not caring if the statement sounded a little smug. 'Which is why we're thinking of becoming foster parents.'

'You are?' Ruby's smile returned. 'That sounds like a great idea.'

'We think so. It's early days yet, but we're both excited about it. Cooper runs free snorkelling classes at the marina for kids with...' she paused '...challenging home situations.' Something he knew far too much about himself. 'Anyway, one of the social workers who escorts the kids suggested it to him—because she's seen how well he handles them. So we've started the ball rolling. There's a lot of paperwork and we have to do a...'

The sound of a toddler's crying reached them, interrupting Ella's enthusiastic reply. She sat up, seeing her husband strolling towards her across the sand, with Jem clinging to his neck and rubbing his eyes—his little head drenched in seawater.

'Oh, dear, what happened?' she said as they approached, trying not to smile, Jem looked so forlorn.

'We had to retire from the field,' Coop announced,

casting a stern eye at Ruby. 'Thanks to a sneaky stealth attack from Super-Splash-Girl.'

'I should have warned you.' Ruby smiled, handing Coop a towel to wipe Jem's face. 'Ally takes no prisoners, and she always plays to win. I'm afraid it's the curse of having two brothers.'

'Want ice cream, Daddy,' Jem wailed as if he'd just undergone an extreme form of water torture.

'OK, buddy.' Coop handed Ruby back the towel. 'I guess you earned one.' He rubbed his son's back as the small head drooped onto his shoulder. 'As well as a lecture on the wiles of women.'

Ruby chuckled. 'Good luck with that.'

'Do you want me to take him?' Ella asked, reaching for the exhausted child.

'Nah, he's good. I'll see if I can sneak a scoop of strawberry past Inez, then I'll put him down for his nap.' Holding his son securely against his chest, he leant down to press a kiss to her lips, whispering as he drew back, 'Then maybe we can have *our* afternoon nap?'

The heat sizzled happily down to her core as she caressed her son's damp blond curls and grinned up at her extremely hot husband. 'Possibly, as long as I don't have to listen to a lecture on the wiles of women.'

'No problem.' He winked. 'I've got a whole other lecture planned for you, sweetheart.'

Saying goodbye to Ruby, he headed towards the beach steps up to the house.

Ella studied his broad tanned back, the muscular,

capable shoulder where her drowsy son's head was securely cradled, and then let her gaze drift down to the wet board shorts clinging to tight buns.

She let out a contented sigh as her happiness combined with the hum of heat. While her husband would still rather have his teeth pulled than talk about his feelings—when it came to lectures in bed, she'd never been able to fault his energy, enthusiasm... Or his expertise.

* * * * *

CHARLOTTE PHILLIPS

has been reading romantic fiction since her teens, and she adores upbeat stories with happy endings. Writing them for Harlequin is her dream job. She combines writing with looking after her fabulous husband, two teenagers, a four-year-old and a dachshund. When something has to give, it's usually housework. She lives in Wiltshire.

THE PLUS-ONE AGREEMENT

Charlotte Phillips

For Gemma, who makes my day every day.
With all my love always.

ONE

—

Q: How do you tell your fake boyfriend that you've met a real one and you don't need him any more?

A: However you like. If he's not a real boyfriend, it's not a real break-up. Hardly likely that he'll start declaring undying love for you, is it?

Chance would have been a fine thing. This Aston Martin might fly before arm candy addict Dan Morgan developed anything more than a fake attraction for someone as sensible and boring as Emma Burney, and it wasn't as if she hadn't given it time. Getting on for a year in his company, watching an endless string of short-term flings pout their way through his private life, had convinced her she was never going to be blonde enough, curvy enough or vacuous enough to qualify. In fact she was pretty much the opposite of all his conquests, even dressed up to the nines for her brother's art exhibition.

She glanced down at herself in the plain black boat-neck frock and nude heels she'd chosen, teamed as usual with her minimal make-up and straight-up-and-down figure. Romance need not apply.

She did, however, possess all the qualities Dan wanted in a supportive friend and social ally. As he did for her. Hence the fake part of their agreement.

An agreement which she reminded herself she no longer needed.

Not if she wanted to move forward from the suspended animation that had been her life this last year. Any residual hope that what was counterfeit between them might somehow turn genuine if she just gave it enough time had been squashed in these last few amazing weeks as she'd been swept off her feet by a whirlwind of intimate, luxurious dinners, expensive gifts and exciting plans. What was between her and Dan was now nothing more than a rut that needed climbing out of.

She watched him quietly for a moment from the passenger seat of his car, looking like an aftershave model in his dark suit and white shirt. His dark hair was so thick there was always a hint of spike about it, a light shadow of stubble lined his jaw, and his ice-blue eyes and slow smile had the ability to charm the entire female species. It had certainly worked on her mother, whose ongoing mission in life was to get Emma and Dan married off and raising a tribe of kids like some Fifties cupcake couple.

Perpetuating her gene pool was the last thing Emma

wanted—a lifetime in the midst of her insane family had seen to that. Having Dan as her pretend boyfriend at family events had proved to be the perfect fob-off.

But now she had the real thing and the pretending was holding her back. All that remained was to explain that fact to Dan. She gathered herself together and took a deep breath.

'This has to stop,' she said.

'You're dumping me?'

Dan shifted his eyes briefly from the road to glance across at her, a mock grin on his face. Because of course this was some kind of joke, right? She simply looked back at him, her brown eyes serious.

'Well, technically, no,' she said. 'Because we'd have to be in a *proper* relationship for me to do that, and ours is a fake one.' She put her head on one side. 'If it's actually one at all. To be honest, it's more of an agreement, isn't it? A plus-one agreement.'

He'd never seen fit to give it a name before. It had simply been an extension of their work dealings into a mutually beneficial social arrangement. There had been no conscious decision or drawing up of terms. It had just grown organically from one simple work success.

Twelve months ago Emma, in her capacity as his lawyer, had attended a meeting with Dan and a potential client for his management consultancy. A potentially huge client. The meeting had overrun into dinner, she had proved a formidable ally and his winning of the contract had been smoothed along perfectly by their double act. She had seemed to bounce off him effortlessly, predicting where he was taking the conversation, backing him up where he needed it. He'd ended the evening with a new client, a new respect for Emma and the beginnings of a connection.

After that she'd become his go-to ally for social engagements—a purely platonic date that he could count on for intelligent conversation and professional behaviour. She'd become a trusted contact. And in return he'd accompanied her to family dinners and events like this one today, sympathising with her exasperation at her slightly crazy family while not really understanding it. Surely better to have a slightly crazy family than no family at all?

He'd never been dumped before. It was an odd novelty. And certainly not by a real girlfriend. It seemed being dumped by a fake one was no less of a shock to the system.

'It's been good while it lasted,' she was saying. 'Mutually beneficial for both of us. You got a professional plus-one for your work engagements and I got my parents off my back. But the fact is—'

'It's not you, it's me?' he joked, still not convinced she wasn't messing around.

'I've met someone,' she said, not smiling.

'Someone?' he said, shaking his head lightly and reaching for the air-conditioning controls. For some reason it was suddenly boiling in the car. 'A work someone?'

'No, not a work someone!' Her tone was exasperated. 'Despite what you might think, I do have a life, you know—outside work.'

'I never said you didn't.'

He glanced across at her indignant expression just as it melted into a smile of triumph.

'Dan, I've *met* someone.'

She held his gaze for a second before he looked back at the road, her eyebrows slightly raised, waiting for him to catch on. He tried to keep a grin in place when for some reason his face wanted to fold in on itself. In the months he'd known her she'd been on maybe two or three dates, to his knowledge, and none of the men involved had ever been important enough to her to earn the description 'someone'.

He sat back in his seat and concentrated hard on driving the car through the London evening traffic. He supposed she was waiting for some kind of congratulatory comment and he groped for one.

'Good for you,' he said eventually. 'Who is he?'

'He was involved in some legal work I was doing.'

So she *had* met him through her job as a lawyer, then. Of course she had. When did she ever do anything that wasn't somehow linked to work? Even their own friendship was based in work. It had started with work and had grown with their mutual ambition.

'We've been on a few dates and it's going really well.' She took a breath. 'And that's why I need to end things with you.'

Things? For some reason he disliked the vagueness of the term, as if it meant nothing.

'You don't date,' he pointed out.

'Exactly,' she said, jabbing a finger at him. 'And do you know *why* I don't date?'

'Because no man could possibly match up to me?'

'Despite what you might think is appealing to women, I don't relish the prospect of a couple of nights sharing your bed only to be kicked out of it the moment you get bored.'

'No need to make it sound so brutal. They all go into it with their eyes open, you know. I don't make any false promises that it will ever be more than a bit of fun.'

'None of them ever believe that. They all think they'll be the one to change you. But you'll never change because you don't need to. You've got me for the times when you need to be serious, so you can keep the rest of your girlies just for fun.'

She looked down at her hands, folded in her lap.

'The thing is, Dan, passing you off as my boyfriend might keep my family off my back, and it stops the swipes about me being single and the comments about my biological clock, but it doesn't actually solve anything. I didn't realise until now that I'm in a rut. I haven't dated for months. All I do is work. It's so easy to rely on you if I have to go anywhere I need a date that I've quit looking for anyone else.'

'What are you saying?'

She sighed.

'Just that meeting Alistair has opened my eyes to

what I've been missing. And I really think our agreement is holding us both back.'

'Alistair?'

'His name is Alistair Woods.'

He easily dismissed the image that zipped into his brain of the blond ex-international cycling star, because it had to be a coincidence. Emma didn't know anyone like *that*. He would know if she did. Except she was waiting, lips slightly parted, eyebrows slightly raised. Everything about her expression told him she was waiting for him to catch on.

'Not *the* Alistair Woods?' he said, because she so obviously wanted him to.

He stole a glance across at her and the smile that lit up her face caused a sorry twist somewhere deep in his stomach. It was a smile he couldn't remember seeing for the longest time—not since they'd first met.

The glance turned into a look for as long as safe driving would allow, during which he saw her with an unusually objective eye, noticing details that had passed him by before. The hint of colour touching the smooth high cheekbones, the soft fullness of her lower lip, the way tendrils of her dark hair curled softly against the creamy skin of her shoulders in the boat-neck dress. She looked absolutely radiant and his stomach gave a slow and unmistakable flip, adding to his sense of unreality.

'Exactly,' she said with a touch of triumph. 'The cyclist. Well, ex-cyclist. He's in TV now—he does presenting and commentating.'

Of course he did. His face had been a permanent media fixture during the last big sports event in the UK. Dan felt a sudden irrational aversion to the man, whom he'd never met.

'*You're* dating Alistair Woods?'

He failed to keep the incredulity out of his voice and it earned him a flash of anger that replaced her bubbling excitement like a flood of cold water.

'No need to make it sound so unbelievable,' she snapped. 'You might only see me as some power suit, great for taking on the difficult dates when one of your five-minute conquests won't make the right impression, but I do actually have a dual existence. As a woman.'

'How long have you been seeing him?' he said.

'What are you? My father?' she said. 'We've been out a few times.'

'How many is a few?'

'Half a dozen, maybe.'

'You're ending our agreement on the strength of half a dozen dates?'

'Yes, well, they weren't dates in the way you think of them. He hasn't just invited me out for an impressive dinner as a preamble to taking me to bed. You can actually get to know someone really well in half a dozen dates if you approach them in a more...*serious* way.'

The thinly veiled dig didn't escape him and indignation sharpened his voice.

'OK, then, if he's so bloody marvellous, and you're so bloody smitten, why the hell isn't *he* on his way to look at your brother's wacky paintings and meet the parents? Couldn't you have dumped me on the phone and saved me a load of time and hassle?'

He pulled the car to a standstill outside the gallery steps and turned off the engine.

'I'm not dumping you! How many times? It's a *fake* relationship!'

A uniformed attendant opened Emma's car door and she got out. Dan threw his keys to the parking valet and joined her on the steps.

'So you keep saying,' he said, keeping his voice low. 'I could have spent this evening working.'

'Like you don't spend enough of your life doing that.' She led the way through the high arched doorway into the gallery. 'You can easily afford an evening. Alistair's out of the country until next week, and I need this opportunity to draw a thick, black and irreversible line under the two of us for my parents' eyes and undo the tissue of fibs I've told them.'

They walked slowly down the red-carpeted hallway, his hand pressed softly at the small of her back—the perfect escort as always.

'I really don't see why I need to be there for you to do that,' he said, smiling politely at other guests as they passed, maintaining the perfect impression. 'Especially since it's only a *fake* relationship.'

Even as he piled heavy sarcasm on the word *fake* he wondered why the hell he was turning this into such a big deal. Why should he care? It had simply been a handy arrangement, nothing more.

'Because the problem with it being a fake relationship is that it was a pretty damn perfect one,' she snapped. 'And so now I need a fake break-up.'

She outlined her suggestion as they walked down the hall and it sounded so insane that his mind had trouble processing it.

'You can't possibly be serious. You want to fake an argument in front of your family so you can make some kind of a righteous point by dumping me?'

'Exactly! Shouldn't be too hard. I'll choose a moment, start picking on you, and then you just play along.'

'Why can't you just tell them we broke up? That things didn't work out?' He ran an exasperated hand through his hair. 'Why do I need to be here at all?'

'Because I've spent the last year building you up as Mr Perfect, bigging you up at every opportunity. You've no idea what it was like before we started helping each other out. The constant questions about why I was still single, the hassle about my body clock careering towards a standstill, the negativity about my career. Introducing you as my boyfriend stopped all that like magic. They think you're the son-in-law of their dreams—a rich businessman who adores me, good-looking, charming, not remotely fazed by my mother. They'll never just take my word for it that we broke up amicably. I'd spend the rest of my days being questioned about what I did to drive you away. You'd be forever name-dropped as the one that got away.

No man I bring home would ever live up to your perfect memory.'

'You don't think you're going a bit overboard?'

'Are you really asking me that? You've met my mother. You know what she's like.'

He had to concede that Emma's mother was without a doubt the most interfering person he'd ever come across, with an opinion about everything that was never wrong. Her relationship with Emma seemed to bring out the critic in both of them. Mutual exasperated affection was probably the nearest he could get to describing it.

'This way your fabulous reputation will be ruined, by the time Alistair and I finish our trip to the States you'll be a distant memory, and they'll be ready to accept him as my new man.' She shrugged. 'Once I've... you know...*briefed* him on what they can be like.'

Trip to the States? His hands felt clammy. He stopped outside the main gallery and pulled her to one side before they could get swept into the room by the crowd.

'You're going on holiday?'

She looked at him impatiently.

'In a few weeks' time, yes. I'm going to meet some of his friends and family. And then after that I'm going to travel with him in Europe while he covers an international cycling race for American TV. I'm taking a sabbatical from work. I might not even come back.'

'What?' His mind reeled. 'You're giving up your life

as you know it on the strength of a few dates? Are you mad?'

'That's exactly it! When do I *ever* do anything impetuous? It isn't as if sensible planning has worked out so well for me, is it? I work all hours and I have no social life to speak of beyond filling in for you. What exactly have I got to lose?'

'What about your family?'

'I'm hardly going to be missed, am I? My parents are so busy following Adam's ascent to celebrity status with his art that they're not going to start showing an interest in my life.'

She leaned in towards him and lowered her voice, treating him to the dizzying scent of her vanilla perfume.

'One of his pictures went for five figures last month, you know. Some anonymous buyer, apparently. But two words about *my* work and they start to glaze over.'

She leaned back again and took a small mirror from her clutch bag.

'And you'll be fine, of course,' she went on, opening the mirror and checking her face in it, oblivious to his floundering brain. 'You must have a whole little black book of girls who'd fall over themselves to step into my shoes. You're hardly going to be stuck for a date.'

True enough. He might, however, be stuck for a date who made the right kind of impression. Wasn't that how this whole agreement of theirs had started? He didn't go in for dating with a serious slant—not any more. Not since Maggie and...

He clenched his fists. Even after all these years thoughts of her and their failed plans occasionally filtered into his mind, despite the effort he put into forgetting them. There was no place for those memories in his life. These days for him it was all about keeping full control. Easy fun, then moving on. Unfortunately the girls who fitted that kind of mould didn't have the right fit in work circles. Emma had filled that void neatly, meaning he could bed whoever the hell he liked because he had her for the serious stuff—the stuff where impressions counted.

It occurred to him for the first time that she wouldn't just be across London if he needed her. He felt oddly unsettled as she tugged at his arm and walked towards the main door.

'You've had some mad ideas in your time, but this...' he said.

As they entered the main gallery Emma paused to take in the enormity of what her brother had achieved. The vast room had a spectacular landing running above it, from which the buzzing exhibition could be viewed. It had been divided into groupings by display screens, on which Adam's paintings—some of them taller than her—were picked out in pools of perfect clear lighting. A crowd of murmuring spectators surrounded the nearest one, which depicted an enormous eyeball with tiny cavorting people in the centre of it. His work might not be her cup of tea, but it certainly commanded attention and evoked strong opinions. Just the way he always had done.

She took two crystal flutes of champagne from the silver tray of a pretty blonde attendant, who looked straight through her to smile warmly at Dan. For heaven's sake, was no woman immune? Emma handed him one of the flutes and he immediately raised it to the blonde girl.

'Thanks very much...' He leaned in close so he could read the name tag conveniently pinned next to a cleavage Emma could only ever dream of owning. 'Hannah...'

He returned the girl's smile. Emma dragged him away. Why was she even surprised? Didn't she know him well enough by now? No woman was safe.

Correction: no curvy blonde arm candy was safe.

'For Pete's sake, pay attention,' she said in a stage whisper. 'You're meant to be here with me, not eyeing up the staff.'

She linked her arm through his so she could propel him through the crowd to find her parents. It wasn't difficult. Her mother had for some insane reason chosen to wear a wide flowing scarf wrapped around her head and tied to one side. Emma headed through the crowd, aiming for it—aqua silk with a feather pin stuck in it on one side. As her parents fell into possible earshot she pasted on a smile and talked through her beaming teeth.

'They'll never just take my word for it that we've just gone our separate ways. Not without a massive inquest. And I can't be doing with that. Trust me, it'll work better this way. It's cleaner. Just go with everything I say.'

She speeded up the end of the sentence as her mother approached.

'And you don't need to worry,' she added from the corner of her mouth. 'I'll pay for the dry-cleaning.'

'You'll what? What the hell is *that* supposed to mean?'

He turned his face towards her, a puzzled frown lightly creasing his forehead, and his eyes followed her hand as she raised her flute of champagne, ready to tip the contents over his head. She saw his blue eyes widen in sudden understanding and realised far too late that she'd totally underestimated his reflexes.

Dan's hand shot out instantly to divert hers, knocking it to one side in a single lightning movement. And instead of providing the explosive beginning to her staged *we're finished* argument, the glass jerked sharply sideways and emptied itself in a huge splash down the front of her mother's aquamarine jumpsuit. She stared in horror as champagne soaked into the fabric, lending it a translucent quality that revealed an undergarment not unlike a parachute harness.

She'd inadvertently turned her mother into Miss Wet T-Shirt, London. And if she'd been a disappointing daughter before, this bumped things up to a whole new level.

TWO

—

'Aaaaargh!'

The ensuing squawk from Emma's mother easily outdid the gallery's classy background music, and Dan was dimly aware of the room falling silent around them as people turned from the paintings to watch.

'An accident—it was an accident...' Emma gabbled, fumbling with a pack of tissues from her tiny clutch bag and making a futile attempt at mopping up the mess.

As her father shook a handkerchief from his pocket and joined in, her mother slapped his hand away in exasperation.

'It'll take more than a few tissues,' she snarled furiously at him, and then turned on Emma. 'Do you know how much this outfit *cost*? How am I meant to stand next to your brother in the publicity photos now? I've never known anyone so *clumsy*.'

Emma's face was the colour of beetroot, but any sympathy Dan might have felt was rather undermined by the revelation that she'd intended, without so much as a word of warning, to make a fool of him in front of the cream of London's social scene. *That* was her plan? *That?* Dumping him publicly by humiliating him? If he hadn't caught on in time it would have been him standing there dripping Veuve Clicquot while she no doubt laid into him with a ludicrous fake argument.

No one dumped him. *Ever.*

'An accident?' he said pointedly.

She glanced towards him, her red face one enormous fluster. He raised furious eyebrows and mouthed the word *dry-cleaning* at her. She widened her eyes back at him in an apologetic please-stick-to-the-plan gesture.

Emma's brother, Adam, pushed his way through the crowd, turning perfectly coiffed heads as he went, dandyish as ever in a plum velvet jacket with a frothy lace shirt underneath. There was concern in his eyes behind his statement glasses.

'What's going on, people?' he said, staring in surprise at his mother as she shrugged her way into her husband's jacket and fastened the buttons grimly to hide the stain.

'Your sister has just flung champagne *all over me,*' she snapped dramatically, then raised both hands as Adam opened his mouth to speak. 'No, no, don't you go worrying about it, I'm not going anywhere. I wouldn't *hear* of it. This is your night. I'm not going to let the fact that my outfit is *decimated* ruin that. I'll soldier on, just like I always do.'

'I've said I'm sorry. I'll pay for the dry-cleaning,' Emma said desperately.

Dan's anger slipped a notch as he picked up on her discomfort. Only a notch, mind you. OK, so maybe he wouldn't have it out with her in public, but he would most certainly be dealing with her later.

Emma closed her eyes briefly. When did it end? Would everything she ever did in life, good or bad, be somehow referenced by Adam's success? Then again, since her mother was already furious with her, she might as well press ahead with the planned mock break-up. Maybe then at least the evening wouldn't be a total write-off.

She drew Dan aside by the elbow as Adam drifted away again, back to his adoring public.

'We can still do it,' she said. 'We can still stage the break-up.'

He stared at her incredulously.

'Are you having some kind of a laugh?' he snapped. 'When you said you needed a fake break-up I wasn't expecting it to involve my public humiliation. You were going to lob that drink over *me*, for heaven's sake, and now you think I'll just agree to a rerun?'

She opened her mouth to respond and he cut her off.

'There are people I *know* in here,' he said in a furious stage whisper, nodding around them at the crowd. 'What kind of impression do you think that would have given them?'

'I didn't expect things to get so out of hand,' she

said. 'I just thought we'd have a quick mock row in front of my parents and that would be it.'

'You didn't even warn me!'

'I didn't want to lose the element of surprise. I wanted to make it look, you know, *authentic*.'

He stared at her in disbelief.

There was the squeal of whiny microphone feedback and Adam appeared on the landing above the gallery. Emma looked up towards her brother, picked out in a pool of light in front of a billboard with his own name on it in six-foot-tall violet letters. She felt overshadowed, as always, by his brilliance. Just as she had done at school. But now it was on a much more glamorous level. No wonder her legal career seemed drab in comparison. No wonder her parents were expecting her to give it all up at any moment to get married and give them grandchildren. Adam was far too good for such normal, boring life plans.

His voice began to boom over the audio system, thanking everyone for coming and crediting a list of people she'd never heard of with his success.

'I can't believe you'd make a scene like that without considering what effect it might have on me,' Dan said, anger still lacing his voice.

The blonde champagne waitress chose that moment to walk past them. Emma watched as Dan's gaze flickered away from her to follow the woman's progress and the grovelling apology she'd been about to give screeched to a halt on the tip of her tongue. Just who the hell did he think he was, moaning about being dumped, when *his* relationship principles were pretty much in the gutter? OK, so they might not have actually *been* a couple, but she'd seen the trail of broken hearts he left in his wake. He had no relationship scruples whatsoever. One girl followed another. And as soon as he'd got what he wanted he lost interest and dumped them. As far as she knew he'd never suffered a moment's comeback as a result.

Maybe this new improved Emma, with her stupid unrequited girlie crush on Dan well and truly in the past, had a duty to press that point on behalf of womankind.

'Oh, get over yourself,' she said, before she could change her mind. 'I'd say a public dumping was probably long overdue. It's just that none of your conquests have had the nous or the self-respect to do it before. There's probably a harem of curvy blonde waitresses and models who've thought about lobbing a drink over you when you've chucked them just because you're bored. And I didn't actually spill a drop on you, so let's just move on, shall we?'

Adam smiled and laughed his way back through the crowd towards them, and she seized the opportunity as he neared her proudly beaming parents.

'Same plan as before, minus the champagne. I'll start picking on you and...'

The words trailed away in her mouth as Adam clamped one arm around Dan's shoulders and one around her own.

'Got some news for you all—gather round, gather round,' he said.

As her parents moved in closer, questioning expressions on their faces, he raised both hands in a gesture of triumph above his head.

'Be happy for me, people!'

He performed a jokey pirouette and finished with a manic grin and jazz hands.

'Ernie and I are getting married!'

Beaming at them, he slid his velvet-sleeved arm around his boyfriend and pulled him into a hot kiss.

Her mother's gasp of shock was audible above the cheers. And any plans Emma might have had of staging a limelight-stealing break-up went straight back to the drawing board.

Emma watched the buzzing crowd of people now surrounding Adam and Ernie, showering them with congratulations, vaguely relieved that she hadn't managed to dispense with Dan after all. From the tense look on her parents' faces, as they stood well away from the throng, dealing with the fallout from Adam's announcement wasn't going to be easy. And despite the fact that it was a setback in her plans to introduce Alistair, there was no doubt that her mother was much easier to handle when she had Dan in her corner.

Dealing with her parents without him was something she hadn't had to do in so long that she hadn't realised how she'd come to rely on his calming presence. They might have only been helping each other out, but Dan had had her back where her family were concerned. And he'd never been remotely fazed by her overbearing mother and downtrodden father.

She wondered for the first time with a spike of doubt whether Alistair would be as supportive as that. Or would he let her family cloud his judgement of her? What was that saying? *Look at the mother if you want to see your future wife.* If that theory held up she might as well join a nunnery. Alistair would be out of her life before she could blink.

She couldn't let herself think like that.

Calling a halt with Dan was clearly the right thing to do if she was so ridiculously dependent on him that she could no longer handle her family on her own. But she couldn't ruin Adam's excitement. Not tonight. She'd simply have to reschedule things.

And in the meantime at least she wasn't handling her mother's shock by herself. She took a new flute of champagne gratefully from Dan and braced herself with a big sip.

'I'm sure it must just be a publicity stunt,' her mother was saying.

Denial. Her mother's stock reaction to news she didn't want to hear.

'It's not a publicity stunt,' Adam said. 'We're getting married.'

He beamed at Ernie, standing beside him in a slim-cut electric blue suit. He certainly *looked* the perfect match for Adam.

Her mother's jaw didn't even really drop. Disbelief was so ingrained in her.

'Don't be ridiculous, darling,' she said, flicking an invisible speck of dirt from Adam's lapel. 'Of course you're not.'

Adam's face took on the stoic expression of one who knew he would need to press the point more than once in order to be heard. Possibly a few hundred times.

'It's the next logical step,' he said.

'In what?' Her mother flapped a dismissive hand. 'It's just a phase. You'll soon snap out of it once the right girl comes along. Bit like Emma with her vegetarian thing back in the day.' She nodded at Emma. 'Soon went back to normal after a couple of weeks when she fancied a bacon sandwich.'

'Mum,' Adam said patiently, 'Emma was thirteen. I'm twenty-nine. Ernie and I have been together for nearly a year.'

'I know. Sharing a flat. Couple of lads. No need to turn it into more than it is.'

Emma stared as Adam finally raised his voice enough to make her mother stop talking.

'Mum, you're in denial!'

As she stopped her protests and looked at him he took a deep breath and lowered his voice, speaking with the tired patience of someone who'd covered the same ground many times, only to end up where he'd started.

'I've been out since I was eighteen. I know you've never wanted to accept it, but the right girl for me *doesn't exist.* We're having a civil partnership ceremony in six weeks' time and I want you all to be there and be happy for me.'

'I'm happy for you,' Emma said, smiling tentatively.

Happiness she could do. Unfortunately being at the wedding might be a bit trickier. Her plans with Alistair lurked at the edge of her mind. She'd been so excited about going away with him. He'd showered her with gifts and attention, and for the first time in her life she was being blown away by being the sole focus of another person. And not just any person. Alistair Woods had to be one of the most eligible bachelors in the universe, with an army of female fans, and he had chosen to be with *her.* She still couldn't quite believe her luck. Their trip was planned to the hilt. She would have to make Adam understand somehow.

He leaned in and gave her a hug. 'Thanks, Em.'

She had grown up feeling overshadowed by Adam's achievements. Just the look of him was attention-grabbing, with his perfectly chiselled features and foppish dress sense. And that was just now. She couldn't forget the school years, where for every one of Emma's hard-earned A grades there had been a matching two or three showered effortlessly on Adam. His flamboyant, outgoing personality charmed everyone he came into contact with, and her mother never ceased championing his successes to anyone who would listen.

It hadn't been easy being her parents' Plan B. Competing for their interest with someone as dazzling as Adam was an impossible, cold task.

'I blame you for this, Donald,' her mother snapped at her father. 'Indulging his ridiculous obsession with musical theatre when he was in his teens.'

Sometimes Emma forgot that being her parents' Plan A was probably no picnic either.

Adam held up his hands.

'Please, Mum. It's not up for discussion. It's happening with or without your approval. Can't you just be pleased for us?'

There was an extremely long pause and then her mother gave an enormous grudging sigh.

'Well, I can kiss goodbye to grandchildren, I suppose,' she grumbled. 'We'll have to count on you for that now, Emma. *If* you can ever manage to find a man who'll commit.'

She glared pointedly at Dan, who totally ignored the jibe. Emma had been wondering how long it would be before her biological clock got a mention. Terrific. So now Adam could carve out the life he wanted without bearing the brunt of her parents' wrath because they had Emma lined up as their biological backup plan to carry on their insane gene pool.

Going away with Alistair was beginning to feel like a lucky escape. She just needed to get her plans back on track.

Dan scanned an e-mail for the third time and realised he still hadn't properly taken it in. His mind had been all over the place this last day or two.

Since the night of Adam's exhibition, to be exact.

There was a gnawing feeling deep in his gut that work didn't seem to be suppressing, and he finally threw in the towel on distracting himself, took his mind off work and applied it to the problem instead.

He was piqued because Emma had ended things with him. OK, so her plans to dump him publicly hadn't come off, thankfully, but the end result was the same. She'd drawn a line under their relationship without so much as a moment's pause and he hadn't heard from her since. No discussion, no input from him.

He was even more piqued because now it was over with he really shouldn't give a damn. They were friends, work colleagues, and that was all there was to it. Their romantic attachment existed only in the impression they'd given to the outside world, to work contacts and her family. It had always been a front.

His pique had absolutely nothing to do with any sudden realisation that Emma was attractive. He'd always *known* she was attractive. Dan Morgan wouldn't be seen dating a moose, even for business reasons. That didn't mean she was his type, though—not with her dark hair and minimal make-up, and her conservative taste in clothes. And that in turn had made it easy to pigeonhole her as friend. A proper relationship with someone like Emma would be complex, would need commitment, compromise, emotional investment. All things he wasn't prepared to give another woman. Tried, tested and failed. Dan Morgan learned from his mistakes and never repeated his failures.

It had quickly become clear that Emma was far more useful to him in the role of friend than love interest, and all thoughts of attraction had been relegated from that moment onwards. It had been so long now that not noticing the way she looked was second nature.

But the gnawing feeling in his gut was there nonetheless. Their romantic relationship might have been counterfeit, but some element of it had obviously been real enough to make the dumping feel extremely uncomfortable.

He'd never been dumped before. *He* was the one who did the backing off. That was the way he played it. A couple of dinner dates somewhere nice, the second one generally ending up in his bed, a couple more dates and then, when the girl started to show signs of getting comfortable—maybe she'd start leaving belongings in his flat, or perhaps she'd suggest he meet her family—he'd simply go into backing-off mode. It wasn't as if he lied to them about his intentions. He was careful always to make it clear from the outset that he wasn't in the market for anything serious. He was in absolute control at all times—just as he was in every aspect of his life. That was the way he wanted it. The way he *needed* it.

He was amazed at how affronted he felt by the apparent ease with which Emma had dispensed with him. Not an ounce of concern for how *he* might feel as she'd planned to trounce him spectacularly in front of all those people. His irritation at her unbelievable fake break-up plan was surpassed only by his anger with himself for actually giving a damn.

Feeling low at being dumped meant you had feelings for the person dumping you. Didn't it?

Unease flared in his gut at that needling thought, because Dan Morgan didn't *do* deep feelings. That slippery slope led to dark places he had no intention of revisiting. He did fun, easy, no-strings flings. Feelings need not apply. Surely hurt feelings should only apply where a relationship was bona fide. Fake relationships should mean fake feelings, and fake feelings couldn't be hurt.

That sensation of spinning back in time made him feel faintly nauseous. Here it was again—like an irritating old acquaintance you think you've cut out of your life who then pops back up unexpectedly for a visit. That reeling loss of control he'd felt in the hideous few months after Maggie had left, walking away with apparent ease from the ruins of their relationship. He'd made sure he retained the upper hand in all dealings with women since. These days every situation worked for *him*. No emotion involved. No risk. His relationships were orchestrated by *him*, no one else. That way he could be sure of every outcome.

But not this time. Their agreement had lasted—what?—a year? And in that time she'd never once refused a date with him. Even when he'd needed an escort at the last minute she'd changed her schedule to accommodate him. He'd relied on her because he'd learned that he *could* rely on her.

And so he hadn't seen it coming. That was why it gnawed at him like this.

You don't like losing her. You thought you had her on your own terms. You took her for granted and now you don't like the feeling that she's calling the shots.

He gritted his teeth. This smacked a bit too much of the past for comfort. It resurrected old feelings that he had absolutely no desire to recall, and he apparently couldn't let it slide. What he needed to do now was get this thing back under his own control.

Well, she hadn't gone yet. And he didn't have to just *take* her decision. If this agreement was going to end it would be when *he* chose—not on some whim of hers. He could talk her round if he wanted to. It wouldn't be hard. And then *he* would decide where their partnership went.

If it went anywhere at all.

He pulled his chair back close to the desk and pressed a few buttons, bringing up his calendar for the next couple of weeks with a stab of exasperation. Had she no idea of the inconvenience she'd thrust upon him?

Not only had Emma dumped him, she'd really picked a great moment to do it. *Not.* The black tie charity dinner a week away hadn't crossed his mind the other evening when she had dropped her bombshell. It hadn't needed to. Since he'd met Emma planning for events like that had been a thing of the past. He simply called her up, sometimes at no more than a moment's notice, and he could count on the perfect companion on his arm—perfect respect for the dress code, perfect intelligent conversation, an all-round perfect professional impression. There was some serious networking to be had at such an event, the tickets had cost a fortune, and now he was dateless.

He reached for the phone.

It rang for so long that he was on the brink of hanging up when she answered.

'Hello?' Her slightly husky voice sounded breathless, as if she'd just finished laughing at something, and he could hear music and buzzing talk in the background, as if she were in a crowded bar or restaurant.

From nowhere three unheard-of things flashed through his mind in quick succession. Emma never socialised on a work night unless she was with him; she never let her phone ring for long when he called her, as if she was eager to talk to him; and in the time that he'd known her she had never sounded this bubblingly happy.

'What are you doing a week from Friday?' he said, cutting to the chase.

'Hang on.'

A brief pause on the end of the phone and the blaring music was muted a little. He imagined her leaving the bar or the restaurant she was in for a quiet spot, perhaps in the lobby. He sensed triumph already, knowing that she was leaving whoever she was with to make time to speak with *him*.

'Tying up loose ends at work, probably. And packing.'

So she was storming ahead with her plans, then.

The need for control spiked again in his gut. He went in with the big guns.

'I've got a charity ball in Mayfair. Black tie. Major league. Tickets like hen's teeth. It promises to be a fabulous night.'

He actually heard her sigh. With impatience, or with longing at the thought of attending the ball with him? He decided it was definitely the latter. She'd made no secret of the fact she enjoyed the wonderful opulence of nights like that, and he knew she'd networked a good few new clients for herself in the past while she was accompanying him—another perk of their plus-one agreement.

For Pete's sake, she had him giving it that ludicrous name now.

Their usual dates consisted of restaurant dinners with his clients. Pleasant, but hardly exciting. Except for Dan's own company, of course. Luxury events like this only came up occasionally. He waited for her to tear his arm off in her eagerness to accept.

'What part of "it's over" did you not understand, Dan?' she said. 'Did you not hear any of what I said the other night?'

It took a moment to process what she'd said because he had been so convinced of her acceptance.

'What I heard was some insane plan to desert your whole life as you know it for some guy you've known five minutes,' he heard himself say. 'You're talking about leaving your friends and family, walking out of a job you've worked your arse off for, all to follow some celebrity.'

'It would be a sabbatical from work,' she said. 'I'm not burning my bridges there. Not yet. And you make me sound like some crazy stalker. We're in a relationship. A proper grown-up one, not a five-minute fling.'

He didn't miss the obvious dig at his own love life, and it made his response more cutting than he intended.

'On the strength of—what was it?—*half a dozen dates?*' he said. 'I always thought you were one of the most grounded people I know. You're the last person in the world I'd have expected to be star-struck.'

He knew from the freezing silence on the end of the phone that he'd sunk his foot into his own mouth up to the ankle.

'How dare you?' she said, and a light tremble laced her voice, which was pure frost. 'It was obviously too much to hope that you might actually be *pleased* for me. Yes, Alistair is in the public eye, but that has *nothing* to do with why I've agreed to go away with him. Has it occurred to you that I might actually like him because he's interested in *me* for a change? As opposed to the grandchildren I might bear him or the fact I might be his carer when he's old and decrepit. Or...' she added pointedly '...the fact that I might boost his profile at some damned work dinner so he can extend his client list a bit further because he never quite feels he's rich or successful enough.'

She paused.

'You're saying no, then?' he said. 'To the all-expenses-paid top-notch Mayfair ball?'

He heard her draw in a huge breath and then she let it out in a rude, exasperated noise. He held the phone briefly away from his ear. When he put it back her voice was Arctic.

'Dan,' she was saying slowly, as if he had a problem understanding plain English, 'I'm saying no to the Mayfair ball. I'm through with posing as your professional romantic interest so you can impress your damned client list while you date airhead models for a week at a time.'

Had he really thought this would be easy? It occurred to him that in reality she couldn't be further from one of his usual conquests, of which currently there were two or three, any of whom would drop everything else at a moment's notice if he deigned to call them up and suggest getting together.

You didn't get as far up the legal career ladder as she had by being a 'yes' girl. But her easy refusal bothered the hell out of him. He'd expected her to agree to resurrect their agreement without even needing persuasion. Had expected her to thank him, in fact.

The need to win back control rose another notch with her unexpected refusal of his offer, and also her apparent indifference to it. It put his teeth on edge and gnawed at him deep inside.

'How about helping me out with this one last time, then?' he pressed, confident that in an evening he could quickly turn the situation around. Reinstate their agreement and then decide what he wanted to do with it. End it, change the terms—whatever happened it would be up to him to decide, *not* her.

'Dan, you don't need my help,' she said patiently. 'I'm in the middle of dinner and I haven't got time to discuss this now. It's not as if you're short of dates. Grab your little black book and pick one of your girlies from there. I'm sure any one of them would love to go with you.'

There was a soft click on the end of the phone as she hung up.

That went well. *Not*.

THREE

——

'Let me just recap. You're in a relationship with Alistair Woods—*the* Alistair Woods, the man who looks a dream in Lycra—and you're not planning on mentioning it to Mum and Dad?'

Adam's eyebrows practically disappeared into his sleek quiff hairstyle and Emma took a defensive sip of coffee. The fantasy she'd had of disappearing around the world on Alistair's arm and calling up her parents from Cannes/LA/somewhere else that screamed kudos, to tell them she would be featuring in next month's celebrity magazine, had turned out to be just that. A fantasy.

Because Adam was getting married.

Her big brother, Adam—who never failed to make her laugh, and who was so bright and sharp and funny that she'd never for a moment questioned her role in family life as the forgettable backing act to his flamboyant scene-stealer. Of *course* she had paled into insignificance in her family's eyes next to Adam—not to mention in the eyes of schoolteachers, friends, neighbours... But only in the way that everyone else had faded into the background next to him in her own eyes. He was simply someone who commanded success and attention without needing to put in any effort.

She couldn't exit her life without telling Adam, and she'd asked him to meet her for coffee to do exactly that. She'd even tried to sweeten the news by buying him an enormous cream bun, which now sat between them untouched. If she'd thought he'd simply scoff the bun and wave her off without so much as a question, she'd been deluded.

'You're not going yet, though, right? You're at least waiting until after the wedding?'

'Erm...'

He threw his arms up theatrically.

'Em! You can't be serious! How the hell am I going to keep Mum under control without you? I can't get married without my wingman!'

'Woman,' she corrected.

He flapped both hands at her madly.

'Whatever. You saw what Mum was like the other night. The wedding is in Ernie's home village. He's got a massive family, they're all fabulously supportive, and if you don't come along our family's big impression on them will be Mum telling everyone I'll get over it when I get bored with musical theatre and meet the right girl.'

'Dad will be there,' she ventured. 'Maybe you could

talk to him beforehand, get him to keep Mum on a short leash.'

'He'd be as much use as a chocolate teapot. We both know he's been beaten into submission over the years. Since when has Mum ever listened to him? She just talks over him. I *need* you there.'

His voice had taken on a pleading tone.

'It's not as simple as that. Alistair's covering another cycling race in a few weeks' time. We're meant to be having a break before it starts because it's pretty full-on. I'm flying out to the States, meeting some of his friends and family, relaxing for a couple of weeks. It's all been arranged.'

She looked down at her coffee cup because she couldn't bear the disappointment on Adam's face.

Adam had never made her feel insignificant. Any inability to measure up was her failing, not his. And she was the one who let it bother her.

'Then there's no problem! Bring Alistair to the wedding,' Adam said, clapping his hands together excitedly. 'You've already said he's got time off from work. The guy's probably got a private jet. You could zoom in and zoom out on the same day if you had to.' He made a soaring aeroplane motion in the air with his hand.

She suppressed a mirthless laugh.

'You mean introduce him to Mum and Dad? A whole new person for Mum to drive insane?' She narrowed suspicious eyes at him. 'It would certainly take the heat off you and Ernie.'

He held his hands up.

'You'll have to introduce him at some point anyway. OK, so you might travel with him for a while, maybe even settle in the States with him, but you'll have to come home to visit, won't you?'

She didn't answer. Visiting wasn't something she'd thought about much in her excitement about getting away. It hadn't crossed her mind that she'd be missed that much.

'Bloody hell, Em.'

She sighed. She couldn't say no to Adam any more than the rest of the world could. He just had that gift.

'It'll be a nightmare if I bring Alistair,' she said. 'Mum will be all over him like a rash, demanding marriage and grandchildren and mentioning my biological clock. He's a free spirit. He'll run a bloody mile.'

Adam was on the comment like a shot.

'Then you definitely *should* bring him. You're talking about leaving your whole life behind to be with him— don't you think he ought to prove himself a bit before you take that kind of plunge? If he's really the guy you think he is—if he's really going to put you first above everything else in his life—then he'll love you no matter what crazy relative you introduce him to, right?'

She couldn't help latching on to that thought—that desire for a level of regard where she would come absolutely first with someone for a change. Was that what this was really about? Was she afraid to bring Alistair to the wedding because of some stupid subconscious conviction that he might see through her? Might see that she really was a plain and inferior mousy girl, despite all the years she'd put in on breaking away from that persona?

'He does love me,' she insisted, mainly to bat away the prickle of unease that had begun in her stomach. It was all Adam's fault for questioning her perfectly laid plans.

'Great. Then put your man where your mouth is. Introduce him to Mum and watch him prove it.'

Dan clicked his phone off with ill-suppressed irritation.

Cancelling a working lunch at a moment's notice was extremely bad form. Focused to a pinpoint on work performance himself, he found it difficult to tolerate lateness or bad planning in others. Especially when it meant he'd interrupted his day to turn up at a restaurant when he could have eaten lunch on the run or at his desk.

He gave the menu an uninterested glance and was on the point of calling for the bill for the two drinks he'd ordered while waiting for the no-show client when he saw Emma cross the restaurant. A waiter showed her to a table by the window and she sat down alone, so engrossed in scrolling through her phone that she didn't even notice he was in the room.

The news that she was leaving seemed to have given him a new heightened perspective, and he picked up on tiny details about her that had simply passed him by before. He saw her objectively for once, as someone else might. Alistair Woods, for example. This time his gaze skimmed over her usual business dress when previously it would have stopped at observing the sharply cut grey suit. Instead he now noticed how slender she was. How had he never picked up before on the striking contrast of her double cream skin with her dark hair? The ripe fullness of her lower lip? When you had reason to look past the sensible work image she was unexpectedly cute. He'd been so busy taking her presence for granted he'd failed to notice any of those things.

Maybe this lunchtime wouldn't be a total waste of time after all. Dealing with her on the phone had been a bad choice. A face-to-face meeting might be a better approach to talking sense into her.

He picked up his drink and crossed the room towards her. His stomach gave a sudden flutter that made him pause briefly en route to the table—then he remembered that it was lunchtime. He was obviously just hungry, and since he was here maybe he should take the chance to grab a sandwich as well as a drink and a smoothing-over session with her. Not that his appetite had been up to much this last week or so.

'Dan!'

Her eyes widened in surprise as he slid into the seat opposite her and put his drink down on the table. She glanced quickly around the restaurant, presumably for a waiter.

'Really glad I bumped into you,' he said. 'Just wanted to say no hard feelings about the other night.'

A smile touched the corner of her lips, drawing his

eyes there. She was wearing a light pink lipstick that gave them a delectable soft sheen.

'The other night?' she said.

'The charity ball.'

'I hadn't realised there *could* be hard feelings,' she said, toying with her water glass. 'It was just a work arrangement we had after all, right? Not like I broke off a date, is it?'

She held his gaze steadily and for the first time it occurred to him that it might take a bit more than sweet-talking for him to regain the advantage between them. His own fault, of course. He was judging her by the standards of his usual dates, who seemed to fall over themselves to hang on his every word. Emma was a different ball game altogether. Taking her for granted had been a mistake.

He gestured to the waiter for a menu.

'How did it go, then?' she said.

'How did what go?' he evaded.

'The charity ball?' she said. 'No-expenses-spared Mayfair hotel, wasn't it? Who did you take?'

'Eloise,' he said shortly.

She had to bring it up, didn't she? When what he'd really like would be to erase the entire evening from history.

'Which one's that?'

She cranked her hand in a come-on gesture and looked at him expectantly until he elaborated.

'She's a leg model,' he said. 'You know—tights, stockings, that kind of thing.'

The woman had the best legs in the business. Unfortunately she was entirely defined by that one physical feature. Tact, sense and reliability didn't come into it.

'Did you make any new contacts?' Emma said. 'Normally charity bashes are great for networking, aren't they? Perfect opportunity for a shared goal, loads of rich businessmen?'

'Normally they are,' he said. 'But normally I have you with me, oozing tact and diplomacy and class.'

It had been kind of hard to hold a professional conversation with Eloise's arms wound constantly around his neck like a long-legged monkey. The one time he had begun to make headway with a potential client she'd returned from the bar with two flutes of pink champagne and positioned herself between them by sitting on his lap.

He watched Emma carefully, to see if his compliment had hit its mark, and was rewarded with the lightest of rosy blushes touching her high cheekbones. Hah! Not so easily dismissed after all. A proper in-depth talk about her whirlwind plans and he was confident he could sow a few seeds of doubt. From there it would be a short step to convincing her to stay put, reinstating their working agreement, getting things back to normal.

He was giving her a quick follow-up smile when he realised her eyes were actually focused somewhere over his shoulder and the blush had nothing to do with him. A wide smile lit up her face and suddenly she was on her feet, being drawn into a kiss by a tall blond man with a deep golden tan and perfect white teeth. No matter that he was wearing a sharply cut designer suit and an open-necked silk shirt instead of clinging Lycra cycling shorts and a helmet. He was instantly recognisable—by Dan and by the room at large.

Alistair Woods was on the premises.

The surrounding tables suddenly appeared to be filled with rubberneckers. Clearly basking in the attention, he offered a wave and a nod of greeting to the tables either side of them before sitting down—as if he was a film star instead of a has-been athlete. Dan felt an irrational lurch of dislike for the guy, whom he'd never met before but who clearly made Emma brim with happiness.

Jealous? his mind whispered.

He dismissed the thought out of hand. This wasn't about jealousy. Emma was clearly star-struck and on the brink of making a rash decision that could ruin her working life and her personal life before you could say *yellow jersey*. If anything, he would be doing her a favour by bringing her back down to earth.

'Alistair, this is Dan,' Emma said, taking her seat again, her hand entwined in Alistair's. 'Dan, this is Alistair Woods.'

She glanced pointedly at Dan.

'Dan happened to be here meeting someone,' she said. 'He just came over to say hello.'

She didn't want him to join them. It couldn't be clearer.

'Heard a lot about you, friend,' Alistair said in a

strong American accent, stretching in his seat. 'You're the platonic plus-one, right?'

Of all the qualities he possessed that Emma could choose to reference him by she'd chosen that. Just *great*.

'Did you get my phone message?' Emma asked Alistair eagerly. 'I know it means rejigging our plans a little, but I just can't let my brother down. It's his wedding day. And it'll be a good chance for you to meet my family.'

She was taking Alistair to Adam's civil partnership ceremony?

Dan felt a deep and lurching stab of misplaced envy at the thought of this guy slotting neatly into his recently vacated place—fake though it might have been—in regard to Emma's family. OK, so they were opinionated and mouthy, and in her mother's case that translated as being downright bigoted at times, but he'd never felt anything but welcomed by them, and their simple mad chaos had been something he'd enjoyed.

An unhappy flash of his own childhood rose in his mind. His mother, hardly more than a child herself. No father—at least not in any way that mattered to a kid. Plenty of 'uncles', though. He hadn't been short of those. And plenty of random babysitters—friends of his mother's, neighbours, hardly the same person twice. What he wouldn't have given for an interfering nosy mother at the age of thirteen, when babysitters had no longer been required and he'd been considered old enough to be left home alone.

He dismissed the thought. Things were different now. He'd learned to rely only on himself, without influence from anyone else. Maggie had been the one time he'd deviated from that course, and it had turned out to be an agonising mistake that he had no intention of repeating. He had no need for family. Past or future.

'Got your message, baby, but there's no way we're going to be able to make the gay wedding,' Alistair said.

Dan watched Emma's smile falter and suppressed an unexpected urge to grab Woods by the scruff of the neck.

'Why not?' she said. 'I can't miss Adam's wedding. I promised him.'

Dan recognised her tone as carefully neutral. She was upset and trying to cover it up. Did this Alistair know her well enough to pick up that little nuance? *Hardly.*

Emma took a sip of her coffee in an effort to hide her disappointment. Had she really thought it would be that simple? That he would just agree to her every whim?

'We're spending that weekend in the Hamptons,' Alistair was saying. 'I've been in talks to land a movie role and one of the producers is having a garden party. Can't miss it. Lots riding on it. I'm sure Arnold will understand. Career first, right?' He leaned in towards her with a winning expression and squeezed her hand. 'We agreed.'

His career first.

'Adam,' Emma corrected. She could hear the disappointment, cold and heavy, in her own voice. 'His name is Adam. And I really *can't* miss his wedding.'

Alistair sat back and released her hand, leaving it lying abandoned in the middle of the white tablecloth. His irritation was instant and palpable, and all the more of a shock because he'd never been anything but sweetness and light so far. But then, she hadn't demanded anything from him so far, had she? She'd been only too eager to go along for the ride. *His* ride.

'You do whatever you have to do, baby,' he said dismissively. 'You can fly out and join me afterwards.'

'But I really wanted you to be there, to meet my family.'

'Sorry, honey, no can do.'

Alistair turned to the waiter to order a drink. She noticed that Dan was looking at her with sympathy and she looked away. Everything was unravelling and it was a million times worse because he was here to witness it. She tried to muster up an attitude that might smother the churning disappointment in her stomach as her high hopes plummeted.

From the moment she'd met Alistair he had made her feel special, as if nothing was too much trouble for him. But it occurred to her that it had only related to peripheral things, like flowers and restaurants and which hotel they might stay in. Now it had come down to something that was truly important to her he hadn't delivered the goods. It wasn't even up for discussion. Because it clashed with his own plans.

Disappointment mingled hideously with exasperated disbelief. She felt like crashing her head down despairingly on the table. Would she ever, at any point in her life, meet someone who might actually put her first on their agenda? Or was this her lot? To make her way through life as some lower down priority?

'Look, I don't want to interfere,' Dan said suddenly, leaning forward. 'But how about I step in?'

'What do you mean, step in?' she asked, eyes narrowed.

Suspicion. Not a good sign, Dan thought. On the other hand Alistair was looking more than open to the suggestion.

Dispensing with Alistair to some swanky party on a different continent was far too good an opportunity to pass up. All he needed to do was step into Alistair's shoes as Emma's date and he'd have a whole weekend to make her rethink her actions and to get the situation working for him again.

'I got my invitation to the wedding this morning,' he said, thinking of the gaudy card that had arrived in the post, with *'Groom & Groom!'* plastered across the front in bright yellow, very much in keeping with Adam's usual in-your-face style.

'*You've* been invited?' she asked with obvious surprise, as if their interaction had been so fake that all the connections he'd made with her family were counterfeit, too. But he genuinely liked Adam—they'd always had a laugh.

'Yes,' he said. 'So if Alistair is away working I can fill in if you like—escort you. It's not as if I haven't done it before. What do you think?'

She stared at him.

'For old times' sake?' he pressed. 'I'm sure Alistair won't mind.'

He glanced at the ex-cyclist, who held his hands up.

'Great idea!' he said. 'Problem solved.'

Emma's face was inscrutable.

'That won't be necessary,' she snapped. 'And actually, Dan, if you don't mind, we could do with a bit of time to talk this over.'

She looked at him expectantly and when he didn't move raised impatient eyebrows and nodded her head imperceptibly towards the door.

All was no longer peachy with her and Mr Perfect and that meant opportunity. He should be ecstatic. All he needed to do was leave them be and let the idiot drive a wedge between them, because one thing he knew about Emma was that her parents might drive her up the pole but Adam meant the world to her. Yet his triumph was somehow diluted by a surge of protectiveness towards Emma at Alistair's easy dismissal of her. He had to force himself not to give the smug idiot a piece of his mind.

He made himself stand up and excused himself from the table.

Give the guy enough leeway and he would alienate Emma all by himself. Dan could call her up later in the role of concerned friend and reinstate their agreement on his own terms.

Bumped to make room for Alistair's career?

Her mind insisted on recycling Adam's comments from the day before. *'Don't you think he ought to prove himself before you take that kind of plunge?'* Was it really so much to ask?

The insistent 'case closed' way Alistair had refused her suggestion told her far more about him than just his words alone, and it occurred to her in a crushing blow of clarity. How had she ever thought she would come first with someone who had an ego the size of Alistair's? An ego which was still growing, by the sound of it, if he was trying to break into the movies.

The waiter brought their food and she watched as Alistair tucked in with gusto to an enormous steak and side salad, oblivious to the fact that there was anything wrong between them. He'd got his own way. For him it was business as usual. His whole attitude now irked her. It was as if she should be somehow grateful for being invited along for the ride. She'd been too busy being swept away by the excitement of someone like him actually taking an interest in her to comprehend that being with him would mean giving up her life in favour of his. Where the hell did she come first in all of that?

It dawned on her that he'd have a lot of contractual issues coming his way with his broadening career. Was that what made her attractive to him? The way she dealt so efficiently with legal red tape on his behalf? Had he earmarked her as his own live-in source of legal advice?

This wasn't a relationship; it was an *agreement*. All she'd done was swap one for another. She could be Dan's platonic plus-one or Alistair's live-in lawyer. Where the hell was the place for what *she* wanted in any of that?

'It's all off, Alistair,' she said dully. It felt as if her voice was coming from somewhere else.

He peered at her hardly touched plate of food.

'What is, honey? The fish?'

He looked around for a waiter while she marvelled at his self-assurance that her sentence couldn't possibly relate to their relationship. Not in *his* universe. Alistair probably had a queue of women desperate to date him, all of them a zillion times more attractive than Emma. He had international travel, a beach home in Malibu, a little getaway in the Balearics, his own restaurant and a glittering media career in his corner. What the hell did she have that could compete with that? Interfering parents and a tiny flat in Putney? Why the hell would he think she might want to back out?

'Us,' she said. 'You and me. It's not going to work out.'

He gaped at her.

'Is this because I won't come to your gay brother's

wedding? Honey, have you any idea how much is riding on this new contract? This is the next stage of my career we're talking about.' He shook his head at her in a gesture of amazement. 'The effort that's gone into lining up this meeting. I'm not cancelling that so you can show me off to your relatives at some small-town pink wedding. And it's not as if I'm stopping you going. That Neanderthal platonic pal of yours has said he'll step up to the plate.'

She was vaguely aware of people staring with interest from the surrounding tables. His slight about Dan irked her. Neanderthal? Hardly. He looked like an Adonis, and he was smart, sharp and funny. She clenched her teeth defensively on his behalf.

'I want *you* to come with me. I want you to meet my family.'

'And I will, honey. When the time's right.'

'It's a family wedding. Everyone who knows me will be in one place for the first time in years. When could the time possibly be more right than that?'

His face changed. Subtly but instantly. Like the turning of a switch. The easy, open look that had really taken her in when she'd first met him, the way he'd listened to her as if she mattered and showed her real, genuine interest, was gone. That look was now replaced by a sulky, petulant frown.

'Because it's all about *you,* of course,' he said. 'No regard for *my* career. You have to make these opportunities, Emma, and then follow them up. You don't mess people like this about, because there are no second chances. I can't believe you're being so selfish.'

For a moment the Emma she'd grown up to be actually questioned her own judgement on the strength of that last comment of his. The insecure Emma, whom she'd begun to push out of her life when she'd at last moved away from home and gone to university—a place where she had finally been accepted without reference to Adam or anyone else. With her own successes not watered down but recognised. After university she'd moved to London instead of going home to the West Country, in case that old, pessimistic Emma was somehow still there, lurking, ready to take over.

No way was she going back to *that* mindset now.

She pushed her plate to one side and leaned down to pick up her bag and take out her purse. She took enough money to cover her own meal and put it down on the table. She didn't throw it down. She wasn't going to resort to stupid tantrum gestures—she was a professional.

'I'm sorry, Alistair.' She shook her head at him. 'I don't know what I was thinking. I thought there would be more to us than being driven by your career. You want me to travel with you so I can iron out your legal issues, don't you? Maybe draw up the odd contract, or just hand out advice where you need it?'

He didn't say anything.

'Come on—be honest with me. Is that what this has really been about?'

A long pause.

'Well, you can't deny it's an advantage,' he said eventually. 'But only in the same way as if you were a hairdresser or a stylist.'

'I thought we were having a relationship. I didn't realise I was joining your entourage,' she snapped. 'I should never have let myself get swept away by this. Have a nice trip back to the States.'

She left the table and aimed her shaky feet at the exit, determined not to look back. When she did, inevitably, she saw that he was signing autographs for the people at an adjacent table. No attempt to follow her or talk her round. But why would he? He undoubtedly had a queue of people waiting to take her place.

She pressed her teeth hard together and concentrated on them to take her mind off the ache in her heart and the even worse heat of stupidity in her face.

She'd bigged up her relationship with him beyond all reason. How could she have been such a fool?

Now she had to face the climb down.

FOUR

—

Emma glanced around the half-empty office, grateful that her colleagues had finally drifted out for lunch. She'd informed HR first thing that her new, glamorous life as the jet-set girlfriend of Alistair 'White Lightning' Woods was no longer happening and the news had quickly filtered through the staff. At least she hadn't jacked her job in completely. That would have made things a whole lot worse. And it was best to get the humiliation over with, right?

Except that she wasn't sure how many more sympathetic stares she could take.

Her phone blared into life and she looked down at the display screen.

Dan. Again.

She pressed her hot forehead with the heel of one hand, as if it might help her think clearly. There'd been rather a lack of clear thinking around her lately.

What the hell had possessed her to let Alistair Woods sweep her off her feet? She was a sensible professional. She knew her own mind and she never took risks. Was she so bogged down in a stupid teen inferiority complex, in a lifetime of failed one-upmanship with Adam, that she'd momentarily lost all common sense? She'd built a life here in London, where she blended in. She'd excelled at not being noticeable and her professional life had flourished. And now, the one time she'd ventured out of that safe box, the same old outcome had happened. Her judgement had been rubbish, she hadn't measured up and it had all come crashing down around her ears. Why had she ever thought things would be different with Alistair?

Defensive heat rose in her cheeks even as she picked up the phone. By extreme bad luck Dan had been there in the restaurant to see that her romance with Alistair wasn't such a bed of roses after all. The thought of filling him in on all the details made a wave of nausea rise in her throat and her eyes water.

'Hello.' She shaped her voice into the most neutral tone she could muster.

'Hey.'

His voice was warm, deep and full of concern, and her heart gave a little flutter because as a rule Dan Morgan didn't do concern. He did sharply professional business demands, he did high expectations, he did arm's length.

'Just checking that you're OK.'

I blabbed to everyone who knows me in London that I was on the point of eloping with the most desirable man in sport. I've made the biggest fool of myself and now I have to tell everyone that, actually, he's an arse and it's not going ahead. So, yes, thanks, I'm just peachy.

Climbing down in front of Dan was somehow worst of all. And not just because she was embarrassed at her own poor judgement when she should have known better. There was a tiny part of her mind that was busy pointing out that for the first time ever Dan was showing interest and support for her beyond what she could do for him and his work. Had he suddenly realised he valued her as more than just a handy plus-one? How many missed calls from him had she had since lunchtime? Five? Wasn't that a bit excessive?

'Why wouldn't I be?' she said.

'Things just seemed a little tense at lunch yesterday.'

As if you could cut the atmosphere with a chainsaw.

'Did you get everything sorted with Alistair?'

A rush of bitterness pelted through her as she answered. 'Oh, yes. I *definitely* got everything sorted with him.'

'He's changed his plans, then? He's coming to the civil partnership?'

Oh, bloody hell, the civil partnership.

An unsettling wave of trepidation turned her stomach over. The biggest Burney family get-together in years and she no longer had a date. Could her crushed and battered ego survive a whole weekend of jibes from her mother about the race for grandchildren being hampered by her inability to keep a man?

'Not exactly,' she said.

'How do you mean?'

There was a sharp over-interested edge to his voice that she recognised from the many work dinners she'd accompanied him to. This was how he sounded when he was on the brink of nailing a new client—as if nothing could distract him from his goal. *Five missed calls and now he was hanging on her every word.*

Oh, hell.

She leaned forward over the desk in exasperation and pressed her hot forehead against its cold wooden surface.

'Alistair and I are off,' she blurted out. 'He's a total *arse.* He wouldn't even talk about making it to the wedding.'

'You broke up because he won't come to your brother's wedding?'

'Pretty much, yes,' she said.

She couldn't bring herself to tell him the truth—that Alistair had only treated her like a princess because he'd wanted a live-in lawyer. Her cheeks burned just at the thought of it.

'I couldn't let Adam down and he just couldn't see that. It made me realise that work will always come first for him.'

'Sorry to hear that.'

Was there a twist of cool I-told-you-so about his voice? She pulled her head from the desk and narrowed her eyes, trying to decide. He was probably glad it was all off. Wasn't that exactly what he'd wanted? For things to get back to normal? Then again, at least he wasn't saying it out loud.

She tightened her grip on the phone.

Wallowing in self-pity was one thing, but it didn't change the fact that in a week's time she had to keep her parents in check while surrounded by Ernie's family. Knowing Adam, it would be the most stuffed-with-people event of the year. She'd become so used to relying on Dan at family get-togethers that the prospect of coping with that by herself filled her with dread.

With her dreams in tatters there was a warm tug of temptation just to scuttle back to the way things had been. And wasn't that exactly what Dan had been angling for all along? Why not resurrect the old plus-one agreement? That nice, safe social buffer that had stood between her and humiliation until she'd stupidly given it up. Her reason for ending it was on its way back to the States right now. She'd dipped a toe in the murky waters of proper dating and it had turned into a train wreck.

She thought it through quickly. Dan was brilliant with her mother, never remotely fazed and the epitome of calm. Exactly what she needed to get her through that scary event. And maybe then she could begin to look forward, put Alistair behind her, make a fresh start.

'Actually, about the wedding...' she said.

* * *

'You want to reinstate the plus-one agreement?' He might as well give it its proper ludicrous name.

'Yes. I know it's a bit of a turnaround.'

Just a bit.

He couldn't quite believe his ears. So *now* she wanted him to step back in as her handy fake boyfriend, as if the last couple of weeks had never happened? What about her insane plan to dump him in public? And she hadn't done him the one-off favour of going with him to his Mayfair charity ball—oh, no. He'd had to spend the evening peeling Eloise off him. But *now* she needed *him* things were different.

And he wasn't about to make it easy for her.

'I thought having each other as a social backup was *holding us back?*' he said. 'Your words.'

A pause on the end of the phone, during which a hint of triumph coursed through him as he reclaimed the upper hand. He was back in control. How they proceeded from here would be *his* decision, not hers.

'I may have been a bit hasty.'

He didn't answer.

'Please, Dan. Ernie has a massive family and his father's a High Court Judge. Our family is me and my parents plus a few distant relatives that my mother's alienated over the years. I've promised Adam I'll keep my mum in check, and the thought of doing it on my own fills me with horror. *Please.* You're so good with them.'

She paused again, and when he didn't immediately leap in to agree, deployed the big guns of guilt.

'I thought this was what you wanted—everything back the way it was? I know I screwed up, and I'm sorry. But how many times have I helped *you* out at the last minute? What about that race meet where you landed your biggest client? You called me two hours before and I stepped in. Won't you even consider doing this one tiny event for me?'

He hesitated. She had a point about the race meet.

'Please, Dan. I want to make sure everything runs smoothly for Adam. You know how hard it is to please my mother.'

She'd lowered her voice now and a pang of sympathy twisted in his gut because he *did* know.

He could tell from her defeated tone that she thought he was going to refuse. This was his opportunity to bring things right back to where he wanted them. Their agreement had paid dividends—there was no denying that—but he'd let it run on far too long. He'd become complacent and let her become too important to drop easily. He couldn't have someone like that in his life, even if it *was* supposed to be under the heading of 'work'. She wanted a fake boyfriend for the wedding? He'd be the best fake boyfriend in the world. For old times' sake. And then he'd dump their agreement without looking back for a second.

'OK,' he said.

Emma took a deep breath as sweet relief flooded

her. It had absolutely nothing to do with the prospect of Dan's company of course. She was way past that. It was just the thought of having an ally in what was bound to be a social minefield.

'Really?' she said. 'I wasn't sure you'd agree after I said no to your charity thing. Thank you *so* much. And you know I'm happy to step in next time you need someone—'

'Please let me finish,' he cut in. 'I'll do it. But this is the last time. I'll stand in for you in acknowledgement of all the times you've stepped in for me at the last minute. But when we head back to London after the wedding, that's it. Our agreement is over. I'll manage my own socialising going forward, and you can carry on as before.'

Emma took a sharp breath, because for some reason that hurt in a way that the Alistair debacle hadn't. He didn't sound inclined even to retain a friendship between them. They would revert to being Mr Morgan and Ms Burney, businessman and lawyer, nothing more. Had she really meant so little to him?

It was a stupid, stupid pang of disappointment because she'd already *dealt* with the idea that nothing would ever happen between her and Dan. Her ridiculous crush on him was a thing of the past. She'd been planning to travel the world with Alistair, for Pete's sake, never looking back.

It had somehow been much easier to deal with when *she'd* been the one making that choice.

* * *

Emma glanced around the lobby of the Cotswolds hotel that Adam and Ernie had chosen as their wedding venue, surprised at the stunning old-world charm of the place. Huge vases of spring flowers softened the dark wood panelling of the walls. Beautifully upholstered chairs and sofas stood in cosy groupings around the fireplace, which was taller than she was.

She would have expected Adam to want to make his vows somewhere screamingly modern in the midst of the buzz of London. Apparently Ernie's family were a lot more old-school than that. They'd lived here in this honey-coloured stone village for generations. She felt a stab of envy at the give and take in her brother's relationship. It seemed *Adam* didn't have a problem putting his partner's family first.

On the other hand it might have been less nerve-racking if the wedding *was* taking place on home ground. Here they would be surrounded by Ernie's nearest and dearest, all eagerly awaiting the impression the Burney family would make. Her stomach gave a churn of unease at the thought.

'What name is it?'

The blonde receptionist ran a manicured fingernail down her computer screen.

'Burney,' Emma said. 'I'm part of the Burney-Harford wedding party.'

Adam had made a block reservation.

Dan strode through the door, fresh from parking the car. He rested one hand on the desk and ran the other through his dark hair, spiking it more than ever. His blue eyes crinkled as he smiled his gorgeous lop-sided smile—the one that had melted half the female hearts in London.

The manicured fingernail came to an instant stand-still and the receptionist's jaw practically fell open as she gazed at him.

'Mr and Mrs Burney?' she asked.

Emma sighed.

'No, that would be my parents.' Mercifully they weren't here yet. 'It will be under Miss.'

The girl handed over keys—proper old-fashioned ones—and a wad of check-in paperwork.

Emma gave Dan an expectant look.

He smiled at her.

'Great venue.'

'What about you?' she said.

'What *about* me?'

'Your booking,' she whispered.

In her peripheral vision she picked up the inter-ested change in the receptionist's posture. She'd seen it a hundred times before. She took in her appearance. Blonde hair—*check*. Sleekly made-up face—*check*. Eager smile—*check*. She knew exactly what would come next.

She waited for Dan to confirm loudly that he had a separate booking—ergo, he was free and single, and in possession of a hotel room and a shedload of charm. Instead he held her own gaze steadily, as if his radar no longer picked up pretty blondes. Not a hint of a flirt or smoulder. Not so much as a glance in the girl's direction.

'Didn't make one,' he said cheerfully.

Emma stared at him incredulously for a moment, before realising that the receptionist was watching them with an interest that was way beyond polite. She walked away into the corner and when he didn't immediately follow gave him an impatient come-on beckoning gesture. He sauntered over. The receptionist made a poor attempt not to watch the laconic grace of his movements.

'What do you mean, you didn't make a booking? You had your invitation—where did you think you were going to sleep? On the lawn?'

He shrugged. 'I never got round to booking a room and then, when you asked me to step in as your date, I didn't need to. I'll be staying in your room, won't I?' He put an arm around her shoulders and gave her a squeeze. 'All part of the façade, right?'

She was rendered momentarily speechless by a wave of spicy aftershave and the sudden closeness of him, and then his assumption about their sleeping arrangements slammed into her brain.

'You can't stay in *my* room,' she squeaked.

'The whole weekend takes place at this hotel. It's hardly going to give a loved-up impression if we sneak off to separate rooms at the end of the night, is it?'

'In the Burney family we'd fit right in,' she said, thinking of her parents, who'd had separate bedrooms since she was in her late teens.

He ignored her and turned his head sideways to read the number on the key fob in her hand.

'Eighteen,' he said, heading for the stairs. 'First floor.'

She stumbled after him, her mind reeling. The thought of their sleeping arrangements hadn't entered her head. This was the first time they'd faked their relationship for longer than a couple of hours. She'd simply *assumed* he would have a separate booking.

An image of her vanity case full of embarrassing toiletries danced through her mind, swiftly followed by the fact that her hair looked like a fright wig when she woke up. She gave herself a fast mental slap, because she absolutely did *not* care whether she looked attractive or not, and any attempt to make herself look good was *not* for the benefit of Dan Morgan.

She made a grab for his arm and he turned round on the landing and looked at her, an expression of amusement on his face.

'I don't see what the problem is,' he said. 'This is a professional arrangement, right? We'll treat it as such. Or were you thinking that I might take advantage of the situation and jump your bones?'

His ice-blue eyes crinkled at the corners as he grinned at her and a flare of heat crept upwards from her neck.

'What am I supposed to think?' she snapped defensively. 'I know what you're like with your five-minute flings. So don't be getting the wrong idea. I am most definitely *not* interested in any shallow no-strings fling. If I'd wanted that I would have stuck with Alistair.'

'I wouldn't *dream* of suggesting one,' he said, holding his hands up. 'The thought never even occurred to me. You're perfectly safe with me.'

Her face burned hotter than ever, because if that wasn't a knock-back she didn't know what was. He was basically telling her she was arrogant for assuming he would *want* to hit on her. Of course he wouldn't. He'd had a year's worth of chances and he'd passed them all up. Her toes curled and she turned away, because her face undoubtedly looked like a tomato right now.

'Look, it's no big deal,' he said. 'We can just shelve the idea. I'll head back to London and you can go it alone.'

A sudden bolt of dread made her stomach lurch as a familiar bugling voice drifted through from Reception.

'Booking for Burney. It'll be one of the higher-end suites—parents of the groom.' A pause. 'The *real* groom, that is...'

Her parents were on the premises and her mother was obviously on her usual form. Poor Adam. He was relying on her.

She glanced back at Dan. He spread his hands questioningly.

'Your call. Do you need a plus-one or not?'

'This is gorgeous, isn't it?' She sighed as she turned the huge key in the lock and walked ahead of him through the door.

Their cases and bags stood waiting for them at one side of the room, efficiently delivered by the porter. It was everything that a country house hotel bedroom should be. The floorboards were suitably creaky, the dark wood panelling of the walls gleamed, the bed had four posts draped with a soft voile fabric, and there was a pile of squashy pillows and a floral bedspread that matched the silk curtains. Behind a door to one side was a luxurious *en-suite* bathroom.

Dan had to bend slightly to avoid smacking his forehead on the doorjamb. He followed her into the room. She hovered awkwardly by the window, clearly still on edge at the whole room-sharing thing.

'Very nice,' he said and, unable to resist the tease, added, 'Nice, large bed.'

He found his gaze drawn to her face as she dropped her eyes and saw faint colour touch her pale cheekbones. Her obvious awkwardness was seriously cute. His usual dates were pretty full-on—a fast track to the physical. Shyness didn't come into it. It was an odd novelty to be sharing a bedroom with someone without bed actually being on the agenda.

He took pity on her and held his hands up.

'You don't need to worry. I'll take the couch.'

There was a squashy sofa to one side of the window, upholstered in a lavender floral fabric. It would be too short for him, but for a couple of nights it would do.

'We can take it in turns,' she said. 'You take the couch tonight. I'll take it tomorrow.'

Momentarily surprised at the counter-offer, he nodded. Not that he would let her.

'Deal.'

She clapped her hands together and took a businesslike breath, as if she were about to start a work meeting.

'Right, then, let's get organised, shall we? This can be my space...' she moved one of the smaller pieces of her vast luggage collection onto a dark wood bureau with an ornate mirror '...and this can be yours.' She waved a hand at the antique desk. 'You get the desk and complimentary Wi-Fi. Should be right up your street. I can't imagine you needing much else.'

'You make me sound like some workaholic.'

'I hate to break it to you...' she said, nodding at his minimal luggage, which included a laptop bag. 'It's hardly a get-away-from-it-all minibreak, is it? You've brought your office with you!'

'Only out of habit,' he protested. 'I take the laptop everywhere. Doesn't mean I'm going to use it.'

She turned back to him and pulled a sceptical face. He held his hands up.

'And somewhere in here...' she shuffled through the wad of check-in bumph '...is the itinerary for the weekend. Might as well know what we're up against. Blimey, we'll hardly have time to draw breath.'

He took it from her—a piece of stiff white card decorated in eye-watering yellow. He was suddenly very aware as he looked at the packed agenda that he would be joined at the hip with her pretty much twenty-four-seven for the next couple of days—a situation he hadn't really considered properly when he'd made light of the room-sharing thing.

It all seemed a bit less amusing now they were actually in the room and she was talking him through their shared personal space and unpacking what seemed like endless belongings. He avoided guests at his flat as much as possible. One night was his limit, with sex the sole item on the agenda. Conversation and space-sharing didn't come into it. He simply didn't *do* the give and take required to cohabit. Not any more. He'd done it once and he had no inclination to be reminded of the lash-up he'd made of it.

Just a weekend. He latched on to that thought.

'Certainly not doing a small quickie wedding, are they?' he commented, speed-reading the itinerary.

Emma leaned in close to look at the card with him and he picked up a soft, sweet wave of the scent she always wore as she tucked a stray lock of hair behind her ear. His pulse stepped up a notch in response.

He wasn't used to her looking dressed down like this. That was all it was. Their usual encounters involved smart, polished business dress or the occasional evening gown for gala dinners and the like. Even then her outfits were always reserved, and he couldn't remember a time when he'd seen her in jeans or when she'd worn her hair down. Now it fell softly to her shoulders in waves, framing her heart-shaped face. When you took the time to look behind her uptight attitude, she was actually very pretty.

'When has Adam ever done anything on a small scale?' she said. 'It just wouldn't be him, would it?'

He refocused his attention on the itinerary.

'So, this evening there's welcome drinks on the terrace. Then tomorrow the wedding is here in the grounds, followed by a night of celebration. And then a slap-up cooked breakfast the morning after. That marquee must be for the wedding.' He nodded out of the window.

She followed his gaze, then moved away and sat down on the edge of the bed.

'Adam must be mad,' she said. She bounced up and down on the mattress approvingly.

Dan leaned against one of the posts at the foot of the bed, watching her. Diaphanous fabric softly draped over it—white with a tiny pale yellow flower print.

'Why? Because his wedding's the size of an elephant or just because there *is* a wedding?' he said.

She looked up at him, a tiny smile touching the corner of her lush mouth, and he had a sudden image of himself leaning her slowly back onto the floral quilt and finding out what she tasted like.

He stood up straight and gave himself a mental shake. What the hell was he thinking? This was a last-ditch platonic date—not one of his conquests. The fact that the venue involved a bedroom instead of a boardroom didn't change the fact that their relationship was work-based. It also didn't seem to stop the slow burn that had kicked in low in his abdomen.

'Both,' she said, and shrugged.

'Is that because of Alistair? I mean, you've got to admit he was a bit of a curveball. You *never* date. Not in all the time I've known you. And then suddenly in the space of a few weeks you're packing up and leaving.'

She didn't answer for a moment. There was a distant expression on her face, as if she was thinking it over.

'Partly because of Alistair,' she said at last. 'But really what happened with him was probably inevitable. Meeting the right person isn't something I've excelled at so far. He was so attentive and considerate that I thought for once I'd really cracked it. I really believed it was something special. But it was the same old story.'

She smiled at him, an I-don't-care smile that was just a bit too small to be convincing, and he felt a sudden spike of dislike for Alistair.

'Same old story?'

She sighed. 'Maybe you had a point when you said I was a bit star-struck—I don't know,' she said, picking at a loose thread on the floral quilt.

There was an air of defeat about her that made him want to kick Alistair's butt.

'I got a bit swept up in all the excitement of it. It wasn't so much him as the idea of *life* with him. It was exciting. It was glamorous. It was everything that I'm not.'

'It was two-dimensional Hollywood claptrap. Who wants to live in a shallow world like that? You can't be the first person to get sucked in, but you're the most grounded person I know. You'll soon get over that card-board idiot.'

That made her smile, lighting her face. He liked her looking happy like that. He liked that he'd *caused* her to look like that.

'I won't be making the same mistake again,' she said. 'I'm going to put *myself* first from now on. But even if one day I do find the right person I won't be getting married with my parents in tow. *No way.* Nice plane trip to a beach somewhere with a couple of ran-dom witnesses.'

He grinned.

'What about you?' she said, wiping the smile right off his face.

'What *about* me?'

'Come on—surprise me. What kind of wedding would you have if you could choose?' She leaned back on her palms and narrowed her eyes at him. 'Some beach thing in the Maldives?' She flapped a hand. 'No, no, let me guess... It would be something small. You could probably do it in a lunch hour if you wanted to—take an hour or so out and nip to the registry office. Quick glass of champagne, handful of confetti, and then you could get back to work.'

'Very funny.'

Terrific. He should have seen that coming. The last thing he needed right now was a chat about marriage aspirations. He just wanted to get through this week-end and get on with his life. And he didn't even have his own hotel room to retreat to.

He moved away from the bed to look out of the window, his back to her.

'Of course you'd have to stick at a relationship for longer than a month, then, wouldn't you?' she teased.

He didn't look round. 'It has nothing to do with sticking at a relationship. I have to prioritise. The business is growing at a massive rate. I need to put all my energy into that.'

'Nobody needs to work twenty-four-seven,' she said. 'Not even you. Maybe you should think about slowing down, or at least taking a breather. I just don't get why you're so crazy for work. I've never known anyone so obsessed. And it's not like you've got anyone to share the rewards with. None of your girls last five minutes.'

He stared across the hotel lawn at the dense woodland right in the distance on the skyline. Stared at it but didn't see it.

Another image flashed through his mind in its place. *Sticking at relationships. Sharing the rewards. Maggie.* Dark-haired Maggie with her gentle smile and her kindness.

Maggie and—

He stamped hard and fast on that thought before it could multiply. What the hell was his stupid brain doing, dragging that old stuff up?

At the faint sound of voices and car doors slamming he glanced down onto the gravel drive as Adam emerged, beaming, from a yellow Rolls-Royce, quiff cemented in place, wearing dark glasses like a celebrity. Ernie was right by his side. A gang of porters staggered under a stack of luggage. Obviously overpacking ran in the family.

'Your brother's here,' he said, to distract her, because he couldn't imagine a time when he'd be keen to discuss his future wedding plans.

Emma scrambled off the bed and joined Dan at the window.

'We'd better get ready for the drinks party,' she said, turning to her heap of luggage and proceeding to unzip.

He checked his watch.

'But it's *hours* away.'

As if that mattered...

'I need to make a good impression,' she said. 'I hate being late. And you have to help me keep my parents in check.'

She looked up at him, suddenly feeling awkward, with a bottle of pink shower gel in one hand and a loofah in the other.

'Do you want to use the bathroom first? I mean, perhaps we should work out some kind of rota.'

'For Pete's sake, we don't need a rota,' he said, his tone exasperated. 'It's two days. You take the bathroom first. You're bound to take longer.'

'What's that supposed to mean?' She made an indignant face. 'That you look great just the way you are but I'm some hag who needs work?'

He laughed out loud.

'No. It means I've never met a woman who takes less than half an hour to get ready.'

She turned towards the bathroom, her arms now full of toiletries.

'And you don't look like a hag,' he called after her. 'You never have.'

It was the nearest thing to a compliment he'd ever given her.

FIVE

—

Dan gazed out of the open hotel room window and listened to the soft sound of falling water from the shower in the *en-suite* bathroom. It had kicked in five minutes after Emma had shut the door firmly and twisted the lock, as if she thought he might burst in on her.

The marquee was now bathed in early-evening golden sunshine. The sweeping lawns were perfectly manicured, and a lily pond lay on the far right of his view. If he leaned forward far enough he could see an ornate wrought-iron bench set to one side of it. He wondered how many brides' backsides had been plonked there over the years. It really was the perfect photo opportunity.

He was at the cream of wedding venues in the south of England and it was only natural that it might whip up a few passing thoughts of his one and only brush with marriage, right? Just fleeting thoughts... That was all.

Maggie and Blob.

The name filtered back into his mind before he could stop it.

Blob, he had called him—or her—after the fuzzy early scan which had been completely unintelligible to both of them except for the blob with the strong and speedy heartbeat. It had made Maggie laugh. An interim holding name while they bandied about proper full-on names. Andy or Emily. Sam or Molly. To delete as appropriate once they knew the gender, at a later date that had never arrived.

Four months hadn't been later enough.

Maggie and Blob.

An unexpected twist of long-suppressed dull pain flared in his chest—the blunt ache of an old injury. He wrenched his mind away forcibly. For Pete's sake, what was he *doing*? He did *not* need a pointless trip down memory lane right now.

He rationalised madly. He hadn't been near a wedding in donkey's years. Without a family to speak of, things like weddings didn't crop up all that often, and this place was Wedding Central. It was bound to stir things up. But that was all this was—just a momentary blip. He had dealt with Maggie and Blob. They were part of the past and he'd left them there with admirable efficiency. He'd dealt with it all and moved on.

Perhaps that was part of the problem. His life was drifting into predictability, leaving his mind free to wander where it shouldn't be going. He needed to up the stakes at work—perhaps a new business venture. Work had always been the solution before.

The shower splashed on and on, and judging by the enormous bag of toiletries Emma had heaved in there with her she wasn't going to be emerging any time soon. There was no time like the present when it came to refocusing your mind. He unzipped his laptop bag and sat down at the antique desk.

Emma gave her reflection one last glance in the steamy-edged mirror and paused to let her heart reconsider its decision to take a sprint. She knew she'd spent far too long rubbing in scented body lotion and blitzing body hair, telling herself it was because she wanted to make a good impression on Ernie's family. For Adam. It had absolutely nothing to do with the fact that Dan was on the other side of that door. He was fully rationalised. Whatever there was between them, it would always have terms. It would always be about work.

But he could easily have refused to accompany her here. I mean, really, what was in it for him? She knew she'd annoyed him with the public break-up thing, but he had no real understanding of how things were with her parents—how the pursuit of an easy life had become the norm for her. It was her defence mechanism against the endless nagging, and that was what Dan had been. Her route to an easy life. Shame it had all been fictional.

But still he was here.

And now there was that tiny nagging voice, whispering that he might just have come to his senses since she'd broken the news that she was leaving. He might have suddenly realised she meant more to him than a handy work date. Could that be why he now *wanted* the arrangement to end, despite his reluctance to let it go at first? Perhaps this weekend could lead to something more than a platonic agreement between them.

It was a *stupid* nagging voice. To listen to it, or even worse to act on it, would be to set herself up for humiliation. Was the Alistair debacle not enough evidence that she had warped judgement when it came to decoding male behaviour?

The twisty lurch of disappointment in her stomach when she opened the bathroom door told her she'd been stupid to read anything into his presence here.

He was still wearing the same jeans and T-shirt, he'd clearly made zero effort to unpack his minimal luggage, and worst of all he was leaning into his laptop where it stood open on the desk, surrounded by the usual scattering of work papers.

Had she actually thought for a moment that his presence here might have anything to do with an increased regard for her? What a fool she was. Nothing had changed between them at all. She was imagining the whole damn thing just because he'd shown her some support. Clearly she was desperate for attention now Alistair had humiliated her.

At best, Dan wanted to part on good terms—*that* was why he'd decided to accompany her to the wedding and help her out this last time. There was nothing more to it than that.

Undoubtedly the fact that the hotel had complimentary Wi-Fi had made the decision a whole lot easier for him.

Dan stared at her as she stood in the doorway, the deliciously sensual scent of her body lotion mingling with steam, epically failing to register the look of resigned disapproval on her face because of her transformation from office starch.

Her dark hair fell in damp tendrils, framing her heart-shaped face, and there was a pink hue to her usually pale skin. She was totally swamped by one of the enormous white his 'n' hers hotel bathrobes, and his mind immediately insisted on debating what she might or might not be wearing underneath.

He stared hard at the e-mail on his computer screen until his eyes watered, in the hope that his stupid body would realise that they might be sharing a bedroom and a bathroom but their interaction was limited to the professional—just the way it always was. For the third time he read it without taking a single word in.

'You're working,' she said with ill-hidden disappointment. 'Don't you ever take a break?'

He felt a surge of exasperation.

'What else was I meant to do? Take a stroll round the grounds? Sit and watch the bathroom door? It's just a couple of e-mails while I waited for you to be finished.'

'Well, there's no need to snap,' she said, crossing the room to the bureau and squeezing a handful of her hair with the corner of a towel. 'You could have gone first if you'd wanted to.'

Oh, for Pete's sake! He hadn't counted on the inconvenient need to be constantly polite that their space-sharing had caused. Without the shared goal of sleeping together it boiled down to a *you-go-first-no-you-I-insist* awkwardness about using the facilities.

With a monumental effort he curbed his irritation.

'I'm sorry,' he said. 'I'm just not really used to sharing my personal space, that's all. I'm used to doing what I like whenever I want to.'

She glanced at him and smiled.

'That's OK.'

She began combing her long hair out, looking at her reflection in the mirror.

'You have a different girlfriend every week,' she said. 'I'd have thought bedroom etiquette was your speciality.'

He watched as she sprayed perfume on her neck and pulse points. The intense scent of it made his senses reel.

'That's different.'

'I don't see how.'

He shrugged.

'There's no give and take needed. They stay over and the next morning they leave. There's no personal belongings cluttering up every surface.' He glanced at the bed, currently festooned with her clothes. 'There's no pussyfooting around each other over who's hogging the bathroom. It's done and dusted, with minimal disruption.'

And minimal emotional input. Which was exactly how he liked it.

'You make it sound *so* romantic,' she said sarcastically, dipping her finger in a pot of pink make-up and dabbing it gently over her mouth.

His eyes seemed to be glued to the tiny movements and to the delicious pink sheen it gave her luscious lower lip. She didn't notice, focusing on what she was doing in the mirror.

'It isn't *meant* to be romantic,' he said. 'It is what it is.'

A temporary and very enjoyable diversion, with no lasting repercussions.

'So it's fine for them to stay over until you get what you want, and then they're ejected from the premises at breakfast time? Is that it?'

'You make it sound callous,' he said, snapping his laptop shut and gathering up his work papers. 'When actually it's fun.' She threw him a sceptical glance and he couldn't resist adding, 'Hot, steamy, no-holds-barred fun,' just to see if he could make her blush again.

'You have no scruples,' she complained.

He saw the flush of pink creep softly along her cheekbones, highlighting them prettily. Sparring with her was actually turning out to be enjoyable.

'I don't need scruples,' he said. 'We're all adults. I

never make any promises that I don't keep. I'm honest with them about not wanting anything serious and they appreciate that.'

'No, they don't,' she said. 'They might say they're fine with it, but in reality they're hoping it will turn into more. It's not the same for women. Sleeping with someone isn't some throwaway thing. It's a big deal—an emotional investment. And, anyway, if you always put those limits in place when you meet someone you're cutting out the chance of ever having a proper relationship. You could meet the perfect person for you and she'd just slip through your fingers unnoticed.' She fluttered her fingers in the air to press her point. 'You'd never even know. You'll be perpetually single.'

'And that,' he said, grabbing his bag and making for the bathroom, 'is exactly the point.'

He smiled at the roll of her eyes as he closed the door.

Emma didn't usually go in for a second coat of mascara. Or a second squirt of perfume just to make sure it lasted the distance. But then she didn't usually go in for room-sharing. She wished someone would tell her stupid pulse rate that it was supposed to be platonic.

He had the speediest bathroom habits she'd ever come across, and as a result she was still balancing on one leg, one foot in her knickers and the other out, when the lock clicked and the bathroom door opened. Heart thundering, she thanked her lucky stars that she'd decided to keep the bathrobe on while dressing, and covered her fluster by whipping her panties on at breakneck speed, clamping the robe around her and then giving him a manic grin that probably bordered on cheesy.

Her entire consciousness immediately zeroed in on the fact that he had a fluffy white towel wrapped around his muscular hips and absolutely nothing else. The faint hint of a tan highlighted his broad chest and the most defined set of abs she'd ever seen outside a magazine. He rubbed a second towel over his hair, spiking it even beyond the usual.

She forced her eyes away, snatched the bathrobe more tightly around her and crossed to the bed.

'I think we should have a quick round-up of the ground rules for tonight,' she said, flipping through some of the clothes laid out on the bed, not really seeing them, just aiming to look busy.

'Did you just say "ground rules"?'

She glanced up and had to consciously drag her eyes upwards from his drum-tight torso. His amused grin told her that unfortunately he'd clocked her doing it, so she pressed the platonic angle hard to show him that they might be sharing a hotel room but she had no romantic interest in him whatsoever. None. Zilch.

'I did. We need to pull off being the perfect couple.'

He let out an amused breath. 'I think you can count on *me* to know how to do that,' he said.

She silently marvelled. He obviously thought a few posh dinners and hot sex was all it took.

'This is a whole different ball game. When you've

been my date before it's mostly been an hour or two alone with my family in a restaurant. A trained chimp could probably pull that off. This is going to be a lot more full-on. The place is going to be stuffed with Ernie's family. We need to make a good impression for Adam. We have to look totally together but in an *über*-normal way, so we can counteract my parents' dysfunctional relationship.'

He looked briefly skyward. One hand rested on the desk; the other was caught in his hair. By sheer will she didn't look at the towel, held up only by a single fold. Instead she fixed her eyes on his face.

'You're over-analysing,' he said. 'Trust me on this.'

He pulled a few items from his bag and headed back to the bathroom with them slung over his arm.

'I know how to pull off loved-up,' he called over his shoulder, with not a hint of trepidation at the evening ahead when *she* was a bag of nerves. 'Just like you know how to pull off professional couple. Just leave it to me.'

A couple of hours' work had certainly done the trick in terms of refocusing him. He'd fired off a ton of important e-mails, had a look through some figures, and if he needed any more of a distraction to stop his mind dredging up the past, looking at Emma as he emerged from the bathroom again was it.

Fully dressed now, she was wearing her hair long again, this time brushed to one side, so it lay gleaming over one shoulder of the soft green maxi-dress she wore. Her newly applied perfume made his pulse jump and she wore more make-up than usual, high-lighting her wide brown eyes and the delectable soft-ness of her lips.

Playing the part of boyfriend to *that* for the evening was hardly going to be a chore.

He could tell she was nervous just by the way she was behaving. Give her a room full of professionals and she could network her way around it with the best of them, holding her own no matter who he introduced her to. But with the prospect of a weekend with her own family she was reduced to a quivering shadow of her work self.

That very jumpiness seemed to heighten his aware-ness of her on some level, and it felt perfectly natural for him to lean in close to her on the way down the passage towards the stairs. He rested his hand lightly around her waist, conscious of her slenderness beneath the light flowing drape of her dress.

Emma was hotly aware of him next to her as he es-corted her along the landing. As his arm curled around her waist she picked up the spicy scent of his after-shave on warm skin and her stomach gave a slow and far too delicious flip. Everything about him seemed to be overstepping the lines of her personal space in a way it never had before. The way he stood just a frac-tion closer to her than strictly necessary... The way he'd held her gaze a beat too long when he'd teased her about wanting ground rules.

'Er...there's no one actually here to see us,' she

pointed out, glancing down at his hand, now resting softly on her hip. She looked up at him questioningly.

'Just getting into character,' he said easily, not moving his hand.

'I'm determined to inject a bit of tradition if it kills me, Donald,' she heard suddenly.

Her mother's distinctive tones drifted down the corridor from behind them and she froze next to Dan. And then they were getting louder.

'I think I'll have a word with Ernie's parents about top tables and speeches. It's a family occasion. They'll be expecting us to have some input.'

Emma's heart began to sink at the thought of her mother instigating a cosy chat about traditional wedding roles with Ernie's clearly far more liberal parents and she stopped at the top of the stairs, intending to intercept her and suggest a new approach of just enjoying the celebrations without actually *criticising* any of them.

The coherence of that thought dissolved into nothing as Dan suddenly curled his hand tighter around her waist and propelled her back against the nearest wall. Before she could so much as let out a squeak, he kissed her.

SIX

—

Nigh on eight months of condition-
ing herself that her attraction to him was just a stupid crush, and all it took to get every nerve-ending of
attraction right back in action was one kiss. One kiss
that made her toes curl and her stomach feel as if it
might have turned into warm marshmallow.

He caught her lower lip perfectly between his own
lips and sucked gently on it, his hand sliding lower to
cup the curve of her bottom. The smooth wood panelling of the wall pressed against her back. She could
feel every hard, muscular contour of his body against
hers, and sparks danced down her spine and pooled
deliciously between her legs.

Her eyes fluttered dreamily shut—and when she
opened them she was staring right into the disapproving gaze of her mother, a vision in purple sequins, a
few feet away over Dan's shoulder.

Reality clattered over her like a bucket of ice cubes
and she wriggled away from him, the flat of her hand

against the hardness of his chest, her heart racing. He made no effort to disengage whatsoever, so she added an extra pace's worth of space between them herself.

He was watching her steadily, the petrol-blue shirt he was wearing making his eyes seem darker than usual, a grin playing about his lips. Her heart raced as if she'd just sprinted up and down the creaky stairs a few dozen times.

She tore her gaze away from his.

'Mum!' she gabbled.

'Hello, darling.' Her father leaned in to give her a kiss and shook Dan's hand.

Her mother glanced at him disapprovingly.

'Really, Emma,' she remarked. 'A little class would be good. *Anyone* could walk along this corridor and how do you think it would look to find you two in a clinch?' She radiated criticism, despite the fact that she was intending to steam in and openly re-evaluate the wedding plans. When it came to social etiquette she could be remarkably selective. 'You're not sixteen, you know. A little decorum would be good. Thank goodness Adam can rely on your father and me to make a good impression.'

She swept past them down the stairs.

Emma stared after her incredulously and then rounded on Dan.

'What the hell was that about?' she snapped. 'What did you think you were *doing*?'

'We've got an image to keep up,' he said, shrugging as if he'd done nothing wrong.

So he'd just been playing a part, while her knees had turned to jelly. There had been a moment back there when she'd thought she might simply fold into a hot puddle on the floor.

But he didn't need to know that, did he?

'I don't think we need to take things quite *that* far,' she said, trying to breathe normally.

'Are you complaining that my kisses are somehow substandard?' he said, his gaze penetrating, a grin touching the edge of his mouth and crinkling his eyes.

Her blush felt as if it spread all the way from the roots of her hair to her toes, because as kisses went it had been utterly off-the-scale sublime.

'Of course I'm not saying that,' she snapped. 'It's just that when I said we were aiming for perfect couple I obviously should have specified that I didn't mean perfect couple at honeymoon stage.'

'What *were* you aiming for, then?' he said, blue eyes amused. He rubbed his lips thoughtfully with his fingers, as if he was savouring the taste of her.

She ran a hand self-consciously over her hair. Perhaps if she could smooth the muss out of it she could smooth the fluster out of the rest of her.

'I was thinking more comfortable in each other's company. You know the kind of thing. More the on-the-brink-of-settling-down stage.' She shrugged, her pulse returning to normal now. 'Then again, you're clearly drawing on your own experiences. When did you last have a relationship that made it past loved-up? You go from meet straight to dump. You miss out everything in between.'

He laughed, clearly amused by the whole affair.

'You gave it one hundred and ten per cent when you were staging our "break-up",' he pointed out, making sarcastic speech marks in the air with his fingers. 'Right the way down to the spectacular drink-throwing. What's the matter with that approach now?'

She could hardly say it made her knees unreliable, could she?

'Because the whole point of this is to stop my parents showing Adam up,' she said. 'And they've actually as good as just told *us* to get a room. I think we might have taken it a *teensy* bit too far.'

She led the way down the stairs

'Spoilsport,' he called after her, kick-starting her blush all over again.

As they walked out through wide-open double doors onto a stone-flagged terrace she was more aware than ever of his hand pressed softly in the hollow of her back. It seemed to generate sparks of heat that climbed tantalisingly up her spine. Her mind insisted on re-playing his kiss on a loop, making her feel completely flustered.

Fortunately she had the reality check of Adam's flamboyant styling to smack her between the eyes. The terrace was softly lit by hurricane lamps on tables and pin-lights strung along the stone balustrade. A band were set up to one side, playing jaunty music to which none of the guests were dancing because they were all crowded around the centrepiece in the middle of the terrace.

For a moment she had to lean back and narrow her eyes while her brain processed exactly what it was.

Adam and Ernie had apparently commissioned a life-size ice sculpture of themselves. It gleamed in the floor-level spotlighting. It depicted Adam with one finger pressed against his temple in a thoughtful pose while Ernie looked on.

Her parents were standing to one side, and her mother's face was a stunned picture. On the bright side, at least it appeared to have rendered her speechless. As soon as she saw Emma and Dan she crossed to them, the beads on her purple evening dress shimmering as she walked. She wouldn't have looked out of place in a ballroom dance show.

The real Adam and Ernie joined them, wearing complementary head-to-toe designer suits, with a group of Ernie's relatives flanking them.

'Aren't they *fabulous*?' Adam was gushing, clasping his hands together in delight. 'And the best thing about having yourself carved is that you can tweak the way you look. So I made myself taller and we had a bit shaved off Ernie's nose.'

'Well, I've got to be honest, I'm not that impressed,' her mother sniffed, deploying her usual tactic: if it was outside her comfort zone then she was suspicious of it. She leaned backwards appraisingly. 'They've made your ears stick out,' she remarked to Adam. 'How much did you pay for them?'

'Mum, you can't ask things like that,' Emma said, smiling nervously at the group.

Her mother drew herself up to her full height and pursed her lips. 'Of course I can. Adam's my son. We're parents of the groom. I'm entitled to my opinion.'

'They were a gift,' Adam said, pink-cheeked. 'From Ernie's aunt. She's a sculptress. She spent *hours* working on them. In a freezer.'

There was an ensuing pin-drop silence, during which Emma's father took a canapé from a passing waiter and attempted to lever it into his mouth.

'No more of those tartlets, Donald,' her mother said, leaning in as if with a sixth sense. She expertly took the canapé out of his hand and his teeth closed over thin air. 'Cholesterol!' she snapped.

Ernie dragged a blushing Adam away to circulate, and Emma did her best to stand in as sounding board for her mother's stream-of-consciousness opinions on every minuscule aspect of the proceedings. She was vaguely and gratefully aware of Dan's calming presence at her side.

How would she manage at things like this in future, without him watching her back? The thought of losing that comfort gave her a needling sense of dread.

A couple of hours later she was worn out with smiling and small talk and her mother seemed to have reconnected with a kindred spirit in the shape of Emma's spinster aunt Mabel, last seen at a childhood

Christmas before moving up north. Emma watched them across the terrace, their arms folded in matching poses, matching critical expressions on their faces. Although her voice was drowned out by the music, she saw her mother's lips form the word *grandchildren* as the pair of them looked her way.

She turned to see her father surreptitiously sliding food from the buffet table onto an already heaped plate while her mother was preoccupied.

'Your mother's got me on a diet,' he said when he saw her disbelieving stare.

'Doesn't sound like much fun,' Dan said.

He shrugged.

'It's not so bad. I have a second lunch down at the golf club most days. They do a fantastic pie and crinkle-cut chips. What she doesn't know, and all that.'

Oh, for Pete's sake, she'd had just about enough of this.

'I need a walk,' she said, heading for the steps down from the terrace and onto the lawns.

'I'll come with you.'

Dan followed her away from the party, grabbing a couple of champagne flutes from a passing waiter.

It was a beautiful clear summer night, the velvety cropped lawn silver in the moonlight. Strings of pearly pin-lights lent the trees a fairy-tale quality.

Emma walked on her toes at first, to stop her three-inch heels sinking into the grass, then gave up and took them off, walking barefoot, with the hem of her dress sweeping the grass. Dan was acutely aware of the change in their height difference. Now she seemed small and fragile as she walked next to him.

The faint sound of music and laughter drifted after them on the night air as the party carried on up on the terrace. The lawn swept gently downwards towards a small lake, molten metal in the moonlight. The fresh, sweet scent of dewy grass hung on the cool night air.

'And you wonder why marriage doesn't appeal to me,' she said as he fell into step beside her. 'If I ever found the right man why the hell would I marry him, if that's what it does to you? They lead separate lives. Separate rooms, separate friends. He spends his life trying to exist below her radar and she's got zero excitement in her own life so she makes up for it with gossip and by meddling in Adam's life and in mine. And yet they think they're presenting the image of joint marital solidarity.'

She warmed to her subject, flinging up an exasperated hand.

'Is that how I'll end up if I have kids? With them arguing over who *isn't* going to have the annoying old cow over at Christmas?'

He couldn't keep in a grin. She was so indignant.

'It's not all bad,' he said. 'At least they *are* interested in you.'

She sighed.

'On an interfering kind of a level, maybe.'

He shook his head.

'Maybe it comes across like that. OK, OK—it *does*

come across like that,' he said as she gave him an incredulous look. 'But still you're lucky to be part of a family. I couldn't believe it when you said you were thinking about throwing it all away for some guy you'd known five minutes.'

Emma hid her fluster at his unexpected mention of Alistair by zeroing in on his other point. *Family* and *Dan* weren't really two words she thought of in the same sentence.

'That was part of the attraction,' she said. 'The idea of having some fun, for a change, with someone who put me first without criticising, without comparing me—who put me ahead of everything else. And with Alistair there was no prospect of settling into anything like my parents' take on domesticity. It would have been loads of travel and excitement, minimal chance of ending up in separate bedrooms living my life through my kids.'

'So the whole thing with Alistair was about you proving a point to your family? Why does it bother you so much what they think?'

Dan's comment made her feel as if she was being sloshed with cold water—especially as it was so astute. She *had* been blinded to Alistair by the desire to impress her parents.

'It had nothing to do with proving a point,' she lied. 'I'm a grown-up. What bothered me when I was a kid is just an exasperation now.'

She stopped to sit down on the bench he'd seen earlier from the bedroom window. He sat down next to her, the hard wrought-iron pressing cold through his shirt. He handed her one of the champagne flutes.

'Then what is it?' he said. 'You handle yourself brilliantly back in London. You're a real slick professional. You don't need to let anyone's criticism bother you.'

She stared across the silvery lawn. Faint laughter drifted across from the terrace.

'Ah, but that's exactly the point,' she said. 'When we see each other it's usually for some work reason or other. When it comes to work I know I can hold my own. I know what I'm talking about. I make sure I won't get caught out or make a slip-up.' She paused. 'It hasn't always been like that for me.'

'So what *was* it like, then?'

Emma looked at him, trying to gauge whether his interest was real or counterfeit. He'd never shown an interest in finding out more about her before—not unless it was related to work, of course. His blue eyes held hers steadily. She took a sip of her drink and smiled a little, remembering, letting the years fall away.

'Growing up, I was the clumsiest kid you can imagine,' she said. 'If anyone was going to make a fool of herself it was me. And it was even more difficult because Adam's always been such an overachiever. I started out at school trying to work hard, but it never seemed to matter how much effort I put in. I was never quite good enough to earn Adam's level of interest or praise. He was picking up A grades, winning competitions, excelling at everything. After a while I learned not to put myself in a position where people could notice I was falling short.'

A memory returned to her in all its cringeworthy glory.

'I had a part in the school musical once.' She looked up at him. 'When I was thirteen. Can you imagine me doing that?'

He shrugged, a small smile on his face. A polite response.

'They used to do a musical every year. It was so popular. Everyone would come and watch—parents, locals. And that year they were doing *Grease*. Loads of singing and dancing. I was so excited by the whole idea. I just wanted to be part of it. It didn't occur to me that there could be a negative side, that things could go wrong. I was so naïve.'

'What happened?'

She put her head in her hands and pulled a cringing face.

'I forgot my lines. I stood on that stage and looked out at the hall, knowing it was packed, and I couldn't remember a word. And I don't mean I stumbled over my lines. I didn't just have a bit of a blip and then pick things up. My mind went completely blank. I froze. The lights were bright in my face, but I could still see the shadows of all the people. The music was so loud I could hardly think.'

'What did you do?'

'I ran off the stage and refused to go back on. They put the understudy on instead. My parents were in the audience and my mother gave me hell. She still brings it up now and then. I think in some part of her mind I'm still that nervy thirteen-year-old who had a public meltdown onstage and showed her up.'

She took a sip of her champagne, thinking back. The bright lights in her eyes. The cold horror rushing through her as she tried and failed to make her panicked brain work. The slick of sweat on her palms.

She looked across at Dan, easily pasting a smile on her face. She'd had years of practice at doing it. She was an adult now, with her own life, and she didn't need to be defined by that awful feeling of failure—not any more. Yet on some level maybe it could never be erased.

'That's awful.'

She shrugged, smiling a little.

'It was at the time. I was mortified. And it never happened again—not to that extent. I never put myself out there again after that—not in any situation where I couldn't trust myself to get it right. I concentrated on academic stuff instead of the arts. Left all that to Adam. And, well, you can see how good *he* was at it. That's partly why I decided to study law. A lot of it is about bulk learning. If you know the rules you can apply them. If you put the work in you can build a career. It isn't left to the whim of anyone else liking what you do in order to secure your success.'

He watched her, looking down at her hands, her skin silvery pale in the moonlight, contrasting with her gleaming dark hair. The air of vulnerability about her made his heart turn over softly. He had an unexpected urge to sweep her into his arms and erase all that self-doubt, make her feel special.

'You care far too much what people think of you,' he said.

She frowned.

'Isn't that what everyone wants, though? Validation from everyone else? Or at least from the people you care about.'

'Maybe. But sometimes love doesn't show up as hugs and presents,' he said. 'Not everything is that in-your-face in life. Your mum, for example, shows she cares by—'

'By being the most interfering woman on the planet? Maybe. But just a little...' she searched for the right word '...*positivity* might be nice now and then.'

She leaned back a little, surveying him with interest.

'I didn't think you had such strong feelings about family,' she said. 'It's not like I see you jumping through any hoops to see yours. You never seem to visit them— you never even mention them. They can't be any more of a nightmare than mine are, and even I do my duty and see them every few months.'

'Why?'

'What do you mean, *why*?'

'Why do you do your duty and see them? It's perfectly clear you don't relish spending time with them. Why don't you just cut them out of your life if they're that much of a chore?'

He made a slicing motion with his hand while she stared at him, momentarily speechless.

'I couldn't do that,' she said at last. 'They're my family.'

'You mean you care about them?'

'Of course I do. I've kind of got used to the criticism in a way. It's who they are. They might be a nightmare, but at least they're mine.'

'And there's your answer.'

She shook her head faintly at him.

'To what?'

'You were wondering why I never mention or see my family. There's your answer. That's the difference between you and me. I don't really have a family—not as such. And what I did have of one was never remotely interested in me, even in a critical way.'

She dropped her eyes from his.

'Look, I'm sorry...' she began.

He smiled at her.

'Don't be. I'm fine with it. It's always been that way. I don't *need* a family, Emma. What you don't have you don't miss. When I was a kid we didn't do overbearing parents or criticism or sibling rivalry.' He paused. 'We didn't actually *do* family.'

His mind waved the memory of Maggie before him again with a flourish and he clenched his teeth hard. Talking about family with Emma wasn't so difficult when it related to his mother. His feelings for her had progressed over the years to end up somewhere near contempt. But family as related to Maggie meant something completely different. That had been his hope. That had been their plan. Losing that planned future had somehow been so much worse than losing any excuse for a family he might have had in the past.

She was staring at him. He could feel it. He stood up, began walking back to the terrace, deliberately not looking at her.

'What do you mean, you didn't do family?' she said, catching him up, her long skirt caught in one hand.

He thought fleetingly about simply closing the conversation down, but found that on some level he didn't want to. When had he last talked his childhood over with anyone? His usual conquests were happy to go along with however much he told them about himself—or, more to the point, however little. There had never been any need to give much away. Dinner and a cocktail or two seemed to be all that was needed to get to first base, quickly followed by second and third.

'Exactly that,' he said. 'My upbringing wasn't in a nice suburban house with a mum and dad, siblings, pets. Out of all those things some of the time I had a mum.'

'What about your dad?'

'I've never known him.'

The look of sympathy on her face was immediate and he instantly brushed it away with a wave of his hand.

'I've never needed to know him. It's no big deal.'

It was a billion times easier to talk about the family

he'd actually had than the one he'd wanted and lost. The two things were worlds apart in his mind.

'Yes, it is. That's awful.'

He shrugged.

'What about your mum, then? You must have been close if it was just the two of you.'

He could feel his lip trying to give a cynical curl.

'Not especially. She wasn't exactly Mother of the Year.' He caught sight of her wide-eyed look and qualified resignedly, 'Oh, hell, she was very young. It can't have been easy, raising a kid by herself. It just was what it was.'

Maggie flashed through his mind again. They'd been young, too, and totally unprepared for parenthood. But walking away had never been an option for him. He'd known that from the very first moment she'd told him about her pregnancy.

'She worked on and off,' he said. 'Bar work, mostly. When I was smaller I used to stay with a neighbour, or one or other of her friends. There was never any consistency to it. Then when I got older it was just me.'

He paused for a second, because that couple of sentences didn't really sum up what it had felt like in that house by himself. It had been cold, with a musty smell of damp that had never gone away, even in the summer. Never tidy. Ready meals and late-night movies because no one cared if he stayed up late or if he was getting enough sleep for school. Sometimes his mother had stayed out all night until he'd wondered if she'd return at all. What would happen to him then? Where would he go? The uncertainty of it all had made him constantly on edge.

'I'd never have known,' she said. 'You've done so well to get out from under all that.'

Emma felt a sudden stab of shame at her fussing about her own childhood. She must sound like some dreadful attention-seeker to him, with her comfortable middle-class upbringing, moaning that she'd never seemed able to please her family when he'd barely had one.

'Not especially. I think it did me a favour. I was so determined to find a way out of there, and when I went to college I found it. Not long after that I had the idea for my first business. It was a coffee kiosk. The cafeteria on campus really sucked. It was poorly run, and there was no facility for grabbing a coffee on the go. So I plugged the gap. It wasn't much more than a trolley at first, but I could see what worked and what didn't. I developed the business, ran it during my free periods, and pretty soon I was making good money. And that was when I *really* knew.'

'Knew what?'

He glanced across at her then, and the look in his eyes was intense in the moonlight, making her pulse flutter.

'That work can be your ticket out of anything,' he said. 'Anything at all.' He smiled at her, a half smile that was steely and determined. 'I just grabbed the coffee kiosk success and ran with it. Built it up, sold it, invested and started over. You can be in control of your own destiny through work. And that's why work will always come first with me.'

So that was why his relationships never amounted to anything. She saw now why their agreement had been of such use to him. She'd furthered his work. She'd provided a date so he didn't need to be distracted.

There had never been any prospect of him wanting more, then. She swallowed as she took that in.

'You'll meet someone one day who'll make you want to put work second,' she said. 'You won't know what you're missing until then.'

He shook his head.

'The moment someone becomes that important you start to lose focus. And things start to go wrong. I just don't need that kind of complication.'

She had the oddest feeling he wasn't just talking about overcoming his childhood.

'I think I'm going to turn in,' she said as they neared to the hotel. 'It's getting late now.'

The music continued on the terrace, more mellow now, and the crowd had dispersed a little. Adam stood to one side, mobile phone clamped to his ear, a stressed expression on his face.

That didn't come as any surprise to Dan. He could think of few things less stressful than getting married. Emma's parents were nowhere to be seen, but obviously just their presence on the premises was enough.

In the centre of the terrace the ice sculpture continued its slow melt.

'I'll come with you,' he said.

The memory of kissing her danced slowly through his mind as they made their way inside. He'd known it might put her on edge—that had rather been the point...proof that he was calling the shots now. He hadn't thought it through any further than that. He hadn't counted on the way she would feel in his arms, all long limbs and fragile bone structure, such a contrast to the voluptuous curves that had always been his short-term fling diet. Or the way that satiny full lower lip would feel tugged between his own. There was a hotly curious part of him wondering how it might feel to take things further. He crushed that thought—hard.

His perception of her had changed. And not just because of the kiss but because of tonight. When had they ever discussed anything before that didn't have the ultimate goal of helping them in their jobs? It had been all insider tips from her. Who might be tendering for this contract, what their bid might be, who in her work circles might be looking for troubleshooting services. From him it had been handy introductions—name-dropping Emma to contacts who might want or need legal advice. All of it professional on one level or another.

This weekend was meant to be all about him taking charge, making the point that *he* was the one doing *her* the favour and then breaking off their arrangement the moment the wedding was over. The plan had seemed so easy in the wake of her insulting dumping of him—the perfect way to redress control and get rid of the gnawing feeling that he'd let her become indispensable in his life.

But the connection between them now felt more complex instead of more detached. The idea of walking away from it felt suddenly less gratifying. He'd been so busy taking what he could get from their agreement, manipulating it to suit his own ends so he could avoid close relationships, that he hadn't considered what might be in it for *her* beyond the shallow work reasons they both had.

For Emma it had been a way of making life easier. Because to be 'good enough' she believed she had to fit a certain stereotype. He wasn't sure which was worse—using their agreement to escape past failures or using it to avoid any remote likelihood of ever having any.

As they walked up the stairs to their room Emma realised suddenly that he still had his arm loosely draped around her. There was no one around them to see it. No family members, no staff. Just what did that mean? Or did it mean anything at all?

She wondered if it felt as natural to him as it felt to her and gave herself a mental slap for even *thinking* about reading something into it. Really? This was Dan—Mr Two-Week Relationship himself. Even if that arm resting on her shoulders right now meant something—which it didn't—it would only ever be that.

Nothing meant anything to Dan Morgan except his work. He'd made that crystal clear this evening. And she wasn't in the market for anything that could be described as a fling. What would be the point? She'd had that with Alistair. What she wanted was not to be some throwaway bit of arm candy but to feel special, to come first, and she wasn't going to get that from Dan.

A hot kiss followed by a night sharing a room with him... The stuff of her dreams a few months ago. And now she had it, it was all for show. How par for the course of her life. They'd been alone together *loads* of times and he'd never had any intention of making a move. Pretend Emma got the hot kiss and the envious glances from female wedding guests over her gorgeous male companion. Real Emma got the awkwardness of bunking in with a work colleague.

She wriggled away from his arm and fumbled in her bag for the room key.

It had taken *months* to get over her stupid crush on him and to reinstate it now would be madness. She was just flustered, that was all, over a stupid fake kiss and a bit of a personal conversation. It didn't mean *anything*.

SEVEN

—

When had he last shared a bedroom with someone for a reason that had nothing to do with sex? Dan couldn't actually remember. It must have been Maggie. Way back when he was still at college and anything had seemed possible.

Had he now become so accustomed to room-sharing being about sex that his body simply expected it as part of the deal? Was that why he felt so damned on edge as he waited for Emma to change in the bathroom? Every nerve in his body was wound into a tense knot.

The air of awkwardness from earlier was back. But now there seemed a new, deeper edge to it. It was more than just the logistics of sharing a small space with someone you only knew on a work basis. His growing attraction to her was heightened by his new understanding of her. A few feet away from him in the velvet-soft darkness she would be there, lying in that bed, with her long, slender limbs and her silky dark hair.

His body matched his racing mind with a rigid, hot tension the like of which was going to make sleep an impossibility.

His pulse jolted as the bathroom door clattered open and she crossed the room to the bed, not looking at him. Her dress was now lying over one arm, her hair loose and gleaming in the soft glow of the table lamp next to the bed. She was wearing a sleep vest and shorts which showed off the most impossibly perfect pair of long, slender legs.

He made an enormous effort not to stare at them as his mind insisted on wondering what other glorious secrets she might be hiding under her sensible work dresses and wide-leg trousers. He stared hard out of the window. His preoccupation became slightly less fake as he noticed movement in the grounds.

'Is that your brother down there?'

He immediately regretted mentioning it because she tossed the dress over the back of a chair and crossed the room to join him at the window, padding across the deep carpet in bare feet. What he *really* needed right now, with his entire body wound up like a coiled spring, was her standing next to him in her flimsy shorts and vest combo. Without her heels she just about reached his shoulder...

'Where?'

He pointed and she craned closer to him to see the lily pond bench. A figure was sitting and staring at the ground contemplatively, a bottle of champagne in one hand and a glass in the other. Her sudden nearness let Dan pick up the faint trace of vanilla perfume still clinging to her hair and his stomach gave a slow and delicious flip in response.

'It's Adam, all right,' she said. 'Even in silhouette that quiff is unmistakable. He's probably taking a break from negotiating family. Can't say I blame him.'

The soft breeze drifting in through the open window ruffled her hair lightly. She turned away from the view and smiled up at Dan.

'Don't snore,' she said, her eyes teasing.

'I *don't* snore.'

She was close enough that in one swift tug she could be in his arms. He swallowed hard, his throat paper-dry.

Oblivious, she narrowed her eyes at him, considering.

'How do you know?'

'I've never had any complaints,' he said. Her lips, scrubbed of lip gloss, were a soft pale pink in the muted light. His eyes were drawn to them.

'That doesn't mean you don't snore,' she said. 'It just means no one's wanted to put you off them by telling you.'

'Whereas you...?'

'Will have no compunction whatsoever about lobbing a pillow at you.' She pressed an emphatic finger against his chest that made a wave of heat pulse through his veins. 'I'm not afraid to tell you what I think.'

'I know.'

For some reason the novelty of that was alluring. It occurred to him that the willingness to please of his usual girlfriends was something else besides easy and no-fuss. It was also very bland. When had he last felt on his toes with a woman?

He'd become slowly more aware of her looks this evening: the fragility of her skinny frame, her dark-hair-pale-skin combo—such a contrast to his usual choice—and now there was her liveliness, her cheek, sucking him in all the more.

For the first time he picked up on her physical similarities to Maggie. She was taller and slimmer, but the smooth dark hair was the same. Was that what this was about? Was that why she seemed to have slipped through his careful filter? Was that why it had been so easy to keep her at a distance and categorise her as a work colleague? Because his knee-jerk avoidance of any thought of attraction to a girl who might remind him of Maggie had gone on so long it had become automatic?

But he hadn't had the complication of being at such close quarters with her back then. Nuances and habits were laid bare now. The fun-loving, cheeky side of her was so much more obvious outside the work environment, where everything needed to be serious and professional. This weekend he'd begun to see what lay beneath. And it drew him in as no woman had. Not since Maggie had walked away.

She was smiling cheekily up at him, her brown eyes wide, and he marvelled again at how softly pretty she was when you took the time to look past her stiff outer layer. Her face was tilted up to his, at the perfect angle for him to kiss her. The warm, sweet scent of her hair filled his senses, and without taking time to think he lifted a hand to touch her cheek—just to see if it felt as satiny as it looked.

That one tiny connection with her gave his pulse an immediate leap and hot desire rushed through him. And in that fleeting moment he knew he had no chance.

Knowing he was acting off-plan now—and not just off-plan for this weekend but for his whole damned philosophy on life—was suddenly not enough to stop him. His mental filters weren't working. She'd already got past them. This was physical now, and there was nothing he could do about it.

Her eyes widened as he let his fingers trace further, around to the soft skin at the nape of her neck, beneath the fall of her hair. All thought of consequences gone, he lowered his mouth towards the silk of that tantalisingly full lower lip. He pulled her closer, melded her body hard against his, felt the contours of her long, slender limbs through the thin cotton of the shorts and vest she wore.

Sparks of hot longing fizzed in his abdomen as he let his hand slide lower, to find the soft cream of those long, slender thighs. Desire flooded through him, deeper than he was used to, steeped in the familiarity of her, the laughs they'd had together, their newfound closeness. This was not his usual throwaway date. He'd stepped outside the norm. The very novelty of that seemed to hike up his want for her to a new level.

A squeak of shock caught in Emma's throat as his thumb stroked along her jawline, his fingers tangling in her hair.

She hadn't imagined the shift in balance between them after all. She hadn't been seeing things that weren't there.

Despite all the flirting and the signs, the new feeling of intimacy as they started to get to know each other beyond the barriers of their previous life, she now realised that she'd never truly believed he could ever be interested in her. Not in *that* way. She'd quit any delusions about that months ago as she'd observed his repetitive dating habits, certain that unless she happened to morph overnight into a pouting curvy blonde, boring old plain Emma Burney simply wouldn't do it for him.

Her pulse had upped its pace so acutely that she felt light-headed. As his lips met hers she could taste a faint twist of champagne on them, warming her mouth as his tongue slipped softly against hers. Hot sparks began to tingle their way through her limbs to simmer hotly between her legs.

How many times had she dreamed of this moment in the dim and distant past when they'd first met? Every nerve-ending was tinglingly aware of him. She was drowning, every sense in her body filled with him. The lingering spicy notes of his aftershave made her senses reel. She let her fingers sink into his hair, its thick, soft texture exactly as she'd imagined it so many times.

The desire that had bubbled beneath the surface of her consciousness until she had abandoned all hope of it ever being reciprocated made a heady comeback, and she grabbed at the last thread of sense before it slipped away.

It was utterly, sublimely delicious, but none of it really counted because he was ending their agreement.

She latched on to that thought. Was that what all this had been about? The warmth of his newfound support and interest in her had delighted her, but she'd assumed it was simply down to friendship. His kiss was something she'd dreamed of, but if he'd wanted to snog her because of *her* he'd had *months* to do it.

All those months waiting for him to notice her, taking extra care with her hair and make-up when she knew she was going to see him, dropping everything to fit in his last-minute work dates. Months when he'd barely noticed she was alive. Months of opportunity, time alone together, work dinners out. None of it had been enough because he'd needed her for work then.

It had taken *this* for him to make a move on her. The fact that he was ending their agreement and had no need for her any more. Dan only slept with dispensable women. And now she was dispensable.

None of this had anything to do with real feelings for her.

With a monumental effort she stopped her arms

from entwining around his neck and groped for his hands, grabbing them at the wrists and disentangling herself from his embrace. The sensation of loss as she took a step back made her suck in a sharp breath and she steeled herself against it. She was *not* going to be sucked into another bad decision because of some stupid age-old crush. She was in full control here.

'Why now?' she panted at him.

His eyes seemed a darker blue than ever, a light frown of confusion touching his forehead. She could hear that his breath had deepened.

He reached for her.

'What do you mean, why now?'

She took another step back, away from his hands, because if she found herself in those arms again she wasn't sure her resolve would stand up.

'We've known each other for months,' she said. 'And in all that time you've never looked twice my way. No matter what I did. No matter how many times I swung business deals for you or put myself out on your behalf. No matter how I tried. And then you decide we're going to go our separate ways, and out of the blue suddenly I'm fair game? Well, I'm not interested.'

She took a slow step back, shaking her head, avoiding his eyes, looking everywhere except at his face. Everything about her told him a very different story. Her shortness of breath, the flushed cheeks, the hard points of her nipples beneath the thin fabric of her vest.

His mind zeroed in on her words. '*No matter what I*

did.' The meaning of that slammed into his brain and turned it to mush. Their agreement had always been about more than platonic convenience for her and he'd never even noticed. His stupid work tunnel vision had neglected to pick up on that point. The surge of excitement it now evoked shocked him to the core, telling him his belief that he was in control here was seriously misplaced.

'I'm not going to be your alternative choice because there's no handy blonde available and you're stuck sharing a room with me,' she said.

Clearly, to her, he was the same old work-obsessed confirmed bachelor.

'This has nothing to do with that.'

She gazed up at him, wariness in her wide brown eyes, and then they both jumped at a sudden flurry of knocks on the bedroom door.

She took a couple of fast paces away from him, her fingers rubbing slowly over her lips as if echoing his kiss. Another surge of desire flooded through him at the sight. She cut her eyes away from his.

Another mad cacophony of knocks sliced through the tension.

She made an exasperated noise and turned away from him towards the door, one hand pushing her hair back from her face in a gesture of fluster.

'Who the hell is that?'

'Emma, ignore it,' he said. 'We need to sort this out. You've got it wrong.'

The knocking graduated to a muffled banging of the

kind a fist might make, and she shook her head lightly at him and moved towards the door again.

He glanced down at himself. In a sudden flash of clarity it occurred to him that the visitor might feasibly be Emma's mother, and his arousal would be obvious to her in the space of one look. He glanced at the door to the *en-suite* bathroom, thinking vaguely that he might take refuge in there for a couple of minutes while Emma got rid of whoever it was and then they could pick up where they'd left off.

He was on his way across the room when she opened the door and Adam, who had clearly been leaning on it, stumbled into the room, performed a twisty lurching pirouette and threw up into the nearest pot plant.

Oh, just bloody *perfect!*

'For Pete's sake, help me get him to the bathroom!'

Emma had managed to pull Adam to his extremely unsteady feet and struggled to hold him upright as he lurched about. Dan rushed in and took over, throwing one of her brother's arms around his neck and heaving him into the bathroom before he could collapse again. She followed them in.

'The wedding's off!' Adam groaned, slumping over the sink. His always-perfect hair hung in a dishevelled mess and his face was a sickly shade of green.

'What the hell's happened?' she said.

He lifted his head and pointed an emphatic jabbing finger at her as he swayed drunkenly.

'I'm a has-been, darling,' he drawled. 'It's all over. It's all gone.'

His knees gave way unexpectedly and Dan made a lunge to catch him before he hit the white-tiled floor.

'He's absolutely wasted,' Emma said, staring down at him. 'What the hell do I do?'

'Call down to Room Service,' Dan said. 'Black coffee. He needs to sober up.'

She left the pair of them in the bathroom and went to use the phone, her mind reeling. She'd never seen Adam lose his cool before. He had no worries that she knew of. His life was only ever full of things to celebrate. As she replaced the receiver there was the sound of gushing water from the bathroom and a piercing shriek of shock. Dan had obviously stuck him in the shower. She grinned in spite of her worry. Whatever she had to cope with now, at least Adam might be more lucid.

Adam emerged from the bathroom, still hideously pale, but his shocked eyes were now wide and staring. Water dripped from his face and his hair and he was clutching a towel and madly rubbing it at his front.

Dan followed him, his hands spread apologetically. 'Look, I'm sorry,' he said. 'I know cold water's a bit of a shock to the system, but it's great for sobering you up and I couldn't think what else to do.'

'Cold?' Adam wailed. 'It's not the bloody *cold!*' He cast horrified hands downwards at his sopping wet purple suit. 'What the hell have you done? This jacket's *designer!*'

EIGHT

—

Dan turned over for the fiftieth time on the sofa, knees bunched up because the damn thing was too short for him. Unfortunately that wasn't the only reason why sleep was totally elusive. The way Emma had felt in his arms had been far too delicious, far too enticing, for him to simply brush it out of his mind. Add in to that the way she'd put an end to it without having time to give a proper explanation and every nerve in his body was on full-scale alert, his arousal refusing to stand down even in her absence.

And, as interruptions went, needy family crises just about ticked his worst possible box. His stomach lurched between desire for her and the more rational desire to run a mile. It was bad enough to be in the middle of a huge family event when the last thing you wanted to be reminded of was the fact that you couldn't actually *do* family. He'd thought he was holding his own on that front pretty well, but now family complications were seeping in at every turn and he couldn't think of anything worse...

Somewhere in the small hours, after he'd finally given up on her returning to the room—not that it had made any change to his sleepless state—there was a soft click as the door opened. The benefit of his eyes being used to the velvet darkness meant he could watch the silhouette of her every move, while she had to feel her stumbling way from one piece of furniture to the next. Had he ever been more wide awake?

She muffled a yelp as she tripped over a chair and he took pity on her and reached to turn on the table lamp. She blinked at him in the muted golden light. She wore a sweater over her sleep shorts and vest that wasn't long enough to hide her gorgeous legs. His pulse immediately picked up where it had left off a couple of hours ago.

He heard her sigh as she clocked that he was still awake. He watched her run a hand through her already dishevelled hair as she sat down hard on the bed. Her face was a pale oval and there were dark shadows of tiredness beneath her eyes.

'You're still up,' she said.

He sat up on the sofa, the sheet bunched around his waist.

'I wasn't sure you were coming back tonight,' he said.

'Neither was I,' she said. 'I think Adam's drained the hotel's supply of black coffee.'

'He's sobered up, then?'

She nodded.

'He's sobered up. I thought that stuff about calling off the wedding was just cold feet—the usual night-before thing, down to him having drunk too much champagne. But there's more to it than that.'

She held his gaze for a moment.

'He's in financial trouble, Dan,' she said.

Worry etched her face and tugged at his heart.

'He's going under unless he can come up with a plan pretty damn quick.'

'For Pete's sake, what's he gone and done now? Spent a huge wad on a purple Bentley?'

She didn't smile.

He sat up straighter.

'Didn't you tell me his pictures sell for five figures?' he said, scratching his head and trying to think clearly. Tiredness was kicking in now. He had absolutely no desire to discuss Adam's spending habits at two in the morning.

'One of his pictures was supposed to. A month or so ago. Adam borrowed a wodge of cash on the back of it and then the sale fell through. He's been so in vogue recently that even *he* believed the hype. Instead of being productive he's been spending money he doesn't have like water. A new swanky flat here, a shedload of designer furniture there... And now things have reached breaking point. He only found out this afternoon.'

'Can't Ernie bail him out? I thought his family were swimming in cash.'

She frowned at him.

'That's exactly why he doesn't want to *tell* Ernie. He doesn't want him to think he's marrying him for a bail-out. And, more than that, he doesn't want Ernie to think he's a failure. You can't imagine what that means to Adam—he never fails at anything. *Ever.* He's refusing to change his mind about calling off the wedding. It was all I could do to make him promise not to do anything until the morning. I need to think of a way to persuade him by then.'

Dan looked at the worry darkening her face and saw a flash of hope in her eyes as she fixed them on his.

'What he really needs is some sound business advice,' she said, with a pointed tone to her voice that really wasn't necessary. 'From someone who knows what they're doing.'

She wanted him to step in. The unspoken request hung in the air as clearly as if she'd shouted it.

Cold clarity immediately took over his brain with the automatic response that had been honed and conditioned in him over the course of the last ten years.

Not his problem.

He didn't *do* family problems. That was actually the one big advantage of not having a family—not getting sucked into other people's dramas, not having anyone rely on him for help. He'd thought he'd done a pretty good job of distancing himself from the blasts from the past that the whole family wedding ambience kept lobbing his way this weekend, but this was a step too far.

'You want *me* to talk to him?' He could hear the note

of frosty defensiveness in his own voice. 'I'm not convinced that would be a good idea. It's his private business—nothing to do with me. He needs to discuss it with Ernie. Isn't that the whole point of marriage—shared problems and all that?'

He dropped his eyes from hers so he wouldn't see the disappointment seeping into them. He ran a hand awkwardly through his hair.

'There isn't going to *be* a marriage unless someone gets him back on track,' she hissed.

'What makes you think that someone should be *me*? I don't think Adam would thank you for involving a stranger in his personal problems. This isn't down to me,' he said.

'A stranger?'

He glanced up and caught her gaze again. Bitter disappointment lurked there. Deep in his stomach a spike of regret kicked in unexpectedly at the idea of letting her down. He steeled himself against it. He shouldn't care about this.

She paused a beat too long, during which he held his position and didn't give in, and then she exploded.

'Fine. Absolutely fine,' she snapped, leaping to her feet.

Had she really thought he would step up to the plate? Why the *hell* had she assumed that? Because he'd kissed her? After months of zero romantic interest he'd kissed her. OK, so she'd thought there had been something more than their usual work relationship growing between them this last day or so, but clearly she'd imagined that. Her first instincts had been spot on and she'd been totally right to stop him in his tracks.

Her mistake had been in hoping that what was between them was in any way about more than the kiss and what he'd obviously intended to follow that kiss up with if Adam hadn't interrupted them spectacularly.

'You didn't even ask me what was wrong with Adam,' she said dully. Her head ached tiredly and she rested her hand against her scalp, lacing her fingers through her hair to pull the roots back from her face, trying to clear her thoughts. 'I thought you were waiting up for me all this time to make sure I was OK, to be supportive, but you weren't actually wondering for one second what the problem was. If I hadn't just told you, you would never have asked me about Adam, would you?'

She glanced down at her fingers.

'That's not what you were waiting up for at all, is it? You just wanted to pick up where we left off earlier. You thought I'd sort Adam out, get him over his hissy fit, and then we'd have the rest of the night to make it into that bed.'

She nodded across the room at the four-poster.

For a moment she got no response and she raised her eyebrows at him expectantly. See if he could talk his way out of this. Or if he would even be bothered to try.

'This has nothing to do with what happened earlier,' he said, not meeting her eyes. 'I just think Adam is big enough to sort out his own problems. I don't get why you need to get sucked into this. His overspending isn't down to you.'

She stared at him, incredulous at his lack of concern.

'Because that's what families do,' she said. 'You know, I always thought nothing could ever touch Adam. He's led a charmed life. As if everything he ever touches is sprinkled with happy dust. When I was a kid I sometimes used to wish for just one time when he would stuff up, show everyone that he wasn't perfect.'

She paused briefly, thinking of how upset Adam was now. There was no joy in that for her. She wasn't a stupid kid any more.

'For once I'm not the one who's screwed up, but I have no good feeling about that. What good would it do if my parents knew what had happened? I just want him to go back to his usual crazy self.'

She made a conscious effort to curb her voice. It was so late now the hotel was pin-drop quiet. Every word she spoke felt amplified in the silence.

'Of course you do,' he said. 'You're comfortable in his shadow, so you're hardly about to want that shadow to get smaller, are you?'

She stared at him.

'Just what the hell is *that* supposed to mean?' She wanted to shout it. Her voice felt shaky on her tongue. She kept her tone measured with great difficulty.

He shrugged.

'It's safer, isn't it? Believing that you're always going

to be inferior? Means you don't have to put yourself out there. You rely on Adam being the star that he is in every possible way because it's an excuse for you to take the safe option.'

'That's not true.'

'Isn't it? Look at our plus-one agreement. I know what *I* was getting out of it—easy networking, work contacts. But what about you? Your dates were all about presenting a front to your family, because that way you didn't have to put yourself there in reality. With me you couldn't fail.'

For a moment she had trouble comprehending what he meant because it came as such a shock. A sharp, hot lurch hit her in the stomach. She shoved away the thought that this was what it felt like to have someone touch a nerve. Refusing to engage in one-upmanship with Adam was a way of avoiding grief from her over-interested parents, *not* a way to embrace the safe option because she was afraid of failure.

Dan saw the dark, defensive anger flush her face and wondered for a moment if he'd gone too far. She'd made him feel such a lightweight for not pitching in instantly to help Adam—who, frankly, was responsible for his own cock-up. Discomfort at the situation had stopped him holding back, and second thoughts seeped in a moment too late.

Her hands flew to her hips, her eyes flashed in anger and her previous attempts to speak in a low voice went totally out of the window.

'You're twisting things!' she yelled. 'I don't know where the hell you get off, preaching to me about family bloody values. Your concern gene is mutated. All this has been about—all anything has *ever* been about for you—is getting someone into bed. In this case, in the absence of any willing curvy blondes, that happens to be me. Well, I'm not interested in being one of your dispensable little-black-book girlies. I don't need you as a boyfriend—not even as a fake one. If this wedding goes ahead—which, the way it looks right now, is unlikely—I'll go it alone. I don't need you. So first thing in the morning you can get back to your sad workaholic singleton life in London.'

He'd never seen her lose her temper. Her voice shook with the force of it and she stood at her full height, her eyes wide and her cheeks flushed. Even in his amazement at her overreaction—which told him he'd not only touched a nerve but had held on to it and twisted it hard—the most visceral part of him zeroed in on how utterly beautiful she looked in that animated moment.

Then admiration fell flat as she turned her back on him, stalked into the bathroom and slammed the door so hard he was surprised the hotel didn't collapse into rubble around them.

Not the delicious uninhibited night of passion he'd expected when he'd kissed her a few hours earlier. Admittedly at the time his mind hadn't been working ahead by more than a few minutes. He certainly hadn't thought about the consequences—it had been very easy to discount those. Any possible repercussions had seemed very far away when the silk of her skin had been beneath his fingers.

If he'd been lying in a regular bed he would have been ramrod-straight. Instead he was cramped into a hunch with his knees up. His body was one big throb of pent-up sexual energy. Every muscle was tightly coiled up with it. And did he really think he could pass the whole night like this?

She'd spent an hour in the bathroom before she'd re-emerged into the darkened room and stalked past him into bed. No attempt to make conversation. Now a silver shaft of moonlight filtered through a chink in the curtains and fell on her bare shoulder as she lay with her back to him. The long legs were drawn up; she was curled beneath the sheet.

For an endless length of time he had felt sure, despite her silence, that she was awake. Her angry vibe had been palpable. Tension still filled the room. He shifted again, in a vain attempt to get comfortable, and wondered what exactly he was bothering with all this for.

He should be looking on Adam's rubbish timing as a very fortuitous wake-up call, shouldn't he? He'd been completely focused on the overwhelming physical pull of her. If he'd stopped for a second to analyse it he would have assumed it would be a one-night stand. After all, he'd made it clear that their agreement had run its course, and that had removed any benefit of keeping things platonic between them. He'd been thinking quick weekend fling.

Hadn't he?

If his interest in her was purely physical, dispensable, then why did her furious criticism of him gnaw at his insides like this? He had no obligation to her or her family, and yet somehow she'd managed to instil guilt because he didn't want to get involved in Adam's undoubtedly crazy problems.

He didn't *do* guilt. That was one of the main benefits of keeping his relationships shallow. He and Emma didn't even *have* a relationship and he couldn't bloody sleep. He had no idea how she'd managed to do this to him.

There was a part of him that was halfway back to London in his head already, keen to do exactly as she had suggested.

She shifted gently in her sleep and he sat up on the sofa, throwing back the crumpled sheet. He could see the smooth pool of her dark hair on the pillow. The quality of the light in the room had changed almost imperceptibly and he glanced at the luminous face of his watch. Dawn would be kicking in before he knew it. He could be back in his Docklands flat in an easy couple of hours if he left now. No need to battle London traffic if he left this early. Why the hell was he even still here?

You want to help. You want this involvement with her and her family.

He absolutely *did not.*

Every sensible instinct told him to get some serious distance from this situation but he rationalised furiously. A brief chat with Adam—and a brief chat was all it *would* be, too—might be the perfect way to take control of this situation. He wasn't about to quietly slink back to London on her say-so, leaving her with the upper hand.

He ignored the inner voice whispering that he didn't like being labelled as selfish, because labels were to him completely irrelevant. Results mattered. Successes. Not good or bad opinions. Even if they happened to be *her* opinions.

Help Adam out and Emma would be in his debt. The fact that after that kiss she felt very much like unfinished business was beside the point. He was not about to fall for her. He was in total control here. When they got back to London he would end their agreement, as planned, in full possession of the moral high ground. It wasn't as if she wasn't expecting him to. He'd made it clear this was their last outing together. There would be no need to see her again after that. It would be over.

There was a chink in the curtains that let the sunlight in.

It took a moment for her brain to process the fact that the bedroom window of her flat in Putney looked out onto a tiny enclosed yard which the sun penetrated for roughly ten minutes somewhere around noon. Additional details seeped into her consciousness. This bed was hard, where hers was soft, and was that *bird-*

song she could hear? Where was the roar of rush-hour traffic?

This was *not* her flat in Putney.

Reality rushed in. Luxury country house hotel. Adam's mad-as-a-box-of-frogs wedding. Disastrous room-share with her crush of the year.

She sat bolt upright and stars swam in front of her eyes at the unexpected movement. She turned instantly to look at the sofa. Every bone in her body ached with tension and her eyes felt gritty when she blinked. She could have sworn she'd been awake all night. Yet that couldn't be so. Last seen lying on the sofa as she climbed back into bed at two-thirty and turned her back on him in fury, at some point Dan had managed to get up and exit the room without her noticing.

She checked the time and that was enough to get her out of bed in a split second. How the hell had she managed to sleep in? Her stomach kicked into churning with a sudden sense of urgency. She needed to get up, check on Adam and find out if the wedding was going ahead or not.

The thought of dealing with the fallout if his world imploded filled her with dread. Adam would be in the doghouse and the spotlight would be right back on her life—her failure to keep a man, her failure to produce grandchildren. Her mind stuttered on that thought with a sharp stab of shame. Surely her only concern should be for Adam, for how she could best help him sort out the mess that was his life, how she could support him through the stress. The thought of the effect it might have on *her* shouldn't even be entering her mind.

Dan's accusation from the previous night rose darkly in her mind. Could he have a point about her living in Adam's shadow because it was safer there?

She crossed the room swiftly to the *en-suite* bathroom, knowing from the silence that Dan wasn't there but sticking her head around the door anyway to check.

Nothing.

She glanced at the hotel information brochure on top of the bureau. Breakfast had been running for at least an hour already—maybe he'd gone down to the dining room. The possibility that he'd upped and left lurked at the very edge of her consciousness but she delayed any consideration of it. And then, as she turned, her eyes took in the antique desk and her heart gave a miserable lurch that she refused to acknowledge.

His holdall wasn't in the room. And, worse, nor were his laptop and all the associated office stuff which basically provided his identity. All of it was gone.

She threw on jeans and a T-shirt and speed-walked down the deep-carpeted hall to the honeymoon suite. Ernie had spent the previous night at his parents' home and had planned to get ready there, so Adam should still be alone.

He opened the door on her first knock and stood aside to let her in before crossing the room back to the full-length mirror. He was wearing an ivory crushed velvet slim-cut suit with gold piping and super pointy shoes that even *she* would think twice about squashing her toes into. He looked her up and down, an eyebrow cocked.

'I do hope you're not wearing that,' he said, waving a hand at her jeans-and-old-T-shirt combo. 'This is a classy event.'

'Of course I'm not wearing this,' she snapped.

There was something incredibly exasperating about the way he was acting, as if the events of the previous night had never happened when they'd caused her a stress-fest of monumental proportions.

'I didn't see the point in putting on a swanky wedding outfit and doing my hair when the likelihood of it going ahead was somewhere around fifty-fifty. At least it was when I left you in the small hours.'

She sat down on the enormous bed. Everything in the honeymoon suite was supersized, albeit in a country hotel kind of a way. The four posts were taller, the swags of fabric bedecking them were bigger and sweepier, and through the door of the *en suite* she could see an enormous sunken bath.

'Oh, that!'

Adam flapped a dismissive hand at her and turned back to his reflection in the mirror. He looked a little tired and drawn but otherwise remarkably like his usual upbeat self. She caught sight of her own reflection behind him. She looked an exhausted wreck. How bloody unfair.

'That's all sorted now.'

She stared at him in disbelief.

'What about last night's meltdown?' His lack of re-action combined with her tiredness made her temper strain to breaking point. 'You puked in my plant, for Pete's sake! You had a total emotional meltdown. Your life was *over*.'

'Oh, that,' he said again, glancing back at her.

At least he had the good grace to look sheepish now.

'Sorry about that, sweetie. Glass of champagne too many. Still, there were compensations. In fact some might say it had elements of stag night perfection.'

He grinned at her mystified expression.

'Sharing a shower room with the gorgeous Dan, for example,' he said mischievously, spraying a toothbrush with hairspray and smoothing his already perfect quiff into place. 'Even if he did ruin my suit.' He tapped the side of his nose with one finger in a your-secret's-safe-with-me gesture. 'Lucky old you. I know you thought you hit the jackpot with Alistair Woods, but I've always thought Dan was in a league of his own. Nice work.' He winked at her and turned back to the top of the bureau, which was groaning under the weight of male grooming products. 'I never did think Lycra cycle wear was a good look—didn't like to mention it.'

He lavishly sprayed a five-foot-high cloud of ori-ental spiced aftershave into the room beside him and stepped into it.

Emma pinched her nose to stifle a sneeze. She shook her head in automatic denial.

'It's not like that. We're just work friends.'

He cackled mad laughter.

'Sure you are! That's why he's just given me an *enormous* business loan with zero interest and his personal phone number so I can tap him for strategic advice whenever I need it.' He winked. 'Either that or maybe he's got the hots for *me*. Maybe you've got competition, sweetie.'

She stared at him in disbelief and he obviously mistook incredulity for angry possessiveness.

'I'm joking!' He held his hands up and laughed. 'For Pete's sake, where's your sense of humour?'

'*When?*' she said, as if in a dream. 'When did he do all this? His stuff's gone from the room. I can't find him anywhere.' She paused. 'We had a bit of a disagreement.'

Adam shook his head.

'He'll be back. He turned up here around dawn, woke me up, ordered a gallon of black coffee and forced me to come clean about my debts.' He coloured a little. 'It wasn't pretty. Then he talked me through a business plan for the next three years and touted unbelievable terms for a loan. I thought he'd want a cut of everything I make for life at the very least, and I would have agreed to it, too. Frankly, I would have put up my *granny* as security to dig me out of this hole. But no.' He shook his head wonderingly. 'He is *so* into you.' He pointed the toothbrush at her.

Her brain was spinning, trying to process what all this meant.

'Where is he now, then? He didn't come back to the room.'

Adam shrugged. 'Around, I think. He was going to make a few calls, draw up some papers and get the ball rolling. I'm sure he'll show up once it's all organised, sweetie. He's probably in the lobby soaking up the free Wi-Fi.'

Or en route back to the city and deliberately avoiding her. Her heart gave a half plummet at the thought and she gritted her teeth. She tugged her fingers through her hair, as if she could somehow smooth some sense into her muddled brain.

She'd told him to go back to London and instead he'd stayed to put together a bail-out package for Adam. Her heart turned over meltingly and she desperately tried to rein it in, to come up with an alternative explanation to the one that was slamming into her brain.

He'd done this for her.

He'd done it to prove her wrong about him.

She cringed inwardly as she remembered the awful things she'd said to him in the throes of her enormous meltdown tantrum. What possible other explanation could there be? It was way above and beyond Dan's normal remit. Dan didn't step in to fix other people's crises. Ever. Since he kept the world at arm's length it was usually impossible to get close enough to his shoulder to cry on it.

He'd stepped outside the box. And what the hell was she meant to make of that?

NINE

—

Dan ran a hand through his hair distractedly as his phone kicked in for the third time in the last ten minutes. Each of the calls had been from Emma. For the third time he pressed 'call reject' on the dashboard and fixed his expression on the road. The motorway would still be pretty clear this time of the morning, but he'd hit traffic when he reached London. It was a Saturday so would be marginally better.

Dealing with Adam had taken a good deal longer than he'd thought it would. Still, it was done now. Loan organised, cash transfer organised, soul sold. Point made. The wedding would go ahead without a hitch and he would return to his work in London. The ridiculous plus-one agreement would be discharged exactly as he'd planned. They would move forward separately, but Emma would go with the knowledge that she'd been wrong about him.

Sad workaholic singleton.

Was that really what he boiled down to? His mind

gnawed at it relentlessly and, try as he might, he couldn't shake the feeling that the reason it bothered him so much was because *she'd* said it. He, who didn't give a toss about how he came across to people so long as the job got done, *cared* what she thought of him.

A miserable, dark churning was kicking into his stomach with every mile he drove further away.

Emma pelted back up the stairs for the third time, having performed a whirlwind circuit of all the public rooms and lounges in the hotel, her heart sinking lower by the second. The marquee was teeming with hotel staff transforming it from plain tent into what was, by the look of it, to be some kind of yellow-themed fairy grotto, all under the supervision of a pristinely dressed wedding coordinator with a clipboard and a voice like a sergeant major.

There wasn't another guest in sight, she hadn't showered, washed her hair or applied a dab of make-up, and she only had an hour or so left to get ready before pre-wedding cocktails and nibbles were served. Her mother was probably already wearing her mother-of-the-bride outfit and preparing herself for an afternoon of wedding critique. Wherever Dan had disappeared to, catching up with him and sorting things out would have to go maddeningly on hold now that the wedding was going ahead as planned.

Maybe he'd come back while she was getting dressed...

...owered and changed with minutes to spare
and ...e was still no sign of him.

Maybe he had no intention of coming back at all
while she was there. She had told him he was selfish
for not helping out a friend, that he cared about no
one but himself. Without him here there was only one
conclusion. This wasn't about any regard for *her*—it
was about making a point, showing her she was wrong
about him and then exiting her life with the moral
high ground.

The finished marquee turned out to be a yellow
flower explosion. Huge floral arrangements stood
on plinths in every spare space. Yellow silk bunting
decked the roof, and the chairs were wrapped in huge
yellow bows, standing in twin rows separated by a wide
aisle covered with a thick-pile yellow carpet. At the
very front a perfectly dressed white table was decked
in yellow flowers.

She was one of the last people to take her seat, earn-
ing a glare from her mother, who was perched in the
front row rubbernecking at the other guests. Her furious face was topped by an enormous salmon-pink
feather hat which clashed eye-wateringly with the mad
overuse of yellow.

In a sudden burst of exasperated defiance Emma
stood straight up again. She could just nip outside and
try his phone again. And maybe while she was there
check the car park. At least that would be conclusive.

She sidestepped out of her row and turned back
down the aisle to the door. She had to get hold of him.

She wasn't about to let this go now—wedding or no wedding. She was stopped in her tracks by a deafening funked-up version of the 'Bridal March' as Adam and Ernie blocked the door in front of her. They were both wearing dark glasses, probably in defence against the major overuse of yellow. Ernie's small niece walked at their feet, lobbing yellow rose petals. The eyes of everyone in the room bored into her back and she had no choice but to slink back to her seat.

What was she thinking? She might as well face facts.

The wedding was under way. And he was clearly not coming.

The wave of sadness that realisation evoked took her breath away and made her throat constrict. The assumption that he'd helped Adam for her, because he *cared* about her, seemed unlikely now that he hadn't hung around to soak up her gratitude. The surge of excitement she'd felt when Adam had told her what had happened took a nosedive into stomach-churning disappointment. She would have to resign herself to coping with the ceremony and its aftermath by herself.

It was an odd novelty to be stressed about something else for a change, instead of the usual prospect of mad parental behaviour. The thought of being without him beat all her other problems into submission. Nothing seemed to bother her now. Her parents could do their worst, and probably would.

And then, just as she mentally gave up on Dan and tried to steel herself to get through the day without losing her sanity, her stomach gave an unexpected and disorientating flip as he walked into the marquee.

He strode casually down the aisle behind Adam and Ernie, crushing the trail of yellow rose petals under his feet, and slid into the seat next to her as if he was just a couple of minutes late instead of having gone AWOL for the last twelve hours. Any possible annoyance with him was immediately sidelined by her heart, which went into full thundering mode. To hide it, she immediately faked irritation.

She spoke from the corner of her mouth as Adam launched into his personally written over-emotional vows. Ernie was gazing at him adoringly.

'You're late,' she whispered.

He stared straight ahead. In his dark suit and crisp white shirt he looked ready for cocktails at some trendy London wine bar. A yellow carnation had been pinned to his lapel by one of the super-efficient attendants. There was a hint of stubble lining his jaw and one tiny sign that he'd cut it fine—the spikes of his hair were still slightly damp from the shower.

'I'm not. I'm bang on time.'

'I thought you'd gone back to London.'

This time he looked her way and gave her a half smile that made her stomach go soft.

'Just because you told me to? You don't get rid of me that easily.'

Her stomach gave a slow and delicious flip. What the hell did *that* mean? That he wanted to stay or that he was making a point?

* * *

The service progressed at the front of the room and she barely heard a word of it. Her mind continued to whirl while cheers rang out around them and a shower of yellow confetti fluttered over Adam and Ernie as they raised triumphant hands above their heads. She hardly took in any of it. All she wanted was to drag Dan somewhere quiet to talk.

Nerves twisted inside her as she followed the rest of the guests back up the yellow-ribbon-lined aisle and into the hotel's conservatory for drinks while the marquee was reset for dinner. A string quartet kicked into action at one side of the room as waiting staff with trays of canapés began to mingle with the guests. Dan nodded around, smiling and winking at people, working the fake plus-one wedding guest image to a tee, and suddenly she could stand it no longer.

She grabbed him by the elbow and tugged him to a quiet corner of the room.

'Where *were* you all morning, then?' she said. 'You don't get off that easily.'

She waited for him to regale her with how he'd single-handedly solved Adam's problems and then sit back to watch her eat her words.

Instead he shrugged easily and took a sip of his champagne.

'Around. I'm an early riser. You were dead to the world, snoring away.'

He grinned broadly as she aimed an exasperated slap at his shoulder.

'I do *not* snore.'

So he was clearly not immediately going to volunteer what he'd done. What was the point of actually *doing* it, then, if it hadn't been to impress her?

She ran her hand through her hair, trying to think straight. She was so confused.

Dan watched her over the rim of his glass, trying to maintain a relaxed air of mingling wedding guest when all he wanted to do was stare at her. She looked prettier than ever in a silver-grey silk dress that set off her creamy complexion. Her hair was lying in soft waves, one side held back from her face by a sparkly clip. His desire for her was as strong as it had been the previous night. Nothing had changed. Had he really thought it would?

She held his gaze boldly and he heard her take a deep breath.

'You helped Adam,' she said. 'I know about the loan. I thought you didn't want to get sucked into family stuff.'

He deliberately didn't meet her eyes and kept his tone light.

'Yeah, well, I wasn't thinking straight when you first suggested it,' he said. 'Maybe I just wasn't crazy on Adam's timing.'

He watched the blush rise on her cheeks at his reference to the previous night and heat began to pool deep in his abdomen.

'Well, if you think I'll just hop into bed with you

now, because you stepped up to the plate with Adam, you're wrong,' she said.

If only that were the limit of his need for her.

'If I'd wanted to go to bed with someone I wouldn't have wasted half the night counselling Adam. I would have been down in the lobby chatting up the receptionist.'

If he needed any reminder that he was in over his head here, there it was. This was *not* just about getting her into bed.

He'd actually done far more than he'd intended when he'd left her sleeping in the small hours. The plan to just give Adam some kind of rousing pep talk had gone out of the window when he'd realised the monumental size of the mess he was in. Within five minutes it had become clear that a couple of websites and the number of a debt helpline were simply not going to cut the mustard, and the temptation had never been stronger to simply bow out of the situation and leave all of them to it while he went right back to his safe and organised life in London.

But all he'd been able to think about was Emma floundering the next morning, trying to pick up the pieces, and he simply hadn't been able to do it to her.

And what that decision meant filled him with far more trepidation than practically writing out a blank check to her lunatic brother.

He had feelings for her. Beyond anything he'd felt since Maggie. And even she now seemed to be taking on a vagueness in his mind that she hadn't had before—as if the edges of her memory were being softened by the reality of the present.

'To prove a point, then,' she said, narrowing her eyes. 'You can't stand being wrong and I touched a nerve.'

He cocked an eyebrow.

'With your "sad workaholic singleton" comment, you mean? I think I've had a few worse insults than that over the years.'

'Then what? Why would you do that about-face if it wasn't so you could have the last word?'

The cynical tilt of her chin finally tipped him into irritation.

'I notice you haven't asked me if I just did it out of the goodness of my heart. It hasn't occurred to you that I might just want to *help*.'

'Of course it hasn't. Because there's always an ulterior motive with you. Normally it's to do with work. Or possibly sex.'

'Emma, are you so used to being second best that you have to find some negative reason when the truth is staring you in the face? Why is it that you can't possibly contemplate that I might have just done the whole bloody thing for *you*?' he blurted in exasperation. 'You're maddening, your family are insane, you snore and your luggage habits are scary. But for some reason I'd rather commit myself financially to your mad brother and stay here with you instead of going back to London and my nice, peaceful, "sad workaholic singleton" life. Do you think I don't want to run for the hills? Truth is, I can't. I've realised there's nowhere I'd rather be than here.' He paused for breath. 'With you.'

She was staring at him.

His pulse vaulted into action as he met her wide brown eyes. He could see the light flush on her cheekbones. All the unrequited tension of the night before seeped back through his body. All around them the socialising carried on, and the urge raced through him to ignore the lot of them, grab her by the hand and tug her upstairs—let this crazy charade go on without them.

He closed the gap between them and lifted a hand to her cheek. The softness of her skin was tantalising beneath his fingers.

'Dinner is served.'

The Master of Ceremonies' curt tones cut through the background buzz of chatter and snapped him out of it.

'Do stop dawdling, darling,' Emma's mother called as she swept past them in her ghastly coral ensemble, undoubtedly en route to the top table.

Oh, for Pete's sake...

By the time the meal was over the presence of Adam's entire social circle was beginning to seriously annoy Emma. It was extremely difficult to have an in-depth personal conversation while seated at a table of eight overenthusiastic art groupies.

Dinner finished with, the marquee was cleared of the tables in the centre to reveal a glossy dance floor. Strings of fairy lights and candelabra supplied a twinkly, magical ambience. You couldn't move without tripping over a champagne waiter. And this after the most sumptuous four-course meal she'd ever been too strung-out to eat. Clearly there had been no expense spared. She wondered just how big Dan's loan to Adam was. If this was the level of his spending habits he'd still be paying it off when he was drawing his pension.

'I mean, really—no speeches? No best man. No bridesmaids. No tradition whatsoever! I just want to *know*—and I'm sure I'm not alone in this—' her mother glanced around for confirmation '—what happens about the name-change? Who takes whose name?'

She looked expectantly at Adam, standing nearby, who shifted from foot to foot.

'Mum, it's no different to any other wedding. You can take or not take whatever name you please,' Emma said, pasting on a smile to counteract any offence that might be caused. 'You're living in the past.'

'I don't agree. I don't see why Adam should change his name.'

'I'm not,' Adam said. 'And neither is Ernie.'

Her mother rounded on Ernie, who took an automatic defensive step backwards.

'Why not?' she demanded. 'Is our family name not good enough?'

'Mum, please...' Emma said.

Ernie held his hands up.

'It's perfectly fine, Emma. It's nothing to do with family names.' He looked kindly at her mother. 'I'd walk over hot coals for him, darling, but I cannot possibly be known as Ernie Burney.'

Adam took his arm and they moved away. Her mother gaped for a moment, and then took refuge in her usual critical safe bet in order to save face.

'Of course if *you* could only find a man who would commit there wouldn't be any of this lunacy,' she snapped at Emma. 'We could have a proper wedding with all the trimmings.'

The band chose that moment to launch into full-on swing music, mercifully making it impossible to hear any further argument, and the compère took to the glossy parquet floor.

'Ladies and gentlemen, I give you...the groom and groom.'

Her mother's mouth puckered and then disappeared as a pool of light flicked on in the centre to reveal Adam and Ernie striking a pose. A kitsch disco track kicked into action and they threw themselves into a clearly pre-rehearsed dance routine.

Dan stared in amazement as Adam danced past them, finger stabbing the air above his head, back to his full quota of sweeping flamboyant enthusiasm. Ernie skidded across the parquet on his knees, snapping his fingers above his head. A circle of guests began to form at the edges of the dance floor, clapping along. The room worked itself into a crescendo of rhythmic toe-tapping. It was bedlam.

'And...the parents of the happy couple...'

Ernie's father, completely unaware of what he was

letting himself in for, held out a hand to Emma's mother and began propelling her around the floor. Emma watched her mother's stiff and obvious fluster with a grin.

'She can't complain. She did want a bit more tradition after all,' she said.

'And...family and friends...please take the floor...'

Dan held his hand out, a smile crinkling his eyes. She stared at him, her heart skipping into action.

'I don't dance,' she said, shaking her head.

He totally ignored her. Before she could wriggle free he'd caught her fingers in his own and tugged her against him, curling his free hand around her waist.

'Just hang on, then,' he said.

The jaunty music demanded a lot more balance and rhythm than a swaying slow dance, and Emma silently cursed Adam for his disco obsession.

Dan turned out to be an excellent dancer. He propelled her smoothly around the floor in perfect time to the music and she somehow managed to hold on to him instead of falling over. Then at last the music mercifully slowed and embarrassment slowly gave way to consciousness of him. She could feel the hard muscle of his thighs moving against her own. Sparks jumped from her fingers as he laced them through his. His heartbeat pressed against hers.

'Why now, then?' she said, looking up at him, a light frown shadowing her face. 'You haven't answered that question. You had *months* to make a move on me if you were interested. Months of work dates back in London. Why now? Why here? Because you'd made it clear our agreement was over? Is that it? You were pretty keen to draw a line under our relationship when this weekend finished, so did that make me fair game?'

'If I'd known you were interested maybe I would have made a move before,' he said, knowing perfectly well he'd never have allowed himself to do so.

She made an exasperated sound.

'That's crap. I'm *so* not your type.'

'In actual fact you're *exactly* my type. And that's why I never made a move. I met you in your work role and you were so bloody good at it I wasn't about to ruin that by sleeping with you. I needed you too much.'

She pulled away from him a little as she processed what that might mean.

'And now you don't need me any more, sleeping with me is suddenly back on the agenda? Is that it?'

'That's not it at all. This weekend is the first I've spent with anyone at such close quarters without sex being the only thing on the agenda. And it isn't a piece of cake, I'll be honest with you. Nothing about you is easy. You're a pain to share a room with, and your family are more bonkers than I realised, but for the first time in I don't know how long work isn't the first thing I'm thinking about.'

She looked up at him and met his eyes, his expression clear and genuine.

'When I talked to Adam I realised there would be a

massive fallout if the wedding didn't go ahead. I could imagine the embarrassment, the fuss, having to send the guests away. It wasn't about Adam. He's got himself into trouble and he should dig himself out of it. It might even be character-building. When I couldn't walk away I realised that the person I was really doing it for was you. And that's when I knew that, whatever I felt about you, platonic work colleague didn't really cover it any more.'

He carried on talking, thinking vaguely that they seemed to have lost time with the jaunty beat of the music. Other guests began to whirl past them.

She stopped dancing. He attempted a couple more steps before giving up and joining her. The thing about dancing was that you needed your partner at least to *attempt* to engage—otherwise it was akin to dragging a sack of potatoes around the floor at speed. Trepidation spiked in his stomach at the look of disbelief on her face, telling him that his feelings for her had climbed way further than he'd thought. He'd been kind of banking on a smile at the very least.

'Say that again.'

'Emma, we're in the middle of the bloody dance floor. Let's go and sit down, get a drink.'

'I don't want a drink. Say that again.'

'I couldn't give a toss about Adam getting into trouble?'

She punched his shoulder.

'Not that bit.'

He saw the mock-exasperated smile on her lips, saw it climb to her eyes.

'Platonic work colleague didn't cover it any more?'

The smile melted away. She was looking up at him, brown eyes wide, soft lips lightly parted, and the madly circling dance floor around them disappeared from his consciousness.

'Yes. That bit.'

He tightened his grip around her waist and slid his fingers into her hair, stroking his thumb along her jaw-line as he tilted her lips to meet his.

Emma's heart was thundering as if they'd done another disco turn instead of swaying languorously around the dance floor.

The Dan she'd known for a year and long given up on would never have helped Adam out for nothing in return—would never have taken the time to explain his feelings to her. And he would never have turned back having driven halfway to London—not when he'd made his point before he left. She'd bucked his little-black-book no-strings trend. He'd put her first.

Sweet excitement began to swirl in her stomach as her mind focused on the feel of his body hard against hers and she breathed in the scent of spicy aftershave and warm skin as he kissed and kissed and kissed her.

At last she opened her eyes to see the *déjà-vu* disapproving stare of her mother across the room. Necking on the dance floor, this time, instead of in corridors—

how common. Except that this time she found she really couldn't give a *damn*.

She laced her hand through his and tugged at his arm.

'Let's go upstairs.'

TEN

―

She followed him into the hotel room, buying a bit more time and space for her skittering nerves by leaning gently back against the door until it clicked shut. The party carried on in the marquee below them and music and faint laughter drifted in through the window, open a crack. The closed curtains fluttered lightly in the night breeze.

Delicious anticipation fluttered in her stomach as he turned back to her in the soft amber glow of the table lamp and tugged her into his arms, his mouth groping for hers, finding it, sucking gently on her lower lip and caressing it softly with his tongue.

His fingers slipped beneath the fall of her hair to find the zip of her dress and he pulled it slowly down in one smooth motion, sliding the fluttering sleeves from her shoulders, his mouth tracing the blade of her collarbone with tiny kisses. He smoothed her dress lower, until it fell from her body into a gleaming puddle of silk on the floor. And then her mind followed his hands as they explored her body, as he unhooked her bra, cast it aside and cupped her breasts softly in his palms. Her nipples were pinched lightly between his fingers, sending dizzying flutters down her spine where they intensified hotly between her legs.

Then came brief unsteadiness as he slid his hands firmly beneath her thighs and lifted her against him. She could feel his rigid arousal press against her as she curled her legs around his waist and he carried her the few paces across the room to the antique desk. He held her tightly against him and she leaned sideways as he swept her belongings carelessly onto the floor. Body lotion and hairbrush fell with meaningless thuds onto the deep-pile carpet, and then there was cool, smooth wood against her skin as he put her down on the desk in just her panties.

She'd had a few boyfriends, yes. In the dim and distant past she'd done the rounds, albeit in a minor way, at university. None of it had felt like this. And if during the last year she'd let herself imagine what it might feel like to be with him it had never touched this reality. His every touch made her heart leap and her stomach flutter. His touch was expert, but there was nothing by rote about this. He seemed in tune with her every need and desire, as if he could read her mind.

His hands found her thighs again, parting them softly, and then he was tracing kisses down her neck, his mouth sliding lower until he closed his lips over her nipple, teasing it softly with his tongue. Heat simmered in her stomach and pooled meltingly between her thighs as he sank to his knees and traced his mouth lightly over the flat of her stomach. She sucked in a sharp breath as his lips sank lower still and the heat of his breath warmed her through the lace of her panties. She gasped as his fingers teased the thin fabric aside and his tongue slipped against the very core of her.

Her hands found his hair and clutched at it as he stroked and teased until she ached for him to go further, and then delicious pleasure flooded her veins as he slid two fingers inside her in one slow and smooth movement. She moaned softly as he found his rhythm, moving his fingers steadily as his tongue lazily circled the nub of her, moving with her, until she cried her ecstasy at the ceiling and he moved both hands beneath her, holding her against his mouth, wringing every last second of satisfaction out of her.

Anonymity was gone. That inconsequential, easy gratification wasn't there. Because for once this wasn't about quick fun, satisfaction. Dispensable satisfaction.

This was about her. Wanting to please *her*. And that was a real novelty that knocked his senses sprawling.

The light change in her breath as he ran his fingertips over the softness of her thighs, the way she gasped and clutched at his hair as he moved them higher— all those little gestures delighted him and turned him on all the more.

Dan got to his feet in the hollow between her parted legs and pulled her close. She curled her arms around him, tugging him against her, her fast, short breaths warm against his lips. Her evident excitement, such a foil to her usual carefully controlled attitude, thrilled him to the core, and in the all-encompassing heat of his arousal he marvelled at the surge of excitement pleasing her elicited.

He had been going through the motions all this time. His dates, his easy flings... Plenty of them, but all a simple good time means to an end. The cost of that had been the detached quality about them that meant pleasure had failed to touch him below the physical surface. The combination of his visceral hot need for Emma, his delight at her eagerness to please him and his own desire to please her took him way beyond that level. There was nothing run of the mill about this.

The thought crept through his mind, tinged with fear at the deeper meaning of it, but he moved on regardless, powerless to stop.

He lifted her, his hands sliding across the cool satiny skin of her lower back, the sweet vanilla scent of her hair dizzying his senses, and crushed his mouth hard against hers. His desire for her was rising inside him like a cresting wave, driving him forward. Her legs wrapped around his waist as he carried her the few paces from desk to four-poster and eased her down gently onto the softness of the quilted bedspread.

And now he moved with intimate slowness, the better to savour every second, to explore. She slid gentle hands over his back and sparks of arousal jumped and flickered in his abdomen as her fingers found his hard

length and stroked with deliciously maddening softness. A guttural moan escaped his lips as he tangled
a hand in the silk of her hair and crushed his mouth
against hers, easing her lips apart with his tongue.

Before he could be consumed by the deliciousness
of it he caught her hand and moved away briefly to
find a condom. And then control was his again as he
moved against her, and her gasp thrilled him as he
eased slowly into her. As she raised her hips with a soft
moan, urging him on, sliding her hands around him to
push him deeper into her, greedy for more, his spirits
soared. And only as she clutched at his back and cried
her pleasure against his neck did he finally let himself
follow her over that delicious edge.

Bewildering *déjà vu* kicked in as Emma woke to bird-
song and sunshine for the second time in a weekend.
And then all thoughts of her surroundings disappeared
as she came fully awake in one crushing instant of consciousness. She turned her head slowly on the pillow.

Not a hallucination brought on by wedding stress
and too much champagne.

Dan was in the bed next to her. And they'd spent the
night exploring every inch of one another. Hell, her
cheeks fired just at the thought of what they'd done
and she pressed her face against the cool top sheet.
Had that *really* been her? Super-cool, professional
Emma? Brazen—that was what she was.

His dark hair was dishevelled even beyond its
usual spikes by action and sleep, and there was a light

shadow of stubble now defining his jaw. She lifted a hand to her dry mouth as her gaze ranged down the defined muscles of his torso to the sheet that lay haphazardly over his hips. He was the stuff of dreams.

But the cold light of day was streaming in right through that window. She'd joined the ranks of Dan's little-black-book girls. How long did he usually leave it before he did his backing off? A day? Two?

She held her breath and without sitting up began wriggling inch by slow inch towards the edge of the bed, not really thinking much further at this point than getting some clothes on. They might have spent half the night screwing, but that didn't mean he'd have the chance to ogle her cellulite in daylight.

She was right on the edge of the bed and just thinking about how to manoeuvre her feet onto the floor when he took a deep, relaxed breath and opened his eyes.

She froze like a rabbit in headlights.

'You look surprised,' he said, stretching easily.

He gave her that slow, laconic grin that never failed to make her stomach do flip-flops. Clearly she had the *look* of a rabbit in headlights, too.

'Is it such a disappointment to wake up next to me?'

She clutched the top of the sheet a modest few inches above nipple height and tried to move her bum cheeks back fully onto the bed so he wouldn't realise she'd been trying to make an exit.

'I wasn't sure I would,' she said. 'I half expected you to make a swift exit under cover of darkness. Didn't you tell me that was your usual modus operandi? Not to make it through to breakfast?'

He pulled himself up onto one elbow and smiled down at her. The benefit of having hair that naturally spiked was that he actually looked *better* first thing in the morning. How typical. She could just imagine the fright wig on her own head after the active night they'd spent.

'Emma, nothing about this is my usual modus operandi.'

His blue eyes held her own and her stomach gave a slow and toe-curling flip as the delectable things he'd done to her last night danced through her mind. He reached a hand out to stroke her cheek softly and a surge of happiness began to bubble through her. He was right. None of this fitted with him acting to type. Yet still it was hard to let herself trust him.

'I know you too well,' she said. 'That's the thing. None of your usual lines will work on me.'

'I wasn't aware I'd used any,' he said.

He had a point. He'd bailed her brother out, he hadn't washed his hands of her and disappeared to London after she'd called him selfish, he'd carried himself brilliantly through her brother's crazy wedding and he was still here at breakfast time. She let her guard slip.

Self-doubt. Any other reaction from her would be a surprise, wouldn't it?

Just looking at her lying next to him, all long limbs

and messy hair and uncertainty, made heat begin to simmer again deep inside him. The night they'd spent replayed in his mind on a loop—the way she'd slowly put her trust in him, shedding her inhibitions, giving as much as taking. He wanted to smooth every kink of doubt out of her, convince her that this was far more than the throwaway night she clearly thought it might be.

He reached across and pulled her into his arms, fitting her long, slender body against his own, breathing in the faint sweet vanilla scent that still clung to her hair. His mouth found hers and he parted her lips hungrily with his tongue and kissed her deeply.

Desire rippled through her, peaking at her nipples and pooling between her legs as he gently turned her over, his mouth at her shoulder.

In her dreams of all those months ago he had been skilled. In reality he was melt-to-the-floor perfect. How did he know how to make her feel that sublime? Where to touch her? How hard to stroke? How softly to caress?

He lay behind her now, her pleasure his sole focus. One hand was circling her waist, his fingers easing slowly between her thighs, softly parting them to expose the core of her. She felt his moan of satisfaction against her neck as he discovered how wet she was. His thumb found her most sensitive spot and circled it with tantalising slowness. His fingers slid lower, teasing until she ached with emptiness and desire.

And then he was turning her expertly, one hand pressed flat beneath her stomach, the other cradling her breasts as he moved behind her. A moment of delicious anticipation as he paused to grab a condom, then she felt him press against her. And then he was thrusting smoothly deep inside her, filling her deliciously, his free hand teasing her nipples to rock-hard points, his mouth at her neck. As she cried out in uncontrolled pleasure he moaned his own ecstasy against the smooth contours of her back, not slowing or changing pace until he knew she was satisfied.

Afterwards, she lay in his arms, the warm length of his torso against her back, his soft breath against her hair. His hand circled her body, lightly cupping her breast, caressing it. They fitted together perfectly, as if they were meant to be together. For the first time she let herself tentatively believe that they might be. He'd made love to her again instead of making a sharp exit. He was still here with her. Yet still there were things that needed to be said.

'I didn't say thank you, did I?' she said softly. When he didn't answer she turned her head slightly, to catch his expression at her shoulder. 'For restoring Adam's shadow for me.'

She felt him tense briefly, then he tugged gently at her shoulder until she turned over in his arms and lay facing him. His mouth was inches from her own and his gaze was holding hers steadily.

He looked at her resigned expression and mentally kicked himself.

'I didn't mean that,' he said. 'It was a crappy thing to say. I know how difficult your family can be.' He paused as if groping for the right words. 'It wasn't a personal dig at you. It was more about reacting to your telling me where to get off.'

'You always have to have the last word,' she said quietly. 'I've noticed that about you. Why is that? Why is it so hard for you to accept anyone else's agenda? People *do* have them, you know—it's not just *you* living in a bubble.'

Was that how she really saw him? Was he really that blind to other people's feelings?

'It wasn't intentional,' he said. 'I'm sorry if it seemed that way to you. It was...' He groped for a way to explain that wouldn't sound totally crap. 'I like staying in control,' he said at last. 'Being the one that makes all the decisions. Perhaps it's become a bit of a habit.' He paused and added, 'A defence mechanism.'

The same one he'd used so successfully since childhood.

'If the only person you look out for is yourself, you can't be hurt.'

'I don't understand.'

He looked at the ceiling, at the blank white expanse of it.

'There was someone once,' he said. 'I'm not talking about one of the girls I see now. They're just dates. Nothing more to it than that. There was someone else a long time ago.'

He didn't look at her. It felt easier, not doing that.

'Maggie and I were housemates at college,' he said. 'There were six of us. Couple of girls, four blokes, each of us renting a room and sharing a kitchen and bathroom. You know the kind of thing. Student accommodation. For the first time I was living away from home.'

He remembered how liberating it had felt that his life was finally his own. An escape route.

'We were friends, Maggie and me, then one night after a party we ended up sleeping together. We kept it really casual, though. Both of us had big career plans. She was training to be a teacher. Primary school kids, you know?'

He glanced at Emma and she nodded acknowledgment, not interrupting. That was a good thing. If he stopped talking about this now he might never start again.

'And she lived up north, had a big family there, and she was going to be moving back once she'd finished her course. It wasn't serious. It was never *going* to be serious.' He laughed. 'Hell, I'd just got *away* from home life, finally tasted a bit of freedom. I wasn't about to get myself tied down to someone before I'd even finished my first year.'

She looked puzzled.

'But you did? You must have for her to have made such a big impact on you. What happened?'

He paused, gathering his thoughts. Who had he told about the baby? Anyone at all? He stormed ahead before he could think twice.

'Maggie got pregnant,' he said simply.

He felt the change in her posture as she shifted in his arms. She lifted herself on one elbow to look at him. He steeled himself to glance at her and read the response in her face, ready for the questions that he was sure would follow.

She said nothing. Her eyes were filled with gentleness but she didn't speak, didn't pry. She was letting him talk on his own terms.

'And that changed everything,' he said.

He took a sharp breath as he recalled the memory. It came back to him easily, in such perfect clarity that it made a mockery of his conviction that he'd done such a great job of putting it behind him.

'At first I was horrified. I thought it was the last thing I could possibly want. Maggie had strong views. She was going to keep the baby whether I was involved or not.' He sighed. 'She made it sound like she was offering me my freedom, but looking back I think to her I was dispensable even at the outset.'

'And were you? Involved, I mean?'

He could see the puzzlement in her eyes. She was wondering if he had a secret family stashed away somewhere.

'Once I got used to the shock I was more and more delighted. The longer it went on the more I bought into it. With every day that passed I had a clearer idea of what the future would be like. I was going to be the best bloody husband and father the world had ever seen.'

'You've been married?'

He gave a rueful smile and shook his head.

'It was my one and only brush with it, but, no, it never happened. I wanted it to be as different to my experience of family as I could make it. Proper commitment, hands-on parents with a strong, healthy relationship.' He paused. 'I probably envisaged a white picket fence somewhere. And a dog. Sunday roasts. All the stereotypes. I was right in there with them.' He took a breath. 'And then it all disappeared overnight because we lost the baby.'

The wrenching, churning ache deep in his chest made a suffocating comeback. Dulled a little at the edges over time, like an old wound, but still there, still heavy.

She was sitting up now, reaching for his hands, her eyes filled with sadness.

'Oh, bloody hell, Dan. I'm so sorry.'

He waved a dismissive hand at her, shaking his head, swallowing hard to rid his throat of the aching constriction.

'It was a long time ago,' he said.

In terms of years, at least.

'I'm over it.'

'I never imagined you being remotely interested in kids or family,' she said. 'I mean, it isn't just the way you keep your relationships so short or the fact you never see your own parents. You're the most un-child-friendly person I've ever known. You have a penthouse flat with a balcony and it's full of glass furniture and white upholstery. Your car is a two-seater.'

'Why would I need a family home or a Volvo?' he said. 'I have absolutely no intention of going down that road again. I gave it my best shot and it didn't work out.'

A worried frown played about her face and he gave her a reassuring *I'm-over-it* smile.

'That's why I didn't step straight up to the plate when Adam needed a helping hand. That's why I made it into the car before I realised I couldn't leave for London. I was trying to play things the way I always do. I don't get involved with people. I like keeping things simple.'

'At arm's length.'

'Exactly. Arm's length. After Maggie I decided relationships weren't for me. Family wasn't for me. I threw myself into work instead. After all, it had always worked at digging me out in the past. And it worked again.' He shrugged. 'But maybe it's become a bit of a habit. I never wanted to come across as selfish or unkind when I said you liked your comfort zone. It was a retaliation, nothing more.'

He pulled her back down from her elbow into a cuddle. Her head nestled beneath his chin. She shook her head slowly against his chest.

'Maybe it *was* just a retaliation but actually you might have had a point,' she said quietly.

He pulled away enough to give her a questioning look and she offered him a tiny smile.

'A *small* point,' she qualified. 'Did you ever know

I had a crush on you for months, like some stupid schoolgirl?'

That flash of clarity kicked in again, the same as he'd felt the night before, as if something he wasn't seeing had been pointed out to him. A wood instead of a mass of trees, maybe.

'You did?'

'Why am I not surprised that you never noticed?' She sighed and rolled her eyes. 'I think maybe part of the reason I was so struck on you was because of what you're like. I knew you'd never look twice at me. I didn't fit your remit.'

'My *remit*?' He grinned and tugged her closer.

She snuggled into his arm. 'Blonde, bubbly, curvaceous. That's your type.'

'Dispensable, simplistic, inconsequential,' he said. 'Those were the real qualities I was aiming for. None of which apply to you.'

'That's exactly my point. I got to know you over months, I saw the kind of girls you went for and I knew none of your relationships lasted. I knew you'd never be interested in me and that made dreaming about the prospect from afar a very nice, safe thing to do.'

She held a hand up as if it was all suddenly clear to her.

'Plus it was a great reason not to get involved with anyone else, and it gave me the perfect way to fob off criticism from my parents when they asked about my life. So there you are, you see. When you said I was happy living in Adam's shadow, staying under my parents' radar, you kind of had a point. My choices were all about keeping an easy life.'

'You must have hidden it well,' he said, scanning his mind back over the last twelve months. Little signs jumped out at him now that he had that hindsight— the way she'd always been available for any work engagement, no matter how short the notice, the effort she'd always made with her appearance. He'd assumed those were things she did for everyone. Because that was what he'd *wanted* to assume. The alternative hadn't been allowed on his radar.

'Then again, I'm not sure I would have noticed unless you'd smashed me over the head with it,' he conceded. 'I had you filed very comfortably under "Work Colleague". That was what I needed you to be. I never intended things between us to be more than that.'

'Our plus-one agreement.'

He didn't respond, although the ensuing silence was heavy with the unspoken question. What would happen now with their ludicrous arrangement? He'd told her it would be over when they got this weekend out of the way and went back to their London lives. With every moment he spent with her, sticking to that decision and riding it out felt more and more difficult.

ELEVEN

'You want to try and get to breakfast?' he asked.

Emma felt the light brush of his kiss against her shoulder. Even after the night they'd spent, followed by the delicious intimacy of this morning, his touch thrilled her.

She wriggled against him. Her arms fitted around his neck as if they were meant to be there. She smoothed the dense spikes of his hair through her fingers.

'Let me think,' she said, smiling into his eyes. 'Would I rather sit opposite my parents and watch my father drool over a full English while my mother force-feeds him muesli, or would I rather stay here with you?'

He laughed and pulled her tighter.

'Adam's married now. I think he's grown-up enough to manage without me watching his back through one little breakfast.' She dropped her eyes briefly. 'And I think you've done enough for him. We can catch him before he goes.'

Was it just that? Or was part of it that she didn't want to leave this gorgeous little bubble where he was hers for fear that it might burst? After wanting him for so long, all the while convinced nothing would ever come of it, to actually have her crush requited made it seem all the sweeter.

Needling doubt lurked at the edge of her consciousness despite the gorgeous night they'd spent and the way he'd opened up about his past. She knew Dan—knew the way he played relationships. Despite his reassurances there was no getting away from the fact that pretty soon after you made it into Dan's bed you made it just as quickly out of it, never to be heard of again. Was this like some holiday romance? Would the magic be theirs as long as they didn't leave? What would happen when they got back to London?

She'd noticed that her mention of the old plus-one agreement hadn't been picked up by him. His intention to cut all ties with her after this weekend gnawed at the edge of her consciousness as she tried to push it away.

Adam and Ernie stood at the hotel doorway, waving madly. Those who had made it down to breakfast clustered in the lobby. Emma had dragged Dan downstairs with moments to spare and eased her way through the group of smiling friends and relatives, her hand entwined in his.

Emma's mother dabbed a tear from the corner of her eye.

'Well, it wasn't the most traditional set-up,' she sniffed, 'but still...it's been a lovely weekend.'

She kissed Adam's cheek and then leaned in to do the same to Ernie.

'Tradition?' Ernie said. 'I think we can stretch to a bit of that before we go.'

He grabbed at a bunch of yellow lilies standing in a huge vase on the side table near the door, turned his back on the gathered crowd of guests and lobbed them high in the air over his head to the sound of claps and squeals, showering the guests with drops of water. As the flowers plummeted, twisting and turning, faces turned to watch their progress.

Dan shot out a hand and caught them on autopilot, to prevent them from smacking him over the head.

He stared down stupidly at the bunch of flowers in his hand as cheers and mad clapping rang out all around them. Even Emma's mother was smiling.

'You're next!' Adam hollered from the doorway. 'Great catch, sweetie!'

Dan glanced at Emma and saw the look of delight on her face. Her eyes shone. Her smile lit up her face. She radiated happiness.

Shock flooded into the pit of his stomach.

You're next!

Was he? Was that where this led?

He'd had a game plan way back in London, before they'd even set foot in the West Country. A plan to be a last-time-pays-for-all fake boyfriend stand-in for Emma and then go back to London. Back to work. Back to what *worked*. And somehow he'd been caught up in the moment, had lost sight of what was important to him.

He'd ended up standing here with flowers in his hands to the sound of excited applause because the path ahead of him led down the aisle. Maybe not now, maybe not even in the next few years, but *that* was the destination.

If they made it that far.

That was the risk. A risk he'd vowed never to take again after the months of despair that had plagued him when Maggie left.

This was way off-plan. Yet the thought of losing Emma now made his heart plummet and misery churn in his stomach.

He followed the rest of the group outside to watch Adam and Ernie pile into a yellow Rolls-Royce. Maybe he could find another way forward. A way to keep her that still minimised risk. A compromise.

She'd been right.

There really was more between them than one of his casual flings. They'd been back from the wedding for nearly a week now and he was a different man. He was in touch with her daily, and with every phone call and text she felt more secure. Flowers arrived from him at her workplace, eliciting envious stares and buzzing interest from her colleagues. He hadn't so much as mentioned their old plus-one agreement, but that was because it was obsolete—right? Past history. OK, so she wasn't expecting him to propose...let's not get ahead of ourselves—although a girl could dream. But she'd been the one to change his behaviour. He really *was* different with her. They were a couple now—not just work contacts.

Dan didn't *do* flowers and phone calls. He did swift exits and dumping by text. And now she was seeing him tonight and her stomach was one big ball of excitement and anticipation. She couldn't wait.

The doorbell. On time.

She checked her appearance one last time. A new dress, a less austere one than usual, with a floaty, feminine skirt. Deep pink instead of her usual black or grey choice of going-out outfit. Because going out with Dan was about pleasure now, not business. About getting to know each other instead of working the situation for every career advantage they could get out of it.

She opened the front door and excitement at seeing him brought an instant smile to her face—one she couldn't have held back. He stood on the doorstep, leaning against the jamb, his crisp blue shirt deepening the tones of his eyes as he smiled at her, a perfectly cut business suit and silk tie sharpening the look.

Not the same relaxed designer look he'd had at the wedding weekend. Her mind stuttered briefly. *Business suit.*

From nowhere cautionary unease jabbed her in the ribs and a wave of disorientating *déjà vu* swept over her. She could have rewound to a couple of months before Adam's wedding, before Alistair had put a stop to their agreement, and Dan would have looked exactly like this when she'd opened the door for one of their business engagements.

He slid an arm around her waist and kissed her softly on the mouth, starting up all the latent sparks from the weekend.

She pulled herself up short.

Jumping at shadows—that was what she was doing. She was so used to being doomed to failure when she put herself out there that now she was pre-empting problems before they even happened. She'd ruin things herself if she wasn't careful. Already he had a puzzled expression on his face—no doubt because her first reaction on seeing him since their gorgeous weekend at the wedding was to hesitate.

He'd called her. He'd sent flowers. He'd texted. And now she was spooked because of the *suit* he wore? She really needed to go to work on her own insecurities if she was going to move forward with her life.

'Where are we going, then?' she asked when he started the car.

'Dinner first,' he said easily, putting it in gear and moving smoothly into the early-evening traffic. 'I've got a table booked at La Maison.'

Another jab of unease.

'La Maison?'

It was Dan's choice of venue for work dinners. She'd been there with him too many times to count, always as his stand-in date, always with a work objective in mind. Maybe it would be a new contact to impress, perhaps a sweetener before he put in a tender for services. Whatever it happened to be, she'd been there to help smooth the path.

He glanced across at her.

'For starters, yes. If that's OK with you? Then maybe later we could go on somewhere else? End up at my place?'

'Of course.'

She smiled brightly at him and pressed her palms together in her lap. They were damp.

He parked the car and escorted her into the restaurant. The usual subtle piano music played in the background, and the usual perfectly dressed dark wood tables and soft lighting provided the perfect ambience for discussion, which had always been the point of coming here.

His usual table. She felt Dan's hand rest gently on her hip as he guided her between the tables towards it.

Usual restaurant. Usual table.

It didn't mean anything, did it? The restaurant was a good one after all.

Usual quick run-through of background?

'Roger Lewis and Barry Trent,' he said in a low voice at her shoulder. 'Medium-sized business providing bespoke travel packages specifically aimed at the over-fifties. Looking for advice on growing their business to the next level.' He gave her shoulder a squeeze. 'Could be in the market for a change in legal services, too—you could be in there!'

As they arrived at the table she turned to stare at him and he actually *winked* at her. It felt as if her heart was being squeezed in a vice.

'Table for four,' she said dully, stating the obvious.

He looked at her as if she might be mad. As if there was nothing spot-the-deliberate-mistake about this at all.

'Of course it is,' he said. 'Just a bit of business to discuss and then the evening's ours. They'll be along in a minute.'

The waiter pulled a chair out for her and fussed over her as she sat down hard, her mind reeling. Dan gave him the nod and he poured them each a glass of champagne, replacing the bottle in the ice bucket to one side of the table.

Her throat felt as if it might be closing up and she swallowed hard. She clasped her hands together on the table to stop them shaking.

'I thought we were going on a date,' she said, making her tone as neutral as she could manage when what she wanted to do was grab him by the shoulders and shake him. 'Just you and me. But this is basically the same old set-up, Dan.'

She waved a hand at the extra two table settings, at the surrounding quiet tastefulness of the restaurant.

'Is that it, then? Now we're back in London it's back to the same old routine? Were you actually going to discuss that with me, or did you just assume I'd go along with it?'

He reached for her hands but she removed them to her lap.

'I don't know what you mean,' he said.

'What this looks like to me is the same old plus-one agreement,' she said, forcing the words out, voicing her worst fears. 'Just with sex thrown in.'

He grimaced and leaned across the table to touch her cheek.

'This is *not* the same old plus-one agreement,' he said, 'and I really wish we'd never given the damn thing a name. It makes it sound like we signed something official when all we really did was get into a routine over time. Because it worked so well for *both* of us.'

A routine? She pressed her lips together hard and pushed a hand through her hair as anger began to course through her. It felt suddenly uncomfortably hot in here. She hadn't missed the emphasis there on the word *both*. No way was she letting him lump her in with this as if it were some joint bloody venture.

When he next spoke it felt as if he'd tipped the contents of the ice bucket over her head.

'But if we *have* to call it that,' he continued, holding out a hand, 'for what it's worth I don't think we should be too hasty about changing how we relate to each other when it comes to work. Why end something that's worked so well for us just because you and I have got closer? What do you think about varying it a little? Adding in a few amendments?'

His tone was jokey—teasing, even. As if he were proposing something exciting. As if she ought to be taking his arm off in her eagerness to say yes.

'Different rules this time—it'll be fun. We can still do work engagements together, give it everything we've got just like we always have, but without the need to limit it. There'll be no need to *pretend* we're a couple any more—no need to go our separate ways at the end of the night.'

He wanted to carry on seeing her but without any full-on legitimacy. Work would continue to come first with him, just the way it always had. He would expect her to carry on acting as his plus-one, smoothing the way for his business prowess at charity dinners and the like. The difference would be that this time she would get to share his bed, as well.

Well, *lucky, lucky* her.

All the pent-up excitement that had built this week as she'd looked forward to seeing him again had quit bubbling and dissipated like flat champagne. The flavour would still be there—the tang of white grape and the sharp aroma reminiscent of the effervescent drink it once was—but when you got right down to it, it was past its best. What you were really getting was the dregs.

And one thing she knew without a shadow of a doubt was that she was not going to be the dregs. Not for anyone.

Not even for him.

* * *

She stood up, a veil of calm slipping over her. She'd wanted him to be hers so much she'd believed she'd give anything to keep him.

But when it came to it she found that her self-respect just wasn't up for grabs.

He looked up at her, his expression confused, as she picked up her handbag and lifted her wrap from the back of her chair, making it obvious this wasn't just a visit to the ladies' room. She was leaving.

'Where are you going?'

'Home,' she said, not looking at him.

She pushed her chair back into place. Sick disappointment burned in her throat, blocking it. She wasn't sure she could stop it transforming into tears if she looked at him. She absolutely was *not* going to cry. No way.

He stood up immediately, his hand on her elbow.

'Why? What's wrong? Are you ill?'

The look of concern in his eyes touched her heart and she almost faltered. But this was just too bloody reminiscent of the last guy she'd met for dinner, thinking she was on her way to a happy ending. Dan was just like Alistair after all.

'No, Dan,' she said. 'I'm not ill. I'm stupid. Stupid for thinking there might actually be more between us than *work*.'

She made a move to leave and he grabbed her by the hand.

'Hey, we can talk about this. That's what this is

about? You're annoyed because I factored a work dinner into our date night?' He shrugged. 'I'm sorry. Maybe I should have talked to you about it first. I just didn't think you'd mind. Before last weekend you were all for carrying on with the agreement, and you'd gone back to work instead of taking that sabbatical, so I just assumed you'd be all for it.'

'That was before the weekend,' she said.

She looked down at her hand, encased in his.

'This isn't what I want. Some half-arsed excuse for a relationship. I thought you understood that. I don't want some relationship where we both have our own agenda and factor the other person in wherever they happen to fit. You know where that kind of relationship ends up?' She didn't wait for his answer. 'It ends up with separate bedrooms and separate interests and separate bloody lives. If we can't even get that right now, what hope do we have? I want you and me to be the priority—not an afterthought to whatever work ambitions we might happen to have.'

'It never bothered you before,' he pointed out.

'Because it was all I *had* before,' she said. 'It was the only way I could have some level of relationship with you. But I want more than that now. And after last weekend I thought you wanted that, too.'

Two business-suited middle-aged men were being ushered between the tables towards them. The over-fifties leisure break people, she assumed.

'Don't go,' he said. 'Let's get this business discussion out of the way and then we can talk this through properly.'

She gave a wry laugh and flung her hands up.

'That's the problem, you see. Right there. You *still* think I might actually sit down and put your work meeting first—before we get to talk about what's happening between us. I'm not doing it. Whatever this is for you—plus-one bloody agreement, quick fling, friends with benefits—it's over.'

She'd raised her voice and some of the diners seated nearby rubbernecked to stare at them. She didn't give a damn. She had no intention of ever visiting this restaurant again. In fact, the way she felt right now, she might not go out socially again. Possibly ever. Maybe she'd embrace her inner workaholic and make senior partnership by thirty-five. A new goal. One that was attainable. One that relied solely on her and so wasn't doomed to failure.

She walked away from the table.

He moved after her as she passed the two businessmen, one with his hand outstretched. She heard Dan apologise briefly before he ran after her. He caught her near the door, took her arm, turned her to face him.

'You're dumping me?' A grin lifted the corner of his mouth.

Her heart twisted agonisingly in her chest.

'Yes,' she said.

'What? No champagne-throwing?' he joked, as if he still couldn't believe she was making such a fuss.

She didn't smile. It felt as if her veins were full of ice water.

'That was a *fake* break-up, Dan,' she said. 'All for show. This is the real thing.'

She walked out of the restaurant without looking back.

TWELVE

—

Dan stared at the city skyline from the balcony of his flat. Grey today, misted in drizzle. The fine rain was the kind that coated and his hair and skin were slowly soaking; the boards were slick beneath his feet.

So she'd dumped him.

No one dumped him. *Ever.* And now she'd done it twice in the space of a couple of months.

The confused feeling of a loss of control which had buried him the first time, back at the art gallery, kicked right back into action. Had that really only been a month or two ago? It felt like years.

He wasn't going to make the same mistake again—grappling for control of the situation and leaving himself open to a second body blow.

Except it really hadn't been just a body blow, had it?

Let it go.

In the first defiant moments after she'd left him to sort out the embarrassment in the restaurant that had felt doable. He didn't need this kind of chaos in his life. That had been the whole point of keeping relationships distant. He'd had a lucky escape.

In the ensuing days it had become more and more difficult to keep himself convinced of that. It wasn't as if he'd let her have an access-all-areas pass to his life after all. Their paths crossed at work functions, they communicated via e-mail and the occasional phone call. Businesslike. At arm's length. She'd visited his flat on two or three occasions—never when it was just the two of them. So it wasn't as if her absence left a gaping hole in his life where she'd previously been. How could you miss something that you never had?

He knew that was possible better than anyone.

Somewhere in the depths of his consciousness he understood that what he was missing was the way she'd made him feel—the way she'd altered his take on life.

He'd spent so long making sure no one became important to him, but she'd somehow managed to get past that barrier. She'd done it so quietly that he hadn't realised how much he needed her until she was gone, so perfect had his conviction been that he had everything under control.

It had seemed like the perfect solution—the perfect way to keep things at the comfortable distance he'd thought he needed. Why not just reinstate the old social agreement? Keep their relationship grounded in something that was tried and tested? Keep some areas of his life untouched rather than investing his entire soul in something that might fail?

And in his stupid arrogance he'd just expected her to go along with his every whim, just to accept that their relationship had a work slant to it. Especially after her revelation about her age-old crush on him. She'd taken whatever he'd thrown her way for the last year, never asking for anything in return, and he saw now that he'd just taken that for granted.

If anything he admired her all the more for finally standing up for what she wanted. She'd wanted out because she wasn't prepared to settle for second best. After years of playing second fiddle to Adam and then being trounced by that moron Alistair Woods she'd been ready to risk everything to be with him and he'd failed her. He'd been too afraid to reciprocate.

The flat that she'd barely visited now felt empty where it had always felt relaxing. So far removed from any family vibe, he'd been able to look around him and know he'd built a new life—one that was successful, one that couldn't collapse under emotional rubble. The prospect of living here now felt empty. He'd had a taste of a different life. He'd tried to keep it in check. But apparently a taste was all that was needed to suck him totally in.

He was in love with her. And it was too late now to guard against loss because the damage was done. He'd screwed up.

He glanced around the balcony—hot tub with its cover on in the corner, railings with a sheer drop below.

What had she said—his life was child-unfriendly? It was. Deliberately so. Only now he began to question whether he still wanted that. Whether he ever truly had.

He moved back inside and slid the double doors shut. The flat was totally silent and devoid of character. No mess. No clutter.

He could let this go. See if he couldn't put it behind him. Hell, work had done the trick before—it might do it again. Perhaps if he ceased eating and sleeping and all other essential functions, doubled the effort with his business, he could crush her from his mind.

Or he could take a risk.

He glanced around him again. What, really, did he have to lose?

'...and Adam and Ernie are heading back from Mauritius. Adam's already got a ton of interest in his new planned collection of pictures and there's talk of them being immortalised on table mats and coasters. Can you imagine?' Her mother paused a moment to let the enormity of that fact sink in. 'That's the kind of mass appeal he has.'

Emma held the phone briefly away from her ear. Dan should have held out for a share in Adam's business in return for helping him. He could have made a mint. Then again, it would have been another tie, another responsibility, another link to a family he wanted to keep at a distance. Of course he wouldn't have wanted that.

She gritted her teeth hard and forced Dan out of her mind, to which he seemed to return at the slightest opportunity.

She put the phone back to her ear.

'What about you? Any news?' her mother was saying. 'Is that Dan showing any signs of making an honest woman of you?' She gave the briefest of pauses, clearly believing the answer was a foregone conclusion of a no. 'Thought not. Work, then?'

How many times had Emma had varying versions of this same conversation? Made the right noises just to avoid interest and interference, just to keep her comfort zone comfortable? She never had any new successes to hold up to her mother's scrutiny, but she never had any epic failures, either. Comfortable, uncomplicated middle ground. And where exactly had it got her?

She opened her mouth to give her mother some stock fob-off—something that would buy her another couple of months below the radar before she had to repeat this whole stupid fake conversation all over again. Probably it would be something about her legal career boring enough to have her mother fast-forwarding onto her next gossip morsel before she could scrutinise Emma's life beyond the surface. It had worked like a dream these last few years.

For the first time in millions of conversations she hesitated.

She was the most miserable she could ever remember being and the hideous pain was sharpened to gut-wrenching level because she'd known that brief spell of sublime perfection before Dan had reverted to type. In actual fact there had been no reversion. He'd never left type. It had all been a façade.

Was there *any* aspect of her life left that was real or of value?

'Dan and I aren't together,' she blurted, then clapped a hand over her own mouth in shock at her own words. 'We never were.'

Except for a week or two when I thought I was the stand-out one who could change him.

'We work together and we had an agreement to stand in as each other's dates at parties and dinners.'

For the first time ever there was stunned silence on the end of the phone and Emma had the oddest sensation in her stomach. A surge of off-the-wall indignant defiance. She picked it up and ran with it.

She really had been wallowing in the role of Adam's underachieving sibling all these years, kidding herself about how hard that was, when in reality it had been the easy option. Pigeonholing herself as failure meant she had absolutely nothing to live up to.

She didn't need to define herself by her childhood inadequacies—she had known that for years—but knowing it really wasn't enough. The real issue was whether or not she'd truly bought into that. Or had a part of her remained that sweaty-palmed kid on the stage in spite of the passing years?

For the first time she took a breath and really did buy into it. Just how much of her inadequacy was she responsible for? Who had put Adam on a gilded pedestal and kept him there? Guilty as charged. It had been easier to live in his shadow than to prove herself in her own right.

Had it in some way been easier to accept the categorisation of herself as the clumsy one? The underachiever? The let-down? The singleton? No relationships for her, because that would lead to rejection. Just oodles of work, because that was the one thing she could feel good at, because it depended only on her. Had it been easier to blame her family for her failures instead of living an actual functional, healthy life?

'I'm taking a sabbatical from work,' she said. 'I'm going travelling.'

All that excitement she'd had about going away with Alistair, about escaping her dreary old life where everything was safe and secure and devoid of risk, made a cautious comeback. When she'd finished with him she'd finished with all of that, too. But now that Adam's wedding was over and the train wreck that was her friendship, relationship, romance with Dan was finished—she wasn't even sure what the bloody hell to call it—what exactly was there to keep her here? Why the hell did she need Alistair on her arm to have an adventure of her own?

She had absolutely no idea what she wanted in life any more, so why not take the time to find out?

She slid her bag from her shoulder and sat down at a pavement café overlooking the harbour. She ordered coffee and watched the bustle of tourists passing by, queuing for boat trips, browsing the local shops, fishing. The sun warmed her shoulders in the simple linen dress she wore. Just time for a coffee before her own boat trip departed—a day cruise around the island.

She looked up as someone snagged the seat opposite her with their foot, and her heart leapt as they pulled it out and sat down.

She must be seeing things. Maybe that was what happened when you missed someone enough—no matter how stupid and pointless missing them might be.

He took his sunglasses off and smiled at her, and she knew instantly that for all her telling herself she was way over him her thundering heart had the real measure of things.

'How did you find me?' she said.

He motioned to the waiter, ordered coffee.

'I had to ask your mother.'

Damn, he'd been serious about tracking her down, then.

'And how did that work for you?' She kept her voice carefully neutral.

'Well, it was no picnic, I can tell you.'

'She doesn't know where I'm staying,' she said. 'I've been picking up accommodation as I go along, depending where I want to go next.'

'I know. Didn't sound like you. What—no agenda? No travel itinerary?'

She grinned at that. At how well he knew her.

'My life's been one massive agenda these last few

years—all about what impression I want to give to this person or that person. I needed a change. My mistake was waiting for someone else to come along and instigate that instead of biting the bullet myself.'

'She told me you'd been e-mailing her, and she knew you'd booked a boat trip from here today. She just didn't know what time.'

She stared at him.

'You mean you've been hanging around here all day on the off-chance I'd show up?'

He shrugged.

'It was a good chance, according to your mother.' He paused. 'It was the best shot I had.'

Bubbles of excitement were beginning to slip into her bloodstream. She gritted her teeth and took a sip of her strong coffee. Nothing had changed. Nothing would. He might have jetted out to see her but it was still the same Dan sitting opposite her. He probably just wanted the last word, as usual. He earned a fortune. A plane trip to the Balearics was hardly going to break the bank. She wasn't going to get sucked back into this—not now.

'It wasn't particularly easy to persuade her to help me, actually,' he added. 'Since you told her our relationship was fake.'

She looked sideways at him, one eye squinting against the sun.

'It was, Dan,' she said.

He leaned forward, his elbows on the table, and for the first time she saw how strained he looked.

'Don't say that.'

'Why did you come here?' she said. 'To make some kind of a point? To finish things between us on your terms? Go ahead and have your say, if that's what you need for closure. Get yourself the upper hand. I've got a boat to catch. I've got plans.'

She moved her hands to her sides and sat on them to maintain some distance between them.

'I know that's how I've behaved in the past.' He held his hands up. 'I hated it when you met Alistair and pulled out of our stupid agreement. I've spent years making sure *I'm* in charge in every relationship I have. I've built a life on controlling everything around me. When you just dumped the whole thing without a moment's thought I just couldn't let it slide. I manipulated the situation until it worked in my favour—agreed to bring the agreement back just so that *I* could be the one to pull out of it. I thought I'd totally nailed why it bothered me so damn much. I thought it was about calling the shots. But really I think you've always meant more to me than I realised.'

He paused, held her gaze.

'I didn't track you down so I could make some kind of a point. I came to apologise and to try and explain.'

Her stomach was doing mad acrobatics and she moved one of her hands from underneath her legs and pressed it hard.

'Go on,' she said.

'I told you how things were with Maggie,' he said. 'The thing is, it wasn't just a break-up with Maggie—

something that's tough but that you reconcile in time. There was this underlying feeling I've never been able to shake—that there was my one chance and I lost it. I never had that sense of belonging when I was growing up, and when Maggie got pregnant it felt like a gift. It was my opportunity to have a family and I would have done whatever it took to protect that.'

He sighed.

'Of course what it really boiled down to was an idea. I had this whole idealistic future mapped out in my head. Birthdays, holidays, where we were going to live. My family was going to want for nothing. I think Maggie understood the two of us better. If I'm honest, when she walked away, I think losing that whole dream future I'd been cultivating hurt a hell of a lot more than losing Maggie. I knew it, too, you see. It wasn't really working between us. If she hadn't got pregnant we might have carried on seeing each other for a few more months, then we would have gone our separate ways—wherever our work ambitions led us. We were fun. We were no-strings. It was never meant to be anything serious. Her pregnancy changed all of that. A baby on the way is one hell of a big string attached. Maggie didn't want me to look out for her. After we lost the baby it became very clear that for her any future we had together was gone. There was no alternative future—not for Maggie. She found it easier to cut all ties than to stick it out with me. And I knew that she was right. Because family hasn't exactly been my finest hour, has it?'

She held his gaze. She couldn't stop her hand this time as she reached across the table and touched his arm lightly.

'None of that means you're some kind of failure. It just means you haven't given yourself a proper chance.'

'I had absolutely no desire to give family a proper chance. Not when it ended up like that. It just seemed easier to accept that I'm not a family guy. And there were compensations.'

He gave her a wry smile. She smiled back.

'You mean your little black book of girlies?'

'I thought if I was going to cut myself off from family life I might as well make the most of what the bachelor lifestyle has to offer. Don't get the idea that I've wallowed in misery for the last ten years or so, because I haven't. I've had a brilliant time. It's only very recently that...' He trailed off.

'What?'

He looked at her then and the look in his eyes made her heart flip over.

'That it began to feel...I don't know...hollow. Nothing seemed to give me the buzz that it used to. I kept trying to up the stakes—pitching for tougher contracts, brainstorming new business ideas. Dating just lost its appeal. I felt like I was doing the rounds—the same old thing, the same old conversations. I couldn't work out what it was I needed to fix that. And then you met Alistair.'

She glanced along the harbourside. The queue for her boat trip was gradually diminishing as people stepped into the boat. She should wrap this up...crack on with her plans.

But hearing him out suddenly felt like the most important thing in the world. She told herself it didn't mean her resolve was weakening, and for Pete's sake there were other boat trips.

'I don't think I'd considered you in that way before. I hadn't let myself. I'd conditioned myself to centre everything in my life on work. But suddenly you had all these big plans—you were buzzing with happiness, you were taking a risk—and I was stuck there on the same old treadmill. I didn't like it. I think I was fed up with my own life. But it's been so long. I've really typecast myself as bachelor playboy. I thought that was who I am. I didn't think I could be anyone else.'

She covered his hand with hers and squeezed it.

A sympathy squeeze. Not a leaping-into-your-arms-is-imminent squeeze. The hope that had begun to grow in his heart when she hadn't simply left the table at the get-go faltered.

'Alistair did me a favour,' she said. 'Until I met him I think I could quite easily have carried on in that same old rut I was in, pretty much indefinitely. Thinking one day you might come to your senses and show some interest in me—'

'Emma...' he cut in urgently.

She shook her head and held up a hand to stop him.

'The crazy thing about that was that I *knew* exactly what you were like. I'd seen it first-hand for months. Different women, same old short-term thing... You never changed for any of them. I used to think they were mad—couldn't they *see* what you were like? Didn't they *know* it was a recipe for disaster, getting involved with you? And then I went right ahead and did exactly the same thing.'

'It wasn't the same. You and I are different. *I'm* different.'

She was shaking her head.

'We don't want the same things, Dan. We're fundamentally mismatched. If I've managed to salvage one thing from the stupid mess with Alistair it's that I know I want to be with someone who puts our relationship first, above anything else. Above some stupid dream of a film career.' She paused. 'Above a crazy work ethic.'

'I want us to be together.'

'Back at the wedding...what you said about me and Adam...' She looked down at her fingers. 'You told me I *liked* living in Adam's shadow. That I was wallowing in always being the one who didn't measure up. And you were right. Knowing I'd be perceived as a failure was the perfect excuse for not trying things, for staying safe. All this time—right back since school, where it felt like nothing I did was right—I've been living in Adam's shadow, and somewhere along the way I learned to prefer it. It made everything easier. Doomed not to measure up, so why bother trying?'

'But you've done brilliantly at work. You're sought after. You do a great job.'

She shook her head, a rueful smile touching her lips.

'The one area I knew I could succeed at, yes. That was a safe bet, too. I made sure I picked a job that doesn't depend on other people's perception of you for success. And something as far removed from Adam's work as possible. I don't even think it was a conscious decision—it was more of an instinctive self-preservation thing that I've been cultivating since I was a stupid, oversensitive teenager.'

She looked up at him then and the look in her eyes wrenched at his heart.

'I even deluded myself, Dan,' she said. 'I thought the single most essential thing, if I was to find someone, was for them to put me first for once. That was my bloody dating criteria, for Pete's sake! Being important to someone. Anyone.'

She threw a hand up.

'Alistair would've done. An idiot like him! If he'd carried on treating me like a princess I'd probably still be there with him, feeling smug and telling myself I was happy with that self-centred moron. I was missing the point completely. The person I really want to be important to is myself. *I* never thought I was worthwhile, but it was easier to put that on other people. I thought I could get self-esteem by keeping away from my parents, moving to London, fobbing them off with a fake life of the sort I thought I should have. But all along that was part of the problem. I liked my fake life better than my real one, too. I never really wanted to be me.'

'I want you to be you,' he said. 'There's not one single thing I'd change about you. Not even your obsessive overpacking for one weekend, which fills me with horror at what you might be like to actually *live* with— how much *stuff* you might bring into my life. I've never wanted anything more. I was scared. Too scared to give our relationship everything I've got because I didn't want to risk losing it. My track record sucks. I couldn't afford to buy into it completely because I couldn't bear to lose you.'

He reached a hand out and tucked a stray lock of her hair behind her ear. She reached for his hand, caught it and held it against her face. But her eyes were tortured, as if she were determined to stick to her decision regardless of how much it hurt.

'What about kids?' she said quietly, and his heart turned over softly. 'What about your glass furniture and your bachelor pad and your determination never to have a family of your own? Because that stuff *matters*, Dan. I'm only just starting to find myself here, but what if I want to have kids in the future? Are you going to run for the horizon?'

A smile touched his lips at that, but her face was deadly serious. Inside his spirits soared.

'I never thought I'd have another chance at family,' he said. 'I know I've built a life that reflects that, but it's all window dressing—all peripheral stuff that I've built up to convince myself as much as anyone else that I'm living the bachelor dream. Truth is, the bachelor dream is pretty bloody lonely. I want to be with you— whatever that involves.'

The thought of a future with her by his side, the

possibility of a family of his own with her, filled him with such bittersweet happiness that his throat constricted and he blinked hard and tried to swallow it away.

'So what are you suggesting?' she said, her eyes narrowing. 'Another crack at the plus-one agreement, just with a few more terms and conditions? Maybe with me living in?'

He shook his head, looked into her eyes in the hope that he could convince her.

'The agreement is dissolved,' he said. 'It's over—just like it should have been after that weekend. Months before that, even. I was just looking for a way to keep seeing you that held something back.' He paused. 'But by doing that I've undervalued you. I didn't know until I lost you that I'd taken that risk already. Trying to keep some distance couldn't change that. I love you, Emma. I'm *in* love with you.'

Silence as she looked into his eyes, except for the faint sound as she caught her breath. The guarded expression didn't lift.

'That's all very well, but you've got your business to think of. I'm going travelling. I'm doing something for *me* for a change. I want my life to go in a different direction. I don't want to end up some bitter, twisted woman trying to live my kids' lives for them because I've done such a crap job at living my own life that I'm totally dissatisfied with it. You can't just expect me to throw in the towel on all my plans because you've decided you want to give our relationship a proper go. Not after everything that's happened.'

'I don't expect you to back out of all your plans. I'll come with you.'

She laughed out loud at that and he realised just how entrenched his work ethic had seemed to the outside world.

She shook her head. 'That's never going to work and we both know it. What would happen to your business? You can't even leave it alone for a weekend without carting your laptop and your damn mobile office with you. You're the biggest work control freak in the universe.'

She stood up then and his heart dropped through his chest.

'I'll do delegation for you!' he blurted.

'You'll what?'

She looked back at him, her nose wrinkled, amusement lifting the corner of her mouth.

'I'll delegate. For you, I'll delegate. Give me a few weeks to promote someone to manager and do a handover and then I'll fly out and join you. Doesn't matter where you are—you choose the itinerary. We'll have a sabbatical together.'

A moment passed during which he was convinced he'd lost her, that there was nothing he could do or say that would persuade her.

He stood up next to her, took her hand in his, tugged her back down onto the seat beside him. The fact that she went willingly he took as a positive sign.

At least she wasn't running for the boat without hearing him out.

'Please, Emma,' he said. 'I know how it sounds. I know I haven't got a great track record when it comes to taking time off work. But this is different. This isn't just some holiday. This is *you*. You're more important to me than the business. You're more important to me than anything.'

She looked down at his hand in hers, tentative happiness spreading slowly through her. He was ready to put her first. And she knew how much that must cost him after what had happened to him in the past. He'd spent the last decade not letting anyone or anything become important to him.

She laced her fingers through his, finally letting herself believe, and offered him a smile and a nod.

'You realise that if you take me, you take my family, too?' she said, and then he was kneeling in front of her.

'Your mother can organise the wedding,' he said, taking both her hands in his.

* * * * *

JUST CAN'T GET ENOUGH

ROMANCE

Looking for more?

Harlequin has everything from contemporary, passionate and heartwarming to suspenseful and inspirational stories.

Whatever your mood, we have a romance just for you!

Connect with us to find your next great read, special offers and more.

Facebook.com/HarlequinBooks

Twitter.com/HarlequinBooks

HarlequinBlog.com

Harlequin.com/Newsletters

⊕ HARLEQUIN®

A *Romance* FOR EVERY MOOD™

www.Harlequin.com

"I gather you want to talk."

Nik spun back to her with the liquid grace of movement
that always caught her eye, and frowned at her, black brows
drawing down, wide sensual mouth twisting in dismissal.
"No. I don't want to talk," he told her abruptly before he
tossed back the finger of whiskey he had poured neat and set
down the empty glass again.

"Then *why?*" she began in confusion.

Months ago she would have shot accusations at him,
demanded answers, and would have thoroughly upset herself
and him by resurrecting the past that consumed her, but that
time was gone, she acknowledged painfully, well aware that
any reference to more personal issues would only send him
out the door faster. Nik had always avoided the personal,
the private, the deeper, messier stuff that other people got
swamped by. From the minute things went wrong in their
marriage she had been on her own.

Nik scrutinised her lovely face, willing himself to find fault, urging himself to discover some imperfection that would switch his body back to safe neutral mode again. Nor could he think of anything that could quench the desire holding him rigid, unquestionably not the tantalising awareness that Betsy, all five foot nothing of her and in spite of her lack of experience before their marriage, was absolutely incredible in bed.

"*Se thelo*…I want you," he heard himself admit before he was even aware that the words were on his tongue.

So Nik, *so* explosively unpredictable, Betsy reasoned abstractedly, colour rushing into her cheeks as a hot wave of awareness engulfed her. Jewel-bright eyes assailed hers in an almost physical collision, and something low and intimate in her body twisted hard. Her legs turned so weak she wasn't convinced they were still there to hold her up, but she was held in stasis by the intensity of his narrowed green gaze.

"And you want me," he told her thickly.

* * *

Read
CHRISTAKIS'S REBELLIOUS WIFE
by Lynne Graham
in July 2014!

HPEXP0614-I

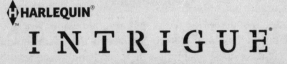

ALISON DELAINE

**brings you the thrilling tale of a hellion on the run...
and a gentleman determined to possess her.**

Lady India Sinclair will stop at nothing to live life on her own terms—even stealing a ship and fleeing to the Mediterranean. At last on her own, free to do as she pleases, she is determined to chart her own course. There's only one problem....

Nicholas Warre has made a deal. To save his endangered estate, he will find Lady India, marry her and bring her back to England at the behest of her father. And with thousands at stake, he doesn't much care what the lady thinks of the idea. But as the two engage in a contest of wills, the heat between them becomes undeniable...and the wedding they each dread may lead to a love they can't live without.

Available wherever books are sold!

Be sure to connect with us at:

Harlequin.com/Newsletters
Facebook.com/HarlequinBooks
Twitter.com/HarlequinBooks

New York Times phenomenon

LUCY KEVIN

returns to Rose Chalet, the most romantic wedding venue in San Francisco, bringing three more of her beloved wedding stories together in one volume!

Dive into fun, sweet and undeniably dreamy stories about women who get swept off their feet when they least expect it!

Be sure to connect with us at:

Harlequin.com/Newsletters
Facebook.com/HarlequinBooks
Twitter.com/HarlequinBooks